NO DESIRE?

Kane knew he would be a fool to believe there was *anything* innocent about this Francesca Rossetti . . . and he sure as hell had no reason to feel *any* desire for this woman.

So why do I?

She lifted her gaze, her eyebrows shooting upward. "Is there a reason you are scowling at me, Mr. Fairchild?"

Yes, damn it, you're driving me crazy! Too many more nights alone together, and he just might fall completely under this temptress's spell and do something stupid—like forget who she really is, and make love to her as he had in his dreams when he'd finally dozed off in the early hours this morning.

"No," he answered, as much in response to her inquiry as to chase away the memories of those dreams. "Just anxious to be on our way, is all." Anxious to be done with *her,* too. The longer he stayed in her company, the more she addled his senses.

Kane reached down and grabbed the bedroll, then placed it on top of the saddlebags, tying it down. He motioned to her to step closer and mount the horse.

His heart thudded faster at her nearness, at the sparkle in her amber gaze. She ran the tip of her tongue along her bottom lip. Heat charged through Kane with a burning need to follow the same path, to know if she still kissed with a passion that could knock a man senseless.

She offered no resistance when he pulled her closer and dipped his head. Her eyes fluttered shut a split second before he closed his own and lowered his mouth over hers . . . and fell into a pool of glorious delight.

<u>BOOK YOUR PLACE ON OUR WEBSITE</u>
<u>AND MAKE THE</u>
<u>READING CONNECTION!</u>

We've created a customized website just for our very
special readers, where you can get the inside scoop on
everything that's going on with Zebra, Pinnacle and
Kensington books.

When you come online, you'll have the exciting
opportunity to:

- View covers of upcoming books
- Read sample chapters
- Learn about our future publishing schedule
  (listed by publication month *and author*)
- Find out when your favorite authors will be visiting
  a city near you
- Search for and order backlist books from our
  online catalog
- Check out author bios and background information
- Send e-mail to your favorite authors
- Meet the Kensington staff online
- Join us in weekly chats with authors, readers and
  other guests
- Get writing guidelines
- AND MUCH MORE!

Visit our website at
http://www.kensingtonbooks.com

LOVE'S JOURNEY HOME

JACKIE STEPHENS

ZEBRA BOOKS
Kensington Publishing Corp.
http://www.kensingtonbooks.com

ZEBRA BOOKS are published by

Kensington Publishing Corp.
850 Third Avenue
New York, NY 10022

All Kensington titles, imprints and distributed lines are available at special quantity discounts for bulk purchases for sales promotion, premiums, fund-raising, educational or institutional use.

Special book excerpts or customized printings can also be created to fit specific needs. For details, write or phone the office of the Kensington Special Sales Manager: Kensington Publishing Corp., 850 Third Avenue, New York, NY 10022. Attn. Special Sales Department. Phone: 1-800-221-2647.

First Printing: June 2002
10 9 8 7 6 5 4 3 2 1

Printed in the United States of America

ACKNOWLEDGMENTS

To Ann LaFarge, Barbara Collins Rosenberg, and Elizabeth Doyle Fowler, with my deepest gratitude for your bottomless well of support and understanding.

To my mom, with love. Your strength and fighting spirit are a constant inspiration.

To my children, Diane and Adam, the greatest joys of my life. I'm so proud of you both.

And a special thanks to my dearest friends: Marsha Lewis for inspiring the writing dream in me so many years ago; Beverly Pironti for helping me to stay focused and keep the dream alive; and Anne Tatum and Suzanne Hagen for all the "Girls' Nights Out" when I needed them most.

ONE

Adrenaline pulsed through Kane as he watched the serving girl approach, her lone footsteps resounding against the oyster-shell pavement and echoing off the brick buildings that lined the hazy moonlit alley. He'd been tracking this gal for nigh on a week now.

He intended to haul her off to jail where she belonged, too!

Kane waited until she walked by, then stepped out from the shadows edging the back wall of the Tremont Hotel and clamped one hand on her shoulder, jerking her to a stop. "Whoa there, sweetheart."

With lightning speed she spun around, hands clasped, her stiffened arms slamming against his side. "Remove your hand from me!"

He'd expected resistance, so he wasn't surprised at her rib-rattling defense; but he couldn't say the same about the suspicious thicker accent he heard in her throaty demand. *What is the conniving she-devil up to this time?* He knew from past experience she couldn't be trusted.

"I'm planning to put more than just my hand on you."

Fear paled her smooth, ivory face, and anger blazed in her amber eyes. "Try it, *signore,* and I will see you served up as fish food." She swung at him again.

Kane grabbed her wrists with his free hand before she

could land the intended punch. "Threatening me is only going to make things worse for you, sweetheart."

She continued struggling against his restraint, then shoved one knee upward.

Kane shifted in time to spare his manhood and take the jab high on his thigh. Just as quick, he hauled her up flush against him, pinning her arms between their upper bodies. "Don't even think of trying that again."

She opened her mouth.

"No screaming, either." He tightened his grip on her shoulder in further warning and cast a glance toward the far end of the alley, where couples strolled beneath the string of electric lights hanging along Market Street.

Hunger had driven him inside the hotel restaurant a short while ago, and the unexpected sight of this fugitive in a serving girl's uniform—causing a scene and being publicly fired, no less—had sent him hurrying right back out. Kane's hasty retreat had garnered him some curious stares from a few folks, as well as pointed scowls from the two men he'd shoved aside in his haste to reach the alleyway before the little villainess emerged through the back door. But for the most part no one had paid him much attention, and he was glad to see his luck still holding. He didn't want to waste time with explanations any more than he wanted the local authorities getting involved and delaying his departure.

"What do you want with me?" she said through clenched teeth.

Kane stared down at his prisoner, at her mink brown hair piled in a neat chignon atop her head. Images of the long, silky strands trailing through his fingers, of the loose tendrils framing her pretty face, flashed through his mind. He lowered his stare over the plain black dress that hugged her shapely curves, and frowned as his heart hammered faster. *Damn it!* He didn't want to feel anything but contempt for this woman.

"You know exactly what I want. To cart your cute little butt off to jail."

"Ja . . . jail?"

"Don't worry, sweetheart; it won't be for long. Just until the trial. Followed most likely by a hanging."

"Impiccagione?" She glanced at the badge pinned to his vest. "Why? It was but food. This makes no sense."

Kane agreed. She wasn't making a lick of sense. "I'm not talking about what happened in the restaurant just now, and you damn well know it." A slow grin pulled at his mouth. "But I must say that was one fine performance in there. I've never seen a man come out of a chair any faster. Must have been one hot plate of food you dumped on him."

Indignation tightened her expression. "The *bastardo* should learn where his hand does not belong."

"My guess is you invited that hand, then changed your mind. Just like you pulled with me."

She drew her thin, dark eyebrows together above her small nose. *"Scusi?"*

Does she really think me idiot enough to believe she can't remember? Kane blew out an irritated breath. *Well, why not, given how I've fallen for her phony acts twice already?*

But he was done playing the fool.

"Knock it off," he snarled. "You've had your backside fondled more times than either one of us cares to recall, and we both know you're about as innocent as the devil's spawn." Ignoring her paled shock, Kane released her shoulder and reached around to pull the handcuffs from his back pocket. "You can consider this performance over. You're under arrest, Francesca."

She stared at his badge again, her gaze narrowing as she looked back up at his face with an intense scrutiny that made Kane's insides squirm. "You are who, *signore?"*

His aggravation escalated at her audacity. "You know damn well who I am!"

She jerked back, nodding once. Her small chin rose a

determined notch. "You may unhand me, Mr. Fairchild.
I won't run."

Mr. Fairchild? Kane frowned. She'd always called him
"Ranger" before. *What game is she playing now?* And
he'd bet next month's pay that she would run like a rabbit
if she got the chance—just like last time. But he didn't
intend to give her that chance again. Tensed with caution,
Kane slowly released her wrists.

She stepped back and held her hands out, palms down.
"I am ready. Take me to jail."

He hid his suspicion behind a smile and slapped the
metal bands around her wrists. "With pleasure, sweetheart."

Bounce. *Ouch!* Bounce. *Ouch!* Bounce. *OUCH!*

Bianca grimaced at the sharp pains shooting through
her bottom. She gripped the saddle horn tighter, the
moon's midnight beams turning her knuckles translucent,
the short, silver links between her shackled wrists jangling in grating rhythm with the creaking leather.

Bounce. OUCH!

Oh, what she wouldn't give for a soft pillow. And what
she wouldn't give for the opportunity to speak with her
sister again. Francesca never mentioned one word about
horses being involved in this plan. As much as she loved
her twin, if Bianca had known about *this* she would have
thought twice before agreeing to switch places.

A lone seagull circled above the bay, its flight silhou-
etted in the starlight glittering against the velvet sky. She
watched the bird swoop down and land a good distance
ahead on the metal railing anchored along the highway
bridge, listened to the gentle waves lapping against the
concrete supports buried in the water below. But nothing
could distract Bianca from the discomfort that intensified
with every plodding step the sorrel mare took over the
wooden planks.

She rolled her eyes and inwardly groaned. *Why didn't*

I listen to Papa? How many times had he warned that someday she would regret never learning to ride? He'd been right. That day was today.

Bounce. Bounce. Bounce. *Ouch. Ouch. OUCH!*

Dio! She couldn't take much more. They'd been riding for less than an hour, but already she was well past her fill of this smelly, lame-gaited horse, and she prayed Ranger Fairchild intended to stop for the night once they crossed to the mainland.

Her bottom slapped hard against the saddle again. She moaned aloud.

"Find your seat, damn it."

"I'm trying," she snapped. But Francesca was the one who loved horses and had ridden nearly all of her twenty-two years. Bianca didn't have a clue how to find a comfortable spot on this torture trap.

Stubble coated the ranger's face, heightening the etched lines of aggravation that firmed his jaw. Fire blazed in his narrowed blue stare. "I don't recall you having any trouble when you stole my horse."

Bianca stiffened with shock. Francesca never mentioned anything about stealing his horse. Why?

Because it's not true. The certainty seeped deeper into her consciousness. She knew her sister was guilty of being duped by her ex-fiancé, Jeremy Bartlett, but Francesca wasn't a thief—not of the thirty-five thousand dollars she'd been falsely accused of helping the Bartlett Bunch steal from that bank in Somerville, and not of this Texas Ranger's horse. Bianca's hackles rose in defense. "I did not steal your horse."

Kane furrowed his brow, deepening the half-inch scar that cut a thin path above his left eyebrow. "Have you lost your mind, Francesca?"

"No."

"Good. Then you do recall the way things went. I don't want you displaying any doubts when you stand before the judge."

Bianca swallowed. *What things?* Francesca didn't say

anything about *"things"* going down. In fact, she swore she wasn't anywhere near the Somerville Bank the night Bartlett and his partners dynamited their way into the safe. *Why does this lawman keep talking in riddles?*

Bianca pondered Kane's earlier comment that Francesca had invited his advances, then changed her mind. Francesca had said she barely knew this man, and then only because he was trying to arrest her. Bianca didn't doubt her sister's word about that, either, or about any of this trouble. She and Francesca had always been close, and always honest with each other. Bianca glared harder at Kane Fairchild. This Texas Ranger could make all the bizarre accusations he wanted, but Francesca was the one she trusted, not this stranger who seemed so willing to believe the worst about her twin.

The faint sounds of squawking seagulls and distant waves pounding the island shoreline did little to break the strained silence between them. Bianca followed the moonlight's pale path along Kane's white shirtsleeves, rolled back to reveal the light coating of sandy hairs on his muscled arms; then over the dusty flecks on the black leather vest hugging his broad shoulders and chest. Worn denims outlined sinewy thighs, and the ivory-handled Colt resting in the holster strapped around his hips only added to the rugged strength radiating from his confident manner. What little Francesca had said about him was certainly true. He *was* an intimidating man, and he *did* have his mind set about her guilt. Bianca could certainly understand why her sister was so desperate to get him off her trail.

She sighed and turned her gaze to the milky moonbeams dancing over the blackened bay in accordance with the mild current. When she'd written Francesca four months ago about their father's death from pneumonia and asked her to come home to help settle his affairs, Bianca never imagined her twin would delay her return without a word, or arrive on the run from a boatload of trouble.

In the three years since Francesca had left the island

to join a traveling theater troupe and follow her dream of being an actress, she hadn't returned once. But her letters had arrived with steady frequency, and were always as welcome as the spring sun to Bianca and her papa. They had enjoyed reading about Francesca's travels out west, about the people she'd met and the plays she had performed in, and there was always added excitement in the thick pages of her flowing script when she wrote about the roles she favored playing most. Contentment and joy had always abounded through her words, and Bianca was glad for Francesca's happiness and her success onstage. But having never been apart from her twin before, Bianca also missed her a great deal, and had been waiting anxiously these past months to see her again.

Bianca imagined a joyous reunion. Had imagined them taking walks along the beach the way they used to, grieving for their father together and talking for hours as they caught up on the happenings in their lives since they'd been apart. Bianca was also eager to hear more about Francesca's engagement, which she'd mentioned in her last letter five months ago, and was looking forward to sharing her own plans to open a restaurant once they sold their papa's shrimp boat.

But when Francesca arrived home late this morning in a state of panic, Bianca's picturesque reunion had been quickly shattered. Instead, she'd listened in stunned silence as Francesca explained about learning that Jeremy Bartlett was really an outlaw, and about the lies he'd been describing concerning her and the bank robbery ever since he and his cohorts were captured. Then she heard, with stark disappointment, that her sister intended to leave again right away. Bianca understood Francesca's need to stay ahead of Ranger Fairchild, though. Being the older—even if only by seven minutes—her protective instincts had kicked in as well, along with a fervent belief in her sister's innocence, garnering her quick agreement to switch places so the law would stop looking.

Spending two weeks in the Somerville jail under false

pretenses, while Francesca sought evidence to prove Bartlett's lies, had seemed a small sacrifice in order to help
her twin regain her future.

But I did not expect to be forced to ride this horse!
Bounce. Bounce. Bounce. *Ouch. Ouch. OUCH!*

Bianca frowned, cutting a sideways glance at Kane.
She hadn't expected to see *him* tonight, either. Francesca
had been confident that the Ranger was at least a day
and a half behind on her trail, which would have given
Bianca plenty of time to make excuses for her absence
so her friends wouldn't worry. But obviously, he'd been
much closer. She hoped the lawman didn't have any other
surprises in store.

The seagull squawked as they drew closer, drawing
Bianca's attention. The bird stretched its large white
wings, then with a graceful, swishing flutter lifted itself
from the bridge and flew out over the bay. The mare
snorted and tossed its head back, scaring Bianca out of
her next breath.

Bounce. *Ouch!* She shifted her bottom over the hard
leather. *Dannare!* She wanted off this beast.

"I suggest you stop this act of not knowing how to
ride, Francesca, and settle into that saddle. It's a long way
to Houston."

"Hou—Houston? But . . . that will take all night."

One corner of his brown mustache twitched as he
smiled mockingly. "Not if we hurry." He tapped his black
hat brim down over the short, sandy-blond hairs that
brushed across his forehead, and urged the horses to a
faster pace.

Pain riveted up Bianca's spine. She tightened her
sweaty fingers around the saddle horn. *Dio, how will I
tolerate staying aboard this animal all night?*

They reached the mainland's solid dirt bank and
headed north along the brush-lined road. A scant distance
ahead, a gray rabbit suddenly scurried across their path.
The mare jumped. Bianca screamed as she bounced into
the air and her fingers slipped free of the saddle horn.

The handcuff links caught underneath the rounded leather, the metal cuffs digging painfully into her wrists and stopping her forward flight. She plopped back down onto the unforgiving seat, sending stinging jabs coursing through her thighs and spine. Her heart pounded a gale-force beat. She could feel a thin, warm trail oozing along one arm. Bianca bit her bottom lip and blinked away the tears that threatened to flood her eyes.

The Ranger pulled back on the reins, bringing the horses to a halt, then reached over and took hold of her hands. Bianca detected a look of concern as Kane stared at the blood on her right wrist, but it didn't last long, quickly replaced with suspicion.

He released her with the same speed as a man holding red-hot coals. "I'm not taking them off."

His harshness grated at her temper. "Did I ask you to, *signore?*"

He shook his head in disgust, then grabbed up the reins and set the horses into motion.

Bianca closed her eyes, wondering if it was possible to die from saddle bouncing.

Pink rays faintly hovered above the horizon, tingeing the charcoal sky with a dawning kiss. Birds one by one began to chirp their morning greetings. As the night sky slowly faded to pale blue, the town of Houston grew visible in the distance, drawing Kane's sigh of relief.

This has been one of the longest damn nights of my life.

He glanced down at the woman sleeping in his arms, her head resting on his shoulder and one breast pressed against his chest. Her legs were draped over his thigh, her skirt hem brushing against his boot, her hip rubbing against his groin with every rocking motion of the horse's gait. Kane swallowed at the intimate contact that had been driving him crazy throughout the night, wondering why he couldn't just ignore this woman—why he found her even prettier than he remembered.

Long, dark lashes fanned her smooth cheeks. Her mouth curved up gently, giving a hint of the sweet dimples he knew existed when she smiled. His pulse hammered with aggravation. *Why the hell doesn't she wake up so I can put her back on her own horse?*

He hadn't wanted to hold her to begin with, but as the night had worn on she kept drifting off and slipping from her saddle. Each time she jerked awake, the fear in her eyes had tugged at his conscience, until Kane couldn't stand it any longer. He'd finally pulled her over onto his lap and told her to go to sleep.

And I've been suffering ever since, too.

Hours ago her neat chignon had lost its precarious battle with the horse's pace. Kane had tried to ignore the way her dark hair spilled over his arm, and the soft feel of it brushing against his chin. Tried to pretend he didn't smell her tantalizing flowery scent that mingled with the salty air and assailed his every breath. Tried to keep from staring at the flush in her cheeks, or notice how perfectly her body fit next to his. He'd tried . . . and failed miserably.

She'd been the first woman in a long time to snare his attention beyond a glancing appreciation of beauty. He could still recall the way his heart had jumped into his throat when he first saw her stepping off that train in Somerville, looking all sweet and innocent. Like now.

Kane tensed. She wasn't sweet, or innocent. He'd learned firsthand that she had the venomous heart of a rattlesnake. Sneaky. Deadly. And she had played him for a big fool. He shouldn't feel anything toward her except hatred, and satisfaction at having her in custody so justice could be served. Francesca Rossetti deserved to pay for her crimes, right along with the rest of the Bartlett Bunch.

A low sigh escaped her lips. She slowly opened her eyes halfway and pulled her eyebrows together in a sincere lack of recognition. Confusion swam in her sleep-clouded gaze as she stared up at him.

Damn, she's a good actress. Too bad she didn't stick to the stage instead of hooking up with Jeremy Bartlett.

Her eyes suddenly widened with remembrance. She jerked up, pressing her warm palms against his shirtfront and pushing herself away from his chest. She lowered her hands to her lap and shifted around, creating further havoc with his hardening anatomy.

"Be still."

"I am jus—"

"I don't care what you're doing." Kane clenched his jaw as she inched herself higher up his left thigh. "Stop it!"

"Why must you be so harsh? I've done nothing wrong."

Kane huffed out an irritated breath. "You've done plenty wrong, and you know it." He pulled back on the reins. "And now that you're awake, it's time to get back on your own horse."

Fear rode across her expression as she glanced behind at the mare, but when she looked back only anger burned in her narrowed stare. "Just so you know, Mr. Fairchild, I would have much preferred taking the train from Galveston this morning. And I see no reason why we could not have waited."

Her indignant tone, her continued use of the deeper accent, and that "Mr. Fairchild" again grated at his last thread of patience. "I'm not interested in your opinions, *Miss Rossetti,* or your preferences."

Her thin mink eyebrows darted upward. "Maybe you should be."

Kane bristled at the challenge in her tone. "Maybe I would be, if you hadn't shot my father!"

TWO

Shot his father? Confusion fogged Bianca's mind. Then her breaths came fast and heavy as anger swept in with a clear, driving force. *Impossible!* Francesca wouldn't shoot anyone. Just how many lies was Jeremy Bartlett telling? "I did not shoot your father."

"We both know you did. And I'm getting damned tired of your phony claims of innocence."

Bianca stiffened in defense. Why was he so quick to judge Francesca guilty? "What if my claims aren't phony?"

Incredulity sparked bright in the Ranger's blue stare. "Did you hit your head while you were on the run, Francesca? Because something's sure got you acting crazy."

"You are the one who is crazy, Mr. Fairchild. For believing Jeremy Bartlett's lies."

"The only one who's told me any lies is *you*. And I'm through listening to them." He leaned closer, scowling harder. "I've had enough of your convenient bouts of memory loss, too. So just cut out this act!"

I have bouts of memory loss because you keep talking nonsense! But the retort sat heavy on Bianca's tongue as caution bartered with her fury.

Francesca had assured her that switching places was the perfect plan because Ranger Fairchild didn't know anything about her family. She'd also told Bianca not to say or do anything to press his curiosity, warning that he was a tenacious sort—as his pursuit and belief of her guilt proved—and had expressed her fear that if he suspected something was amiss he might start digging for answers. Possibly in Galveston, since that's where she had run.

In the fourteen years since the Rossettis had sailed from their homeland of Sicily and settled on the small Texas island, they'd made many acquaintances, and were close friends with all their neighbors. Her father had worked daily alongside the other men who shrimped the waters on the small handcrafted boats that were the families' homes as well as livelihoods. Her mother had happily bantered with the other wives as they sorted the day's catch on straw mats along the docks to sell to the passersby, or while hanging clothes to dry on the decks when the boats were anchored side by side in the evenings. The Rossettis had celebrated many joyous occasions with their friends, and had also grieved with them when yellow fever swept through the island nine years earlier and claimed the lives of many loved ones—Bianca's mother and little brother included. Bianca knew Francesca's concern was warranted. It wouldn't take more than a simple inquiry for Kane to learn about their family. And given how she'd already aroused his suspicions, she feared it wouldn't take much for him to make the short leap from there to realizing he'd been duped and had the wrong sister.

"I'll take your silence as agreement that you're done with this game." He nodded his approval.

Bianca clenched her jaw at his gratified smile. It went against her nature to stay silent, especially when it came to defending her family. But knowing it was for the best, this time she forced the defensive words into retreat . . . then choked as the Ranger tugged on the reins, bringing the mare up alongside his buckskin.

Dannare! A deep ache stabbed at her bottom as Bianca recalled his intent to put her back on the four-legged beast. Her legs throbbed with dread. Much as she hated to admit it, she was quite comfortable here with Kane. Her heart beat a rapid staccato. *Perhaps too comfortable,* she thought as disquieting reminders of cradling herself against his strong frame, of the strange warm contentment that had languidly flowed through her blood as she dozed off in his arms last night, came rushing in. She sat up straight, suddenly more than ready to forgo comfort and put an end to this closeness they shared. She stared at the mare, at the hard leather strapped around its middle. But *Dio,* she wasn't ready to be tortured by that saddle again. Certainly not with the call of nature that came rearing up in urgent request for relief.

"*Per favore,* may I have a few minutes to take care of . . . um . . ." She licked at her dry lips. "Personal matters?"

He hesitated, eyeing her with distrust.

Bianca sighed. "You have my promise that I will not try to escape."

He chuckled dryly. "Sweetheart, your promises are about as reliable as a jammed gun. But you can still tend to your personal matters." His muscled thighs shifted beneath her as he nudged the horse into motion, then guided both mounts off the road. "I'm not letting you out of my sight, though."

Surely he isn't serious. Bianca gaped her disbelief, glancing at the town of Houston in the distance, then around at the flat land sparsely dotted with oaks, a few mesquite, and several clusters of trunkless palmettos, their long, fan-shaped leaves rising up from the dirt in green sprays that resembled small waterfalls but offered no privacy. Heavens, it didn't look as though the Ranger would have any trouble keeping her in sight. Bianca rolled her eyes, trying not to think of the humiliation, and strongly wishing she had thought to gain just a few more details about this *"simple trip to Somerville"* that Francesca had proposed.

As they approached the lone, narrow oak, Kane dropped the extra set of reins, ground-tying the mare.

Annoyance at his reinforced distrust rose in Bianca, but was just as quickly replaced with amusement at his wasted effort. Even if she were contemplating an escape, it certainly wouldn't be on that animal!

The ranger rode on for several yards, then reined his buckskin to a stop beneath the oak's long, leafy branches. He released the leather straps and circled his large hands around her waist, lifting Bianca from the saddle as though she weighed nothing. He lowered her to the ground, his long fingers gliding up her sides with a distractingly gentle ease that sent an odd array of warm tingles sliding across her flesh. Bianca swallowed, surprised at the reaction from his touch, then gasped when he released her and sharp tremors shot through her feet and up, shoving all thought aside save for the tide of pain sweeping like fire through her lower body. Her muscles quivered in tortured protest of supporting her weight; her legs felt permanently curved like bows.

Bianca closed her eyes as a low groan whispered past her lips. Saddle bouncing hadn't killed her, but she feared she would never walk right again!

Kane frowned, irked that the agony on her scrunched face drew his concern. He dismounted and stood behind her, staring at her hunched shoulders, none too pleased with himself that he didn't doubt her pain. Which made him a fool, because he knew she had no reason to be in pain. She knew how to ride. Unless . . .

A spark of amusement sizzled through him. Perhaps her little pretense had backfired. He lowered his gaze. Maybe she had smacked that cute little bottom of hers around harder than she should have. He shook his head, annoyed with himself for continuing to notice her nice attributes. Annoyed with her foolishness, as well. And he didn't intend to give her any special treatment just because she was hurting. She might as well get used to paying the consequences for her actions. She was definitely going to be spending a long time paying for her crimes, whether it be a lengthy prison term or a quick trip into the eternal bowels of hell, should the judge decide to sentence her to hang. Kane knew the latter was possible, too, given the lengthy list of charges against her, especially the one for horse theft.

He personally didn't give a damn about the mount she took, but his boss hadn't taken that same view over having Ranger property stolen. And Kane knew that horse theft was still considered as serious an offense as murder by most Texans. Some considered it even worse . . . and that included Gregory Paxton, the presiding judge in Somerville.

Kane stepped around to face his prisoner, swallowing his surprise that the tears swimming in her gaze tore at his heart the way they did. *Damn it!* It was her own fault she was hurting, and he had no reason to feel sorry for her.

He reached into his front pocket, his fingers grazing over the handful of hairpins he'd rescued from being lost when her chignon came apart last night, before settling on the item he sought. He pulled out the handcuff key, then reached over and took hold of her hands. The thin line of dried blood where the metal had cut into her skin showed stark against her pale flesh and nagged at his conscience as he unlocked the shackle from her right wrist and released her. The cuffs jangled accusingly from her still bound wrist as she rubbed her freed arm.

Kane clenched his jaw. *Blast it!* He didn't have anything to feel guilty about. She was an outlaw. A lying she-devil! And she wouldn't be hurt at all if she hadn't been pretending she couldn't ride. "You can tend to your business behind that tree."

She squared her shoulders. "Fine. But there is no need for you to accompany me any further."

It hadn't been his intent to do so, but he considered challenging her demand anyway, just to annoy her. The temptation quickly died. She was the one who enjoyed playing games, not he. He crossed his arms. "You've got two minutes. If you're not back, I *will* come and get you."

She cocked her head, her narrowed gaze burning with the same defiance that sculpted her slender jaw. "If you are in such a hurry, Mr. Fairchild, perhaps we should be traveling by train."

"As a matter of fact, there's one pulling out from Houston in less than an hour." His smug intent to point out also that it was leaving two hours before the first train from Galveston was due to arrive, and that this was the reason for their all night ride, died an unnerving death in the wake of the hopeful smile that creased those small, pretty dimples into her cheeks.

"Are we going to be on it?"

He swallowed and nodded, wondering why he couldn't recall ever seeing that extra softness in her smile before, or that bright amber light in her eyes. Wondering why it made his blood race unwillingly faster. Then memories of all the things she'd done to him—to his father—flashed through his mind as quick as bits of paper tossed into a violent wind, and his pulse slowed. A beautiful smile . . . a poisonous bite. He wouldn't make the mistake of forgetting that again.

The train whistle blasted through the opened windows of the Houston station, momentarily shutting out the blended conversations of those gathered in the lobby, and of others standing at the waist-high mahogany counter conducting business with four railroad clerks. Through hooded eyes, Bianca stared at Kane's imposing presence beside her, grateful he'd come to his senses about their means of travel, and still more than a little shocked at his thoughtfulness in sparing her hairpins from being lost. He'd surprised her even further with his unexpected kindness this morning by pulling a comb from his saddlebag and offering her a few minutes to make herself presentable . . . before he'd forced her to mount that mare again and endure the jarring—but thankfully short—ride to town.

Bianca clenched her hands together in the front folds of her dusty black skirt, trying to ignore the loosened chignon sitting precariously atop her head, as well as the nagging itch in her fingers to reach up and adjust the pins. The last thing she wanted was to draw attention to herself, and she knew the handcuffs locked around her wrists were sure to do just that. She'd already gotten a taste of being stared at when she rode through town beside the ranger, her cuffed hands in full view for everyone to see because she hadn't been able to find the courage to release her grip on the saddle horn. Of course, it hadn't helped either that the tin star on the Ranger's vest had glinted in the early sunlight like a beacon, begging for folks to look over at them.

Since entering the train station, Bianca had made sure to keep her hands hidden in her skirt, glad no one had given her and Kane more than a passing notice. So far, anyway.

She frowned, glancing around the crowded depot. She hadn't thought about being paraded around in handcuffs when she'd agreed to Francesca's plan. Then again, there hadn't been time to think about much of anything, except helping her sister. But there was plenty of time for thinking now . . . and for worrying.

She knew folks came to the island daily for pleasure and business, and that their numbers increased with day-trippers who crowded the special trains that ran from Houston every weekend. What if someone who'd seen her today happened to wander into her restaurant and recognized her? Bianca was certain she'd already stirred up gossip on the island by being publicly fired from the elite Tremont Hotel. Not that she regretted dumping food in that shipping owner's lap. She'd known before she did it that she would lose her job, but she had planned to resign that night anyway. Besides, the man deserved what he got for fondling her backside, and Bianca really didn't mind people knowing she wouldn't tolerate such behavior. However, gossip circulating that she'd once been seen

as a bound criminal was a whole different matter. She
didn't want *that* embarrassment for herself, or for
Francesca—nor the hassle of trying to explain things.

Don't bring on worries that aren't here, sangu miu.
The words whispered from across the years with loving
memories of her *mamma's* guidance and wisdom, and the
reminder of just how much Bianca missed her. Straightening, she swallowed the sadness that threatened, knowing she didn't need to add to her discomfort with sorrow.
Right now, all she needed to think about was helping
Francesca clear her name.

The railroad clerk handed two tickets to the elderly
couple standing at the counter ahead. As they turned to
leave, the white-haired woman met Bianca's gaze and
smiled. Bianca returned the polite gesture, then watched
in growing horror as the older lady lowered her stare and
quickly jerked her head back up in wide-eyed shock.

"Good heavens, you're handcuffed!" she screeched.

Heat flooded Bianca's cheeks as a deathly hush settled
over the depot. *So much for not drawing any attention.*
She stared around at the employees behind the counter
and the men and women scattered in the lobby, all gawking incredulously, their faces frozen in time like subjects
in a bad painting.

The man patted his wife's bony fingers, now clutched
like hawk's talons around his arm. His dark, aged eyes
darted from the shackles to Bianca, then to the Ranger.
"What did she do?"

"Enough that she won't be spending her days free any
time soon," Kane responded.

"Is she dangerous?" Another man inquired from
across the room.

"Of course I'm not dangerous!" Bianca shifted her
gaze over the crowd, her heart sinking at the shocks and
disbelief in their stares.

"Not as long you don't believe anything she tells you,
or let her close to a gun." Kane's caustic tone singed
Bianca's blood.

Men chuckled, women gasped, then heads bent together and a chorus of soft whispers erupted. The elderly
woman lifted a shaking hand to her mouth as the couple
skirted wide around Bianca and hastened toward the door.
The Ranger's sardonic smile cut a deeper path through
her temper. She had done nothing to deserve this kind of
humiliation, and no matter what trouble Francesca was
in, her sister didn't deserve it, either.

"Was that necessary?" Bianca threw the whispered
words at him like stones, silently praying no one would
remember her face once she left here.

He shrugged. "I can tell them the details of your
crimes, if you'd prefer."

"I have committed no crimes."

His humor faded. "I thought you were done with these
phony claims of innocence.

"I guess you were wrong," she snipped. "Just as you
are wrong about many things, Mr. Fairchild."

He straightened. "I'm not the one who's wrong about
anything, sweetheart, and you know it."

Bianca balled her hands into fists to keep from reaching up and slapping the smug satisfaction from his face.
"What I know is that you find much delight in being
cruel."

"Really?" One light-brown eyebrow arched high on
his forehead. "As I recall, you were singing a much different tune about my delights back in Somerville."

Bianca's heart stopped. "What?"

"Did you want to buy a ticket, sir?" the young clerk
inquired. The black-suited employee offered a half apology to Kane in the form of a slight shrug of one lean
shoulder and pointed behind them. "You're, um, kinda'
holding up the line, sir."

Bianca glanced around, heightened embarrassment
flooding in as she saw the interested stares on their spectators' faces, several of whom were standing close enough
to have heard their latest exchange. Kane took hold of
her arm and forced her to walk with him up to the

counter, her embarrassment instantly paling beneath the pain that scorched her muscles at being forced to move. Her legs throbbed with an intensity that threatened to buckle her limbs if she didn't sit down on something comfortable soon.

Kane reached inside his vest and pulled out a black leather wallet. "Two tickets to Flat Rock."

Bianca jerked her gaze up to the Ranger, her thoughts pounding with renewed confusion. "You mean Somerville."

"I know exactly what I mean." His tone registered a strong annoyance at her interruption, and was laced with an underlying command for her to stay silent.

A cold chill crawled up Bianca's spine, proving more powerful than his angered intimidation. "Why are we going to Flat Rock?"

"Unfinished business . . . as you well know," he snarled, then veered his attention back to the clerk. "I've got two horses I need to take along, as well."

The railroad clerk rattled off the amount of the fair, his prying gaze shifting between her and the Ranger as he reached out and gathered up the bills Kane slid across the counter.

Worry churned in Bianca's stomach. *What unfinished business?* Sweat beaded beneath the high collar of her dress.

The train whistle shrilled a short blast; then a deep masculine voice calling "All aboard" filtered from outside the station.

The clerk pushed the tickets across the counter. "You'll need to hurry. That's it getting ready to pull out."

Kane snatched up the tickets in one hand and grabbed her arm with the other. "Let's go." He turned and started to walk away, but was pulled up short when Bianca's feet stayed rooted to the floor. He stepped back, towering in front of her. "What are you doing? I said let's go."

Panic gripped her insides. *What is going on here? I*

am supposed to be going to Somerville. She opened her mouth, but nothing came out.

"I don't have time for this."

Before Bianca could fathom his intent, he bent his knees slightly, wrapped his hand around her waist, and lifted her off the ground, tossing her over his shoulder. Her stomach rammed against his hard muscles. The air whooshed out from her lungs. Bianca reached up and held her hands over her head to keep her chignon from falling. The shocked gasps echoing around the room only fueled her anger at this shameful treatment, but the Ranger was already out the door and on the planked platform running alongside the train before she found her breath enough to protest.

"How dare you! Put me down!"

To her surprise, he stopped and did just that. Then he pulled the key from his pocket and grabbed her hands, removing the shackle from her left wrist and quickly relocking it around the metal rail leading up to one of the passenger cars. Without a word he turned and hurried off, calling out to the portly conductor, who stood consulting his pocket watch up near the front of the train. Kane spoke briefly to the conductor, then hurried off around the side of the station.

Bianca brushed the loose strands of hair away from her face and set about straightening the damage to her chignon as best she could. The conductor stood staring his curiosity at her, his beefy hands planted on his hips, his dark blue suit straining its seams across his ample frame. Bianca stood her ground, resisting the temptation to stick her tongue out at him. After several seconds, he finally swiveled around on one heel, then forged a lumbering path toward the soot-covered man staring at her from where he leaned out of the train engine's window.

Bianca shook her head and rolled her eyes, trying not to think of the humiliation she was suffering, and grateful that at least there wasn't anyone standing outside on the station platform to gawk at her. But there was a wall of

judging faces staring out from the depot windows, and
Bianca sensed that the passengers aboard the train were
gazing with just as much blatant interest. She tugged at
the manacles, wishing she could somehow undo them
and just walk away from this whole mess. Surely there
was some other way to help Francesca.

"Well, now, this is mighty interestin'."

Bianca spun around at the whiskey-smooth voice that
sounded at her back, frowning at the stranger who stood
at the top of the train steps. He wore denims beneath
scarred leather chaps, and a blue chambray shirt as dusty
as the brown hat he tipped in greeting. His long black
hair brushed against his shoulders, and the smile he offered took the edge off the lines engraved on his tanned
face. He climbed down the steps and stood much closer
than she preferred. Close enough that she had to tilt her
head back to look up at him. Close enough to smell the
grime of trail dust that clung to him.

"How'd a pretty lady like yourself get in such a mess?"
He nodded toward the handcuff that bound her to the
railing.

"It is all just a bad misunderstanding," Bianca responded, wary of the interest in the stranger's green eyes.

"That's what I figured." The smile stayed firm on his
mouth. "But then again, I happen to be someone who
knows you're innocent."

Bianca's heart thudded against her ribs. Did this man
know something about the robbery? Had he approached
her because he thought she was Francesca? "How do you
know this, *signore?*"

"Just a gut sense. But my gut never lies," he spoke
casually, shrugging one shoulder, deflating Bianca's hope
that he could somehow help her sister. "And I'm sure
you'll get this all worked out. In the meantime, I'd be
more than happy to get you out of that metal bracelet
and find you a much more comfortable seat on the train
until that Ranger gets back."

"Do it, cowboy, and you'll be heading to jail right along with her."

Bianca jumped at Kane's harsh warning, loudly accompanied by the sound of his gun cocking. The cowboy cut a sharp glance over his shoulder. Bianca leaned sideways to look around the stranger, and swallowed at the anger she saw blazing on Ranger Fairchild's tensed face.

Seething, Kane crossed the last few yards to Francesca's side and grabbed her by the arm, his gaze never leaving the stranger. "Who are you?"

"Devon Carson." The man extended his right hand.

Kane ignored it, instead keeping his gun aimed at Carson's gut, and the six-shooter strapped around the cowboy's hips well in sight. "What the hell were you doing just now?"

Carson pulled his hand back and crossed his arms over his chest. "I saw you lock her up and leave. Just thought I'd pass a little time with the pretty lady."

"Sounded like more than that to me." *A hell of a lot more.* Kane tried to recall if he'd ever heard of Devon Carson before, and came up blank.

"Only tryin' to help. Just thought she'd be a little more comfortable sittin' inside until you got back."

Kane glanced at Francesca, then back at Carson, not buying this weak explanation for a second, and wondering just how stupid they thought him. "I don't need your help with my prisoner, cowboy, so go pass your time elsewhere."

Challenge flared in Carson's eyes, then quickly dissipated. He nodded at Bianca. "Pleasure talking with ya, ma'am." Carson climbed the steps, never once looking back before disappearing through the door into the passenger car.

Kane shoved his gun into his holster and swung toward his prisoner. "Who is that fella?"

She shook her head. "I have never seen him before."

"Don't lie to me." He tightened his grip on her arm, loosening it slightly when she winced.

"I am not." She tried to twist free of his hold.

Kane released her and took several deep breaths. "Why would a stranger offer to set you free?"

"That is a darn good question. But I do not have the answer."

Despite the veiled sarcasm in her tone, he wanted to believe the innocence in her voice, in her words, in her eyes. But he couldn't. She hadn't shot straight with him about anything from the moment he'd met her. Why should he believe her now?

"All set, Ranger?" the conductor called out from where he stood on the steps between two passenger cars ahead.

Kane waved an affirmative response, then quickly fished the key out of his pocket and unhooked the manacle from the rail.

To Bianca's chagrin, the Ranger slapped the handcuff around his left wrist instead of hers. She gathered her skirt and followed him up the steps, then inside the car, loathing the humiliating sight of their outstretched arms linked by the metal bands. Not wanting to meet the curious stares aimed her way, Bianca kept her eyes on the Ranger's back as they headed down the narrow aisle. She grimaced at the odor of sweat and tobacco smoke lingering in the air, thankful that a good number of the windows lining both sides of the train were open.

Kane stepped sideways between two rows of blue brocade-covered seats and sat down next to the window. Bianca lowered her numb bottom onto the thick padding and closed her eyes in welcome relief, sighing as she leaned against the cushioned back and settled deeper into the soft seat . . . until her hip grazed against Kane's solid strength, sending a shocking trail of warmth shivering along her skin. She jerked up and quickly scooted to the side, her effort to put distance between them succeeding beyond her intent when she started to slip off the edge of the cushion. She scrambled to keep from falling, frantically clawing the air with her hands, her cheeks heating at the laughter that issued from the passengers seated around her.

Kane wrapped his hand around her arm and tugged her none too gently back onto the seat. "If you're going to pretend you don't know how to ride a damn train, either, at least wait till we're moving."

Bianca jerked her arm free, fuming. "There is no pretense, *signore*. I simply slipped."

One corner of his mustache twitched in response to the cutting half smile that curled his mouth. "Sweetheart, you don't do anything *simply*." He reached up and pulled his hat brim over his eyes, then scooted down slightly and leaned his head against the seat back. He crossed his arms over his chest, taking her bound wrist along for the ride.

The back of her hand slapped against the hard muscles hidden beneath his shirt. Bianca tugged at the cuffs, but he refused to budge his arm. She finally gave up the useless struggle to have her hand back and stared out the window as the steam engine hissed and billows of white smoke rose from under the iron horse. The train crawled forward, the wheels clacking against the rails with a loud rhythm that started out slow and gained in speed and volume with every turn that took them closer toward their destination.

Their destination being Flat Rock, not Somerville. Apprehension knotted her stomach. *But why?* What unfinished business awaited there?

THREE

Kane fully intended to catch some sleep during this three-and-a-half-hour trip to Flat Rock, but with the interruption of two brief stops in towns along the way, and the nagging thoughts he couldn't silence, he had yet to find a minute's peace. He stared at the darkness beneath the Stetson partially covering his face, still bothered by the fact that Devon Carson had been nowhere in sight when he'd boarded the train with Francesca back in Houston. His instincts hummed with a strong certainty that the cowboy was somewhere close by, though, and likely to turn up again real soon.

Kane pictured Carson's face, trying to recall ever seeing it on a wanted poster. He couldn't. But he wasn't discounting the cowboy's possible outlaw status, or his possible connection to The Bartlett Bunch, any more than he was buying his prisoner's claim not to know the cowboy. From everything Kane knew about this gang, however, there were only four members, and three of them were currently sitting in the Somerville jail. Francesca made number four. *So how did Carson fit into the picture?*

Kane sighed, wishing like hell he knew for sure.

A week after the Somerville Bank robbery, Kane and his friend and fellow Ranger, Caleb Wilson, had successfully tracked The Bartlett Bunch to their hideout at Eagle Pass, capturing Jeremy Bartlett and his two male cohorts. But there hadn't been any sign of Francesca there, or the stolen loot, and Bartlett had hotly accused her of double-crossing him, swearing she'd skipped out the night before with the entire thirty-five thousand dollars in gold and cash. Kane hadn't put much stock in that accusation at first, considering the large quantity of gold too bulky and heavy for a woman to sneak off with by herself. But while Caleb had escorted the three prisoners northeast back to Somerville, Kane had headed south in search of Francesca, finding her trail just a half day's ride from the hideout, and feeling reassured by the deeper prints of a second horse that she could indeed have the stolen loot as Bartlett had claimed.

Kane clenched his jaw, still irked that he'd lost Francesca's trail soon after that, and by the time he had found it again late the following morning she was thirty miles southeast of Austin, and making tracks with only one horse. He'd wondered then where she had stashed the gold . . . and he was still wondering.

He also wondered now if she'd had some help carting the loot off. Were she and Carson partners in double-crossing Bartlett? *Or is the cowboy just someone she met while on the run to Galveston, and who foolishly fell prey to her lying wiles?* Kane knew firsthand just how good Francesca was at fooling a man, and the memories of the last time she'd duped him could still set his blood to boiling.

After rediscovering her trail outside Austin, he'd noticed a worsening limp in her horse's stride. Using that advantage, and his knowledge of the road she traveled that ran through the outer boundaries of his family's ranch, Kane had finally caught up with Francesca. But the conniving she-devil hadn't been alone when he found her sitting in the grass off to one side of the road. To Kane's surprise, his father had been there, kneeling beside her. And like a fool, Kane had believed the same tearful tale of a twisted ankle that she'd waylaid his father with. Worse, Kane had lowered his guard, had gotten too close to her because he'd been concerned. Then, swift as light-ening, she'd grabbed his gun, jumped to her feet, and expertly fended him and his father off with the cocked six-shooter. Before he could find an opening to try to retrieve his rifle or his father's only weapon—a shotgun strapped to a mount several yards away—Francesca had grabbed the reins to Kane's horse and scrambled into the saddle. And when his father suddenly lunged forward to try to stop her escape, she'd fired off the shot that tore into the elder man's chest, then kicked the buckskin into a hard run toward the woods.

Kane had been too worried about his father to go after Francesca at the time, but he'd left the following day, picking her trail up not far from where she'd surprisingly dropped his Colt amid the thick trees. From there, he'd dogged her winding path all the way to Galveston, talking with a handful of people who'd seen her—in particular, a farmer who had bought Kane's stolen horse and saddle, but who had said the woman refused to sell him the rifle, too. And at two of the depots she traveled through, he'd spoke with a couple of railroad employees who clearly recalled that she carried nothing with her but a small reticule. That latter news had alleviated some of Kane's growing concern about her southward flight. He figured she had the five thousand in stolen bills with her, but surely she wasn't planning to jump on the first ship leaving Galveston without the other thirty thousand in gold she'd gone to such trouble to steal and stash away. He frowned, recalling that she hadn't been carrying a reticule when he'd found her this last time. Had she ditched the bag and hidden the money somewhere beneath her clothing? The thought of searching her to find out only served to remind him of the glimpse he'd had of her naked ivory curves before, and it grated at his frustration that he'd been such a fool where this woman was concerned.

Their bound hands rested together on the narrow section of seat between their thighs, her fingers brushing his as the train rolled along, each soft touch sending heat skittering over his skin. Kane swallowed, deeply bothered that he hadn't been able to ignore her closeness during this trip any better than he'd been able to turn off his thoughts. How could he hate her so much in one breath and find her so damned desirable in the next? It also irritated him that he liked this slightly thicker accent she insisted on using this time, though he had to admire her acting ability for not making a single mistake in her tone so far.

The question of why she had hired on at the hotel as a serving girl also continued to nag him. It didn't make sense for her to casually take up a life as though she had nothing to hide from. Then again, she hadn't been behaving like herself from the moment he'd confronted her in the alleyway . . . and it was driving him crazy trying to figure out why. *What is she up to?*

He knew she was capable of anything. Smart. Tough. Beautiful. Seductively sweet and charming when she wanted to be. She had the courage of a lioness and the cunning of a fox. Kane tensed. But he knew her heart pumped pure poison, making her too deadly to enjoy.

"Flat Rock, folks!" the conductor called out from the front of the car, his voice booming above the monotonous, rackety clack of the wheels. "Next stop, Flat Rock!"

Kane straightened on the seat and shoved his hat back up on his head. Caution instantly kicked in as he scanned the passengers, in search of Devon Carson. Several women fanned themselves against the late morning warmth slowly rising with the promise of a sweltering afternoon. A couple of babies fussed; older children squirmed in their seats with the similar impatience of being forced to endure a long Sunday sermon. Two men puffed on cheroots, the hazy white smoke curling into the heavy air, the smell blending with the pine-scented breeze blowing through the windows. The cowboy wasn't anywhere in sight. Kane nodded at the conductor as the man lumbered down the aisle; then he glanced over at his prisoner, arching one eyebrow at the venomous stare she leveled at him.

"Something wrong?"

"Why are we here instead of headed to Somerville?" She kept her voice just above a whisper, but there was nothing held back in her demanding tone.

Kane cocked his head, perplexed at her game. Surely she knew he would want to recover the gold, and he knew as well as she did that it was stashed somewhere within a two-day ride from here. Carson's image flashed through his mind again, sending a thin, icy web spinning up Kane's spine. *Unless the cowboy has already taken it elsewhere.* Still, Kane didn't believe Carson would head back to Somerville with it.

So why was Francesca *really* chomping at the bit to get there?

"Think harder, sweetheart. It'll come back to you."

Gold flames rose in her amber orbs. He braced himself for the fight he saw building in her expression, but then she paused, glancing around at the other passengers, her shoulders slumping in obvious reluctance to cause a scene.

Good. He wasn't in the mood for another public display, either.

The wheels groaned in a loud whine of metal against metal as the train slowed. The whistle blasted its announcement of their impending arrival.

"Let's go." Kane stood, tugging at the manacles when she hesitated before doing the same.

He motioned for her to precede him down the aisle, noting disapproval in her stiffened spine and shoulders as the train's rocking movement forced her to grip the seat backs to steady herself. Kane reached around her and opened the door, then waited for her to pass through before following her outside onto the platform between the two cars.

The second he closed the door, she whirled around. "Why couldn't we wait for the train to stop?"

He wanted to be first off because he didn't trust her and Carson not to have devised some plan of escape, but he wasn't about to hand those thoughts over. "Just wanted to make sure folks got a last good look at you."

"Bastardo," she hissed.

He smiled cockily, rather enjoying the enraged flush that reddened her cheeks. "Coming from *you,* sweetheart, I consider that a compliment." He turned away and stepped over to the railing, giving her no choice but to follow and stand at his side.

Thick, lush forests densely covered the hills sliding past. Beeches and maples fought for space among the pines that dominated, and the magnolia blossoms added a splash of bright white, yellow, and rose amid the greenery. Nature's sweet fragrance kissed the air. Kane took a deep breath, relishing the sight and the smells.

Home.

He released a long sigh. Being barely more than a year old when the War Between the States had ended and his parents left their ravaged Tennessee farm to make a fresh start in Texas, he had known no other. A bittersweet pang echoed through his soul. He had been content growing up in Flat Rock, and at one time in his life had never given a single thought to ever leaving. It was hard to believe he'd only been back twice in the past eight years. Three times if he counted tracking Francesca here.

The train whistle shrilled another blast as the outskirts of Flat Rock drew closer. Several one- and two-story clapboard homes sat scattered on either side of the main road leading to town, and a tall, white church sat atop a grassy knoll. Kane recalled spending many Sundays in that church, most often at the persistence of his mother, who'd been adamant that he and his sister attend regardless of the fact their father didn't. His father had been in attendance at the church the day Kane had gotten married, though, and so was more than half the town. A white iron fence circled the cemetery that stood off to one side of the church. Kane swallowed. Most everyone who had attended his wedding had also been standing with him at the graveside two years later when he'd buried his beloved wife. Kane blinked back the moisture that blurred his vision.

The train lurched slightly as the brakes gripped tighter and, with a loud grinding, slowed the iron monster's speed. The outskirts of town were left behind as the train passed by the livery, then two saloons, before crawling to a squealing stop in front of the depot. Several people stood outside on the station platform. Kane descended the stairs, returning nods of greeting to the few folks he recognized, seeing their curious looks shift to the hand-cuffs linking him to his prisoner, and easily reading their silent speculations that this must be the woman they'd heard shot Sam Fairchild. Kane took the last, much longer step down to the ground, then turned and offered his prisoner a hand. She hesitated briefly before slipping her fingers along his palm. His pulse hammered faster at her warm touch, and his aggravation at the response made him frown. What the hell was wrong with him?

He shook his head, dropping her hand as soon as her feet touched the ground. He turned and headed across the wooden platform, pausing only long enough to speak to a porter about seeing to his horses before resuming his path toward town.

"Where are we going?"

He felt the tug of the handcuffs between them and glanced out the corner of his eye, seeing her forced to take two steps to his one in order to match his stride. He slowed his pace. "Sheriff's office."

"Why?"

Kane rounded the side of the depot onto a narrow lane leading toward Main Street. "That's usually where they keep the jail."

"Why aren't you taking me to Somerville?"

"Why are you in such a rush to get there?" He cocked his head to stare her full in the face, surprised at the panic he saw in her pale cheeks.

"I—I'm not. I just . . ." Her thin eyebrows knitted together. "What are we doing here?"

"Like I already said, unfinished business."

"What unfinished business?"

She sounded so sincerely confused, the uncertainty on her face looked so damned honest, Kane wondered again if she'd hit her head and suffered some sort of memory problem. But then again, this was Francesca, a woman who couldn't be trusted.

The sun beat down on the wagons and riders kicking up dust along Main Street. Businesses lined both sides of the road, and the walkways were littered with folks intent on their errands. Kane stepped up onto the sidewalk that ran in front of Watson's Mercantile, and waited for Bianca to lift her skirt and climb up. His gaze drifted to her hand dangling close to his, to the pink chaffing and dried blood on her shackled wrist. He quickly shoved aside the pang of guilt that tried to wedge its way into his conscience, and walked on.

"Well?"

"Well, what?" he grated. As they came closer to the bank, Kane spotted an older couple he recognized coming out of the building.

"Will you tell me about this unfinished business?"

Kane glanced away and nodded at the Hendersons, offering a brief exchange of greeting as he crossed paths with the couple. Then he turned back to Bianca, his patience with her innocent act wearing dangerously thin. "No. I'm going to let you sit in jail until you *do* remember."

The panic sprang back into her eyes. She bit at her bottom lip. Kane pondered the sincerity of her worry as he crossed a side street, then called himself every sort of fool. The woman was an actress. She was used to pretending, and damn good at it. He was an idiot for wasting a single moment wondering about her odd behavior.

He stopped beneath the short wooden awning that shaded the front of the sheriff's office. The windows on both sides of the door were raised, and the faint smell of tobacco smoke drifted out from the shadowed interior. Kane turned the brass doorknob and stepped inside.

Sheriff Murphy looked up from the papers cluttering his desk, then pulled the cheroot from his mouth and snubbed it out in a square tin. "Kane, am I glad you're back!"

In the fifteen years since Lyle Murphy hired on as town sheriff, Kane had seen that same look of concern sketched on his lean, craggy face enough to know it meant bad news, and his gut tightened. "What's wrong?"

Murphy shook his head, a wayward strand of gray-streaked black hair shifting across his broad forehead. "Marcus rode into town early this morning. He said your pa's running a bad fever." The sheriff's Adam's apple bobbed along his throat as he swallowed. "And that it didn't look good. He was here to fetch Doc Tatum."

A cold wave surged through Kane. His brother-in-law wasn't one to jump the gun about things. If Marcus said it didn't look good, Kane considered that as good as gospel. A wave of anger warred with the pain in his heart. He glanced over at his prisoner, his fury mounting at the worry in her gaze. He figured the little she-devil was concerned about having murder added to her list of charges. If his father did die, Kane would never forgive her . . . and he'd be standing in the front row at her hanging. If his father didn't make it, he'd never forgive himself, either, for giving her the means and the power to end his life.

"I need to borrow your jail, Murphy."

"Sure thing." The sheriff strode out from behind his desk, snatching up a set of keys off one corner, and crossed over to the first of three empty cells. He unlocked the door and swung the bars open, his dark, accusing stare following Bianca as Kane led her inside.

With stiff, deliberate movements, Kane retrieved the key from his pocket and unlocked the cuff around his wrist, then from around hers.

She looked up, her eyes dark with concern. "I will pray for your papa," she whispered.

"Save your sympathy," Kane snapped, not believing there was any sincerity behind it, and not wanting it even if there was. Not from her. He turned and stormed out. Metal clanged noisily as the sheriff closed the door, and in the next moment Kane heard the heavy lock click into place. A spurt of satisfaction quickened his heartbeat. *The little outlaw is right where she belongs.*

He paused at the front door, intending to ignore her as he turned back to speak to the sheriff, but his gaze unwillingly drifted over. She looked so innocent standing there with her hands gripped around the bars, her eyes wide, her face tense with apprehension. Kane closed his eyes, envisioning her instead holding the gun, hearing the blast when she pulled the trigger . . . firing the bullet that might yet cost his father his life.

He opened his eyes and faced the sheriff. "I'll be back tomorrow morning."

Murphy nodded. "I'll keep a real close eye on her." The disparaging note in his voice matched the brief glance he swung toward the cell; then empathy clouded his brown gaze as he looked back. "Lots of folks are worried about your pa, Kane. Know that the missus and I'll be sayin' a prayer for him."

"Thanks, Murph, that means a lot." Kane stepped outside, welcoming the sunlight that beat down on his shoulders and wishing it could heat the cold worry that flowed through his veins. He quickened his pace along the walk, heading back toward the train station to collect the horses.

"Kane! Kane!"

He stared across the road where Walter Coggins stood in the doorway of the telegraph office, frantically motioning with one hand for him to come over. *Damn!* He'd known Walter since they were kids. Unless it was really important, the man didn't get worked up about anything. As Kane forged a path across Main Street, it crossed his mind to wonder if this had to do with the news he already knew about his father, and he grew a little more impatient at the delay.

He climbed the steps up to the walkway. "What is it, Walt?"

"A wire came for you this morning." Walter handed over a slip of paper, an ominous look haunting the expression on his heavy-jowled face. "It's from Caleb."

Kane figured Caleb was either worried about how his father was doing, or had bad news. He read the wire, learning it was the latter, and grumbled a string of curses as he wadded the missive in his fist.

Walter shook his head. "I didn't figure you'd be pleased. Got any message you want sent back?"

Kane nodded, shoving the note into his front pants pocket. "Tell him I've arrested the woman, and we'll be heading back to Somerville as soon as I recover the gold."

Twenty minutes later, Kane looped the reins of the two saddled mounts around the hitching post in front of the jail. Still fuming over the wire, he stomped across the walkway and jerked the door open, then froze.

Bianca quickly removed her foot from the edge of the cot, shoving her skirt down over her leg as she did. *Dio! What is he doing back?* And how much had he seen? Her heart pounded faster at the Ranger's hard scowl.

He looked around the office. "Where's Sheriff Murphy?"

Bianca buried her shaking hands in the folds of her skirt. "He went to get me something to eat. He said he would only be gone a few minutes."

Kane sauntered farther inside, allowing sunlight's golden streamers to rush through the vacated doorway and brighten the room. He stopped outside the cell, suspicion mingling with the tempered blaze in his blue stare. "What were you trying to hide just now while he was gone?"

Bianca squared her shoulders, hoping the facade of

bravado hid the trepidation coursing through her like a river. "Nothing. I was but adjusting my stocking."

"Really?" He arched his eyebrows. "Then you won't mind if I have a look for myself."

Anxiety stabbed at her stomach. That was the last thing she wanted. "Yes, I do mind, Mr. Fairchild."

"Too bad. I *am* going to have a look under your skirts."

For the first time Bianca was grateful for the iron cage that locked her in. Doubly grateful she was standing far enough away that Kane couldn't reach her through the bars, and that she'd seen the sheriff pocket the keys before he left. A very temporary restraint, she knew, but it was enough for now to help steady her nerves and bolster her courage. "Over my dead body will you come in here and lift my skirts."

"Don't tempt me, Francesca." His voice deepened razor-sharp.

Given the news he'd just received about his father, and his misguided belief that her twin had shot the man, Bianca decided she'd pushed far enough, and held her tongue. But she still wasn't willing to show him what she had tucked in her stocking.

"Kane?" The sheriff's tall, lanky form filled the doorway, blocking out the sun. "I wondered whose horses those were tied out front. What are you doing back already?" He strode inside and over toward his desk.

Bianca said a prayer of thanks for the timely interruption, as well as for the mouth-watering smell of fried chicken and apple pie wafting from the cloth-covered basket looped over Sheriff Murphy's arm. Her stomach rumbled its protest at being neglected since early the night before, loud enough for both men to raise their brows in mild surprise.

Kane walked away from the cell. "I got some news that's forced me to change my plans."

No. Bianca tensed. Things were already getting too complicated. She didn't want any more changes in plans.

"Bad news?" The sheriff pushed aside the wanted

posters on his desk and set the basket on top of the dulled wood.

" 'Fraid so. Caleb wired that Bartlett broke out of jail last night."

Bianca's heart skipped a beat. Her mouth went dry with worry for her sister. Francesca had been confident of finding the proof she needed because Jeremy Bartlett was out of the way behind bars and couldn't stop her. Bianca offered a silent prayer for her sister's safety, and success with her mission.

"I decided I'm going to take her along with me out to the ranch," Kane went on to explain.

The sheriff lifted one bushy, black eyebrow. "Think that's a wise move? I mean, she did almost kill your pa."

"I did not." The words were out before Bianca could stop them. Both men shot her thunderous stares that made her wish all the more she could draw back the instinctive defense.

Kane shook his head, lines of aggravation creasing his forehead. "I guess you've also conveniently forgotten that there was a witness to that shooting?"

Bianca's nerves tightened around her throat. *Witness?* "Wh—who?"

The sheriff's jaw dropped open.

Kane's stare narrowed to mere slits. "Me," he grated harshly. "I was standing right there. Remember, Francesca?"

Bianca's blood turned to ice. This didn't make sense. Francesca never said anything about a shooting. *What is going on?* She also couldn't help but wonder if this was the "unfinished business" the ranger had mentioned.

"You sure 'bout taking her with you?" The sheriff eyed her warily.

Goose bumps blossomed on Bianca's arms. Given the murderous look still gleaming in Kane's eyes, she was sure she didn't want to go.

"I'm sure." He looked away from her to the sheriff. "With Bartlett on the loose, I'm only going to stay at the house a few hours, then head on out. Taking her along now will just save me having to backtrack into town."

Murphy nodded. "Makes sense, I reckon." But skepticism deepened the lines on his face.

Kane didn't blame the lawman. He wasn't all that sure himself about the wisdom of taking her to the ranch. But he didn't have a choice. Caleb's wire said Bartlett was suspected to be headed this way looking for Francesca and the money. Kane didn't plan to let the outlaw find either one. "If you'll just hand me the keys, I'll let her out so we can be on our wa—"

"May I have something to eat first, *per favore?*"

Kane paused, not wanting to respond to her soft-spoken request, but his heart beat faster of its own accord. Her eyes pleaded hunger as she glanced from the basket to him, and he had to admit she did look a little peaked. There hadn't been time to bother with breakfast in Houston, and it would take another two hours to reach the ranch. He'd been too anxious about returning home to give his own empty belly any thought, but the last thing he needed was her fainting from hunger or getting sick. He wasn't about to carry her again.

"Fine, but you'll need to eat fast. I'm in a hurry." He picked up the basket and took the keys Murphy handed him, then crossed over to stand facing her through the bars. "And you don't get a bite of anything until *after* I see what you're hiding under your skirt."

FOUR

How dare he bargain with my hunger! Bianca clenched her hands into fists, anger at his impertinence converging with her worry as she wondered again how much Kane had seen when he walked in. Enough to know for certain she was hiding something? Or was it just his habitual distrust of Francesca that made him assume so?

"I have already explained that I was but adjusting my stocking."

"And I told you I want to see for myself." Heavy brown stubble heightened the ruthlessness in Kane's hardened jaw. "Lift your skirt up, Francesca."

The sheriff wrinkled his brow in curious puzzlement at the demand.

Bianca swallowed her apprehension. *Dannare! What am I going to do*? She wasn't the bit least anxious to expose her legs to these men, or to reveal what she had hidden. She bit at her bottom lip, wishing Francesca hadn't insisted she take the hundred dollars . . . wondering again why her sister had stuck the daguerreotype of the two of them when they were eight inside the folded bills and not said anything.

The photograph had been their *mamma's* favorite of her girls, and Francesca had taken it with her when she left to pursue her dream onstage. Bianca made the surprising discovery of its return just after Francesca had boarded the last afternoon train yesterday—this time leaving to seek out proof of her innocence. Since Bianca had gone straight from the depot to the restaurant, and it wasn't her habit to carry a reticule to work, she'd stuck the items inside her skirt pocket. She wished now she had just left them there, too, instead of thinking they would be safer hidden tucked inside her stocking.

"You're wasting time." Kane swung the basket in a slow, taunting pendulum. "And you still want to eat before we leave, don't you?"

Bianca's stomach rumbled at the enticing smells drifting out from the basket, and her fury with Kane rose another notch. She knew she could easily explain the money. Francesca was a good actress and made a fair living at her profession, a fact proven by the money she frequently tucked inside her letters to help out her family. *But what can I say about the photograph?*

Bianca hesitated, locked in a heated stare with the Ranger, her hunger finally winning out over the urge to further argue this predicament—a battle she feared she most likely wouldn't win anyway. "Fine. I will give you the money I am hiding."

The ranger quirked his mouth in a half-smile and nodded his approval at her acquiescence.

Bianca took a deep breath, then hiked her skirt up along her black stockings, heat flooding her cheeks as Kane and the sheriff dropped their stares to her legs. She gathered her skirt to just above her knees, then bunched the material in one hand, and slipped her other hand underneath the hem.

Kane and the sheriff yanked their guns from their holsters at the same time. The sound of both hammers locking into ready reverberated in the silence and sent Bianca's heart leaping into her throat.

"What the hell are you doing?" Kane snarled.

Bianca swallowed. She'd been hoping to slip the daguerreotype farther down inside her stocking and retrieve only the bills, but staring at the end of Kane's gun, she could see that hadn't been such a wise plan. Slowly she straightened and grabbed her skirt with both hands. "I . . . I was just reaching for the money."

Kane shook his head. "Not until I see for sure that's *all* you're hiding." He motioned with his gun for her to raise her skirt up higher.

Bianca hesitated, gripping the black cotton tighter in an effort to still her shaking hands.

"What's wrong, Francesca?" Kane cocked his head, a mocking grin curving his mouth. "You weren't the least bit modest about showing me your goods in Somerville. No need to be shy now."

Bianca blinked her surprise. Francesca would not "show her goods" as he so derisively suggested. Their mother had instilled a deep sense of respectability in both her daughters. But a sudden odd uncertainty fisted in Bianca's stomach and kept her from offering up a defense.

Something is not right. Her heart raced, as rampant as her confusion. Attempted murder . . . horse theft . . . Kane's continued insinuations of a more personal relationship with her sister. A foggy mist shrouded her mind with a cold sensation of being trapped in a bad dream. None of this sounded like Francesca at all. Neither could she deny, however, that Kane appeared just as confident about this accusation as he had about being a witness to his father's shooting. *But if his allegations are true, why didn't Francesca say anything?* Bianca took a deep breath, longing to find the door to get out of this nightmare . . . longing to talk with Francesca again, and find out why the Ranger would make these appalling claims.

"I don't have all day. Either lift your skirt up or I'll come in there and do it for you."

Bianca didn't doubt his threat for a second. Much preferring to take what small control she could, she jerked her skirt up to mid-thigh, exposing a slim line of pale flesh and the money peeking out from the top of her right stocking. She grabbed the folded bills, then quickly dropped her skirt, sighing with relief to be covered once again.

The sheriff holstered his gun.

Kane did the same, then unlocked the cell, strode inside, and placed the basket on the floor near her feet. Bianca's pulse pounded as he snatched the money, as he unfolded the bills and stared at the daguerreotype. He glanced up at her, back at the photograph; then his icy blue gaze locked on her once again.

"Who are these girls?"

"My cousins . . . in Sicily." She hoped the ruse of a close relation would explain any resemblance he noticed, and keep him from suspecting Francesca had family in Galveston. To Bianca's relief, he nodded in seeming acceptance of her explanation.

Then his eyebrows knit together as he fanned the five twenty-dollar bills between his fingers. "Where's the rest of it?"

Bianca shook her head, confused. "That's all I have."

Kane eyed her with disbelief. "I believe you carted away more than this, sweetheart. Thirty-five thousand more."

His unmitigated arrogance sent waves of fury through Bianca's chest. Regardless that this lawman wanted to believe the worst, Francesca wasn't guilty of bank robbery. Bianca had seen the truth of that in her sister's eyes, heard the desperation in her voice, and seen her rage at being conned by her ex-fiancé. "I did not help Jeremy Bartlett rob that bank, and I do not have that stolen money."

Exasperation tightened the Ranger's jaw. "Knock it off, Francesca. I know better, and so do you." Kane pointed down at the basket. "You've got fifteen minutes to eat before we leave." He turned and walked out of the cell, closing the door behind him.

Bianca didn't understand why the Ranger believed Francesca had the stolen money, but that wasn't her biggest concern at the moment. She hurried across the cell, wrapping her hands around the bars. "Mr. Fairchild, wait."

He stopped and slowly turned around.

"May I have the photograph back, *per favore?*"

Kane glanced down at the picture, then shoved it inside his vest pocket, and pinned her with an uncaring stare that chilled her blood. "Just as soon as you clear up that unfinished business and lead me to the stolen loot, Miss Rossetti."

Kane tilted his hat brim down against the sun's noon glare and nearly collided with Francesca's back as she came to a sudden stop.

"No, *per favore.* No, *il cavallo.*"

He didn't need to understand her whispered words. He heard the dread in her voice, saw it in her stiffened spine, and knew without a doubt that she wasn't happy to see the sorrel mare tethered in front of the sheriff's office. He figured her backside must still be smarting. But that was just too bad; she was going to have to climb onto that saddle anyway. Kane placed his palm against the small of her back and nudged his prisoner forward.

Wariness hovered in the glare she shot him. Kane frowned, hoping she didn't plan to continue this foolish charade of not knowing how to ride.

Tentatively she reached up to grab the saddle horn, the handcuff links jangling against the leather; then she fumbled with the stirrup as she tried to slip her left foot in. The mare snorted and shifted sideways. Francesca gasped and jumped back. Kane braced his hands against her shoulders to stop her stumble, aggravation stretching his patience dangerously thin. Not a far stretch, since he was still fuming over her feigned ignorance about the money, and not in any mood for more of her pretenses.

He lowered his hands to her narrow waist and jerked her up off the ground.

"Unhand me, you brute!" She lashed out with her feet,

her boot heels connecting sharply with the lower half of his legs.

"Damn it, stop kicking me and swing your leg over!"

She stilled, glaring at him, then grabbed the saddle horn with both hands and did as he'd ordered. The moment her bottom hit the saddle, her face scrunched with pain, drawing Kane's sympathy—and just as quickly his frustration. He jerked his hands from her waist and stepped back, his gaze lowering to the trim ankle peeking beneath her hiked hem. Flashes of her shapely legs danced across his mind, heating him with desire.

He frowned. *What the hell is wrong with me? I don't even like this woman!*

Kane stomped over to the hitching post and untied both sets of reins, then mounted his buckskin and guided the horses along Main Street, falling in behind several other riders traversing the thoroughfare through town. Hooves and wagon wheels kicked up dust, sending thousands of tiny particles swirling in the brilliant rays that beat down on the town. Kane acknowledged greetings from the few friends and neighbors he recognized, but didn't delay his departure with any conversation, anxious as he was to get home and check on his father. He was just as anxious to leave Flat Rock behind as well, wanting to escape the memories he'd been having trouble keeping at bay ever since he arrived. Memories of the day his wife had died.

Kane quickly shut the mental door on his past, refusing to travel that path again, and nudged the horses into a trot as they neared the edge of town. He stared at Francesca's white-knuckled grip on the saddle horn, at the way her bottom bounced in an ungainly manner that surely had to hurt, and for the life of him he couldn't figure out why she continued to torture herself riding like a novice. Nor how she tolerated the pain.

Foolish woman. He shook his head and looked away, tensing as they approached Hanson's Livery and he saw a familiar figure leading a saddled bay out through the opened doors.

Devon Carson looked up, smiled, and tipped his hat. Kane didn't bother with any return greeting, but let his thoughts race again with speculation about Carson's connection to Francesca and Bartlett. He recalled Caleb's wire about the outlaw's escape last night, particularly the information that Jeremy Bartlett had had help from an unknown accomplice. Kane knew the cowboy couldn't have been in Somerville last night—it was a hard three-day ride from there to Houston, and the train didn't run through Somerville after dark. But neither was he overlooking the possibility that Bartlett had *two* accomplices, nor that the outlaw had sent this cowboy on ahead to find Francesca and the money.

Kane gave some serious thought to locking his prisoner back in jail and having a lengthy chat with Devon Carson. But as he watched the cowboy mount up and head out in the opposite direction through town, his concern for his father overrode the idea. He faced forward, dismissing Carson from his sight but not from his thoughts.

From the corner of his eye, he saw his prisoner peek over her shoulder to watch the cowboy's retreat. Kane couldn't see her expression—not that it mattered. Whatever plan Francesca had cooked up, he was bound and determined the scheming actress wouldn't escape this time.

A few yards off the main road, Devon Carson stood beneath a narrow, bent oak, its spindly branches creating a small patchwork of shade that left him half exposed to the blazing sun. He tugged his hat brim lower over his forehead, pulled a final draw from his cheroot, then tossed the butt onto the grass and rubbed it out with the toe of his boot. He shifted his stare along the southern hills thickly coated with new prairie grass and stands of pine, and over the fields of bluebonnets and Indian paintbrush, then along the dirt road that cut a path through the landscape and sat empty for miles.

Devon reached inside his shirt pocket and retrieved a silver watch. With the pad of his thumb, he stroked the worn leaf engraving, just as he did each time he held the gift his grandfather had given him ten years ago, when Devon had left their Ohio farm to seek his fortune Out West. He frowned, glad the old man had passed on without knowing what a failure his grandson turned out to be.

Devon pressed the small clasp, releasing the lid, and glanced at the dial. One-twenty. He stared down the road again, not seeing so much as a dust cloud in the far distance to indicate any sign of someone coming. Irritation quickened his pulse. Where the hell was she?

When he'd met her briefly at the Houston depot, just before she left on the final train headed out last night, she had been adamant about meeting at *this* tree—two miles south of Flat Rock—at exactly one o'clock. He released a heavy sigh and shook his head as he snapped the lid closed. Then again, it was just like Francesca to keep a man waiting.

Devon returned the watch to his pocket, then strode over and leaned back against the tree's gnarled bark. He crossed his arms and watched the road, glancing around every now and then to search the surrounding area for her approach. As the minutes ticked by, his patience decreased, and his thoughts had too much room to move in.

Not for the first time, he wished he'd never met Francesca Rossetti, or gotten involved in her plan. But he owed the woman a debt and, despite the gambling and occasional lawless path he'd chosen to travel in this life, he was still a man who paid his debts. Not to mention that she'd offered him a hefty fee to help her out. It didn't mean he had to like what he was doing, though, any more than he liked being kept in the dark about what Francesca was really up to.

Catching a movement from the corner of his eye, Devon turned his attention to the horse and rider topping the north hill. She was too far away for him to see her face, but he recognized the long rope of dark hair bouncing against Francesca's back, as well as her skillful handling of the horse she kept to a dangerously swift gait down the grassy slope. She disappeared behind an incline, then seconds later topped the rise, riding down and through the short valley below before finally slowing the Appaloosa as she rode up the hill toward him. Devon straightened away from the tree when Francesca drew near and brought the winded mare to a stop. He watched her dismount, running his stare over the full-legged riding skirt she wore, with a solely male appreciation for the curvaceous figure outlined beneath the brown cotton twill and matching tailored jacket.

Francesca pulled brown leather gloves from her hands as she crossed over to stand in front of him. "Did you see my sister?"

Devon nodded. "She was at the Houston depot this morning, just like you said she would be." And the Ranger had gone to Flat Rock, just as she had said he would. Devon wished he knew how Francesca stayed so well informed of the Ranger's every move. It was a damn good tactic to ensure an outlaw's safety . . . and something he could certainly use if he ever found himself in trouble with the law again. "I got a chance to talk to her for a minute."

"How is she?"

He heard the edge of worry in Francesca's tone, saw it slowly filter into her golden stare. Now that he'd seen both girls up close and knew they were twins, Devon could tell the slight difference in their identical resemblance. Just a subtle, fuller shaping in Francesca's face and a slightly deeper tone in Bianca's voice were amazingly the only contrasts he detected, though.

"She looked tired, but other than that she seems to be holding up just fine. That is, if you don't count the whip-pin' I saw her takin' in that saddle as she rode out of Flat Rock a while ago."

Francesca furrowed her eyebrows. "Bianca isn't all that fond of horses, and even less of riding them."

"She's not very good at it, either, from what I saw. But you did warn her about the possibility, didn't ya?"

"Of course I did." She raised her chin a defiant notch, leveling him with a gaze as bright and honest as her voice, but Devon knew by the slight pink coloring in her cheeks that she was lying.

He shook his head in reprimand, letting his expression reveal his disbelief. Francesca repeatedly slapped the pair of gloves against the palm of one hand, and frowned. "All right, perhaps I failed to mention that little detail."

Devon crossed his arms. It was her beauty that had drawn him to her in the first place, and had prompted him to arrange an introduction with the actress after seeing her onstage in Denver. But it took only a week in her company for him to see through her facades of honesty and innocence, and to figure out that Francesca Rossetti was a sneaky gal with more tricks in her bag than a clown took to the circus. He'd walked away back then, happy to do so. If it weren't for the debt he owed, if he didn't need the money she promised him, he'd tell Francesca to peddle her stories elsewhere, and walk away this time, too. But he did owe this debt, and he felt a little obligated now to continue keeping a watch on Bianca Rossetti. No telling what other pieces of information Francesca hadn't told the poor girl.

Or me. "What else have you failed to mention about this plan you've concocted, Francesca?" He didn't bother to hide the irritation in his voice.

She tapped the gloves lightly against his chest once and smiled up at him, the soft dimples in her cheeks making his heart beat unwillingly faster. "Nothing that concerns your part in it, I assure you."

"You better be right about that," he sternly warned, then lowered his arms to his sides. "Now, if you're done checkin' on your sister, I need to be ridin' out if I'm gonna catch up with them."

"Not yet. There is another matter I wish to discuss. The last part of what I need you to do for me."

He tensed, hating this game she played of feeding him her demands of repayment in bits and pieces. "What is it?"

"Once Bianca is safely in the Somerville jail, you may leave, but I want you to go back there in a couple of weeks. On June first—no sooner—I want you to leave this"—she reached into her skirt pocket and pulled out a small, sealed envelope—"for the sheriff. Do not get caught. I do not want anyone to know where this letter came from. Then we are done, Devon. Your debt will be paid, and we will have no reason to ever see each other again."

Never seeing her again sounded just fine to him. Devon took the envelope from her and flipped it over, expecting to find the sheriff's name written on the front, and surprised to see *Kane Fairchild* penned in flowing script across the parchment instead. "Why am I leavin' this for the sheriff? What are you up to?"

She smiled. "Trust me, darling; you know all you need to."

His gut tightened at the mischievous gleam he saw in her stare before she blinked it away and turned to go. He grabbed her arm and spun her back around. "Not quite, darlin'," he snarled, tightening his grip when she struggled to jerk free. "Here's somethin' I don't know but need to. When am I gonna get my money?"

She stilled, hatred burning in her narrowed eyes, the barrel of the derringer he hadn't even seen her pull now poking in his gut. "When you have fulfilled your debt. Now unhand me, you brute."

FIVE

Every muscle in her body burned with agony. Bianca didn't think she'd last another minute in this saddle, but her only other options at the moment were the hard road below and the long drop to get there. Neither of which sounded any more appealing than this torture she'd endured since leaving Flat Rock two hours ago. She lifted her face into the breeze that had kicked up earlier, welcoming this small salvation that at least made the midafternoon warmth tolerable. But along with the wind also came the hint of rain in the air, the threat heightened by the black mass building on the northern horizon, and the arms of grayish clouds slowly reaching out to blotch the distant azure sky. Bianca hoped the brewing storm would hold off for a while, or skirt around this area altogether. She couldn't imagine anything more uncomfortable than having to ride this rough-gaited mare in the rain.

"How much farther, Mr. Fairchild?"

"Not far." He reined the horses to the south, onto a narrower trail that branched off from the main road they'd followed from town, and pointed ahead. "Just over that next hill."

She dredged up a smile of relief at the news, more than ready for a break, even as a wave of panic crashed across her chest at the thought of the impending reception she would receive from Kane's family. A family who believed she had shot one of their members.

The sound of cattle bawling softly drifted from over

the hillside, growing louder as they rode closer, and the faint scent of hide and dung rose amid the sweet grass and pines that scented the air. True to Kane's word, when they topped the ridge several minutes later the Fairchild ranch came into view and fairly took her breath away. The land stretched flat as far as Bianca could see, the grassy plains dotted with large herds of cattle confined within miles of barbed-wire fencing. At the bottom of the slight incline, a broad two-story barn centered the large ranch operation, and additional lines of interconnecting wooden fences reached out from the red structure, corralling younger longhorns of varying sizes, as well as a fair number of horses. Farther down, bunkhouses and other outbuildings sat in a cluster, and off to the right Bianca spotted a garden large enough to feed a small army, then the two-story white house standing tall behind a sparse grove of trees.

It crossed her mind to wonder why Kane had decided to become a Texas Ranger. Considering the stability and prosperity evident in the size of this spread, surely there was plenty of means to support him here with his family, if he'd wanted to stay.

"You have a nice home, Mr. Fairchild," Bianca offered, sighing her annoyance as Kane's hard, probing stare seemed to search for more behind her compliment than sincerity. She wished he didn't distrust her sister so.

"Thanks," he finally responded, his tone holding as little warmth as his continued gaze. "But you do know you're not going to get any welcome here. Right?"

Bianca nodded, swallowing the knot of worry that caught in her throat.

"Good." He faced forward and nudged the horses to a faster walk down the road.

She gripped the saddle horn tighter to stay astride the mare, as well as to still her shaking hands. What if his family's fury at Francesca was enough for them to want immediate revenge, and the Ranger couldn't—or wouldn't—stop them? Bianca bit at her bottom lip, envi-

sioning a group of faceless people ripping her apart limb
by limb the moment she arrived, wondering if their anger
would be justified. Had Francesca really shot Kane's father?

As far as she knew, Francesca didn't even know how
to use a gun. Bianca had always known her sister to have
a kind heart, too, and couldn't imagine Francesca hurting
anyone. A shudder raced up her spine and shivered across
her shoulders. Unless it was self-defense. But if that was
the case, why hadn't Francesca mentioned it? And why
would the Ranger lie about being a witness to what happened?

Tired of trying to make sense of the confusion, she
tucked her thoughts away for now and shifted her attention to the activity humming about the ranch. Loud cattle
bawls drifted on the breeze, and every now and then a
horse's neigh, or a honking mule's bray, would fill the
air. A handful of men rode among the penned herds, cutting out certain calves and redirecting them to smaller
corrals. A few others were working down by the barn,
fixing a wagon wheel and cleaning tack. Bianca noticed
several of them pause from their work to watch her and
Kane follow the winding road around two large corrals.
The cowboys were all too far away for her to be able to
discern by resemblance if any of them were members of
the Ranger's family, but even though some of them
waved, and a couple even shouted out a welcome home
to Kane, no one made any attempt to ride over and greet
him more personally, as she expected family would.

The road led into the center of a large dirt yard, and
from there the Ranger guided the horses onto another
path that cut through the scattered stand of pines, and
proceeded through a neatly trimmed yard sparsely land-
scaped with magnolias and live oaks. At the end of the
long drive sat the white clapboard home. Its upper and
lower verandahs were edged with white, intricate iron-
work railings, and matching spiral supports braced the
overhangs above both porches. Black shutters decorated

the windows that lined both levels along the front and around the two sides of the house that Bianca could see.

Her parents had instilled the traditional values that a home represents the site and source of all that gives meaning to life, teaching both their daughters to look upon plentiful food as a symbol of well-being, and a well-kept home as representing a sound family. From what Bianca had seen so far, Kane's home boded well for both without being ostentatious. Kane's confident manner also made her believe that inside this home she would find sturdy furniture that lasted—the symbol of a family's stability, and therefore their strength.

Her heart pounded faster as she wondered about the people living here, and wondered again if they would band together, as the Italian families she knew would do, and want immediate revenge. Sweat popped out on the palms of her hands as the front door opened and a tall, broad-shouldered man dressed in denims, a blue shirt, and twin six-shooters strapped around his lean hips stepped outside.

He looked to be near Kane's age, which she guessed was close to thirty, but his short, pitch black hair and square jawline bore no resemblance to the Ranger that she could see. However, the cold look shrouding the stranger's expression when he glanced toward her cuffed hands then back at her with presumed recognition was a familiar sight she'd seen often enough in Kane's stare. Bianca's nerves jangled like a streetcar bell as the man sauntered to the edge of the porch.

Kane noticed his prisoner looked a little jittery—and well she should, given the rancorous look Marcus Caldwell aimed at her. Kane brought the horses to a halt near the bottom of the steps, not surprised when his brother-in-law cast a disapproving look at him. He'd known when he left Flat Rock that his family wasn't going to like having Francesca here, even for a short while.

"Good to see you again, Marcus."

"You, too." The disapproval in his tight expression

faded, replaced with concern as Marcus walked down the short flight of steps.

Kane dismounted, hanging on to both sets of reins, and walked over to shake hands with his brother-in-law.

"I'm afraid I've got some bad news, though."

Kane tensed, praying it wasn't any worse than what he already knew. "I saw Murphy. He told me you rode into town earlier to fetch Doc Tatum because my father's running a fever."

Marcus nodded. "He was delirious with it most of the night. Doc says the wound's infected, and Sam's strength is drainin' pretty fast." His brow furrowed with concern. "And I gotta tell you, Kane, Doc looked worried. Real worried. He's comin' back this evenin' to check on him again."

Kane took several deep breaths as he absorbed the news, willing his pulse to slow, forcing himself not to turn around and drag Francesca from the saddle so he could wrap his hands around her throat for putting his father in this shape. As he saw Marcus cross his arms, Kane wondered if his brother-in-law was restraining himself from similar thoughts. He wouldn't be surprised. He knew Marcus was just as upset about the shooting as the rest of the family. In the ten years since Marcus had first come to the ranch seeking a job, Kane knew he'd developed a deep esteem for the man who'd hired him and was now his father-in-law.

"We've been taking turns sittin' with Sam. Your ma's up there now. Charlotte's resting."

Kane knew his mother was a pillar of strength in any crisis, only falling apart afterward. His sister wasn't as strong, though, especially when it concerned the parent she'd always doted on the most—and she was six months pregnant to boot. Having miscarried her first two babies since marrying Marcus four years ago, this upset couldn't be good for her or the baby.

"How's Charlotte holding up?"

"Doc says she's far enough along now not to worry

this time, and doing fine." Marcus's dark-brown eyes burned with misgivings. "But I wish she'd just stay in bed until this baby is born."

Kane didn't envy Marcus the task of trying to enforce that. He knew his sister could be a stubborn handful at times, and that she'd want to be by their father's side as much as possible right now.

Marcus sighed. "I'm sure I'm just bein' overprotective. That's what Doc says, anyway. She'll be all right, I reckon . . . as long as Sam doesn't get any worse."

Kane shuddered inwardly at the thought of that happening. "I'd like to go up and see him." He hooked one thumb over his shoulder toward Francesca. "Do you mind keeping an eye on her for me?"

Marcus nodded reluctantly, his jaw tightening. "She's the one who done it, huh?"

"Yeah, this is her."

"I'm glad you caught her, but I don't like it none that she's here, and neither will your ma. She needs to be sittin' in jail for shootin' Sam. And since you saw Murphy, why didn't you leave her in town with him?"

Kane quickly explained about Bartlett's escape, and the suspicion that the outlaw was headed this way looking for Francesca and the money. "I'm only planning to stay a few hours, and I didn't want to backtrack into town."

Though his expression still held a tinge of disfavor, Marcus nodded his understanding. "I'll keep an eye on her down at the barn. I can lock her in the tack room there."

Kane briefly placed one hand on the man's shoulder. "Thanks, Marcus." He handed over both sets of reins, then waited for his brother-in-law to mount the buckskin and turn the horses around back down the lane before he headed up the short flight of steps. Kane paused at the top, bothered that he felt compelled to look back at his prisoner, surprised to find her glancing over her shoulder at him.

Her pale face showed signs of sympathy, and worry

now replaced the nervousness he'd seen in her eyes a moment ago. Kane didn't want to believe for a second that she truly cared about what happened to his father— except for how it might affect her sentencing. But *damn,* her empathy sure looked genuine.

He frowned as images of being with her in that hotel room in Somerville flashed through his thoughts. He reminded himself that Francesca Rossetti was a lying thief without an ounce of sincerity . . . unless it worked for whatever performance she needed it to at the time.

Kane turned away and crossed the porch, shoving thoughts of his prisoner aside as he walked through the open doorway and into the large foyer. He stopped, glancing around at the familiar watercolors hanging on the pine walls, and the spring flowers decorating a round oak table. His heart missed a beat as his gaze fell on the broad staircase in the center of the planked flooring. He closed his eyes and swallowed, picturing his wife hurrying down the stairs the way she used to when he'd come home from town, her skirts lifted high, her blond curls pinned back with her favorite tortoiseshell combs, and a welcoming smile on her lovely face. He sighed heavily and opened his eyes, locking out any further memories of Natalie and wondering if he'd ever stop missing her.

He removed his hat and placed it on the table, then took the stairs two at a time, his footsteps muffled on the rose-flowered carpet runner that centered the steps and continued along the long planked hall above. At the top he turned left, glad the room he'd once shared with his wife was at the opposite end. He followed the corridor, stopping at the last door, and rapped his knuckles lightly against the oak wood before circling the brass knob with a trembling hand. When he stepped inside, his gaze instantly riveted to the fourposter bed at the far end of the room, and his father's chest rising and falling sporadically with his fast, heavy breaths, to his fever-flushed face, stark against his blond hair and the white sheet that covered him.

Beth Fairchild paused beside the bed, a white cloth gripped in one hand, a smile creasing lines of relief in her slightly plump face. "Kane." She quickly placed the wet cloth on his father's forehead, then wiped her hands on the apron tied over the green calico dress that hugged her ample frame, and hurried across the room. Her light-brown hair was gently streaked with gray; her short stature barely reached his chest, and she had to stretch up on tiptoes to hug him. "I'm so glad you're here."

"I got back as fast as I could." He hugged her, then held her at arm's length, not liking the fatigue he saw in the darkened skin beneath her hazel eyes, or the worry that pinched her mouth. "I saw Marcus downstairs. He told me everything." Guilt ate at Kane's gut. If he hadn't been careless, his father wouldn't be suffering like this, and his mother wouldn't be grieving over it. "He's going to be all right, Mother. He's strong. He'll pull through this." Kane silently prayed his reassurances weren't a lie.

She nodded and looked toward the bed, wiping away the tear that spilled onto her cheek. "I refuse to believe otherwise." She looked back up at Kane. "Your father will be glad to see you. But Doc gave him some medicine to help him rest easier, and I'm afraid it might be a while before he wakes up."

Kane hid his disappointment. His father had been unconscious after the shooting, and in too much pain when he finally came to after Doc Tatum had operated to remove the bullet, for Kane to be able to talk with him before heading out after Francesca. And the entire time he was gone, Kane had been anxious to get back, not only to check on his father's condition, but to express how sorry he was for causing this. "It's all right," he said. "Rest is the best thing for him."

"Yes, it is." His mother sighed, then drew her thin eyebrows together and wrinkled her nose in derision. "Did you find that horrid creature who shot him?"

Kane nodded and quickly explained his search for Francesca this past week, ending with the reason he'd brought his prisoner home with him. He watched disbelief pale his mother's cheeks when she learned about the latter, then saw the angry flames spark her eyes.

"I'll not have that woman in my house."

"I wouldn't ask you to. Marcus is keeping an eye on her for me down at the barn."

His mother nodded reluctant acquiescence; then sadness drooped her expression. "I wish you didn't have to leave again so soon."

"I wish I didn't, either. But I'll head back this way just as soon as I close this case." He quickly calculated how fast he expected to recover the gold and deposit his prisoner in the Somerville jail. "It shouldn't take me more than three days." *Provided Francesca cooperates, and Caleb finds Bartlett before that outlaw turns up to cause trouble.* He glanced over at his father, vowing to do whatever it took to get back without delay, knowing he'd be worried sick about the man every second he was gone.

His mother placed her small, warm palm against the side of his face. "I wish you'd consider giving up that badge, and come home for good this time, son."

Kane tensed at the familiar plea, first uttered when he'd come home for Charlotte's wedding, and repeated in each of the letters his mother had written since.

"Your father's going to need plenty of time to recover from this and get his strength back. You know what a chore it is to run this ranch. There's more work than Marcus can handle alone. We need you here, Kane. Now more than ever."

Condemnation nagged at his conscience. In times of crisis his family had always banded together, drawing strength from one another. He knew his place was here. He knew he should *want* to stay. Kane loved his family deeply, cherished the happy memories he had growing up here. It wasn't them he ran from, only the memories of Natalie—and the dreams he'd buried with her.

He removed her hand from his face and gently

wrapped his fingers around hers. "I'll come back for a while, Mother. But not for good."

Bianca peered through a gap in the pine logs, staring across the barn and out the open doors, where the heavy gray clouds coated the sky, and rain fell steadily. She wondered if Kane would hold true to his word about leaving. She did not relish the thought of a wet, chilling ride, but was not all that anxious to stay at the Fairchild ranch, either. The hatred she'd seen reflected in Marcus's eyes had been the reaction she expected, and the memory still made her nervous. So did the memory of the hostile stares she'd received from the cowhands when Marcus had brought her down to the barn, explained her identity, and had them cart everything out of the tack room except for the one horse blanket cushioning her numb bottom from the hay-littered ground.

She wrapped her shackled arms around her knees, hugging herself for a bit of warmth against the drop in temperature that had rolled in with the storm and slowly seeped through the log walls to invade her darkening prison. She rested her chin on her knees and curled her nose against the lingering smell of leather and oil, as old now as the boredom that had made the afternoon hours seem to tick by like days. The only excitement had been when the storm first blew in with a howling fury. Then, she'd heard the faint conversations of the men working outside the barn change to a rush of flurried shouts as the cattle's bawling from the pens had suddenly grown more urgent. She had heard Marcus leave when the noise started, and return once the wind died down and the rains finally came, to relieve the hand he'd posted in his absence. Then he had resumed his guard outside the tack room door. Beyond that all had been quiet, except for her thoughts, which were slowly driving her crazy with questions she had no answers for.

She still didn't want to believe that Francesca had shot

Kane's father, any more than she wanted to believe that her sister had kept quiet about something this important. Francesca had never kept secrets from her before, and it choked Bianca to think she would let her walk into this situation ignorant of the truth. Loyalty had always run deep between them, and family blood meant everything. Bianca was more than ready to defend her sister, but *dannare,* confusion sure made a poor arsenal of defense.

The sounds of approaching hooves and a jangling harness made her sit up straight. Bianca stared through the narrow slit again, surprised to see Kane in a small black buggy, drawing a paired team to a halt just outside the barn. He climbed down from the covered rig, then lifted a wooden crate off the seat and carried it inside. Black denims now hugged his long legs, and he wore a clean white shirt under his vest. Bianca glanced down at her dusty dress, envying the Ranger his opportunity to clean up.

"What are you doin' in Doc's buggy?" Marcus's voice filtered clearly from just outside the tack room door.

Bianca stared across the room, barely able to make out the two men's shadows through the small gaps in the wall.

"He's decided to stay the night and keep a watch on Pa's fever. So I borrowed it for you. Thought you'd appreciate not having to walk up to the house in the rain."

"And you not wantin' to get wet comin' down had nothing to do with it?" Marcus chuckled. "Not to mention *I* get to stable the horses now."

There was a brief moment of silence; then Kane responded with a laugh. "All right, I might have had a slight motive in that I didn't want to get wet. But that's it. Stabling the horses just worked out that way."

"An added bonus, you mean," Marcus jokingly responded; then his voice dropped to a somber level. "So, what did Doc say about Sam?"

"Just that he's holding his own." Kane's grim tone reflected a deep worry, and stabbed at Bianca's chest. "Supper's ready. I told Charlotte I'd send you up to the house to join them."

"Aren't you gonna sit down with us? We can get a couple of the hands to stand guard."

"I ate before I came down. Besides, guarding this prisoner is my job, and it's time I got back to it. But I want to thank you again for watching her, Marcus, and giving me time to spend with the family."

"Glad to do it. Did you get a chance to talk to Sam?"

"No, he's been sleeping the whole time."

"You still plannin' to head out?"

"Yeah, if the rain lets up within the next hour. If not, it'll be dark then and we'll just camp out down here and head out at dawn."

Bianca prayed the rain would last. She'd rather sleep on the ground in this tack room than try to do so sitting in a saddle or riding in Kane's lap again.

"Either way, I'll be up to say good-bye before I go."

"Be sure you do."

Bianca heard Marcus's footsteps softly pound the dirt as he walked away, then moments later the leather straps slapping against horse flesh, and the buggy pulling out. She jumped at the sound of a quick scrape against the doorjamb and saw a brief flash as bright as lightning reflected through the gaps. She heard the squeak and rattle of metal lifted off a hook, a glass globe being removed; then pale yellow light glowed through the narrow breeches in the wall. Bianca tensed when the log slat that barred the door was raised. Then the wooden barrier swung open, and Kane's tall presence filled the space, shrouded in a halo of soft light from the lantern sitting on the chair just outside. He'd removed his hat since entering the barn, and she noticed the damp, finger-combed rows that ran through his short sandy-blond hair. She also noticed further evidence of his opportunity to clean up in the missing stubble from his face.

She raked her gaze over his smooth, tanned jaw and square chin, frowning. There was something different

about the way he looked, and it took her a minute to
realize what it was—his mustache was gone. Bianca scru-
tinized him just a little closer, deciding he looked better
without it, then sighed her regret that she hadn't been
afforded the same chance for a bath and clean clothes,
and wondered what other comforts she'd have to go without for the next two weeks.

"You hungry?" He tilted his head toward the wooden
crate he held in his hands.

Bianca sniffed at the warm aroma of soup and fresh
bread that slowly permeated through the tack room's
smells, and felt the sudden ravenous pit form in her stomach. She nodded, grateful for his thought to at least her
nourishment, if not her cleanliness.

His boot heels kicked up small patches of dust as he
crossed the room. He stopped a little more than an arm's
length away from her and squatted down. With quick ef-
ficiency, he soon had the crate placed upside down as a
makeshift table, with a small, open crock of steaming
stew sitting on top. He unwrapped a thin cotton towel,
revealing two golden biscuits and a spoon; then he un-
screwed the lid from a mason jar filled with lemonade
and set it beside the rest of the fare.

Bianca hid her dislike of the sweet drink. She'd grown
up with a developed preference for wine with her meals,
following her parents' belief in the traditional saying that
"a day without wine is like a day without sun." But at
least the rest of the food looked and smelled delicious.
"Thank you, Mr. Fairchild," she said.

"You're welcome." He pushed the crate over in front
of her, then took a slight step back and lowered himself
to a sitting position on the ground, clasping his hands
together around his knees.

Leaning over slightly, she took a bite of the stew, welcoming the warmth that slid down her throat. She took
another, feeling it start to ease the chill inside. She took
a couple more bites, finding it as awkward to eat with
cuffed hands as it was having the Ranger watch her; then

she reached for one of the biscuits, curious about the faint aroma of orange that scented the warm bread. The light, fluffy feel of the small roll impressed her as much as the heavenly hint of sweetness that melted in her mouth when she bit into it. She finished the first biscuit between bites of stew and reached for the second, wondering if there might be a way she could obtain the recipe to serve these in her restaurant.

"These biscuits are very good. Who made them?"

"My sister, Charlotte."

Bianca waved her bound hands over the food. "Judging from this meal, your sister is a fine cook."

The chuckle from deep in his throat took her by surprise. "The fine cook who takes care of fixing meals around here is named Rosa. These biscuits are the *only* thing Charlotte can make that's fit for consumption. My sister really has no talent in the kitchen." His blue gaze burned with memories she wasn't privy to, and sparkled as much with love as with teasing. His wide smile softened his jaw and cut tiny lines into the corners of his eyes . . . and was the kindest look she'd ever seen the Ranger express. He wore it handsomely, too, making her heart skip a startled beat. "But it certainly isn't from lack of trying. I've had to eat some damned awful stuff she's tried to cook."

His humor evoked a smile from her, and it was on the tip of her tongue to reply that her sister wasn't that good a cook, either. But she caught herself in time, hiding both her panic at the near slip and her unexpected attraction to his smile behind another bite of biscuit.

His obvious affection for his sister reminded Bianca of the worry she'd seen in him earlier when he'd asked Marcus how Charlotte was holding up, and their resulting conversation that had hinted at her past problem with childbearing. Bianca had said a prayer for the woman then, able to identify a little with her grief after watching her *mamma* mourn three babies lost to miscarriages before finally giving birth to a son—the little brother Bianca had lost to the fever five years later, just hours after their mother's passing. She blinked away her sudden tears, offering up a prayer that her family was happy in the life beyond, and another for Charlotte's continued good health as well as her child's. Bianca also said a silent farewell to her chance for this biscuit recipe, knowing Kane's sister wasn't likely to share. Certainly not while they all thought she was Francesca . . . and certainly not if her sister had really shot the elder Mr. Fairchild.

Her stomach churned with reminders of her confusion about the shooting, and it chased away her hunger. Bianca set the remaining biscuit back on the towel and wiped her hands on one corner of the cloth.

Kane's face creased back into the scowl he wore most of the time around her. "Something wrong?"

She shook her head and offered a small smile. "Just full."

He pushed himself up and shifted to a kneeling position. Retrieving the lids, he covered the crock and the jar, then rocked back on his heels and rose to his feet. "I'll leave it here in case you want some more later." He turned and strode toward the door.

"Mr. Fairchild?"

He stopped and slowly turned around, then planted his hands on his hips. His narrowed gaze shimmered with puzzlement. "Why is it that you don't call me Ranger, like you did when we were together in Somerville?"

Bianca's heart pounded as hard and fast as the rain pelting the roof. *Why didn't Francesca tell me she called him Ranger?* Kane's comment on their spending time together in Somerville—and Francesca's contradiction that she barely knew the Ranger—also bothered her. She couldn't help but wonder what other details Francesca had left out of her story. Had she really stolen Kane's horse? Shot his father? Had she purposefully failed to mention Bianca would have to ride a horse? Even more unnerving to Bianca was why her sister would lie to her.

"I just did not think of it this time." She shrugged one

shoulder and licked at her dry lips, wishing she had a better reason to offer.

He cocked his head. "It's not a hard question, Francesca. Surely you can come up with a better lie than that." Irritation laced his voice. He squared his shoulders and folded his arms across his chest. "Never mind; I don't really care what you call me, or why. What did you want?"

Bianca rubbed her shaking hands along her skirt. She'd wanted to keep him here a moment longer and try to bring the conversation around to the shooting, with hopes of finding out details without making him suspicious of why she was asking. But it seemed like even less of a good idea now. "I . . . I was wondering if I could have some water to wash with."

He nodded. "Anything else?"

She started to shake her head, then stopped. "Just that I am very sorry about what happened to your papa."

He scowled harder. "It's been my experience that outlaws usually are sorry—when they get caught."

Bianca sighed, wishing he'd believe her sincerity, and sorry to see that glimpse of his more relaxed, lighter side gone so soon. "I assure you, I wish your papa only good health."

"I don't recall you being the least bit worried about his health when you suckered me in with your lies so you could grab my gun and shoot him."

"No," she whispered her shock, not meaning to speak aloud, and wishing she hadn't when Kane's face reddened with anger.

"Stop it! You know damn well you did, Francesca." He lowered his arms; his eyes blazed daggers at her. "I've been trying to be halfway decent to you when what I really want is to put my hands around your throat and choke the living daylights out of you, and I'm getting sick and tired of you treating me like a fool. I believed your little act in Somerville. And I fell for that phony twisted ankle you pulled on me and my father, but that ship has sailed for good. Trust me, sweetheart, I'm not falling for any more of your lies, or this memory-loss act you've got going."

Her blood pumped ice through her veins. *Dio, Francesca, what have you done?* Bianca took several deep breaths, reeling from Kane's accusations that swirled among her confusion, leaving her with more questions and still no answers. But Francesca was her sister. Family. Kane was a stranger. Bianca had no reason to believe a stranger over her own blood. It was not her family's way. They had always stood by each other no matter what.

So why *did* she believe Kane? And why did she feel this odd urge to appease his aggravation? "It is not my intent to treat you like a fool, Mr. Fairchild."

Kane chuckled harshly. "It's always your intent, sweetheart." He turned and walked out, roughly closing the door behind him.

Bianca blinked, feeling the tear slip free and slide down her cheek. *Dio, Francesca, what have you gotten me into?*

SIX

Hundreds of seagulls circled above the bay and flocked around the dozens of brightly colored shrimp boats moored along the pier. Cacophonous squalls blended with the laughter of children playing on the decks, with the fishermen's boisterous voices as they hoisted green-and-white nets over tall, spindly masts to let them dry in the salty air, with the muted sounds of sharp feminine tones amid the clattering of pots and dishes coming from the small cabins that centered each boat.

Hailey Tillman stood near the back of the shrimping vessel tied closest to the wharf and pondered what to do as she gazed out across the bay watching the sun slip from view, its final light capping the horizon in a hazy lavender farewell. She didn't live in the best part of Galveston to be walking home alone after sunset, but she wasn't anxious to leave, either. Not without knowing her friend was all right. Hailey glanced toward the pier and ran her hands along her crossed arms as a shudder of worry rippled through her.

Where are you, Bianca?

She'd been waiting for almost two hours already. Had bided her time listening to the gay banter among the fishermen's wives as they'd spread straw mats along the pier and sorted fresh shrimp and oysters amid their offerings of honey and other goods brought from ports farther up the bayou. Had enjoyed listening to their bartering with the swell of people strolling by in search of the best price

for the best catch of the day. And all the while thinking
that any minute she would see her friend among the
crowd. But the people had thinned out to just a trickle
now, and families were settling in for the night . . . and
trepidation over Bianca's absence tugged a little harder
at her consciousness.

Soon after Hailey had arrived for work at the Tremont
Hotel this morning, she learned about her friend's getting
fired the night before, and was instantly concerned when
she heard *which* shipping owner Bianca had dumped food
on. Hailey knew Avis Murdock. She knew the man had
a violent temper, and she had seen him take revenge before for being publicly embarrassed. Worry for Bianca's
safety had only increased when her friend never sought
her out today as Hailey had expected, to share the truth
about the incident rather than letting her hear only the
gossip.

Hailey sighed, cautioning herself not to overreact. *Just
because I haven't seen Bianca today doesn't mean Murdock has done something to her.*

She skimmed her gaze over the line of boats, reminding herself that Bianca had friends who looked out for
her among this Italian fishing community, as well as her
godparents—the Casales—and their three sons. *There's
nothing for me to worry about.* Bianca was no doubt taking supper with friends or the Casales, as Hailey knew
she often did.

Hailey knit her eyebrows together. *So, why can't I
shake this uneasiness that something isn't right?*

In the two months since she'd met Bianca one afternoon at the beach—when they'd struck up a conversation
that had led to their discovery of a common interest in
shell collecting, and the beginning of a blossoming
friendship—they had spent many afternoons together,
walking along the shore in search of shells, sharing bits
and pieces of their lives, their dreams, and growing closer
in their trust of each other. Bianca had even helped Hailey
obtain her current position as a maid at the hotel. At a

far better wage than she'd made selling painted shells to the tourists, too.

Given what she knew about Avis Murdock, Hailey couldn't make herself leave without finding her friend first and making sure all was well.

She stared at the dozens of boats again, wondering where to begin searching. Although Bianca had often talked about her friends here, Hailey had never met any of them, with the exception of Bianca's godparents' youngest son.

Her pulse pounded faster, as it did every time she thought of Raimondo Casale since meeting him a month ago, when Bianca had invited him to come along on one of their planned outings to the beach, hoping Hailey wouldn't mind the last minute intrusion. And how could Hailey have possibly minded, when her heart was lost to him from the moment she'd gazed into his warm, brown eyes and inviting smile, from the second he told her what a pleasure it was to meet such a lovely girl, and had lifted her hand to his lips for a soft kiss? She'd floated on a cloud of enchantment that afternoon, enjoying his wit and his wonderful gift for spinning a story, enjoying the sight of his lean, muscular body gliding through the waves crashing to shore. And she had thought by his flirtatious attention that he had felt something for her as well.

A sadness pulled at Hailey's chest, for she'd been wrong. Raimondo had made no effort to call on her after that day, and the two times she'd seen him since, he had treated her with nothing more than a gentlemanly politeness. Except for the couple of times that she'd seen him staring at her when he thought no one was looking, and had caught a brief gleam in his eyes that strongly reminded her of the way his gaze had darkened with desire when he'd looked at her that day at the beach. Hailey frowned, chiding herself. Or maybe it was just her heart longing too much for it to be true. For why would Raimondo hide any feelings he carried for her? She had cer-

tainly given him every encouragement to act on them—if
they truly existed.

She'd thought more than once of confiding in Bianca
about her infatuation with Raimondo, and of asking her
friend to talk to him and find out if he did have any
feelings for her. But Hailey had kept silent, not wanting
to use her new friendship with Bianca for such selfish-
ness, or to risk an awkward and embarrassing situation
for them all should she expose her deepening fondness
for him only to have Raimondo verbalize the rejection
he'd been politely delivering by inaction so far.

Hailey took a deep breath and closed her eyes, telling
herself just to forget Raimondo. But with each passing
day she only thought of him more, and wondered if she
would ever be able to get him out of her mind or her
heart. Even now his memory haunted her so deeply that
she thought she could hear the jaunty tune he frequently
whistled drifting on the salty breeze.

Then she heard the soft thud of someone jumping onto
the boat's bow. Her eyes flew open as booted feet landed
hard on the front deck. The whistling stopped.

"Bianca? Where are you?"

Hailey smiled at the heavy accent in his familiar deep
voice, and the thought of seeing him again sent her blood
rushing with heated intensity. She quickly brushed away
from her face the chestnut strands the wind had pulled
loose from her chignon, tucking them behind her ears.
Then she pinched her cheeks for color, and turned just
as Raimondo came striding around the corner of the
cabin.

She thought she saw a slight falter in his step when he
spotted her, thought she saw a spark brighten his eyes.
But in a flash he was cutting a steady pace once again
and the look was gone, and Hailey wasn't sure it hadn't
just been her hope once again playing tricks with her
imagination.

"Hello, Raimondo."

"*Ciao,* signorina Hailey." He reached up as though to

tip the black cap he usually wore. But it wasn't there, and as he cut his eyes up in a quick glance, a tinge of red spotted his smooth, wind-tanned cheeks.

Hailey swallowed her chuckle at his slight embarrassment, thinking how the flush in his face, and his curly black hair cut short and tousled across his wide forehead, made him look younger than the six years in age he had over her nineteen. Through lowered lashes, she raked an admiring gaze over the white shirt hugging his broad shoulders, along his smooth, sun-bronzed neck, and the glimpse of his chest below the open collar. Tan pants encased his lean hips and muscled thighs, disappearing into the tops of his brown boots.

"You are looking well." He stopped in front of her, his smile creasing brackets on the side of his mouth and making her heart skip a beat.

Hailey swallowed. "You, too, Raimondo."

He glanced around the boat, frowning at the darkened cabin. "Where is our wayward friend?"

Apprehension rushed in with a chilling reminder of why she was here, crowding out her pleasure at Raimondo's unexpected company. "I don't know. I've been waiting a while, hoping she would be home any time. But then it started to get dark, and I decided maybe she was having supper with your family."

He shook his head. "We have not seen her all day. Was Bianca expecting you tonight?"

"No." Hailey ran her trembling hands along the sides of her black skirt, glancing toward the other boats. "Has anyone seen her today?"

Raimondo shrugged, his straight, black eyebrows pulling together. "Why? What is wrong, Hailey? What makes you so . . ." He waved one hand about, his forehead wrinkling in frustration as she'd seen him do whenever he had to stop to search for the English words to translate his thoughts. ". . . nervous?"

Hailey scanned the dock again, offering up a quick prayer that she would see Bianca coming home. But she didn't recognize any of the few people hurrying through twilight's increasing shadows, and trepidation's vise gripped her once again.

"Did you know Bianca got fired from her job last night?"

Raimondo jerked up straight, shaking his head. "Why did this happen?"

Hailey explained the details she'd gleaned from the gossip about how Bianca had accused the shipping owner of fondling her backside and dumped food in his lap. As she spoke, she watched Raimondo's hands slowly ball into fists at his sides and his jaw harden with anger. "I thought Bianca would come and see me today and tell me herself what had happened. But she didn't, and I'm really starting to get worried. Avis Murdock doesn't take kindly to being humiliated."

Raimondo's eyes narrowed to slits. "Are you saying he might try to hurt her?"

"I don't know." Hailey tensed, not wanting to think the worst but unable not to. "Maybe. But one thing I *am* certain of is that Murdock is an evil man, and I would feel much better if I knew Bianca was all right."

"How do you know this man is evil?"

"How I know doesn't matter, only that I do."

Raimondo wrapped his hands around her upper arms and pulled her close, stealing her breath with his gentle firmness. Her breasts lightly pressed against his chest, her nipples tingling, her pulse racing at the intoxicating smell of salt and wind that kissed his skin and blended with his spicy male scent.

"It does matter. Tell me what this man has done to you."

"Nothing. I just know his reputation."

Raimondo frowned his disbelief. "Why don't you want to tell me the truth, Hailey?"

She swallowed, puzzled by his persistence and not the least anxious to answer his question. For the past few years, she'd been working hard to build a new life for herself, and Avis Murdock was a part of the past she wanted to forget about forever. "All I'm concerned about right now is finding Bianca. Please, Raimondo, will you help me look for her?"

He clenched his jaw; his dark eyes flashed his desire to demand answers from her as several long, silent seconds ticked by. But he finally nodded, sighing with reluctant resignation. Hailey released the breath she'd been holding.

"We will search among our community first. It will go faster if I get my brothers to help us find out if anyone has seen her. And after we find Bianca, my family will see to it that this Avis Murdock pays for daring to lay his hand on her." Raimondo removed one hand from her arm and placed his rough, warm palm against her cheek. "And I give you my word, Hailey, he will also pay for whatever he has done to you."

The surprising depth of concern and promised defense she heard in his voice and saw in his gaze sent a warm glow cascading over her heart, and her hope soared that perhaps he really did care for her. Then doubts rushed in as Raimondo's stare shuttered closed, as he lowered his hands to his sides and moved away from her.

If he does care for me, then why does he keep backing away instead of acting on those feelings?

Francesca treats me like a fool because I am one.

Kane stared at the blanket barrier stretched over the rope he'd tacked up, his mind conjuring up unwanted images of pale flesh as he listened to the gentle splashes coming from the other side. Despite his aggravation with her for denying having taken his gun and shooting his father, he'd still felt sorry for her dusty, disheveled appearance and had supplied her request for some water with a whole damn hip-tub-full to bathe in. Since the rain had shown no signs of dissipating, either, and the temperature kept dropping, he'd also brought her to this of-

fice at the opposite end of the barn, where the walls were
more solid than the tack room, and a water closet and
stove provided more comfort. Hell, he'd even given her
water to rinse her clothes.

Lamplight illuminated the small, square room, casting
a soft yellowish haze on the rough-hewn walls and the
stockings and chemise he'd spread for her over the back
of a chair near the fired stove. His gaze drifted over the
damp white petticoat and black shirtwaist she'd draped
along the top of the two blankets forming the thin wall.
Kane lifted the half-filled tumbler of whiskey to his lips
and downed the contents, scowling when the fiery
warmth that hit his gut did nothing to erase his thoughts
of her.

Why can't I get this she-devil out of my system? Before
he'd caught up with her in Galveston, he hadn't had a
lick of trouble hating her and hadn't given a damn about
her comfort, or what happened to her—as long as the
latter happened in prison or at the end of a rope. He
grabbed the bottle and poured another measure of whiskey, downing it, then frowning. Nothing had changed. He
still wanted justice. But why couldn't he shake this an-
noying need to be nice to her in the meantime?

Rain beat a steady staccato against the roof, and darkness reigned outside the narrow window as evening
marched closer toward the midnight hour. Kane blew out
a heavy sigh, poured another shot into the glass, then
capped the bottle and stuck the whiskey back into the
side bottom drawer where his father always kept it, trying
not to think about the long night still ahead. But the
sounds of sloshing water reminded him of the woman's
nakedness behind that blanket and created images that
had him shifting uncomfortably in his seat.

He grabbed the glass and closed his eyes as he tossed
the liquor back against his throat, longing for the day
Francesca Rossetti would be found guilty by a jury and
sentenced for her crimes . . . and he'd never have to lay
eyes on her again.

He set the glass down, then leaned the wooden chair back against the wall and propped his feet, ankles crossed, on top of the desk.

"Excuse me, Mr . . . um, Ran—Ranger, could you hand me some more rinse water, *per favore?*"

He cringed as she stumbled over the name with a grating tone that didn't sound even remotely close to the purr he'd heard her use in Somerville. *Why is she doing this?* He shook his head and brought the chair back down on all four legs, then stood. As he crossed the room, he grabbed the porcelain pitcher she'd placed in the wide gap between the edge of the blanket and the planked flooring. Snagging the towel off a wall hook, Kane lifted the kettle from the stove top and filled the pitcher with the remaining hot water, then returned.

He bent over and slid the pitcher back under the blanket. His gaze locked on her backside pressing a soft indentation into the dark wool as she leaned down to reach for the pitcher. He had not realized until then that she'd gotten out of the tub. His eyes traveled to the open space beneath the blanket. He swallowed at the sight of her bare heels and the brief glimpse of her smooth, pale legs, his blood racing with sudden memories of the one time he'd seen the shapely pale flesh of her naked backside.

Kane straightened with a start. *Don't forget that one glimpse landed me in a heap of trouble with the boss, too.* His heart wrenched with guilt. *And nearly cost Pa his life.*

Frustrated strides quickly carried him back behind the desk. He sat down in the chair and ran one hand through his hair, trying to chase away the image of her rinsing herself as he heard the water pour into the tub, trying to ignore the soft rustle of clothing minutes later as she dressed, his tension winding tighter than a coiled snake. He rubbed his fingers against his temples, stewing over the time he still had to spend in her company, not relishing a minute of it, and vowing not to let her little games and pretenses drag it out, either. He decided he'd just set that rule down right now, too, and save them both an argument later. But when she pulled the blanket aside and stepped out, Kane's resolve lodged in his throat.

His heart raced at the sight of her glowing face and soft golden gaze that bared her relief at being clean. Her damp, towel-dried hair hung in a tousled mass, richly dark against her ivory skin, and looked more desirable than any way he'd ever seen her wear it yet. He swept his stare over the black skirt that she'd managed to brush free of the majority of the dust, and over his blue chambray shirt he'd loaned her to wear while her clothes dried, noticing she'd had to roll the sleeves back several times. The shirt swallowed her narrow shoulders and slender frame, but to his chagrin the cotton did little to hide the swells of her full breasts, or her puckered nipples that defined the material.

"Thank you again for the bath . . . Ranger." The name rolled a little easier off her tongue this time, and her smile creased the sweet dimples into her cheeks, both sending heat barreling through his hardening body.

Kane clenched his jaw. *Jesus, what's wrong with me?* He hadn't been this drawn to a woman since Natalie, and he certainly didn't want to be drawn to *this* woman. "You're welcome," he ground out, watching her smile fade at his rough tone. He stood, grabbed the comb he'd taken from his saddlebag and placed on the desk earlier, and walked over to hand it to her. "And why don't you just stick to calling me Mr. Fairchild?"

She snatched the comb from his grasp, then raised her chin a defiant notch. "Fine. I much prefer that, anyway."

Her reddening cheeks and burning gaze suggested she'd prefer to call him something much worse, which was fine with him. He had a few choice names for her, too. Kane walked back and sat down against the front edge of the desk. He crossed his arms, reminding himself he was only keeping an eye on Francesca because he didn't trust her not to try to bury that comb in his back, and he forced himself not to find an ounce of pleasure in watching her work the tangles from her long hair. He tried his best not to stare at her breasts, too, but was doing a damn poor job of it.

He took a deep breath, glad when she noticed the cotton pulling tight against her nipples and turned away, offering him the view of her back instead, but he was a little surprised as well by her action. He'd never known Francesca to display that sort of modesty. It was more her style to flaunt her wares, usually in an effort to con a man out of something. And that's what he'd expected this time: for her to make some attempt to seduce him in an effort to claim his gun and try to flee this prison. He frowned, glad she hadn't, but puzzled nonetheless.

Why does she keep behaving so different from before?

Trying to figure out her act reminded Kane of his intention to inform her that he wouldn't tolerate any delays on the rest of their journey together. "I want you to understand that I'm through with your games, Francesca."

She paused with the comb midstroke and stiffened her back.

"When we leave out from here in the morning," he continued, "I don't want any more of this pretense of not knowing how to ride."

She glanced over her shoulder, determination edging the slender line of her jaw. "I will do my best to ride that horse, if you will promise to take me straight to Somerville."

Kane arched one eyebrow, wondering again what her itch was to get back there so quickly. "Sure, sweetheart, just as soon as you take me to where you hid the gold."

She turned around to face him, lines of exasperation marring her brow. "I have told you I did not help rob that bank." She swung one hand out to her side in an aggravated stroke. "Why do you keep insisting I know anything about this gold?"

Kane's pulse simmered with barely controlled patience. "Because I know you *did* help rob that bank, and I know that Bartlett swears you stole the loot from him.

I also know that you were toting *something* heavy on that second horse you had when I tracked you from his hideout, so I'd say he's telling the truth. Question is, what did you do with it? Because we both know you didn't have anything but one lame horse when you waylaid my father off the road with the intention of stealing his." *Before I happened along to mess up your plans.* Kane's gut tightened. *And to cause this nightmare for my family.*

Her body slumped; her face paled with a bafflement so genuine, Kane believed she truly had no idea what he was talking about—almost. Just for half a second, until the reminders of her acting ability, her lies, and the effort he expected her to put into trying to escape from him and the sentencing that awaited her shoved it out.

"When we head out in the morning, I don't want any more of your confusions, your pretenses, or your lies. I want you to take me straight to the gold, you understand?"

She squared her shoulders, nodding, but there was a hesitation in her gaze that had him doubting the sincerity of her acquiescence. Her bare feet made no sound as she walked over and handed him the comb.

"Grazie." She lifted her chin slightly. "I am tired and would like to go to sleep now."

She didn't look the least bit tired to him. In fact, she looked pretty worried, and he wondered if it was the thought of prison that haunted her, or something else. He pushed away from the desk, then set the comb down on the scarred oak top and retrieved the handcuffs. She held both arms out. Kane reached for her left one, which was less chafed and had no skin broken like the other, and locked the metal band around her wrist. He removed his gun from his holster and placed it on the desk, grabbed a hammer and two nails, and led Francesca over to the bedroll he'd spread close to the stove. He waited until she lowered herself to a sitting position, then knelt at her side.

"Lie down," he ordered.

Her throat rippled as she swallowed. Slowly, she

stretched out on her back on the pallet, her rounded gaze darting between him and the objects he held in his hand.

Kane was surprised he didn't find any satisfaction in her anxiety, considering it was the first time he'd ever had any kind of upper hand with this woman instead of being just an ignorant pawn in her schemes. He gently pulled her shackled arm a short way out from her body, then placed the handcuffs flush against the floor. He set a nail through the center of one of the links, hammered it in halfway, then pounded it over the chain's metal edge, and finished by burying the head solidly into the wood. Kane did the same with the second nail, then tugged at the cuffs, confident when the links didn't budge from the floor that his prisoner was secure enough that he could catch a little sleep himself tonight. Standing, he grabbed the blanket he'd set on the chair earlier, shook it out, and covered her as he handed it down.

She offered a small nod of thanks, then turned on her side toward him and closed her eyes. Kane stared at her, puzzling at the tear he saw slip free and slide over the bridge of her nose—and rankled at his urge to kneel down and offer comfort.

He spun around on one heel and walked away, trading the hammer for his gun, which he shoved back in his holster. He started to sit down in the chair when the door suddenly opened, admitting a rush of the wet, windy chill outside, along with his brother-in-law.

Francesca jerked up, propping herself up on her shackled arm, her face paling with surprise.

Worry charged a path through Kane's chest. He was certain only bad news would bring Marcus out in the weather. "Is my father worse?"

"No." Marcus closed the door and removed his hat, shaking off the excess water before hanging the brown Stetson on a wall peg. "In fact, Doc says his fever is comin' down some."

Kane released the breath he'd been holding, encouraged by the news, though his brother-in-law's expression was still grim. "Nice of you to come all the way down here to tell me."

"I figured you'd want to know." He slipped the yellow poncho from his shoulders, a grin pulling at his mouth as he held the dripping slicker out with one hand. "But I also came to tell you that Sam's awake, and he's asking to see you. I'll keep an eye on your prisoner while you're gone."

Kane smiled, relief coursing through him that the rain had kept him from leaving, from missing this chance to tell his pa how sorry he was for what had happened. "Thanks, Marcus."

Kane rounded the desk, took the slicker and draped it over his shoulders, then grabbed his hat, shoving it on his head as he walked out the door into the rain. Minutes later he entered the house through the kitchen, greeted by his mother, who was dressed in a white gown and blue robe and standing at the stove pouring him a cup of coffee. His sister was there, as well, her pink nightgown draped over her swollen stomach, her short braid of caramel hair swishing about her shoulders as she walked across the room, one hand pressed against her back, the other holding out a towel that she handed to him. Both women wore hopeful smiles that mirrored Kane's own prayers that his father's fever would keep coming down.

They spoke briefly about his condition as Kane shucked out of the wet gear, then his boots, and dried his face. But he was anxious to see his father and didn't tarry long, carrying the cup of coffee with him as he left the kitchen and sipping at it as he made his way up the stairs and down the hall. He stepped through the open door into the dimly lit room, pausing when he saw his father— propped up slightly with pillows now—and choking up at the smile that spread across the elder man's face when their eyes met.

Doc Tatum snapped his black bag closed, grabbed it in one hand, and walked away from the bed, coming over to stand in front of Kane.

"How is he, Doc?"

"Better than I'd expected." A positive spark shone in the physician's blue eyes and relaxed the lines that creased his round, middle-aged face, easing Kane's worry some. "He's breathing much easier now, and the wound doesn't look any worse. If his fever's down by morning, I'd venture to say he'll pull through this."

"Damn right, I will."

The voice was weakened, but Kane still heard the familiar ring of determination in his father's tone and smiled.

Doc chuckled and shook his head. "Good thing stubbornness will only add to the cure in this case." He raised one hand and patted Kane on the shoulder. "Don't stay too long. He needs his rest."

Kane gave his promise he'd only be a minute, then closed the door behind the physician. He set the tin mug down on the dresser, crossed the room, and lowered himself into the burgundy wing-backed chair pulled up close to the bed. He noticed a half-filled cup of what smelled like sassafras tea on the bedside table. Staring at the added gauntness in his father's lean, weathered face, he hoped the appetite his mother had said he'd lost days ago would soon return. "I'm real glad to hear you're doing better, Pa."

He chuckled low. "Your mother didn't give me much choice. She threatened bodily harm if I didn't beat this." He took several deep breaths, his expression turning more serious. "Besides, I'm not ready to journey from this earth just yet."

"No one's ready for you to go, either." Kane blinked away the threatening moisture at the thought of how close he had come to losing his father.

Your mother says you caught that woman who shot me."

Kane nodded. "I intend to see justice served for everything she's done, too."

"Marcus told me about the list of charges against her. Sounds like the woman's nothing but trouble."

Kane frowned. "That's stating it kindly." And his father didn't even know the half of it. Though he'd told his family about the robbery, he hadn't mentioned Francesca's seduction, or his gullibility that had played right into her hands. The only people who knew how he'd been suckered in Somerville were the sheriff, his boss, and Caleb. *And Francesca,* Kane seethed.

He leaned forward, bracing both arms on his thighs and clamping his hands together between his knees. He blew out a weighty sigh and looked straight at his father. "I should have seen through her lie about that twisted shin long before she had the chance to shoot you, Dad. I'm real sorry I let that happen."

"Hell, I fell for her lie, too, son. It's a man's curse to be turned by a pretty face. Can't beat yourself up for that. We were only trying to help. She's the one to blame for choosing to be sneaky."

Kane shook his head. "Yeah, but I knew what she was capable of, Dad; you didn't."

His father placed one hand on Kane's shoulder. "I'm the one to blame for getting shot. I never should've tried to grab the reins and spooked that gal like I did. So just forget any guilt you wanna try to carry around about this. You hear me?"

Kane took a deep breath, slowly nodding. But seeing his father like this, feeling the weakened strength in his grip, he couldn't fully let go of the guilt, and vowed again to make sure Francesca Rossetti paid for her crimes.

His father smiled. "Good." He lowered his hand back to the bed, a grimace of pain briefly clouding his face, then his expression turned somber again. "Your ma also said that she asked you again to come home. I just want to add this time that I hope you'll think real hard about it, son. Because I'd like for you to come back, too."

Kane sat up and cocked his head in surprise at the request. His father had always just expressed his understanding of Kane's decision to leave, explaining long ago how he'd accidentally overheard the argument between his son and daughter-in-law the day she died, and that he knew his son needed time to heal. Kane had deeply appreciated his father's understanding, and to hear the request for him to come back now had him not wanting to let the man down.

"I'm planning to come back for a while and help out until you're well."

"That's what your ma said." He paused, clearing the cough that rattled in his throat. "But I'd like you to consider staying longer than that. This is your home, Kane, and I think it's time you gave serious thought to settling back down here."

Kane tensed. He was willing to come back, and would somehow find a way to live with the memories while he was here, but he wasn't ready to make any deeper commitment than that. Though he found it harder to say no to his father than to his mother, he shook his head anyway.

His father hesitated, breathing deeply, his bushy blond eyebrows pulling into a straight line across his forehead. "I've stayed silent and given you time because you needed it, son. But what happened to Natalie isn't your fault, and you need to put this guilt to rest. You can't beat yourself up forever over one mistake." His tone was stern but still laced with worry and love. "It's time you made some peace with yourself."

Kane sighed, thankful for the words and concern. "I'm trying, Dad." But how could he find peace when he could never forget that he'd selfishly denied Natalie's simple request to accompany her to town? And how could he forgive himself for putting that sad look in her eyes on what should have been one of the happiest days of their lives, then doing nothing to mend their quarrel before she'd left the ranch that day, never to return?

SEVEN

Kane glanced over his shoulder and waved a final fare-well to his mother and Charlotte, who stood on the front porch, then faced front in his saddle and kicked the buck-skin into a trot down the lane. He tipped his hat brim down against the midmorning sun blazing bright across the azure sky, the only remnants of last night's rain evident in the small puddles scattered along the road, and a few glistening drops still clinging to the grass. He hadn't left at dawn as he'd planned, but instead had gotten two hands to stand guard over his prisoner while he gathered around the breakfast table with his family and Doc Tatum and celebrated the good news that his father had sweated out the rest of the fever during the night. The wound was looking much better.

Kane didn't regret spending this extra time with his family. He missed them, and despite the memories of Natalie that had crept in at the dining room table when-ever he let himself think about the empty spot beside him, he had found himself looking forward to coming back for a while. Maybe sticking around long enough to see his new little niece or nephew born.

After talking with his father again this morning, Kane wondered if maybe the elder man was right and coming home *would* help him find a way to put Natalie's mem-ory—and his guilt—to rest.

And maybe it would only make it worse. He hadn't forgotten the house he'd been secretly building for Natalie in her favorite meadow a few miles away, and that still sat unfinished, waiting for him to decide what to do with it. Too clearly he remembered the few things his young wife had ever wanted in her life: a home of her own, children, and the chance to breed horses, which she loved so much. It had been Kane's sole goal in life to give her everything she wanted, too, and he'd failed to give her any of it. All because he'd been stubborn about wanting to stay behind to finish the surprise he had for her instead of going to town that day and being there to protect her when she'd needed him most.

He took a deep breath and released it on a heavy sigh as he rode through the small grove of pines. Marcus was standing off to one side where he'd left him fifteen minutes ago while he'd gone to say his final good-bye to his family. His brother-in-law held one gloved hand gripped around the reins to the saddled sorrel, where his prisoner sat.

Kane slid his gaze to Francesca, thoughts of his family fading as he returned his focus to his job, to staying alert and bringing this fugitive to justice. Though she'd braided her hair and coiled the mink rope at her nape in the style more familiar to him and had climbed into the saddle this morning with little hesitation—albeit a bit slow and stiff—he'd seen an apprehension in her eyes every now and then that had him wondering if her attempt to appear normal was only another part of her act. An attempt to get him to lower his guard while she set some plan into motion.

He tensed. *Not this time, sweetheart.*

Kane reined the buckskin to a stop alongside his brother-in-law. "Thanks again for helping me keep an eye on her."

"You know I'm glad to help you out any time I can." Marcus handed up the reins, which Kane took and wrapped around his saddle horn.

Kane nodded, then reached down and shook Marcus's proffered hand, not for the first time grateful that his little sister had married this hard-working, honorable man. He was glad Marcus had been a comforting presence for Charlotte after the mercantile owner's son she had been courting for two years and her best childhood girlfriend both broke her heart when they left town together, secretly eloping and not even bothering to leave behind a note of explanation or apology.

"See you in a few days."

"Looking forward to it. I'm glad you'll be staying a while." Marcus cut a quick glance at the woman, then looked back at him. "Be careful."

Kane nodded, then started to swing his gaze toward his prisoner, but never made it that far as he spotted a rider reining his horse to a stop down at the barn, and froze. Caution tightened his muscles. Suspicion and anger thrashed around in his thoughts as he watched the rider talk with one of the cowhands, saw the man glance over as the hand pointed their way. Devon Carson kicked his bay into a walk toward them.

"Do you know that man headed this way, Marcus?"

His brother-in-law tipped his hat brim up slightly and planted his hands on his hips, staring. "Nope. Do you?"

"I saw him in Houston yesterday morning. And again after arriving in Flat Rock. He told me his name's Devon Carson." He shrugged one shoulder. "That may or may not be the truth. What really bothers me is that I think he's following us." Kane turned to his prisoner, wondering if her wide-eyed look stemmed from surprise at seeing Carson again, or just seeing him *here*. "You ready to tell me what you know about him?"

She shook her head, her throat rippling into her high-buttoned collar as she swallowed. "Nothing. He is a stranger to me."

Kane arched his brow in skepticism. "No more lies, remember?"

"I am not lying," she insisted with that same innocent tone that he wanted to believe—and knew he didn't dare.

Kane shot her a narrowed look of distrust, then turned

away to watch Carson ride closer. "I don't trust him any more than I do her, Marcus."

"Let's send him packing, then."

Kane nodded his approval of that comment and waited tensely until Carson finally reined his horse to a stop just a few feet from them.

The cowboy sat back in his saddle and smiled. "Nice to see you again, Ranger." He glanced away briefly, tipping his hat. "You too, ma'am."

"What do you want, Carson?" Kane snapped. He kept his prisoner in his corner sight, watching for any sign that she was about to try something funny.

The cowboy pushed his brown hat brim up higher, then leaned forward and crossed his arms over the saddle horn. "I came to talk to that man." He pointed one leather-gloved finger at Marcus. "That is, if you're Mr. Caldwell?"

"I am." Marcus shifted his stance, leaning his weight on one leg, then crossed his arms. "What can I do for you?"

"I'm lookin' for a job. Heard ya might be hirin'."

"What are you really doing here?" Kane's blood simmered with speculation at the cowboy's connection to his prisoner.

"I'm lookin' for work. And I'm talkin' to Mr. Caldwell. Not you."

Kane shook his head. "There's no work for you here."

Carson narrowed his eyes, anger darkening his green gaze. "Look, Ranger, whatever burr you've got under your backside about me, that's just too bad. I'm an innocent man lookin' for an honest day's work, and I enjoy talkin' with a pretty gal now and then. There ain't nothin' wrong with any of that."

Kane shrugged. "Maybe so, but there's no work for you at *this* ranch."

"Well, since it ain't none of your concern, why don't you let the boss here tell me that?"

"I'm sure my brother-in-law will be glad to, won't you Marcus?"

"Kane's right." Marcus unfolded his arms and planted his hands back on his hips. " 'Fraid I've got nothin' to offer you. So you might as well be on your way."

Surprisingly, Carson only smiled, then reached up and tipped his hat. "Good day to you folks, then." He wheeled his horse around and rode off, kicking the bay into a gallop through the ranch yard and back up the winding road.

"You mind sending a couple of the hands to follow him, Marcus? I don't want him easily picking up our trail from here."

"Don't mind a bit." Marcus strode off, calling out to two cowhands as he headed toward the barn.

Kane watched Carson top the hill and disappear, certain the cowboy would turn up again. *And when he does, I'll be ready.* He braced one hand on his thigh and turned to his prisoner.

"All right, sweetheart, which way to the gold?"

Bianca shifted her seat in the saddle, not sure which hurt more—the pain in her backside, or deception's knife twisting in her heart. Why had Francesca shot Kane's father?

Why didn't she tell me the truth about her troubles?

The late afternoon rays beat down from the clear sky with a scorching intensity that rivaled the perplexing questions that had haunted her sleep last night, nagged at her all day, and still left her with only one answer she could fathom: her sister had been desperate. *But why?*

She sighed her frustration, no closer to that answer than she was to understanding why Francesca had lied about how well she knew Kane Fairchild. She was no closer to knowing if he spoke the truth about her sister taking the gold, either. Was this just another of Bartlett's lies about her sister's involvement with the bank robbery?

Or another of the details Francesca had left out of her story.

Bianca still wanted to believe the truth she'd seen in Francesca's eyes when she had claimed innocence of the robbery. Wanted to believe that the hundred dollars Francesca had given her wasn't part of the stolen money. But Kane had sounded so sure of his accusations, and provided too many details for Bianca to stop the niggling doubts about the robbery that kept wanting to creep in. She was certain of only one thing now. She had to get to Somerville and wait for Francesca to meet her there as planned. Then demand the truth from her twin.

Bounce. Bounce. Bounce. *Ouch. Ouch. OUCH!*

Dannare! Even more than the opportunity to talk with her sister again, Bianca wanted to be off this horse and back home, where the most torture she had to endure in a day was from Raimondo's teasing.

The thought of her friend brought melancholy nipping at her heart. She'd known Raimondo all of her life. Their families had been friends even back in Sicily, and had sailed to America together. The Casale boys had always been like protective brothers toward her and Francesca, and she knew they would be worried about her. Her godparents and Hailey, too. Bianca wished again that she'd been given the opportunity to ease their minds with a false excuse for her absence, and couldn't help wondering what they would think had happened to her.

"Well, here we are," Kane stated, jerking Bianca from her musings.

She slumped with welcome relief as he brought the horses to a stop. Then she stared at the grassy meadow that lined both sides of the road—at this spot where Francesca had shot his father—and tensed as an odd sense of fear slithered up her spine. It was a fleeting sensation that vanished as quickly as it came, but it left her with a reinforcing certainty that her sister *had* been desperate when she pulled that trigger.

A twinge of anger wormed its way into her thoughts.

But *desperate* didn't explain why her twin would break the bonds of blood and be deceitful with her about what she'd done.

Kane pushed his hat brim up with one finger, then rested his hand on his thigh. "Now which way?"

Bianca bit at her bottom lip and turned away from his icy blue gaze scanning the sea of grass and groves of trees that covered the prairie for miles.

When he'd asked which way to the gold back at the ranch, she had stalled by saying that she needed to come here to get her bearings, hoping she would find an intersecting road that Francesca might have traveled—not this field that looked the same as all the others they had passed along the way. She took a deep breath to ward off her panic and stared ahead where the road continued westward, glad that curiosity about her intended destination had prompted her to ask Francesca where Somerville was located. But knowing the town lay about a hundred and fifteen miles up from Houston didn't tell her how to get there from here, only that she needed to start heading northeast—and should have been doing so a long while back.

"Which way, Francesca?" Impatience deepened the stern edge in Kane's tone.

What am I going to do? She wasn't the least bit anxious to make her own pathway through the countryside. She was a fisherman's daughter and had lived by the sea all her life; she didn't know anything about tracking her way through unknown territory. Her hands began to shake, and for a brief moment Bianca contemplated just telling Kane the truth: that she wasn't Francesca and didn't know anything about the missing gold. But love stopped her—that and the fact that she wasn't willing to place her sister in more jeopardy than she already faced with Jeremy Bartlett on the loose. Nor could she hand Francesca over to Kane without knowing the truth of her troubles and why she had lied about them. Bianca had also given her promise to allow Francesca time to prove her innocence of the bank robbery, and she had no intention of breaking her word—or of forgetting her inherent devotion to her family.

"What the hell are you stalling for?" the Ranger snapped, furious lines etching his brow and firing his gaze.

Bianca prayed for the strength to get through the next two weeks. "It is just that I am tired from riding." She stalled with the truth. "Could we rest a while, *per favore?*"

Kane hesitated, contemplating a motive behind the request. Despite the fact that he knew the two cowhands that Marcus had sent to follow Devon Carson would slow the man down from finding their trail any time soon, he wasn't lowering his guard against the possibility Francesca was about to hatch some plan of escape, with or without the cowboy. However, he found himself slowly nodding his agreement, giving in because he decided the horses could use another break after the steady gait he'd held them to the past several hours, not from any concern for the weariness evident on his prisoner's face and in her voice. Or so he tried to convince himself as he tore his gaze away from her relieved smile.

He guided the horses off the main road and through the prairie grass, toward the tall pines that he knew surrounded a narrow tributary of the Colorado River. As they reached the edge of the small, shaded grove, a loud noise like dry beans shaking inside a tin can suddenly issued from just ahead and to the right. Kane pulled his gun at the same moment his buckskin jerked to a rough stop at the rattlesnake's warning. The mare neighed and shied away, tugging at her reins. The shaking noise sounded again, louder, closer. Kane tightened his hold on the reins as his horse snorted and tossed its head back, then sidestepped toward the skittish mare. He quickly scanned the grass, spotting the coiled snake just a few feet away, and fired, shattering the reptile's large wedge-shaped head; its long, brown body fell twitching to the ground.

"Aiuto!"

Kane jerked his head around at Bianca's frightened scream just in time to see the mare rearing up as much as the reins allowed, and for his heart to skid to a stop as his prisoner slid off, hitting the ground on her back with a heavy thud. She lay still, her eyes closed, her left foot caught in the stirrup. Kane couldn't get out of the saddle fast enough, unwrapping the mare's reins from the horn as he did. He dropped one set of leather straps, ground-tying the buckskin, then wound the mare's reins around his hand as he inched his way up higher, speaking low, soothing words to calm the sorrel's nervous side-steps. Then he ran his hand along the horse's neck, easing his way closer to the saddle, and took hold of Bianca's foot, gently slipping it from the stirrup. She groaned as he lowered her leg to the ground, but didn't open her eyes. Her chest rose and fell in rapid succession with her short breaths. Kane nudged the mare off to one side, then went back to kneel beside his prisoner, surprised at the depth of caring that overwhelmed him.

"Francesca?" He trailed one hand along her smooth, pale cheek.

Bianca moaned, slowly shaking her head from side to side, then opened her eyes. She blinked several times, dripping tears that ran in rivulets along her temples.

Kane brushed the tiny drops away, sucking in a breath against the puddle of tenderness that wanted to rise in his chest. "You'll be all right. You just got the wind knocked out of you."

She nodded, wincing. "I've hurt . . . my ankle, too," she whispered.

Kane tensed and jerked his hand away, concern vanishing beneath caution. He sat back on his heels. "Don't even think of trying to pull that stunt again."

"It is no stunt. I have truly hurt my ankle."

Annoyance that she would think him fool enough to

fall for this again pounded through his veins. "I don't believe you." Kane pushed himself up from the ground, towering above her. "And I'm not in the mood for your games. Now get up."

Her watery gaze widened. "I swear to you, I play no games."

Kane crossed his arms over his chest, vowing not to give into that silken plea and innocent gaze as he had before. "If you're not on your feet by the time I count to five, I'll put you there myself. One."

Astonishment brushed across her face.

"Two."

She braced herself up on one elbow. "You must believe me, *per favore.*" A slow trail of tears creased lines along her cheeks . . . and nagged at his conscience.

Damn it! A woman's tears ought to be outlawed. They just weren't fair on a man's heart. He shook his head in disgust, anger sizzling through him at his weakness toward this woman. "Nope. To do that is nothing more than asking for trouble, and I'm not sending out an invitation this time. Three."

Her breaths came deep and heavy now; her eyes narrowed to angry slits. Slowly, she rolled onto her right hip, then pushed herself up on her hands and knees, favoring her left leg as she did.

"Four."

She looked over her shoulder at him and snapped, "Leave me alone. I am doing what you ask."

Kane's blood boiled. He sure hadn't asked for this performance she was putting on. He'd sure thought she was done with these damn games, too!

"But not near fast enough, sweetheart. Five." He stepped forward, circled his hands around her waist, and hauled her to her feet, ignoring her squeal of protest. Just as abruptly, he released her and stepped back.

She cried out as her foot buckled and she started to fall to the side. Kane quickly grabbed her around the waist again and pulled her back against his chest, frowning at the teary stare she turned on him. Wondering how far she intended to carry out this fake injury, but unable to completely ignore the genuine pain he saw on her face, either.

He helped her to sit down on the ground, noticing how she kept her left leg out straight and bent the other. She wrapped her shackled wrists around her knee and rocked herself slightly, her tear-streaked face marred with pain.

His caution still high, Kane quickly scanned the area for any sign of Carson, then went over and knelt down on one knee close to Bianca's foot, careful to keep his gun facing away from her and well out of arm's reach. He pushed her skirt a short way up her stocking, then ran his fingers over her ankle, seeing her wince at his touch and feeling the throbbing intensity in the swelling flesh that strained the top of her boot.

"Damn it, you really are hurt," he whispered, his heart thudding with sudden concern.

"And you should do penance for not believing me and being so cruel, *signore.*"

Sure, he felt a little repentant, especially for being so rough with her a moment ago, but not enough to bow to her snippy attitude. "Well, surely you can understand my skepticism, *signorina,* given this is the first time you haven't lied to me."

She pulled her thin mink eyebrows together, her sharp gaze reflecting her struggle to find a plausible dispute to his claim. Her shoulders slumped as she released a heavy sigh. "I am in too much pain to argue with you."

He didn't doubt her about that, but he didn't expect her soft voice to send his aggravation fleeing so quickly, or his concern to come rushing back in with such intensity. "It'd be a good idea to soak that before the swelling gets any worse."

He stood, walked over and grabbed up the reins to the horses, then returned to stand beside her, all the while telling himself he was only worried because he didn't want any delays. He was ready to be done with this woman once and for all. Leaning down, he braced one arm behind her back and the other beneath her legs, then lifted her slight weight.

He shifted her closer to his solid strength, jarring her foot. Bianca groaned at the searing jabs that shot through her ankle and up her leg.

"Sorry," he whispered.

She nodded, biting at her lower lip until the pain subsided a bit, then relaxed in the comfort of his strong arms, tensing slightly at the tingling warmth of her breast pressed gently against his hard, warm chest. She'd fully expected him to put her on the mare again, but he took off through the woods instead, sending relief through her to be spared from that saddle.

She peered up at him through lowered lashes, pondering the uneasiness etched on Kane's tanned face. Was it his distrust of Francesca that put it there? she wondered. Or his more caring side that he so sparingly showed around her? She couldn't deny that she definitely preferred his kindness over the stubborn brute he was most of the time. Couldn't deny that she liked the scent of bay rum that faintly clung to his skin, blending with his manly spice and the pine-scented air that tingled her nose.

She tensed. *Dio, what is wrong with me?* Bianca looked away, startled by her attraction to this lawman, and not welcoming it at all. She'd vowed a long time ago never to get involved with a man who'd once kept company with her sister, and it was obvious from Kane's comments about what had taken place in Somerville that he and Francesca had spent time together. Besides, she didn't even like this man. He was hell-bent on believing the worst about Francesca and intent on seeing her in jail. Even worse, more than once now he'd mentioned the strong possibility of seeing Francesca hang! There was no way Bianca was going to let *that* happen.

She was glad to see the fast-flowing creek cutting a narrow path just ahead, as ready to feel some relief to her throbbing ankle as she was to put some distance between her and Kane. He dropped the reins, leaving the horses behind where the grass still grew thick before giving way to the sandy patches that lined the water's edge, and carried her the last few yards, then gently lowered her down onto the bank. Bianca sighed at the comforting cushion of the soft ground beneath her bottom.

Kane squatted beside her and started to undo the laces on her boot.

Bianca sat up straight and reached down, shoving his hands aside. "I'll do that."

Quick as a flash, he wrapped his hands around hers and pulled her close, his gaze narrowing, his warm breath brushing against her chin. "Why? You hiding something in there?"

"No," she angrily replied, tired of his constant suspicions.

He cocked one eyebrow. "So what, then? Another moment of modesty?"

Exactly so. But his mocking tone sent the truth fleeing from her tongue. "Maybe I just do not like you touching me," she snapped instead.

His eyes darkened with blue-hot anger, mingled with a small flame of sly amusement. "You didn't have any trouble enjoying my touch in that hotel room. And now that you've peaked my curiosity, I *will* have the honor of partially undressing you again."

Bianca gaped her shock. *Just how much had happened between Francesca and this man?*

He released her hands and deftly unlaced her boot. She gritted her teeth against the pain as he gently tugged the black kid leather from her foot; then she sighed, grateful to have the strained confinement removed. Tension was quick to grip her once again, though, as Kane ran his hand up her leg, creating a shocking path of goose bumps that continued even after he stopped just below her knee. He tugged at her stocking, bunching the black cotton down onto her calf; then carefully he pulled it over her ankle, revealing her swollen limb and the small pinkish knot protruding from one side. He tossed her stocking on top of her discarded boot, then slipped one hand beneath her leg and lifted it slightly, his examining gaze riveted on her shin, his warm touch surprisingly tender.

Kane looked over at her, his blue gaze clouded with stark concern, sending heat that had nothing to do with the scorching pain from her injury darting through her body. With gentle ease, he lowered her foot into the stream.

Bianca closed her eyes, welcoming the water's relieving coldness.

"You've hurt it pretty good. We best just make camp here for the night, and let you stay off of it."

She opened her eyes and nodded her thanks, touched by the caring in his deep voice. And sorry to see the familiar scowl suddenly return to his face.

"But make no mistake, Francesca. First thing in the morning you're taking me to the gold. No excuses."

The salty breeze stirred the late afternoon warmth, and the dissonant sounds of buggies and horses could be heard traversing the wooden blocks that paved Strand Street. A flurry of voices rose from the folks strolling the elevated walkways that lined the merchant shops pressed between the tall Victorian buildings owned by the banking and finance companies. Any other day Hailey would have enjoyed strolling along Galveston's busy business district, dreaming of the day she'd have enough money to buy the trinkets she enjoyed looking at. She would have enjoyed breathing in the wonderful scents of French perfume and exotic fruits such as green bananas and South American oranges that sweetly mingled with the headier odors of imported cigars and wool filtering out from the open doorways.

But today annoyance crept in as she was forced to weave a slow path around the flock of people that blocked her from making the mad dash she wanted to the trolley

stop at the corner of Twenty-first Street. She was anxious
to see Raimondo again. Anxious to learn what he'd found
out about Bianca.

Their search among the fishing community and around
the surrounding wharves last night had turned up nothing
except more worry about Bianca's absence—a worry Raimondo and his family strongly shared with her now.
Though Hailey wished it had been under happier circumstances, she'd welcomed the opportunity to meet Raimondo's parents, his brothers, and their families, too, and
had taken an instant liking to all the Casales. She'd also
had the chance to meet several of Bianca's other friends,
and she appreciated the help they'd offered. Hailey knew
the more people keeping an eye out for Bianca, the better
their chances of finding her.

It had been after midnight when Raimondo finally
walked her home, leaving her with his promise that he
would continue looking for Bianca and would meet her
after she finished her shift at the hotel today. Hailey had
spent the day nervously waiting for time to pass, each
second hoping Bianca would come by and ease her mind
that everything was fine. But just like yesterday, her
friend had never shown.

And Hailey feared that when she met Raimondo in a
few minutes he would be bearing bad news.

The dull-edged knife of guilt sawed a little harder at
her conscience. She should have done more to find her
friend. She might not have wanted Raimondo to know
about her past, but she should have at least gone to the
sheriff and told him why she feared Avis Murdock might
be responsible for Bianca's disappearance.

Hailey skirted around an older couple and two men,
then hastened down the steps at the end of the block, only
to pull up short on the side road. She crossed her arms,
tapping one foot impatiently as she waited for the slow
team pulling the lumbering wagon to pass, biting at her
upper lip as she pondered again about going to see the
sheriff.

She didn't have any proof that Murdock had done something to Bianca. She didn't have any doubts that the shipping owner would follow through on his long-ago threat to kill Hailey if she did go to the authorities, either. But could death be any worse than this worry for Bianca that had eaten away at her all day?

The wagon rolled out of the way. Hailey gathered her serge skirt with trembling fingers and hurried across Twenty-second Street, then climbed the steps up to the sidewalk, again weaving around the people in her way. The plump woman in front of her suddenly stopped to stare in the window of Millie's Sweet Shoppe. Hailey jerked her head to avoid the metal tip on the blue-striped parasol resting against her narrow shoulder, and walked around the lady. Then she quickly pulled up short as a rail-thin boy, no more than eight, came running out from the candy store, his bare feet slapping hard against the planking.

A short black-haired woman brandishing a rolling pin darted out after him, shouting, "Come back here, you little thief!"

Dirt stained the boy's thin gray shirt as well as the brown pants that rode high on his ankles. He leaped off the sidewalk, stumbled when his feet hit the road, and fell, landing in the path of an oncoming buggy. Hailey gasped, taking a step forward, then paused and released her breath as the lad rolled out of the way of the wheels just in time and jumped to his feet.

The woman chasing him stopped at the edge of the walkway and waved her rolling pin. "I'm going to the sheriff this time! You hear me, you filthy brat?"

Fear and desperation shimmered in the boy's dark eyes. He spun around and took off running, dodging the traffic as he crossed the road.

"You're going to be staring at the world through a set of bars. Mark my words on that!" she shrieked, shaking her wooden pin higher in the air.

Hailey watched the boy head down a side street that

led toward the docks, then made her way past the spectators, now going on about their business, and stopped beside the woman she assumed was the shop owner.

"I'll pay for whatever he took," she offered.

The woman jerked her chin up, her plump middle-aged face still flushed bright red with anger. "Why? Do you know the little snot?"

Hailey frowned, her hackles rising. "No, ma'am, I don't know the *boy*." But the island was home to many orphans who roamed the streets, and other children born to poorer families. Hailey knew firsthand what it was like to be a child forced to do without life's necessities, such as properly fitting clothes, baths, and regular meals—and luxuries such as store-bought candy. She also understood what it felt like to desperately want those things.

"I just know what it's like to be hungry, and desperate enough to sometimes make foolish choices. And I'd rather not see him get in trouble." She removed the thin strings looped around her wrist and pulled the top of her paisley reticule open.

The woman narrowed her dark-molasses stare. She shoved her free hand on her rounded hip, pulling the cotton seams of her myrtle green calico taut across her shoulders, and pointed the rolling pin at Hailey's chest. "I know what's it like to be hungry, too, young lady. That don't make it right to steal."

"You're right, of course." Hailey stiffened, forcing a smile but unable to fully keep her irritation from filtering into her voice. "It would be *better* if the boy could work for his food. Perhaps you would consider giving him a job sweeping floors for you, instead of sending him to jail?"

The woman shook her head. "This is the third time he's stolen from me. And I know for a fact he's stolen from Mr. Wimbley's produce market a couple of times, too. I don't want no thief working for me." She arched one black eyebrow. "And if you're foolish enough to pay for his mistake, I'll take your money. You paying for just what he took today, or all the other times as well?"

Hailey swallowed, thinking of the four quarters in her reticule and hoping it was enough. "Everything he's taken from you."

The woman straightened, lowering the rolling pin to her side, and cocked her head in contemplation. "Well, let's see, he's carted off about a half pound of my divinity now, a dozen chocolate cookies, and three big handfuls of penny taffy pieces." A calculating smile lifted her mouth. She removed her hand from her hip and held her palm out. "Three dollars should cover it."

Three dollars was highway robbery! And more than half of what Hailey figured was truly owed. She fumed, not doubting in the least that this compassionless woman would follow through on her threat about going to the sheriff. She shoved her hand inside her reticule and retrieved the coins.

"I only have a dollar. I'll bring you the rest on Saturday when I draw my weekly pay." She dropped the quarters into the shopkeeper's flour-dusted palm, surprised to see a man's blunt, tanned fingers scoop them right back out and drop three one-dollar bills there instead.

Hailey trailed her stare over the length of his white shirtsleeve, across his broad shoulder, and up, her breath hitching at the soft smile on Raimondo's handsome face. The familiar black felt cap sat atop his tousled curls, the short bill pressing several wayward locks down along his forehead. He placed the coins back into her hand, his warm fingers brushing against her palm and making her blood tingle.

She tried to give them back to him. "Please, I want to help."

"So do I." He gently forced her fingers closed over the coins and pushed her hand away.

"Makes me no never-mind which one of you pays. Or why." The shop owner closed her fist around the bills.

Hailey watched Raimondo's smile fade as he looked

toward the woman. He reached into the front pocket of his black pants and pulled out another dollar bill. "Here," he shoved it toward the woman.

She jerked her chin up. "What's that for?"

"It is what I think is the real amount owed for what that boy stole from you. So this should give him enough credit to visit your shop three more times without being run off."

The woman eyed Raimondo as though he'd lost his mind, but made no hesitation in snatching the bill from his grasp. "He takes a penny more than a dollar's worth, and I'm going straight to the sheriff." She added a quick nod of assurance that she would follow through on that threat, then headed back toward her shop.

"That was nice what you were willing to do for that boy."

Hailey swallowed, feeling the heat rush into her cheeks at the admiration in Raimondo's deep voice, at the matching gleam in his dark gaze. "He just looked so desperate. I felt sorry for him, and I didn't want him to go to jail." She smiled. "But giving him a store credit was even nicer, Raimondo. Do you know him?"

"Not really. I have seen him selling shrimp down at the docks a few times. He never has more than a bucketful to sell, and he has always been alone."

Hailey stared across the road, down the side street where the boy had disappeared. "Do you think he's an orphan?"

Raimondo gently rested his hand on her shoulder, his heated touch searing through her white blouse to kiss her skin. "I will try to find out, if you would like."

His kind offer only added to her heart's list of reasons for not wanting to let go of her affection for this man. "Would you?" She didn't know why she wanted to know about this boy, but she did.

He nodded, a sensuous light shimmering in his brown gaze, gone as quickly as it came, leaving her wondering if she'd only imagined it.

He removed his hand from her shoulder, a frown pulling at his mouth. "Hopefully, I will have better luck with that than I did finding Bianca."

Ice filled Hailey's veins. "You didn't find her?"

He wrinkled his brow in frustration. "Not a trace. I searched everywhere and talked with everyone I could think of who knows her. No one saw her yesterday at all. Mr. D'Angelo was expecting her to stop by his market, too. She always goes by on Tuesdays to bring him a dozen loaves of bread and whatever pastries she has baked for him to sell for her that week." He jammed his fists on his hips and shook his head. "This is not like Bianca to just disappear. Francesca, yes. She has a reckless heart, like her papa. But not Bianca. She would not leave without telling someone."

Hailey agreed that Bianca was too caring to let her friends worry unnecessarily. Her concern that Murdock was responsible dug prominently deeper, along with her guilt. *I should've already gone to the sheriff.*

"I'm sorry, Raimondo, I have to leave." She grabbed her skirt up in her shaking hands.

He reached out and took hold of her arm, stopping her from turning around. "Where are you going?"

"To see the sheriff."

His jaw visibly tensed. "Why?"

"He should know that Bianca is missing, so the law can help us look for her, as well."

His fingers dug into her arm; his mouth thinned with displeasure. "We do not need *la polizia*. My family takes care of our own. *We* will find Bianca."

"You don't understand how much danger she could be in."

"Then tell me, Hailey."

She bit at her bottom lip, still reluctant to reveal her past to him, but also knowing he cared deeply for Bianca and was just as desperate as she to find their friend.

"Is this about Avis Murdock?" Raimondo sternly

pressed. "Do you still believe he might have done something to Bianca?"

She took several deep breaths of indecision, then sighed and slowly nodded.

"That is as I thought." His eyes narrowed with stony anger. "And why I went to see him today."

Hailey tensed, her pulse pounding as loud in her ears as the jangling bell from the mule-drawn trolley pulling to a stop at the corner. "Did he say anything about Bianca?"

A dark cloud settled over Raimondo's face. "He wasn't there. The man I talked to said Murdock left for Houston yesterday morning on business and would not be back until tonight."

A shudder rippled up Hailey's spine as she recalled Raimondo's words that no one had seen Bianca yesterday. *Dear God, where has Murdock really gone . . . and to do what?*

"I really must tell the sheriff what I know about Avis Murdock."

Raimondo shook his head. "You should tell *me* about that *bastardo*. And we will talk later about going to *la polizia.*"

Hailey hesitated, struggling to put aside her foolish pride to hide her past, knowing it really mattered little in comparison to doing everything possible to find Bianca. She nodded, then glanced around, noticing the stares they were garnering from passersby. "Can we go somewhere more private?"

"Of course." Raimondo slid his hand down her arm and cradled her palm against his, keeping her close to his side as he forged a trail along the crowded walkway. He turned at the corner of Twenty-first Street, heading down the side street away from the people filing off the trolley.

They walked in silence, but Hailey's thoughts swirled as fast as their steps. She hoped she was doing the right thing. Hoped Raimondo wouldn't think any less of her once he knew about her past. Hoped she wasn't placing him in any danger from Murdock by revealing what the man had done. But she knew without a doubt that Raimondo would attempt to see Murdock again, and she also wanted him to know exactly what he was up against in the evil shipping owner.

They crossed the street onto another block, and halfway down Raimondo turned into a narrow alleyway. Their booted steps echoed in the emptiness. He pulled her into the shadows of a tin awning suspended above the back door of a small shop wedged between two larger buildings.

He turned to face her, loosening his hold on her hand but not letting go. "Tell me about Murdock. Did he hurt you?" Tension edged his tone. Anger burned in his gaze, but so did a blaze of concern that made her heart skip a beat.

"Not me." She swallowed, catching her breath. "My mother." She ran her tongue along her bottom lip, stalling as she searched for the words to explain, then sighed, finding no easy way. "She was a prostitute, and Avis Murdock was one of her customers. Six years ago, she made the mistake of commenting to a couple of her friends about the size of his . . ." Her throat went dry as the flush worked its way into her cheeks. She took a deep breath, then another before finding her voice enough to continue. "About his . . . manhood. The comment ended up spreading like a wild vine through several of the brothels on Post Office Street, and found its way to Murdock's ear. He wasn't happy about it and decided to make my mother pay."

"What did he do?"

She reveled in the comfort of his hand gently tightening around hers. "He came to see her late one night, and he brought some man with him who I'd never seen before. They tied and gagged us." Hailey blinked against the tears that rose as the horror of that night broke through the door she'd locked it behind and came crawling back into her mind. "They made me watch them rape my mother. Then Murdock took a knife and cut four deep gashes in her face."

Raimondo spewed a string of Italian she didn't understand, but there was no mistaking the disgust and fury on his face. "Did they touch you, Hailey?"

Her tears spilled over, flowing down her cheeks. "No." And she didn't know why, nor did she care. She only thanked God that they hadn't. "Murdock just warned me to keep silent about that night . . . or they would come back and kill me. They threatened my mother with the same thing."

Raimondo reached up and gently brushed the tears from her face. "Where is your *mamma* now?"

"She died three years ago." From an opium overdose, the sheriff had explained when he'd come to the beach where Hailey was selling her painted shells, and informed her of the discovered death.

"Did your *mamma* raise you in a brothel?"

Hailey shook her head. "We lived in a small house down in Fat Alley." A neighborhood well known for its gambling and prostitution, and she could tell by Raimondo's arched look of surprise that he was familiar with the nickname assigned to Galveston's pesthole. She'd grown up hating that neighborhood, hating the different men who came to visit her mother each night. Hating the assumption folks made that she was "her mother's daughter." She wasn't. And she'd grown weary of always having to defend herself from that, sometimes even being forced to fight to keep her innocence. But as she gazed into Raimondo's warm stare, she saw no judgment, only compassion. "But I left there four years ago and have been taking care of myself since."

"And you have done a fine job," he whispered, stroking her cheek, his warm breath brushing against her chin as he leaned closer.

The heartrending tenderness in his gaze stole her breath away. The first touch of his warm mouth on hers nearly made her faint. She closed her eyes, grateful for the support of his strong arms circling her waist, her limbs melting into a warm puddle from the gentle caress of his lips setting her aflame. She wound her hands around his neck, pressing closer to his hard chest, feeling his heart pound against hers with the same fierce pace. She moved her lips beneath his, parting them to welcome the velvety stroke of his tongue.

Then, suddenly he jerked his mouth from hers, gripped her shoulders, and pushed her away. "This is not right."

Hailey swallowed, dazed and confused. It had felt perfectly right to her, and she would have sworn there was passion far beyond just friendship in that kiss they'd shared. "Why, Raimondo?" A cold child spiraled up her spine. "Is it because of where I come from?"

"Never. I cared for you before, and that has not changed now, except to grow stronger.

Hailey took several deep breaths, stunned that Raimondo had finally expressed his feelings, relieved and delighted to finally know that the affection she'd thought she had seen in his eyes was real. "I care for you, too, Raimondo. Very much."

He lifted his hand partway to her face, then stopped and crossed his arms over his chest. His face tightened. "Do not waste your time caring for me, Hailey."

Shock slammed the breath from her lungs; then the hollowness of rejection filled her chest. "Why?"

He sighed deeply, sadness gripping his expression as he whispered, "Because I have already given my promise to marry someone else."

EIGHT

Bianca sipped at the strong coffee Kane had fixed, then set the still half-filled blue tin down beside her and leaned back against the saddle perched at one end of the bedroll. She lifted her arms to cross them, stopped short by the handcuff locked around her left wrist, the other end attached to one wide leather stirrup. Sighing, she lowered her hands to her lap, refusing to let the metal reminder dampen her momentary contentment as she gazed up at the twilight sky, at the stars popping out with steady frequency to twinkle their brilliant show.

Bianca marveled at how vividly the stars sparkled inland without the electric lights that turned Galveston's streets as bright as day, without the many lamps burning from the boats along the pier, and the water's moonlit reflection to dim them. She closed her eyes, listening to the nearby stream's steady rush, so different from the bay's waves constantly lapping against the boats. She listened to the soft woodland noises mingling with the crickets' songs, and the occasional owl's hoot or a lone wolf's cry that floated on the light breeze. So quietly peaceful compared to the sounds of what she was used to, creaking wood and boats bumping against the pier. So different from the seagulls squawking and the drone of voices along the docks, and the horns blaring as ships moved in and out of the harbor.

She opened her eyes and took a deep breath, missing the smell of the ocean and the oleanders and the blended

scents of imported goods that perfumed the air around
her home. But she found a surprisingly equal pleasure in
the intoxicating fragrance of fresh water and grass and
the pine trees that surrounded their camp. The only taint
to the sweet air that assailed her nose came from the
horses, hobbled at the edge of the light cast by the campfire, and from the wafting scent of pungent meat cooking.

Bianca tucked her chin down, frowning at the skinned
rattlesnake wrapped around a narrow stick and propped
above the small fire. Juices dripped from the browned
meat and hit the low flames with sizzling pops. She swallowed against her rising queasiness. She hated snakes
more than she disliked horses, and contemplated just how
badly she wanted to fill her empty stomach.

"You're looking a little pale. You all right?"

Bianca lifted her gaze to the other side of the fire,
where Kane sat on a blanket with his back against his
saddle, one black-denim-clad knee bent, the small knife
with which he'd been whittling at a narrow piece of wood
now idle in his hand. Yellow flames flicked shadows over
his tanned face and danced with the teasing light in his
blue gaze. It was the same annoyingly irresistible gleam
he'd had earlier, when he answered her voiced disbelief
that he really intended to cook this creature with an assurance that it was perfectly edible meat and there wasn't
any reason to "waste what the Good Lord saw fit to put
in our path."

"By some miracle does this horrid animal taste better
than it smells?"

Kane shrugged. "Depends on how bad you think it
smells."

"Like it has been dead for a week beneath the summer
sun."

He chuckled. "Well, you're in luck. I guarantee that it
does taste better than that."

His wide smile sent heat skittering through her veins.
Dio, he truly is a handsome man. And ever since he realized that she really had hurt her ankle, he'd been noth-

ing but attentive and kind to her, which had only made her enjoy his company more than she knew was wise.

Bianca looked away, her gaze falling warily on the rattlesnake, her skepticism of this meat's palatability still running high. "How much better?"

Kane set the small stick down and brushed the tiny wood shavings from his white shirt, then rose to kneel beside the fire, his expression turning serious. "Actually, it's not bad at all. I think it has sort of a fishy taste to it." He waved the knife in her direction. "You remember Caleb Wilson?"

Hearing more a statement of fact that Francesca knew this man than a question in Kane's tone, Bianca nodded hesitantly—and prayed that she wouldn't be expected to recall specific details.

"Well, he says the taste leans more toward fried frog legs. Since I've never eaten frog, I can't say he's wrong. You ever eaten frog legs?"

"No, but I came close to eating them once."

"What stopped you?"

Bianca shuddered, surprised that the childhood memory was still capable of sending this chilly dislike coursing through her. "I was only six, and when I saw them squirming around in the pan while *Mamma* was frying them, I could not get past being afraid that they were still alive long enough to try one."

Amusement simmered deep in Kane's eyes, and she expected his laughter to follow, but it didn't. "I can see where a sight like that could scare a kid. Hell, even grown I wouldn't want to see my supper taking a last jig around the skillet while it's cooking."

Bianca chuckled, her heart pounding faster with admiration for his effort to be understanding.

Her smile was dangerous, her cute dimples lethal weapons that ran right over his good sense and threatened to make Kane forget the real reason they were spending time together. He looked away before he fell further victim to her beauty, before he started to enjoy her company even more than he already had these past few hours, watching her gaze around at the countryside as though she'd never seen anything like it before, seeing a contentment that she could sit here for days without a complaint settling over her pretty face.

In the short time they'd spent together in Somerville, he had never seen her content to sit still this long, or known her to be so talkative about anything other than herself. But she had kept up a nice pace of conversation since they'd made camp, asking him to name certain trees or plants, expressing an interest in his experiences growing up on a ranch. Even surprising him with a few childhood anecdotes of living in Sicily, and the trials on the ship when her family had sailed to America. And when he'd inquired about the twins in the photograph—still tucked in his vest pocket—she had explained that the picture was old and her cousins now grown, and had fondly mentioned exchanging letters frequently with them, and how glad she was that they were both happy with their lives. He'd also seen the love in her eyes when she had talked about her parents and little brother, and heard the sadness in her voice when she'd told of their demise.

More than once, it crossed his mind to wonder which woman she truly was: the conniving, self-centered actress he'd met in Somerville, or this caring, gracious temptress he had arrested in Galveston.

"Tell you what, Francesca." He dug two tin plates out of his saddlebag and set them on the ground close to the fire. "I only packed a few strips of hardtack and some biscuits. Didn't figure we'd need much before we retrieved the gold and could get a decent meal in Austin." He shifted his gaze along her black skirt to her ankle, propped on a folded corner of the bedroll, her small, pale toes peeking out above the red bandanna he'd wrapped around her foot. He knew it shouldn't, but it still bothered him that he hadn't believed she was hurt at first, and had been so rough with her. "But I'll make a deal with you.

Take just one bite of this rattler, and if you can't stomach it, you can have your portion of what I was saving for breakfast, and we'll divvy mine up in the morning."

Relief sparkled in her golden stare. "That is very generous of you, Mr. Fairchild. I will accept your deal."

Her smile sent his heart pounding at a heightened rate that threatened near explosion and forced him to strongly remind himself again of the robbery, the shooting, and all the other reasons why he didn't like this woman. He pulled a bandanna from his back pocket, used it to wipe the knife blade clean, then cut a small slice of the meat and placed it on one of the plates. Kane walked around the fire and squatted down beside her, watching her slender throat ripple as she took the tin and stared at the snake meat.

She set the plate on her lap, grimacing as she tentatively reached for the meat, gripping the smallest bit of one corner she possibly could between her thumb and forefinger. Then she closed her eyes and quickly popped it into her mouth.

She chewed slowly, and Kane took it as a good sign that she didn't spit it right back out or turn sickly pale. "Well?"

She swallowed, then opened her eyes, nodding. "You're right. It does have a little fishy taste to it. And is not all that unpleasant." Her thin eyebrows pulled together. "But I cannot say that I would want to eat it often."

"No argument here. Give me a two-inch steak any day." He stood, waving the knife he held in his right hand toward the fire. "But since I can't offer you steak tonight, what's it going to be? A little more of that rattler, or hardtack and biscuit?"

"What you have cooked will be fine." She handed him the plate.

Kane crossed over to the fire and cut off several small chunks of meat, which he placed on the plate, then returned it to her. He walked over and knelt down again, filling his own plate. Then he sat back on the blanket and stared across the fire at Francesca, noticing that she still looked a little tentative about the meal every time she took a small bite.

"If you had a choice of anything you wanted, Francesca, what would you rather be eating tonight?"

"Anything?" She cocked her head, tapping one finger against her chin. *"Zabaglione,"* she finally responded.

He didn't understand what she'd said, but he sure liked that accent in her velvety voice. "You want to run that by me again, sweetheart?"

"Zabaglione."

He arched one eyebrow. "And that is . . . ?"

"A custard made with egg yolks, sugar, and marsala." She sighed, a dreamy glow rising in her eyes. *"Un pezzo di cielo caduto in terra.* A piece of heaven fallen to earth."

He could say the same of her, Kane thought. Then quickly chided himself. *If she weren't a conniving outlaw.* "That good, huh?"

She ran her tongue along her bottom lip as she nodded.

Kane swallowed the desire to lean closer and sample the same delicate path—to see if she tasted as good as he remembered.

"My *mamma* made the very best. Her *zabaglione* was always a favored request at the celebration feasts. And of all the things she taught me to cook, it is the only recipe I cannot get exact." Lines of frustration wrinkled her brow. "I keep trying, but I just can't seem to get the right amount of sweet marsala to make it taste the same as hers."

Kane tensed. *Keep trying?* Distrust reared up with a harsh reminder that he'd best remember just exactly whom he was dealing with here and not let his guard down for a second. *Or want to kiss her, either!*

"I recall you saying that you hadn't stood in front of a stove since you set foot on a stage three years ago, and didn't care if you ever did again. Was that a lie?"

Bianca froze, realizing she'd gotten too caught up in her memories, had let herself relax too much in Kane's company, and slipped back into being herself. And unlike her, Francesca hated to cook, had always dreaded their *mamma's* weekly lessons when they were young, and more often than not would try to pick an argument, hoping to be sent from the kitchen. It had rarely worked, but Bianca recalled there were many times her *mamma* ended up waving her spoon in frustration when Francesca burned the food because she'd been forced to stay.

"No. I, um . . . was just thinking back to the years after my *mamma* died, and how I would keeping trying. But since I didn't really like cooking all that much anyway, I *did* give it up when I became an actress. It is not something that I have missed, either." She smiled for added effect to the lie, glad to see the suspicion leave Kane's expression, and a small smile relax his handsome face.

"Think you'll ever give your mother's recipe another try?"

"Not anytime soon." At least not until she was done with this charade and could return home. She took another bite of the meat, trying not to think about what she was eating, but she could feel the images of the rattlesnake coiled and ready to pounce.

"What made you decide to become a Texas Ranger?" she inquired in desperation to redirect her thoughts, getting more diversion than she'd expected in the look of sorrow that suddenly sprang up in Kane's eyes.

He set his plate down and looked up at the sky. No stranger to grief, Bianca wondered who he had lost in his life. He sat silent for a long while. Long enough that she thought he intended to ignore her question.

"Eight years ago, someone I cared about was killed during a robbery at the Flat Rock Bank," he finally said, his gaze still focused upward. "The outlaw responsible got away. After he eluded every posse and lawman on his trail, I went looking for him myself. Finally found him

about a year later, already dead and buried in Arizona."
He stared across the fire at her, the sadness gone from
his eyes, replaced with a distant, cold gaze even the
flame's reflection couldn't penetrate. "I was sort of used
to chasing outlaws by then, so I came back to Texas and
joined the Rangers."

Bianca suspected there was much more behind his decision to become a lawman. She also wondered how
much of the anger in his voice, in his tightened jaw,
stemmed from the missed opportunity to be the one to
put that outlaw in his grave, and how much of it drove
his determination to see her sister pay for shooting his
father.

He relaxed his shoulders and reached for his plate
again, taking a bite of the meat. He swallowed, then
paused, cocking his head. "Since I answered your question, Francesca, answer one for me. Why did you decide
to become an outlaw?"

Bianca frowned, not at the question as much as at the
realization that outside of knowing Francesca had been
duped by Bartlett about his real profession, she didn't
have a good answer for the trouble her sister had landed
in. She sighed, hating that once again she was forced to
rely on a weak arsenal of defense. "I did not *decide* to
become an outlaw, Mr. Fairchild. I just trusted the wrong
man."

"Murdock Shipping Company" was emblazoned in
bold, black lettering across the elongated window that
fronted the single-story building. Off to one side near the
double oak doors, a smaller sign that read "Closed" hung
face out against the pane. But a low haze of lamplight
softly washed the glass and dimmed the gray shadows in
the empty lobby, its glow shining brighter where it spilled
out from the middle of three offices lining the far wall
and illuminated the two men seated across a desk inside.

Dannare, Murdock is a windbag. Raimondo huffed out

an impatient breath and leaned back against the clapboard wall of the darkened button factory across the street, waiting for the chance to get Murdock alone.

But so far, the balding shipping owner had been inside conversing with his clerk ever since Raimondo and his brother arrived an hour ago—just as the sun left for the day and Murdock had ridden up in his buggy, returning from his trip to Houston. Suspicion and fury swirled through Raimondo. He balled his hands into fists.

If that is really where the bastardo went . . .

The elbow nudge his brother delivered drew Raimondo's attention. He took the burning cigar Daniele held out, and pulled a long draw, watching the ashy tip glow bright red in the shadowy moonlight; then he glanced up the roadway, glad the electric lights didn't reach this far down Strand Street. Nor did the stream of people walking along the sidewalks several blocks away, wandering in and out of the shops open late to take advantage of the trade. Raimondo released the smoke into the cool night air, took another draw, then handed the half-gone cheroot back to his brother.

Daniele puffed on the cigar, then slowly released the smoke out one side of his mouth. A muscle flicked in his tightened jaw. His thick black eyebrows formed a straight line of concern along the ridge of his wide forehead. All of the Casale brothers had inherited a short, sloping jawbone and broad brow from their father, but Daniele was the only one who'd also inherited their father's thin, straight black strands and receding hairline.

"The longer Bianca is missing, the more I think you might be right about Murdock, Raimy-boy."

"Murdock will not have long to live if he has done more to Bianca than place his hand on her at the restaurant." Raimondo patted the wooden handle of the .44-caliber Colt revolver stuck in the front waistband of his pants.

Daniele paused with the cigar partway to his mouth and narrowed his coal eyes assessingly. "We are only here to talk, Raimy-boy. Remember that. Once we know Bianca's fate, Papa will decide what we are to do with this *bastardo*."

Raimondo nodded. *Papa.* The head of their family. It was an honored position that came with great responsibility, and demanded respect, both of which his papa did not take lightly. A wise son did not act without the *capo di famiglia's* consent, or go against tradition, either. And Raimondo was a wise son. As far as his family knew, this visit to Murdock was strictly about Bianca.

Only *he* knew how loud his soul was screaming to also take revenge for what the shipping owner had done to Hailey and her mother.

"Just how far do you think this *bastardo* would go to hurt Bianca?"

Raimondo shook his head, not willing to tempt fate with speculation, not willing to break his promise to Hailey to keep silent about what she'd told him. He'd given his word, not because he shared her concern that Murdock might kill him for talking, but because he respected her wish to keep her past a secret. He understood now that she was trying to build a new life, and he admired her courage and fortitude to put the past behind. He was glad she'd confided in him, though her strength, her trust, and her declaration of affection for him had only deepened his love for this young woman—and had made it even harder for him to push her away.

He frowned, thinking how he wouldn't have had to push her away if he hadn't been weakened by her tears and by his overwhelming desire to hold her, comfort her . . . kiss her, as he had longed to do since the moment he'd met her.

But he never meant to let it happen. Never meant to voice his feelings for her. Never meant to break her heart.

Raimondo sighed, guilt gripping him as he recalled the shock and sadness that had clouded Hailey's light-blue gaze when he told her he was promised to another. He'd been surprised that she hadn't slapped him, or walked away and left him alone in that alley. Instead, she'd asked questions and had patiently listened as he explained about his family's tradition of arranged marriages. About his fiancée, a woman he'd never met, but who was already on a boat sailing here from Sicily. About honor, and being a man raised to fulfill his promises.

What he hadn't told her was that he'd struggled for months trying to decide whether he wanted to follow tradition or not; that he'd fought with his parents about it and was finally swayed toward his decision when he learned they had already sent for the girl without telling him; that he'd sent a wire of confirmation to the girl's parents in Sicily—just days before he had met Hailey and fallen in love. Nor did he tell Hailey that he would love her all his life, too. He swallowed against the pain that rammed his heart. But instead, he'd said he was sorry he couldn't offer more than that one kiss, and hoped they could remain friends.

And he silently wondered how he would get through the rest of his days without her.

What he also hadn't told her was that he had every intention of making sure Murdock never bothered her again. His anger boiled hotter every minute he stood there waiting to confront the man, and he had to keep reminding himself to concentrate on finding Bianca right now. And after she was found, *then* he would see to it that Murdock paid for everything he had done.

Raimondo took the cheroot Daniele handed him and took a long draw, filling his lungs as he shifted his attention back across the street. Then he choked the smoke out on a stifled cough when he saw only Murdock through the window.

One side of the front doors opened. Raimondo dropped the cigar, and ground it into the dirt with his boot, then glanced at his brother, seeing Daniele nod his readiness.

The clerk closed the door as he left, then headed off toward the bright lights at a clipped pace.

Raimondo stared through the window, watching Murdock place a liquor bottle on top of the desk, uncork it, and pour the amber liquid into a short glass. When the clerk was a block and a half away, Raimondo headed out across the road, his brother right beside him, their footsteps pounding softly against the wooden blocks. They climbed the two steps and crossed the narrow sidewalk. Raimondo grabbed the door handle with his left hand, pulled the Colt into his right and lowered the gun to his side, then stepped inside. Daniele followed and quickly closed the door behind them.

Raimondo heard the lock click in place.

Murdock looked up, the liquor bottle again poised above the glass he held. "Sorry boys, we're closed," he called out. "Come back tomorrow. We open at eight."

"This will not take long." Raimondo crossed the lobby toward the short wooden railing that separated the offices, and from the corner of his eye saw Daniele walking toward the window to pull the two shades down.

"You boys hard of hearing? I said we're closed." Murdock's pouchy cheeks burned a sickly red in the lamplight. His mouth thinned in a tight, grim line. He set the liquor bottle and glass down and reached his right hand behind the desk.

Raimondo raised the Colt until it was level with the man's head. "Get your hand back where I can see it, Murdock. We are just here to talk." *This time.* Which is why Raimondo had asked Daniele to come along. Unlike his oldest brother, who was more apt to let his temper rule, he knew his middle brother could hold his anger if things started to get out of hand, and would stop Raimondo from giving in to his urge to kill Murdock right then.

The shipping owner's dark eyes widened. Slowly he placed both hands flat against the desktop.

Gun held steady, Raimondo pushed his way through the swinging gate, lengthening his stride between the two desks spaced wide apart, and into Murdock's office, not stopping until he stood at the edge of the wide oak top.

He centered the gun close to Murdock's forehead. Sweat glistened on the man's bald pate, small wayward drops sliding down into the narrow patch of brown hair that ran from ear to ear around his pale scalp.

Daniele came into the room and stopped beside him, his shoulders stiff, fists resting against his hips.

"If it's money you're after, my clerk just left with the day's proceeds." Murdock glanced between them, his smug smile belied by the nervous twitch jerking his left eye.

Raimondo nodded toward the black safe standing wide open against the back wall. "What about those bills stacked on the top shelf. Did he forget those?"

Murdock arched his eyebrows and glanced over his shoulder, frowning with remembrance of the forgotten task of closing the door, his shoulders sagging as he looked back. Angered resignation at the mistake costing him dearly burned in his dark-brown stare. "Fine. Take the money."

Raimondo raised one corner of his mouth in a small, sly grin. "Are you hard of hearing, Murdock? I already told you we are here just to talk."

The man eased himself back into the chair, his barrel-shaped body filling the black leather. "What about?"

"Bianca Rossetti," Daniele answered.

Puzzlement marred Murdock's brow. He shook his head. "Sorry, don't know her."

"You know her, Murdock," Raimondo ground out. "The young waitress from the Tremont Restaurant."

"You mean that bitch who dumped food on me?"

Raimondo pulled the hammer back.

Daniele pressed his hands against the desk and leaned forward. "Watch your tongue, *bastardo*," he snarled.

"Look, whatever she told you about what happened, it was just an accident. All I did was try to move my chair out of the way to give her room to set the plate down. It was a simple brush of the hand. Nothing more." Murdock narrowed his eyes with contempt. "She got fired because she overreacted. Just like you boys are doing. All you dagos are too hot-tempered for your own good."

Raimondo wouldn't argue that his temper was hot, and he was only getting started. "From what I heard, Murdock, your hand did more than brush. It pressed and pinched, too."

The shipping owner shrugged an easy dismissal and raised his hands, palms up in submission. "Obviously, you boys are convinced I've overstepped a boundary here. So, what is it you want? An apology? Fine. Bring her around here tomorrow, and I'll apologize."

"You can make your useless apology tonight," Daniele declared, straightening and crossing his arms. "When you lead us to where you have taken her."

Murdock tilted his head to one side, confusion clouding his expression. "What are you talking about? I haven't seen her since the manager fired her and she stormed off into the kitchen that night."

"Don't lie to us, Murdock," Raimondo warned, waving the gun slightly. "What have you done with her?"

"If that girl's missing, you boys are barking up the wrong tree. I didn't have anything to do with it."

"You were mad over what she had done to you at the restaurant," Raimondo countered.

Murdock furrowed his eyebrows. "Hell yes, I was mad!"

"Mad enough to want to make her pay for embarrassing you?" Derision dominated his tone. Raimondo eyed the man with a knowing look, smiling his satisfaction at the worried suspicion that clouded Murdock's stare.

The shipping owner ran one finger along the inside of his white collar and swallowed, sending his Adam's apple gliding along his throat. "I don't know what you're trying to imply, mister, but I do think that gal deserved to get fired." He leaned forward, the anger that was slowly building in his voice also rising up red in his face. "Beyond that, I haven't given her a moment's thought since then, let alone seen her. And I can prove that I've been

in Houston since that night, too. With a different woman."
In a defiant move, Murdock rose from the chair, his
shoulders tensed, his expression hard as nails. "Now, it's
time for you boys to leave."

Raimondo had to admit that Murdock sounded as if
he was telling the truth about not having seen Bianca.
Glancing over, he judged from Daniele's furrowed brow
that his brother was thinking the same thing. But she *was*
missing, and Raimondo couldn't ignore the few details
he'd pieced together that indicated she never made it
home from work that night but had disappeared some
time shortly after her encounter with this man.

"This is not over, Murdock," Daniele warned. "Not
until we find Bianca and learn the truth."

"Your truth doesn't lie at my doorstep." He stuck one
arm out, pointing toward the door. "Now, the both of you
get out of here."

Daniele took a step back, then another.

Raimondo remained where he was, enjoying the worry
in Murdock's widened eyes as he lowered the gun, aiming
the silver barrel at the shipping owner's groin.

Murdock swallowed. "You wouldn't."

"Do not bet on it, Murdock. *La fortuna* will not be
with you the next time we meet," Raimondo stated low
and evenly, smiling as he backed away from the desk and
followed his brother out the door.

NINE

Kane saddled the mare, then his buckskin, and tossed the saddlebags onto the gelding's back, all the while scanning the trees and listening for any change in the birds' songs or the sounds of nature stirring to greet the new day, alert for any sign of Carson—or Bartlett. He also kept a constant vigil on his prisoner as she washed up at the stream and now sat on the bank with dawn's pale rays shining at her back, the handcuffs jangling softly as she braided her long dark hair. He couldn't deny she was a beautiful distraction, and to his chagrin, he was finding it too damned hard to confine his thoughts of her strictly to business.

He'd stayed up long past midnight watching her sleep, studying the angles of her smooth oval face, pondering why she seemed so different from the woman he remembered knowing in Somerville—and why he was having such trouble controlling his desire for her. He'd also thought about the fear that sometimes paled her cheeks. About the confusion that always looked so genuine on her face. About the innocence in her defensive golden stare that melted his heart every time and created an odd impulse in his gut to protect her.

"I did not decide to become an outlaw . . . I just trusted the wrong man."

He hadn't been able to stop the words from nagging at him since she'd uttered them. At the time, he'd asked her a few probing questions, hoping for more information, but beyond disclosing that she met Bartlett in San Francisco and didn't learn he was an outlaw until they reached Texas, she had refused to say more. He'd left it alone after that, assuming it wasn't any of his business—just as knowing it was his wife he'd lost to that outlaw's bullet hadn't been any of hers.

It hadn't kept Kane from spending a good amount of time speculating on what his prisoner wasn't saying, however, and more than once he wondered if the innocence she claimed about the bank robbery was because Bartlett had somehow forced her to be his accomplice. And each time the thought popped up, aggravation would follow, with a harsh reminder that despite whatever reason bound her to Bartlett, *she* had ended up with the gold and was *solely* responsible for stealing his horse and shooting his father. Kane knew he would be a fool to believe there was anything innocent about Francesca Rossetti—and he sure as hell had no reason to feel any desire for this woman.

So why do I?

She lifted her gaze, her eyebrows shooting upward. "Is there a reason you are scowling at me, Mr. Fairchild?"

Yes, damn it, you're driving me crazy! Too many more nights alone together, and he just might fall completely under this temptress's spell and do something stupid—like forget who she really was and make love to her, as he had in his dreams when he'd finally dozed off in the early hours this morning.

"No," he answered, as much in response to her inquiry as to chase away the memories of those dreams. "Just anxious to be on our way, is all." Anxious to be done with *her,* too. The longer he stayed in her company, the more she addled his senses.

Kane reached down and grabbed the bedroll, then placed it on top of the saddlebags, tying it down. "How far is it to where you hid the gold, Francesca?"

"I . . . I do not know the number of miles."

Kane tensed at the stalling note in her tone, at the way

she tucked her head back down and fumbled with the strip of leather he'd given her earlier to tie a small bow around the bottom of her braid. "Then give it to me in hours."

Bianca shrugged, not looking up. "A day's worth. Maybe two."

"Don't play games with me," he snapped.

She pushed the finished braid over her shoulder, the thick rope falling to rest against her back, then lifted her chin in a stubborn tilt. "I am not. And I wish you would not always assume that I am."

"Then answer my question. How long before we get to the gold?"

"I cannot say for certain." She glanced around, frowning. "I buried the gold beside an oak tree somewhere north of here. But this countryside all looks the same to me. All I am saying is that it might take me a little time to find the same spot again."

Kane arched one eyebrow. "I don't believe you stashed thirty-five thousand dollars and don't know exactly where every dime of it is."

"I was in a hurry to get away from you. And I am afraid I did not think to draw a map."

There was total sincerity in her voice, and fire mingled with the look of innocence in her eyes, but Kane wasn't sure how much of this explanation to believe. He recalled again how he'd lost her trail outside Austin after following her from Bartlett's hideout, and he knew that in that day's time it was possible she could have backtracked north to hide the gold. His gut tightened. Or had Carson done it for her? He knew it was also possible that she'd been in a hurry and might have deemed the small detail of a map unimportant at the time. If she'd only been in Texas with Bartlett a couple of months, as she had claimed last night, it was highly feasible that she probably *didn't* know the countryside all that well. But on the other hand, this was Francesca Rossetti, and he knew the true she-devil that lurked beneath that pretty face. A detail he'd be a fool to forget.

"Your memory better be damn good, sweetheart, because I meant what I said about being through with your games."

She nodded, biting at her lower lip. Then she looped her arms around her right leg as she bent it upward, and began tying the strings on her kid boot.

Kane patted the horse's hindquarters once before walking behind the animal. Tipping his hat brim down against the morning glare, he strode the short distance to the water's edge, stopping in front of Francesca as she carefully eased her left boot onto her stockinged foot. There hadn't been any swelling when he'd checked her ankle earlier, and she'd said it felt much better; she had even been up walking some, though barefoot and with a slight limp. But seeing the slight wince mar her face as she slipped her heel down inside the leather, he wondered if she was in more pain than she was saying.

"Your ankle still feeling all right?" he inquired, wondering why this concern ran deeper than he wanted—why it even mattered to him at all.

"It is a little sore. Not bad, though." She tied the laces, then pulled her black skirt down over her ankle. "You have been kind to let me stay off of it all this time. *Grazie.*"

He nodded, his throat going dry. *God, how he liked her accent!* Damn, how her smile could radiate through his chest with the force of a lightning bolt and fill him with such intense—and unwanted—desire. Kane stretched his right hand out to her, offering assistance as she made to rise, his blood turning to liquid fire when she lifted her shackled hands and slid her warm, satin skin against his roughened palm. He gently gripped her delicate fingers and pulled her to her feet.

Her left foot buckled under, and she dipped sideways. Kane tightened his hold on her hand and quickly wrapped his other arm around her narrow waist to keep her from falling.

"You sure your ankle's not hurting too bad?"

She nodded, straightening in his hold. "I just have to remember not to put my full weight on it yet. But I am fine now. You may let go." She whispered the last, but made no move to pull away.

And for the life of him, he couldn't, either.

His heart thudded faster at her nearness, at the smoldering desire in her amber gaze, shining brighter and with a much deeper honesty than he remembered seeing her express in Somerville.

She offered no resistance when he pulled her closer and dipped his head. Her eyes fluttered shut a split second before he closed his own and lowered his mouth over hers . . . and fell into a pool of glorious delight.

Oh God, she tasted even better than he remembered. Softer. Sweeter. He kissed her slowly, exploring every curve of her warm, luscious lips, surprised at her shy response, even more surprised that he found it as intoxicating as the faint scent of roses from the soap he'd given her to use back at the ranch and that still lingered in her hair. He rubbed his thumb lightly along the back of her hand, felt the palm of her other hand flatten against his chest, her warmth searing through his shirt and making his pulse hammer with excitement. Gently he traced his tongue along the line of her closed lips, anticipating the journey inside even more by her weakening reluctance to admit him in.

Reluctance? Shy? Francesca? Warning bells clanged in his head, instantly cooling the heated flow in his veins. *And what the hell am I doing kissing her, anyway?*

Kane tore his mouth away, abruptly releasing her as he stepped back and crossed his arms, his breath coming as fast and heavy as hers. Her paled cheeks and the hurt look on her face tightened his gut with an odd guilt, annoyingly adding to his bafflement at what he'd just done.

She's an outlaw. She shot my father, for Pete's sake!

He had a job to do. A job he *wanted* to do. The only thing he wanted from this woman was for her to guide him to the stolen gold—and to pay for her crimes.

He swallowed the sour taste of once again playing the fool around her and made a fast sweep of the area, sighing his relief that nature stirred at an undisturbed pace, and his momentary lack of judgment hadn't resulted in the opportunity for an ambush by Carson or Bartlett. He looked back down at Francesca.

"Rest assured, sweetheart, what just happened was a mistake, and I won't repeat it."

She narrowed her gaze; color flooded her cheeks once again. Before Kane could take his next breath she stepped forward, reached up, and clumsily slapped his face with her cuffed hands.

Damn it, I knew he was gonna kiss her. In fact, he'd been so sure of it that had the opportunity presented itself, he would have placed a thousand dollar bet on the outcome. The slap had come as a surprise, though. Devon would have applauded Bianca's strike, but he didn't want to risk giving away his presence.

He held his gun sighted on the Ranger, his muscles tensing as he lay on his belly in the grass and peered through the parted branches of the sweetleaf shrub, waiting to see how Fairchild would respond. Devon could see the reddened fury burning on the Ranger's face, and the fists clenched at his sides, and hoped Fairchild wasn't the sort to strike a woman in anger, or try to force himself on her. Devon wouldn't have any choice but to step in if that happened, and he wasn't anxious to face several years in a dank prison cell for assaulting a lawman.

"I'll let that pass, because I deserved it," Kane hotly snapped. "Now get on the damn horse. We're leaving." He turned away from her and stormed off.

Devon released a sigh and uncocked the hammer, slowly returning the six-shooter to his holster. He released the branches, letting them fall back into place, and rolled onto his back, close to the blue-gray trunk of the tall beech tree. He fumed.

What the hell is going on with these two? Had Bianca kissed the Ranger as herself, or as her sister? But of even more concern to Carson was how this new development might complicate his job of making sure she reached the Somerville jail unscathed.

This is turning out to be more trouble than I want. And making him strongly question whether the fifteen hundred dollars Francesca had promised him was really worth it. Sure, he needed the money to pay off a couple of gambling debts, and to be able to stake his next game. Sure, he owed Francesca a huge favor. If she hadn't barged into his Denver hotel room and warned him about the angry husband on his way up to kill him, Devon never would have gotten out of that bed—and away from that conniving blond actress who'd told him she was unattached—in time to climb out the window and save his hide. But he'd let the temptation of the money, and his honor, sucker him in and make him forget—no, *ignore*—that cutting *any* deal with Francesca was only one small step above signing his soul away to the devil.

Through the thick leaves and yellowish flowers that coated the tree limbs overhead, he stared at the clear morning sky. It had taken him most of yesterday to finally lose those two cowhands who followed him from the Circle F Ranch, and from then until just before dawn this morning to find where Fairchild and Bianca had made camp. He blinked back the aching tiredness in his eyes, wanting nothing more than to catch some sleep. He could easily find a thousand reasons to stay right here, too, and forget his deal with that sneaky little Francesca. But honor wouldn't let him.

Devon frowned. Honor, and the fact that he couldn't find a single reason to make himself abandon Bianca Rossetti. Especially knowing that Francesca had been even less honest with her sister about this plan than she'd been with him.

No, he was stuck with this job for the time being, whether he wanted it or not.

Rolling back onto his stomach, Devon parted the scrub again, then uttered a sharp oath as he stared at the now empty camp on the other side of the stream. He scanned the distant trees, spotting the retreating horses in the shadows, then sat up and grabbed his hat, shoving it on his head. *Time to go.*

The sun made its slow, sweeping journey through the sky and now hung low on the western horizon, and still Bianca's thoughts raced at the same swift pace that they had all day. Her heart pounded faster each time she recalled Kane's tantalizing kiss, his soft, warm lips so tenderly caressing hers. She glanced over at the Ranger, sitting tall in the saddle as they rode side by side through the grassy meadow, her gaze locking on the firm set of his mouth.

Why did he kiss me? She frowned. No, it hadn't been *her* but Francesca Kane had kissed. Which only confused her more. Why had he wanted to kiss Francesca, given that everything he'd said and done so far spoke of nothing but his strong dislike, and definite lack of trust, for her sister?

Bianca sighed. *And why do I care so much what his reasons are?* No matter how handsome he was, or how much she liked and admired the kinder side that he kept hidden behind his scowl, or how his touch had scorched her blood and made her long for more, she knew she had no business wishing his breath-stealing kiss had been for her. She certainly had no business wishing he would kiss her again!

So why couldn't she stop?

Even if she wasn't deceiving the Ranger with this switch, even if he wasn't determined to put her sister in jail—or worse, see her hang, as he had mentioned more than once—he'd definitely had some sort of relationship with Francesca in Somerville; and Bianca knew better than to let herself be attracted to a man who'd shown any interest in her twin first. She'd made that mistake once already, four years ago.

His name was Antonio, and Bianca had been smitten with the fisherman from the moment he sailed into their lives. But it was Francesca he had courted first. Their stormy relationship had only lasted a few short weeks, however, and when he turned his attention to Bianca, courting her for six months, she had foolishly believed his words of love for her were genuine. Painfully but thankfully, she had learned the truth just a week before their wedding, when they had sneaked away to the beach one night, and in the heat of his passionate pressuring for her to give in and make love with him, he'd called her Francesca.

Bianca clenched her jaw, the memory still powerful enough to rankle her. She'd vowed then to never travel that road of pain again. In the years since, she had focused her attention on saving money and planning for her restaurant, and though she'd met a couple of men who had garnered her attention enough to spend time with them for a brief while, the temptation to give her heart away had never risen again—until now.

She raked her gaze over Kane's solid jaw, his broad shoulders, and muscular legs. His kiss had been unlike anything she'd ever experienced and, not for the first time today, had her wishing that she had met this lawman under different circumstances. Bianca looked away, chiding herself for the foolish thought, and for feeling bad about the slap she'd delivered, still deeply bothered that it had stemmed from pain rather than anger. She didn't understand why, but it had hurt to hear Kane say the kiss had been a mistake. It had bruised her heart to hear him so vehemently declare it wouldn't happen again.

Of course, it won't happen again. Kane had been right:

that kiss *was* a mistake. So why was she having such a hard time convincing herself of that?

"Any chance we're going to reach the gold within the next hour?" Kane inquired, his tone as coldly distant as it had been all day—a match for the brooding expression he'd worn as well.

Bianca shook her head.

Kane braced one hand on his thigh, his eyebrows arching high as he cocked his head at her. "Now, why am I not surprised at that answer?"

She tightened her grip on the saddle horn to still her nervous shaking, praying she could stall Kane long enough to reach Somerville, hoping he would be so frustrated with her by then that he'd just lock her in jail and go look for the gold on his own. Or, if luck was with her, perhaps they would run across a freshly dug hole on the way and she could claim that Jeremy Bartlett must have come along after escaping from jail and taken it. Bianca frowned. Of course, *la fortuna* had not smiled down on her from the moment Kane had accosted her in the alleyway, so she wasn't holding out much hope for the latter.

"I told you it might take a couple of days for me to find this place."

Skepticism hovered in his blue gaze. "And you're still positive north is the direction we need to be going?"

She nodded, sweat beading beneath the high collar of her black shirtwaist. It was the third time today he'd asked that, and she assumed it had something to do with his comment last night about having planned to get a meal in Austin. *But why did he expect us to head west to Austin?* Francesca never mentioned anything about being there, only about being in Somerville. Then again, Francesca hadn't mentioned anything about stealing Kane's horse and shooting his father, either. Frustration tensed Bianca's shoulders. Her sister had a lot of explaining to do about how this simple plan had turned into such a complicated mess.

"We'll find a place to make camp up ahead." He pointed toward the grove of oaks and pines at the edge of the meadow.

Bianca offered a small smile of relief. She was more than ready to get out of this saddle, though she had to admit she'd finally learned to brace her knees against the sides to keep from bouncing so hard, and her backside wasn't feeling as sore today. She wondered if that meant she was getting used to riding this beast. Or if her bottom was just in a permanent state of numbness.

Thin shafts of sunlight filtered through the canopy of branches and leaves as they rode into the forest's shadows. The sound of rushing water from the winding creek ahead blended with the woodland noises. Kane brought the horses to a stop a few feet from the stream, then dismounted. Since he hadn't offered her any assistance climbing onto the mare, or dismounting when they had stopped for a short break at noon to dine on blackberries and a few chinquapin nuts from the small tree they'd found, Bianca didn't expect anything different now. So when she again gripped the saddle horn with both manacled hands and awkwardly swung her leg over the horse's hindquarters, it came as a surprise to feel Kane's strong hands circle her waist and lift her down to the ground. She noticed that he wasted no time releasing her, though.

He unwrapped the mare's reins from his saddle horn, then led the horses the rest of the way to the water's edge, leaving the pair to drink their fill as he returned to stand in front of her. Then he fished the handcuff key from his pocket and unlocked the left band.

"Turn around and put your hands behind your back."

"Why?"

"So it'll be harder for you to try to get up and run off while I'm setting up camp."

Bianca furrowed her brow. "I am not going to run off."

He lifted one corner of his mouth in a sly smile. "I

know, because I'm not going to let you. Now turn around."

"I could help you set up camp. I know how to build a fire. Or I could skin that rabbit you shot."

"Thanks for the offer, sweetheart." He gently gripped her shoulder and forced her around, then pulled her arms behind. "But rule number one in this business is never to give your prisoner any sort of weapon, like a match or a knife." He snapped the metal band back around her wrist, then led her along the bank away from the horses.

Bianca's legs wobbled slightly from the long hours in the saddle, and a few twinges of pain shot through her left ankle, but to her relief they quickly subsided. He helped her sit down on the grass beside a tall pine.

"You just worry about staying put, or I'll tie you to that tree."

She glared at his retreating back, wanting to yell at him that she was sick to death of sitting. Tired beyond endurance of having nothing to do but think thoughts of him she didn't want, and to wonder and worry about this predicament Francesca had gotten them in. She was used to staying busy, and this idleness was beginning to grate at her as much as the discomfort of being constantly handcuffed.

Bianca leaned back against the narrow trunk, and tried to relax and enjoy the birds' soft chirping, tried to focus on the sunset painting the sky a soft shade of pink. But all too often her gaze drifted over the Ranger's tall, muscular body as she watched him build the fire, then place the skinned rabbit to roast over the flames. All too often her thoughts drifted back to their kiss, to the memory of his strong but gentle hands on her waist.

He pulled the saddle from the mare's back, and slung it over one broad shoulder, then crossed the narrow distance and placed it at one end of the bedroll he'd spread beside the fire. To her surprise, he came and stood in front of her then, leaning down to circle those strong hands around her waist again and lifting her to her feet.

"I'll lock you to the stirrup, so you'll be more comfortable while I see to the horses."

"Grazie." She turned around, her pulse hammering at his nearness, his thoughtfulness, at the feel of his fingers brushing her skin as he unlocked the handcuff from her right wrist. Bianca rolled her stiff shoulders, relishing the freedom, then turned back to face him. "Could I take care of personal matters before you lock me up again?"

"Sure. But don't go any farther than that oak right over there."

She looked where he pointed toward the tree standing about thirty feet away, the only thick trunk amid the dense grouping of spindly pines that were still visible in dusk's fast-fading light, and nodded her promise. Bianca slowly made her way in that direction, glad for the opportunity to stretch her legs, glad her ankle was so much better, and wanting to drag her brief freedom out as long as possible. She rounded the tree, out of Kane's view, and leaned back against the bark—and only then saw the gray coyote standing in the shadows just ahead. Icy fear filled her veins as she stared at the animal's bared teeth and the white froth lining its mouth.

Kane cocked his head at the strangled squeak that sounded from behind the tree. "Did you say something, Francesca?"

Silence.

He took a step forward, his muscles tensing. "Francesca?"

"Aiuto."

Her voice was barely more than a whisper that he caught on the breeze, but the fear in her tone came through loud and clear and chilled him to the bone.

"What's wrong?" Worry had him pulling his Colt and instantly charging ahead; the vicious growl that resounded made him stop before he'd taken half a dozen steps. Coyote or wolf, he didn't know, but there was no doubt in his mind his prisoner was in serious danger.

"Whatever you do, sweetheart, don't move." He issued

the command in a sternly calm and even tone that belied the panic clenching his chest, and resumed his path at a slower pace so as not to startle the animal with noise.

"Hurry," her voice quivered. "He is—he is rabid, I think."

Rabid! Christ, it was even worse than he thought.

Another harsh growl filled the air.

"Oh *Dio,* he is coming at me!"

"Don't move!" Kane broke into a run, gun raised.

Bianca's scream rent his ear at the same moment he came around the tree and saw the coyote lunge forward. He fired. The bullet plowed into the coyote's head, instantly dropping the animal in its tracks. Kane shoved his gun in his holster and spun toward Bianca, drinking in her deathly pale face. He could see the tears shining in her eyes, saw her lips trembling.

"Are you all right?"

She slowly nodded once; then her eyes rolled upward and fluttered closed as she fainted. Kane saw it coming and captured her limp body in his waiting arms.

TEN

Kane jerked up to a sitting position on the blanket, his gun drawn and cocked as he scanned the darkness beyond the glow of the low fire, searching for the source of the noise that had awakened him.

The whimpering sounded again. He glanced across at his prisoner, seeing her shake her head from side to side.

"No," she whispered, her arms raised to ward off whatever was haunting her dreams.

Kane sighed, figuring it was memories of that coyote making her restless, and not surprised.

She had roused from her faint as soon as he carried her over and placed her on the bedroll, and afterward had tried to act as though she could easily brush off the effects of her encounter with the rabid coyote. He admired her attempt, but he'd known better than to believe it and had seen his suspicion confirmed several times throughout the evening when her shoulders would suddenly ripple with a shudder, and in the way she'd darted her eyes nervously about at every little noise.

Hell, he couldn't blame her. He'd had trouble shaking off the incident, too. Not to mention recovering from the overwhelming fear for her that had gripped his heart in a vise and left him wondering why she had such a deep effect on him.

He shoved his gun back in his holster, then rose to his feet. Her moans grew louder as he crossed the distance between them in a few short strides. He knelt down beside her and gently took hold of her flailing arms.

She stiffened, issuing a strangled scream. Her eyes flew open.

"You're safe," he soothingly assured her. "It's just a dream."

She sat up, hindered slightly by the handcuff binding her left wrist to the stirrup, and glanced around with a confused look, blinking repeatedly until the daze cleared from her stare. Then she sighed heavily and her shoulders drooped, but her breaths still came short and fast. "I thought that coyote was back."

"Sorry you had to relive that." He released her arms and reached one hand up to stroke her cheek.

"Me, too," she whispered, her trembling lips forming a weak smile.

Kane couldn't stop himself from trailing his thumb along her mouth, couldn't stop the desire to taste her sweetness again that sizzled through his blood. He forced himself to lower his hand before he gave in to that thought.

"I am sorry if I woke you."

He shrugged. "No matter. There's still a couple of hours left before daylight to catch some more sleep." He saw the look of reluctance to resume slumber spring into her amber eyes, and he released an understanding sigh. "Unless you'd rather we just stay up."

She shook her head, the movement sending a tear spilling from the corner of one eye. "I would not ask that. But would you . . ."

He took a deep breath as he wiped the drop from her cheek, struggling to ignore the strong urge to pull her into his arms. "Would I what?"

"Never mind. It is silly." She tucked her head down.

He placed one finger under her chin, gently forcing her to look up. "Since you and I rarely agree on anything, chances are I won't think it's silly at all. Would I what?"

Her throat rippled as she swallowed. "Would you hold

me?" she whispered so soft he barely caught the words, but the impact on his heart was too hard to ignore.

He replied by twisting around to sit on the bedroll with his back against the saddle, shifting her onto his lap as he did, then cradling her shaking body close to his chest. He lightly rested his head on top of hers, only intending to stay there just long enough for her to fall back asleep. But she felt so good, so right in his arms, that he found himself relaxing against her once her breathing evened out and she drifted off, and promising himself he'd move in just a minute as he closed his eyes.

The next thing Kane knew, he felt the warmth of the morning sun shining on his face, pulling him from the unconscious depths of sleep. He moved slowly toward it, knowing it was time to wake, but reluctant to do so because something felt damn good beside him, and soft in his hand, and he didn't want to let go of the dream.

He opened one eye, surprised to realize it wasn't a dream.

Christ! I'm fondling Francesca's breast!

He froze, taking a second to remember why he was even on this side of the campfire, then wondering when he'd slid down to lie on his side on the bedroll, with her back snuggled against his chest and his arm draped over her. And as he listened to her steady breathing with the hope that he wouldn't be caught in this indiscretion, he was also oddly reminded of how much he'd missed waking up beside a woman in the morning. Slowly and steadily he eased his hand away from her breast, then his arm from around her, and rolled to his back.

Bianca didn't move but quietly sighed her disappointment at the loss of his comfort and protective hold, and of the sensuous feel of his fingers gently stroking her breast and setting her blood on fire. And not for the first time in the past several minutes, she chided herself for not doing exactly what Kane just did: pull away the moment she'd awakened and discovered his hand on her breast.

She listened to him rise and stir about the camp, wondering why she was so drawn to his kindness, to his touch. Wondering why she couldn't stop wishing that she'd met him at another time, in another place—as herself, instead of pretending to be her sister.

Wondering why she had longed for him to try to wake her with a kiss instead of sneaking away.

Moored along Galveston's wharves, tall schooners and steamships towered above the small fishing vessels, and in the distance Hailey saw several more shrimp boats just now sailing into the harbor, the seabirds skimming in their wake thick enough to blot out the late afternoon sky. Amid the squawks and squalls filling the air rose the shouts of sailors and dock workers busy unloading cargo, while other crates were hoisted up in roped nets and stowed on ships soon to depart.

Hailey ignored the few crude calls aimed her way as she hurried by, her attention focused on Pier Twenty up ahead, and on the shrimp boats tied along both sides. She spotted the Casales' red vessel moored three quarters of the way down the dock, and her pulse began to pound with nervous anticipation. She hoped Raimondo wouldn't mind that she had come. He'd told her when he saw her home last night that he would stop by and see her again this evening. But she'd been anxious all day to know if there was any word about Bianca. Too anxious to wait a moment longer, so she'd headed straight here as soon as she had finished her shift at the hotel.

She couldn't deny that she'd been anxious all day to see Raimondo again, as well. Joy and sadness had been waging a war in her heart since she'd last seen him. Ever since he'd been so kind and understanding of her childhood, and so tender as he wiped her tears away. Ever since he'd told her that he cared about her, and had kissed her. Her pulse skipped a painful beat. Ever since he'd told her that he was promised to another.

Hailey admired Raimondo's commitment to his family and to their traditions, but she didn't agree with their belief in arranged marriages. She'd always believed in marrying for love, and had promised herself nothing less. And admiration for Raimondo's integrity hadn't kept her heart from breaking, or her from wishing he would walk away from this promise he'd made to marry a woman he'd never met, and follow his affections for her instead. Hailey sighed, swallowing. But he'd made it clear last night that he was honor bound to follow through with his parents' wishes, leaving Hailey to spend a sleepless night pondering how she could possibly just be friends as he wanted, when she wanted so much more. And finding no answers.

Hailey sighed and blinked back the tears that started to rise. She slowed her pace as she reached the pier, disappointment claiming even more of her heart as she stared at the shrimp boat tied closest to the dock. The dark cabin and silence aboard severed the small shred of hope she'd harbored on the way over that Bianca might have returned home.

She started down the pier, weaving her way through the throng of people shopping for the fresh catch of the day. Hailey recognized several of the fishermen's wives she'd met that night while searching for Bianca, and waved at a couple who didn't happen to be busy with customers when she walked past.

As she made her way near the end of the pier, Hailey was surprised she didn't see the Casale women among the others bartering their wares. Instead, on one side of the pier, she saw the four Casale children playing together on the decks of the two boats belonging to Raimondo's brothers, while their mothers stood at the railings near their respective cabins, each holding a baby perched on her hip, and engaged in a lively conversation that included lots of hand waving. And moored directly across the dock was the vessel where Raimondo lived with his parents.

Hailey saw Rosa Casale on the front deck, taking wash down from two ropes strung between the cabin and the bow with a quick agility that belied her short, amply rounded frame. She stopped at the edge of the dock.

"Good afternoon, Mrs. Casale."

Rosa turned around, a smile lighting up her plump, tanned face. Her thick black hair was parted down the middle and pulled back into a bun. *"Buongiorno,* signorina Tillman. It is nice to see you again."

She dropped the armload of clothes into the basket at her feet, then crossed the deck, shoving the wooden pins into the pocket of the pinafore apron tied over her white blouse and blue calico skirt. *"Veni icca."* She gestured with one hand for Hailey to come onto the boat. "Tell me what you have learned about our Bianca."

"I'm afraid I don't have any news, ma'am." Hailey lifted her gray skirt and carefully took the long step down onto the bow, then down the short flight of steps to the deck. "I've talked with several folks from the hotel, but still no one has seen her since the night she was fired. I came by hoping that Raimondo had found out something today."

Rosa crinkled her brow and shook her head. *"La fortuna* did not shine on him, either. He and Daniele went to see this man Murdock last night." She waved her hands about in frustration. "He claims he knows *niente* about Bianca's disappearance, and says he was in Houston with a different woman. And that this he can prove. So today Papa takes our sons and sails up the bayou, and they discover that Murdock tells the truth about that. But Raimondo still thinks he knows something."

Hailey's gut tightened. "Why?"

"Raimondo says he is certain our Bianca never made it home from the hotel that night that man got her fired. And that Murdock did not leave the island until the next morning. Plenty of time for him to do something to her." Worry gleamed starkly in Rosa's dark eyes. "Raimondo and Daniele have gone to talk to Murdock again. Papa and Vito Junior are at the beach while the sun is still up, searching along the shoreline again. But they are only doing so to keep busy. Truth is, we do not know any more places to look."

Hailey swallowed, pondering whether she should go to the sheriff and tell him why she feared Murdock was responsible for Bianca's disappearance, worrying again that she'd let too much time pass already. The longer her friend was missing, the more Hailey feared that something very serious had happened to Bianca, and her guilt dug deeper that she hadn't done everything she could to help find her. Much as she didn't want to break her promise to Raimondo to let his family handle this matter, Hailey couldn't deny her conscience any longer. She had to get the sheriff involved in the search.

"Mrs. Casale, thank you for telling me what you've learned. Will you please let Raimondo know that I stopped by?"

Rosa placed one hand on Hailey's arm and shook her head. *"Per favore,* do not leave. Stay and have supper with us. Perhaps Raimondo and Papa will have some news to share. Hopefully good news."

"That is very kind of you, Mrs. Casale." Hailey swallowed at the mouthwatering scents that drifted from the cabin and clung faintly to the salt- and fish-scented air. "And whatever you are cooking, it smells wonderful."

"Cannelloni. It is Raimondo's favorite dish. Cheese and meat with pasta. You will like, I am sure."

"I'm sure I would, ma'am. But you are busy." Hailey nodded toward the laundry hanging on the lines. "And I do not wish to intrude on your family."

Rosa smiled. "Friends do not intrude, and you are a good friend to our Bianca and to us. We are grateful that you told Raimondo when you first worried that something happened to her."

"Bianca has been a good friend to me. I could do no less than to return the favor." She needed to stop wasting time and go talk to the sheriff.

"It would be an honor to have you as our guest, signorina Tillman. You will stay?"

Hailey pulled her bottom lip in between her teeth and contemplated what to do. She'd never sat down to a real family meal before; her childhood memories only included eating alone while her mother either slept or worked, and the temptation to stay was strong. But the swaying factor to her final decision was her guilt. She thought it only fair to tell Raimondo first about her decision to go to the sheriff, rather than break her promise and then try to explain her action—and risk making him even angrier.

She smiled. "Please, call me Hailey. And I would love to stay. Thank you, ma'am."

Kane brought the horses to a halt at the edge of a sparse grove of loblolly pines, pecan trees, and scattered oaks of various size and shape. He braced one hand on his thigh, his narrowed glare cutting the distance between them. "Where the hell is the gold, Francesca?"

Bianca swallowed at the impatience in his tone and glanced around at the miles of lush hills and prairie shrouded in a pinkish haze as the day neared its close. "I do not think it is much farther. This area is starting to look familiar to me," she lied.

Kane sat back and pushed his hat brim up. Lines of exasperation furrowed his brow. "You've said that about every meadow we've crossed today. Now stop playing games and tell me where the damn gold is buried!"

Dio, I am in trouble. She raised her chin in a confident tilt that belied the turmoil rolling inside. "I did already. It is under a gnarled oak that sits at the edge of a meadow."

He cocked his head, and waved one hand about. "But not any of these particular oaks, or any of the others we've seen today?" Sarcasm mingled with the skepticism ringing heavy in his tone.

Bianca bit at the inside of her lip and shook her head.

He raised one finger in warning. "You better be telling me the truth, Francesca. And we had better find that gold tomorrow. If not, I'm taking you straight to the Somerville jail, and I assure you that your lack of cooperation in this matter will only make things worse when it comes time for the judge to sentence you."

Bianca nodded, silently shouting for joy that he was finally going to take her to Somerville, even though panic still rioted with the realization that she still had tomorrow to get through, and the days after until Francesca arrived with the needed proof to clear up the questions of her innocence.

"I know a spot not far from here where we can make camp." He gathered up the reins.

She rubbed her sweaty palms on her dusty black skirt, then grabbed the saddle horn tight as Kane set the horses into motion. The grass was a deep, rich green and grew thicker as they rode through the sketchy woodland toward the sound of rushing water. Minutes later the broad river came into view, and Bianca gasped her appreciation for the breathtaking beauty of the falls, bathed in sunset's golden light that shimmered over the frothy water rapidly flowing down the long, sloping ramp of limestone.

Kane stared, transfixed by the radiance beaming on his prisoner's pretty face as she gazed at the falls, confident she'd never seen them before now. Her surprise had been too immediate, her look too genuine for this to be an act. Which only deepened his uncertainty about whether or not she was being honest and truly leading him to the gold as best she could remember. Or was he once again being a fool and playing right into her hands, as his gut suggested?

He turned the horses along the bank, following the Brazos River downstream to where the water moved at a more placid pace. He was a fool, all right. If for nothing more than allowing her to cause him this confusion, when he already knew without a shadow of a doubt that she couldn't be trusted. He reined his horse to a stop, then dismounted and walked around to help Bianca down. He jerked his hands from her waist as soon as her feet touched the ground, trying to force down the memories of her shapely curves pressed against him this morning, of her soft, full breast beneath his fingers.

He shook his head in disgust, having the same lack of success keeping the images at bay now as he'd had all day.

He locked Bianca's hands behind her back and made her sit by the water's edge, keeping her in close sight while he took care of setting up camp. By the time the sun fully disappeared and the moon was making its claim on the night, he'd managed to snare a squirrel—now roasting over the fire—and had the bedding spread out and the horses hobbled. He'd also had the foresight that afternoon to stop at a farm they came across and purchase a small cache of flour, salt, and blackberry jam from a widow with three young children hanging on her tattered skirts, and had taken Bianca up on her offer to fix bread to go along with their supper, figuring she couldn't do much harm with a spoon and a small frying pan.

As long as he didn't turn his back on her, anyway.

That wasn't a problem, though. He frowned. In fact, ever since he'd sat down across the fire from her, he'd been finding it damned hard *not* to keep an eye on her. And it grated at him that it wasn't just interest in the job at hand holding his attention. He whittled another thin shaving from the tip of the stick he held, then paused and stared over to where she knelt beside the fire.

She pressed one finger lightly against the risen dough, seemingly satisfied with the way it sprang back up, then she pushed the skillet near the coals so the bread could bake.

"You sure you don't cook more than you say? That bread looks pretty darn good, and smells great. Better than any I've ever whipped up."

"Some things are never forgotten, even though the skill

is not often used." She shot him a brief grin, then turned her attention back to the bread, adjusting the pan over the coals, slightly back away from the fire. "But I am more used to a stove than a campfire. This bread will have to be watched close, or it will burn on the bottom."

Kane shrugged. "If it does, it'll be just like I cooked it myself."

"Do you burn a lot of bread, Mr. Fairchild?" She chuckled, her wide smile deepening her sweet dimples and stealing his breath.

"My share, that's for sure." The firelight danced across her pretty face, illuminating the white streak on one cheek that he'd found too captivating to say anything about. He tensed. Damn it, he had to stop being captivated with her! "You have some flour on your cheek."

She raised her shackled arms and brushed at her cheek with the back of one hand. "Did I get it?"

Kane shook his head and smiled. "Wrong cheek."

She issued a small huff of annoyance, but there was nothing but amusement shining in her amber gaze as she wiped the other side of her face.

"You want to wash up at the stream?" He set his knife and the stick down and leaned forward, reaching for the saddlebags he'd placed at the end of the blanket.

"I would really like to do more than just wash up. Would it be all right if I take a bath in the river?

Kane froze with the bar of soap halfway out of the leather pouch and snapped his head up. "You mean a bath, like taking your clothes off and getting in?"

She nodded. "And I would like to wash my hair. I won't take long."

Kane swallowed. Christ, he was having enough trouble keeping his mind off of her without her wanting to get naked! "And just where do you plan to take this bath, since I'm not about to let you of my sight?"

Lifting her shackled hands, she motioned toward where the river flowed by just a few yards behind them. "Right here will be fine."

Kane sat up straight and arched his brow. "You going to just undress right here while I watch, too?"

Patches of red rose in her cheeks. "No. I am going to ask you to turn around long enough for me to undress and slip in the water."

Turn around? Sure. And why don't I just give you my gun, too? He chuckled. "Not on your life."

"Look, Mr. Fairchild, I know you have a few reasons to doubt me, but—"

"Definitely more than a few, sweetheart."

"But . . ." She cocked her head, frowning at his interruption. "I have made no attempts to escape when you have let me have privacy. And I am not asking to go any farther than I have at those times. I will be right in sight, so surely you can trust me not to try to escape this time, as well."

No, he didn't have to do any such thing. But his conscience wouldn't let him ignore that she made a valid point. He also had to admit that she'd had ample opportunity to take his gun and try to escape while he'd been curled next to her sound asleep this morning, and she hadn't. And to be honest, with himself at least, he really wasn't nearly as worried about her trying something as he was about controlling his desirous thoughts for her while she splashed around out there in the moonlit water.

"All right, I'll turn my back while you undress and get in. But not a second longer."

She nodded. "That is fine. *Grazie.*"

He rose to his feet, wishing her voice didn't make his blood rush, and that her smile didn't scorch his heart the way it did. Wishing he'd listened about being too close to this case and had let Caleb go after Francesca, as his friend had wanted to do. She pushed up from the ground. He reached her side and cupped her elbow, helping her to stand; then he gave her the bar of soap and dug the handcuff key from his front pocket. He unlocked one band, then the other, and tossed the handcuffs down on the bedroll.

"Don't make me regret this."

"You have my promise."

Kane nodded, but his gut tightened as he recalled how she had said those exact words that night in Somerville, when he'd asked if she was really serious about coming to his hotel room. And what a disaster that had turned out to be.

He crossed his arms as he watched her walk to the water's edge. She looked back at him, cocking her head, her expression one of impatience for him to comply with his agreement. He slowly turned around, alert to every noise she made, vivid images wrestling for space in his thoughts as he heard the soft shuffle of cloth sliding from her body and being tossed to the ground. With every slow second that passed, desire built in his loins and hardened his body, making him wish he'd never agreed to this bath. He sure as hell hadn't agreed to be tortured like this.

He couldn't shake this sense that he was being a fool to turn his back on her, either.

Hurry it up, Francesca. He lowered his hands to his hips and stared down at the fire, then sighed his relief when he finally heard the gentle splashes of her walking into the river. He knew she hadn't had time to reach the deeper section in the middle, but he turned around anyway, not sure what compelled him: the desire to glimpse her beauty again; his distrust; or the simple fact that he was a man and he desired this woman with a need he didn't understand.

Pale moonlight shimmered in her dark hair, the thick, loose strands cascading down her back. Kane's mouth went dry as his eyes skimmed her narrow ivory shoulders, the slimming curve of her tiny waist, the gentle flare of her hips . . .

He paused, frowning. "Wait just a minute there, Francesca."

She squealed, wrapping her arms across her breasts and whipping her head around to look over her shoulder with eyes as wide as saucers. "You broke your promise! I thought you were a man of honor, Mr. Fairchild."

"To hell with honor." Kane stomped over to the water's edge. "Where's that heart-shaped red mark you had on your hip the last time I saw you?"

ELEVEN

Bianca's heart jumped into her throat and pounded so hard she couldn't breathe. She knew there was only one way Kane could know about Francesca's birthmark. *He has seen her unclothed!* Shock warred with the anger that rose at her sister for lying about her relationship with the Ranger.

And now Kane was getting a good eyeful of *her*, too! Embarrassed heat flooded her body. She gave serious thought to stooping down and hiding beneath the water, and would have if her muscles weren't stiff with shock, and if she didn't fear Kane might consider any sort of move she made an attempt to escape and come in after her.

"Well?" he snapped.

She opened her mouth, but no words came out. What could she say? How could she explain the absence that marked the only physical difference between her and her twin without revealing the truth?

The cool water gently lapped against her thighs. She felt the reddening blush sweep up into her cheeks as Kane raked his gaze over her exposed backside. "Would you turn around and let me come out and get dressed, *per favore?*"

"No. I think I stand a better chance of getting the truth if I keep you at a disadvantage." He shoved his hands on his hips and frowned. "Now, tell me why you don't have that birthmark on your hip."

She was cornered, but not yet ready to give up the fight. "What you saw before was just a mark painted on with rouge."

He shook his head. "I know better. So you just keep standing there thinking up lies if you want, sweetheart; I don't mind the view. But you're not coming out of that water until I have the truth."

She looked away from his probing stare and took several deep breaths, trying to calm her nerves and having no success. *Dio,* she'd been a fool to believe Kane would keep his word and not look. She'd been a fool to want to wash the two-days' worth of horse smell off so badly she had agreed to bathe in front of him.

What am I going to tell him? She glanced back at Kane, anxiety knotting her stomach even tighter when she saw him now staring down at the photograph he'd confiscated from her at the jail.

Twins? Kane's heart slammed to a stop. It was all he could do to keep his jaw from dropping open. *What a fool I've been!*

He looked up at the woman he'd captured. "You're not Francesca, are you? And these girls aren't your cousins, but rather you and your sister, am I right?"

She darted her gaze about, her throat rippling as she swallowed.

"You might as well admit it. I know I am." He could see it all clearly now. He understood fully why he kept hearing a subtle difference in her voice, kept seeing a prettier softness in her round face, and a more caring and inquisitive side to her manner. He understood now why she hadn't recognized him at first and had seemed surprised and confused about things he would bring up. It hadn't been an act at all. Francesca had obviously withheld a good chunk of the truth from her sister—something Kane didn't have any doubts Francesca would do. He also suspected that this woman didn't know a damn thing about the hidden gold, but was only trying to stall him by leading him on this fool's errand away from

Austin. Kane frowned. The signs had all been there, but he realized he'd been too wrapped up trying to figure out why he couldn't stop his infatuation for this woman to read them right—until now.

She sighed and finally nodded.

"What's your name?"

"Bianca Rossetti." She shot him a cutting stare from the corner of her eyes, then aimed her gaze down at the water. "Will you let me come out now and get dressed?" she grated through clenched teeth.

"Yes." He spun around and shoved the photograph into his vest pocket as he headed back toward the camp, telling himself not to feel guilty for making her stand there naked but to remember that even though she wasn't that scheming actress Francesca, she obviously knew how to be just as deceptive as her sister. He scooped the handcuffs up from the bedroll, wondering what he was going to do with Miss Bianca Rossetti.

He heard her wading through the shallow water as she neared the riverbank, and couldn't stop the images of her naked beauty from crowding his mind. He shook his head and tossed the handcuffs over by his saddlebags, then knelt down by the fire, and turned the meat to brown on the other side. Memories of her confusion, her claims of innocence, the arguments that had transpired between them kept spinning through his mind, stunning him that he'd been so blind. Stunning him with the realization that she really wasn't Francesca. She wasn't the woman who'd ridden with Jeremy Bartlett's gang, wasn't the outlaw who'd shot his father—nor the she-devil he'd kissed in Somerville.

But rather, the beautiful temptress whose soft, shy kiss yesterday had seared his heart like no other. Kane's pulse pounded at the memory of that sweet kiss and sent his desire rearing up once again: *Bianca.* Her name was as pretty as she was.

He tensed, a frown taking hold as caution cooled his blood. *Don't forget what she's done.* Whether or not she knew the truth about Francesca's crimes, Bianca was still—at the very least—guilty of being an accessory. Not to mention playing him for a fool ever since Galveston!

He heard her approaching up the bank and turned around. Her dusty skirt and shirtwaist covered her once again, and even without the evidence of the wadded bundle of her white camisole and petticoat in her arms and her bare feet peeking beneath her hem, he could tell by the way the black serge clung to her soft curves that she hadn't bothered putting on any underthings. She stopped in front of him and dropped the bundle onto the bedroll.

Kane forced himself not to be sidetracked by her beauty or the apprehension in her golden stare. "I want the truth. What's going on here, Miss Rossetti?"

She hesitated, looking away, then back, sighing. "I switched places with my sister."

"Why?"

"Francesca wanted to get you off her trail so she could find proof that she's innocent of the bank robbery."

"What proof?"

"She didn't say."

"That's because she's not innocent."

"I believe Francesca *is* innocent of the robbery."

"Then you're an even bigger fool than I've been. She's guilty. And there's not a shred of evidence out there to prove otherwise."

Bianca hesitated. Perhaps she had been foolish where her sister was concerned, but she still refused to believe that Francesca had lied about everything. "Maybe you are wrong about that." She lifted her chin in a stubborn tilt. "What I told you about Francesca being duped by Bartlett was true. I am sure of it. Francesca wrote me months ago about their engagement. She mentioned even then that he was a rancher, and she was planning to go to Somerville with him because she thought that was where he lived. She went there to plan a wedding, not to help rob that bank, and maybe she *can* prove it."

Kane shook his head. "She lied to you. The Bartlett

Bunch is wanted for a bank robbery in Fort Worth, and also for robbing a train outside of Denver. Francesca was seen with Jeremy Bartlett in both towns. From the moment she stepped off that train in Somerville, she was doing exactly what she and Bartlett planned, and it didn't have anything to do with a wedding. They somehow found out about the gold one of the local ranchers there was temporarily storing in the bank's vault. They also knew that me and my partner and friend, Caleb Wilson, were in town to find the rustlers who'd been giving that same rancher and several others in the area trouble for months.

"The morning of the robbery, Caleb received a message that his fiancée had been hurt in a buggy accident. He took the next train out and went back to Austin. We found out later it wasn't true. But in the meantime, that just left me and the sheriff to deal with it. It was a well-planned out robbery, Miss Rossetti."

Bianca was shocked by these new details that strongly pointed to her sister's guilt, and sadly, she found it easier to accept that Kane was telling the truth again and that her sister had lied about this, as well. But she still wasn't willing to turn against Francesca. "She swore to me she was not anywhere near the Somerville Bank that night."

Kane nodded. "That's right; she wasn't. She was with me."

Bianca stiffened. "With you where?"

"In my hotel room. It was her job to keep me occupied until the robbery was done. Bartlett and the other two men riding with them overpowered the sheriff and tied him up in the woods outside of town; then they came back and blew up the safe with enough dynamite to shake half the town. The lot of them met up afterwards and rode to a hideout in the hills about fifty miles west of here—a place called Eagle Pass. That's where me and Caleb found them a week later. Most of them, anyway. I followed your sister's trail from there to Galveston."

Kane watched the expressive struggle to accept the

truth slowly cross her face, then the frown of determination still to trust her sister settle in. "If what you say is true, then how did Francesca manage to get away from you after the explosion?"

Kane hesitated, running one hand through his hair, not the least bit anxious to reveal his gullibility. "It doesn't matter."

"Why not?"

"Because I said it didn't."

Bianca cocked her head. "Or is it because my sister is not as guilty as you want me to believe?"

"Your sister is the lowest outlaw I've run across in a long while."

She narrowed her gaze at him. "I am certain Francesca must have had a very good reason for doing what she did."

"She had a reason all right. She's a conniving she-devil!" He stepped forward, impressed that Bianca stood her ground with him, but fast tiring of her arguments and ill-placed faith. "Face it, Bianca, she didn't tell you the truth about the robbery any more than she told you about shooting my father and stealing my horse."

"And you're not telling me the full truth, either. How did my sister get away from you?"

He took several deep breaths, knowing she *did* deserve the full truth, if for no other reason than to take off the blinders about her sister so that she might understand the depths Francesca would sink to, to get what she wanted— and the trouble she had drug Bianca into along with her. But *damn,* he wasn't looking forward to facing this embarrassment. "She handcuffed me to the bed and walked out the door."

Her eyebrows darted upward. "Certainly she did not manage to accomplish that against your will?" She threw her hands out wide, then balled her fists and planted them on her hips.

He swallowed. "No, she didn't. She lured me in with

a promise of a night of passion, and some very good seduction."

"And how far did her seduction go before you agreed to be handcuffed?" Her eyes burned with a spark of jealousy that took him by surprise—and made him want to lean down and kiss her.

Kane stepped back and crossed his arms to keep from reaching over and pulling Bianca into them. "Not as far as she promised it would, I assure you. She's a master at timing, too. She'd lured me into her plan and had her dress undone and half off when the explosion sounded. She didn't bother to take the time to do up the back buttons afterward, and I saw her birthmark as she was hightailing it out of that room." *Taking the handcuff key right along with her, too!* Kane fumed. But at least he'd still had his pants on, so when the sheriff had finally been found two hours later and came looking for Kane to help form a posse, his embarrassment hadn't been as bad as if he'd been lying there naked.

Bianca sighed, more relieved than she wanted to admit that Kane hadn't been intimate with her sister, and angry with Francesca at the same time. Why had she done all these things? She had never acted like this before. *She has never lied to me before, either. Why now?*

"Why did you agree to switch places with Francesca?"

"Because she is my sister. And it is one's duty to stick by their family."

"Do you understand that I have to arrest you?"

Bianca's heart raced. "I understand that you are angry at being deceived, and I am sorry. But it was just a simple pretense to help Francesca. I have committed no crime."

Kane arched his eyebrows high. "Pretending to be your sister to help her elude arrest makes you an accessory after the fact. And that *is* a crime, Bianca."

"How can it be a crime to help your family?" She frowned. "And besides, Francesca is not eluding arrest. She is only postponing it. I know my sister quite well, and it is not like her to act this way. She must have had a good reason for getting into this trouble, and she will find what she needs to prove her innocence."

"If her reasons were so good, then why did she lie to you about what she'd done?"

Bianca took a deep breath. "I do not know." But she intended to find out the moment she saw Francesca again. "All I know is that when I saw her four days ago, she promised to meet me in Somerville in two weeks, on June first. And I know she will be there, Mr. Fairchild. No matter what Francesca has done so far, she is a good person, and she *will* come and clear all this up. She would not leave me to face this alone."

He shook his head. "Sorry, but I don't share your faith in Francesca. And I don't think you better count on her keeping her word."

Bianca did count on it, though, because she deeply believed in the bonds of blood that held her family together. They had always been there for each other. She had come to Francesca's aid in her hour of need, and Bianca could not—*would not*—believe that her twin would do any less for her. "You will see that I am right."

"For your sake, I hope so." He didn't want to stand here and fight about it, or try to destroy her faith in her sister, but Kane didn't doubt for a second that Bianca would be proven wrong. Francesca had a reason for her actions, all right, and he strongly suspected those actions had included using her sister to throw him off track while she made arrangements to get herself and the gold on a ship headed out of Galveston. The question was, did he have time to get back before she fled the country?

And what was he going to do about Bianca? He could understand that she'd wanted to help her sister, and he felt a little sorry for her that she'd obviously walked into this situation on blind faith in Francesca's word. But that didn't make his job any easier. By all rights he knew he had to arrest her. Now.

He gazed down into her fiery, golden stare. But, damn it, that was the last thing he wanted to do. Now that he

knew she wasn't Francesca, wasn't the lying outlaw he'd
thought her to be, the desire he had tried so hard to push
away came flooding back in full force. He didn't question
why he wanted to kiss her and be nice to her any longer.
She was a beautiful, interesting woman, and he liked
her—a lot more than he wanted to admit. But he couldn't
completely shove aside that she'd willingly participated
in this deceptive switch and was still even now trying to
find a way to defend Francesca's innocence. He couldn't
help but wonder just how far Bianca *would* go to help
her twin—or how wise he would be to let his attraction
rule his good sense where she was concerned.

"Well, in the meantime we might as well make the
best of the situation we've got." He spared a quick glance
toward the fire. "The food's not done yet. You've got time
to take that bath if you still want. And I promise I'll keep
my back turned this time." He smiled, deciding to go one
step further since he figured Bianca had been telling him
the truth all along that she wasn't going to try to run off.
"Or you can go upstream a short ways, if you'd rather
have more privacy."

"*Grazie.* I will go upstream. Not because I do not trust
you," she was quick to add, her smile of gratitude widening, her dimples heightening the heated fervor rushing
through his veins. "It is just that since you are giving me
this opportunity, I would like to wash out a few of my
clothes, as well."

He swallowed. "That's fine." And being a man able to
admit to certain weaknesses, he'd just go off in the woods
for a while. Where he couldn't hear her and wouldn't be
tempted to break his promise and sneak over to have a
peek.

Rosa Casale stood on the front deck, frowning her disapproval at the couple walking along the moonlit pier
away from the boat, her instincts humming with a dread
she knew from past experience it would be unwise to

ignore. She glanced over to where her husband sat against the side railing, puffing on the cigar that was his habit to partake of after every evening meal. "I did not know so before, Papa, but that girl is trouble. I am sorry that I invited her to eat with us."

"Signorina Hailey?" Vito furrowed his brow, glancing toward the pier, then back. "Why do you say that, Rosa?" he scoffed. "She is a nice girl. And she has wanted only to be helpful in finding Bianca."

"And she is in love with our Raimondo."

"What?" Vito scrunched his face in disbelief, then waved his hand dismissively. "You are talking *matto, Mamma.*"

Rosa drew her eyebrows together and shook one finger at him. "Do not call me crazy because you are a blind man, Vito. Did you not see it in her eyes every time she looked at Raimondo?" She shoved her hands on her hips. "And I am worried, because I also saw that same look for her in your son's eyes."

Vito shook his head. "I saw none of this."

"That is because they were careful to hide it. They just did not succeed with me."

Vito turned away and stared toward the dock, taking a draw on the cheroot. He looked back at her, blew out a long stream of white smoke, and shrugged one shoulder. "I think you are exaggerating that these looks you saw had anything to do with love. They might be attracted to each other. They are young, It is natural. But it is nothing to be concerned about."

Rosa crossed her arms. "What if you are wrong? What if Raimondo decides again to argue with us about this marriage to Adrianna?"

Vito narrowed his gaze. "He will not. He is a good son. We raised him right, Rosa. He would not shame us by going back on his promise. And even if he had not finally agreed to this arranged marriage, he still would never break our hearts and marry outside of our heritage. There is *niente* for you to worry about."

"I pray you are right, Vito." Rosa blew out several short breaths, then turned to stare at the couple again, narrowing her gaze with disapproval as she watched Hailey reach up and touch Raimondo's face.

"Are you telling me the truth, Raimondo?" Hailey brushed one soft finger along his slightly swollen cheek, heating his flesh. "Did Daniele accidentally give you this bruise, or did you get into a fight with Murdock?"

Raimondo smiled and reached up to take hold of her hand. "Daniele really did hit me with the fish," he admitted, though he would rather have earned the bruise while beating Murdock to a pulp.

His father and brothers had all accompanied him this time to scour Houston, to check out Murdock's fishy story and find a hole in it, any hole that might lead them to Bianca. But it was a wasted journey, completely devoid of clues pointing toward Murdock's innocence or guilt. The Casale men had returned empty-handed and hopeless, brimming with violent frustration, which surfaced in their brusque banter and in the unthinking way Daniele had spun around in the midst of scaling a fish, carelessly swatting his kneeling brother in the eye. They were so consumed by their thoughts and their burning desire to rescue Bianca that Daniele barely apologized for his carelessness and Raimondo barely felt the bruise as he'd muttered, "Dannare! That should have hurt"—if he hadn't been so distracted by his own fury.

Damn Murdock's insistence that he was innocent! He was their only suspect, and that made him their only hope. Raimondo and Daniele had even returned today to corner that *bastardo* at the shipping company on his way home, fully intending to beat him for information if that was what they had to do. But he had only repeated his proclamation of innocence and threatened to call the police if they didn't stop harassing him. It was not the threat of *la polizia* which made them turn around and go. It was the stubborn set of his beady eyes, wedged deeply into his nearly bald head, that convinced them he would never tell them anything, even if he knew—which they were beginning to doubt.

One thing had not changed, though. Whether Avis Murdock had anything to do with Bianca's disappearance or not, he was still the man who had caused Hailey much suffering. And for that alone, Raimondo was willing to pound him to a pulp. Just being so near him, looking at his red, perspiring face and remembering what he had done to Hailey's *mamma,* and how she'd had to watch. To watch. It made Raimondo want to beat him and then hold her, comfort her, and then beat him some more. It was Daniele, cool-headed as always, who had kept him from doing so and finally dragged him home before his little brother did something he might really regret. "He knows nothing," he told Raimondo. "Come. We tried. He doesn't know." Why it looked as though Raimondo wanted to kill him anyway, Daniele really didn't understand.

"I learned something about the boy today." Remembering to tell her helped break Raimondo from his thoughts. "I asked some questions and snooped around." *For you,* he added silently.

Hailey's baby blue eyes narrowed inquisitively. "The boy?"

"Yes. The one you were so kind to, the orphan." The memory of her altruism when she handed the shopkeeper all of her money to help a stranger made him gaze upon her ivory face with even more fondness.

"Oh, the boy!" Her brows shot up expectantly. "What did you learn?" She was eager for any morsel of information about the child who had unwittingly touched her heart.

"The boy has not been on the island long," he said, "What I managed to learn was that his parents were killed, and he came here from Greece several months ago to live with his grandfather."

"Is his grandfather a fisherman too?"

Raimondo frowned. "Yes, but I've heard he is also a drunk and only takes his boat out when he needs money for his next bottle of whiskey."

"How sad for that little boy." Hailey blinked back the tears that swelled her eyes, wishing there was something she could do to help him.

Raimondo caught her chin with a firm knuckle, urging her to look into his powerful dark eyes. "He is not the only child who has known sadness," he said. "It is no wonder you care for him so." Sympathy welled in the darkening tones of his tanned face as he remembered what she, too, once endured.

Hailey didn't wish to speak about that anymore. But the way he gazed at her, as though she were precious and her trials as a child really mattered to him, made her knees tremble. She longed to be kissed. The nearness of his lips, full and shadowed with stubble, made her tilt back her head with hope. But then she reminded herself: he was taken; he could not be hers. It hurt, but she straightened her chin and fought for a change of subject. "I really enjoyed supper," she said, struggling to avert her eyes from his tender, dark gaze.

Raimondo, also consumed by the urge to kiss her, blinked soulfully for a long minute before replying to her mundane remark. "I'm glad you enjoyed it. Papa really likes you, I think." He forced himself to withdraw his hand from her soft chin and appear casual as he crossed his arms.

"What about your *mamma?*" she asked nervously, "Something tells me she is not so fond."

Raimondo shifted awkwardly, favoring his right leg. "I am sure you are wrong. Everyone likes you." *But she knows,* he thought. *My mamma has seen what lies between us and it frightens her.*

"I like them both as well," she said, though it still nagged her that Rosa seemed a tad unsettled. "I hope that they . . ." Her wide eyes met his with vulnerability.

"That is, I'm sure that they . . . they picked a fine bride for you."

His voice cut through the darkness like a foghorn, at least in Hailey's mind. "She'll be here in a matter of weeks, Hailey."

Hailey lowered her gaze and took a hard swallow. He could see the hurt hiding there, and he knew how she felt, because his own hurt burned just as fiercely. Defeatedly he tipped the bill of his black hat in a friendly, chaste gesture and said, "May I walk you home, signorina?"

Her eyes burning with unshed tears, she nodded.

Lanterns flickering from rows of anchored floating homes cast dancing lights upon the waves, competing with the moon for space to sparkle on the water. The air was rich with the scent of sea and sea creatures, and with the salt that rode on the wind. A strong breeze blew Hailey's chignon awry, but it also left droplets of water on her dewy cheeks, making her glow with youth and natural beauty. Raimondo had to fight to look away, to hold her hand in the crook of his strong arm without giving in to the temptation to fondle her warm palm. But the longer they strolled through the windy black night, the harder it was to focus on the docks. He knew he couldn't just leave her at home and walk away. They had to settle this somehow, to talk about their feelings, perhaps even talk one another out of having them. He knew he would not find rest until he had convinced them both that whatever lurked between them was not real, not important, not as strong as the bonds of family.

"Let's stop here," he said as they passed by the vacant rocking boat that was once Bianca's home. "It is private in there. *Per favore.* We must talk."

Hailey was reluctant to talk, but not reluctant at all to spend more time with him. She craved his company so, even knowing that most likely she was only leading herself to heartbreak by lingering in his appealing presence. "Very well."

He helped her onto the shrimping vessel and then into

the cabin, their footsteps echoing on wood, alerting them to their privacy. It took some time for Raimondo to find a lantern in the dark, but when he lit it, he was unhappy to observe the handsome glow it lent to Hailey's tender cheek. Their solitude became even more real. He realized he had her exactly as he'd secretly longed since the day he'd first met her. They were alone, in a private cabin, within each other's reach, and dangerously near a bed. He devoured her with his eyes, drinking in the glimpse of a white petticoat and stockings below her hiked hem, her slender curves shaped beneath the plain black uniform from the hotel, and the mass of chestnut hair falling naturally from her chignon.

"I love you," he heard himself say, not at all according to plan.

The tears his words brought to her eyes told him that she felt the same way. Her heart overflowed like a bubbling goblet at the sound of what she had always hoped to hear. She had not been delirious to think he felt the same way! He really did care for her.

"But I cannot marry you," he reminded both her and himself.

Her overflowing heart dropped to the pit of her stomach.

He stepped nearer, a gesture that did not bode well for his plan to carry on a platonic conversation. He swallowed. He placed one hand on her shoulder, wishing he could permanently erase the sadness from her pretty face. But he could not. "My mamma and my papa are important to me," he explained, "Without family, I have nothing. Surely, you would not even wish me for a husband if I were the sort to take my commitments lightly."

What a cruel irony it was. But he was right. His honor, his determination to be true to the ones he loved, only made her love him more. Not only did she long for him, but he was the sort of husband she had always wished for: faithful to a fault, strong and sure of his duties. With him, she could have had the family she never did. The kind where people have supper together and share stories, where everyone loves one another and honors his commitments. But the same qualities that made him so perfect for her were the ones keeping them forever apart. He had a previous commitment. And it hurt.

When he saw the tear make a trail along her pink cheek, he instinctively caught it—with his lips. Her breasts were pressed against him, her body helpless and compliant in his strong arms, and for a moment he thought he had lost control. His mouth took hers with a heat he had not expected. But before she could part her lips beneath his succulent demand, a noise startled them both.

They froze, gazing at each other in disbelief over what had nearly transpired after all their talk of how this must never be. And then their disbelief turned to the noise over their heads. Someone was walking down the stairs! Feeling caught, Raimondo pulled away. He wished he had brought his gun, but had only his fists to rely on should the intruder try to harm Hailey. He stepped out in front of her, shielding her from whatever was about to appear. But it was a feminine shadow that stretched across the cabin wall.

Hailey screeched for joy. "Bianca!" She saw the long braid and tried to run at her friend, ready to draw her into an embrace, to hold her and thank God she was all right.

But Raimondo caught her arm. "No," he said, trying to still her without bruising her elbow. "Hailey, no."

A dark smile spread across Bianca's honey-warm face as she watched Hailey struggle to tug free.

Raimondo noticed the slight fullness in the cheeks, which plumped over her smile. Sternly he asked, "What brings you back home, Francesca?"

Kane scraped his knife along the stick, slicing off a thin shaving that dropped into his lap, then another. Catching a movement out the corner of one eye, he paused. His gaze hooded, Kane watched Bianca walk from the river back to camp, her hips gently swaying, his desire building as he drank in the sight of her bare feet peeking beneath her skirt, his blue shirt he'd loaned her to wear again—and that still did little to hide the shape of her full breasts—her damp, dark hair that draped about her shoulders and softly framed her pretty face. His pulse pounded faster.

"I cannot believe my bread was burnt to a black crisp." She stopped at the end of the blanket where he sat, a puckered frown drawing her brows together and pinching her mouth tight as she turned the small iron skillet from side to side, staring at it as though it were at fault.

God, she's beautiful. And he wanted her with a need that drove deeper than anything he'd ever felt before, and that surprised him with its unfamiliar intensity. Kane chuckled softly. "I can't believe you're still upset about it." But he'd definitely enjoyed this bantering on the subject that had filtered into their conversation three times now in the past thirty minutes.

She tossed the pan down beside the saddlebags and planted her hands on her hips. "You said you would keep a watch on it."

"I did."

"Then how did it burn?"

Because he'd gone off in the woods and gotten caught up in his daydreams about her and forgotten the damn thing. "It's only bread, Bianca. Forget about it."

She lifted one thin mink eyebrow in a serious arch. "I have been baking bread every week for years. Do you have any idea how long it has been since I have burned a batch?"

"Given your reaction, I'd guess quite a while." His pulse raced at the flame's reflection washing her face in its pale, golden light. He found as much pleasure watching her wave one hand about as he did seeing the passion for this subject that burned in her amber stare. The same look she'd had the other night when he realized now that she had slipped with the truth about trying to get her

mother's recipe for that dessert just right. "And who do
you bake bread for every week?"

"Of course, for my papa before he passed away. Vito
and Rosa Casale. They are my godparents. And Mr.
D'Angelo. He sells them in his market for me."

"Anyone else?" he inquired with an underlying need
to know if she had a special fella she baked for, someone
waiting back home for her—and he found himself hoping
like hell that she didn't.

She shook her head.

His heart pounded faster. "Well, you can stop fretting,
because you didn't burn this batch. I did. So your record's
still intact. But tell me why it's so important to you."

She paused, furrowing her brow in thought for a moment, then shrugged. "A cook's pride, I suppose."

"I take it you don't share your sister's dislike for cooking, then?"

She shook her head, her smile reaching deep into her
eyes. "I have always liked to cook. In fact, I intend to
open my own restaurant in Galveston. I am hoping by
the end of summer."

He liked the determination he heard in her tone, liked
that she seemed a lot more relaxed around him now, too—
more confident being able to be herself and not having
to worry about slipping up. And he found her even more
captivating than he had before he'd known the truth about
her identity. "I'll have to make a point of coming down
and stopping by there when you do."

Bianca nodded, surprised at how much she hoped that
he would follow through on that suggestion. "And I will
make you *zabaglione* for dessert."

"I'd like that."

His warm smile made her pulse skip a beat. *Dio, he
is a handsome man.* Bianca made her way back around
the fire and sat down on the bedroll, needing to put some
distance between them and slow down her growing attraction to this man. He was handsome enough to make
her want to forget the vow she'd taken after Antonio had

broken her heart. But she couldn't fully ignore that Kane had been attracted to Francesca first, or ignore the sadness that thought brought with it. She bent her legs and wrapped her arms around her knees, frowning, unable to forget that he had thought he was kissing Francesca yesterday.

"Now, what's gone and put that sour look on your face?"

She blinked, snapped from her musings. "Nothing. I—"

He shook his head. "You're no good at lying, Bianca. One thing I've certainly noticed in the last few days is the way your eyes turn shadowy like golden twilight when you're confused, or you've got something on your mind you don't want me to know about. Does it have something to do with your sister?"

She wanted to be aggravated with him for being so astute, but she was too busy trying to stem the joy from his poetic words about her eyes—and wondering what else he'd noticed about her.

"I was wondering why you kissed me when you thought I was Francesca, since you do not seem to like her very much." Bianca tensed. *What is wrong with me?* She hadn't meant to blurt that out.

Kane wasn't sure what surprised him more: that she'd been thinking about their kiss, or that spark of jealousy he saw flash in her eyes. But they both sent equal pleasure rushing to form a hot pool of fire in him.

"I don't like Francesca at all. What I feel for her leans more toward hatred and hovers on the border of taking that next step and booting her into eternity myself. But you're two very different women, and I noticed that from the moment we first met in that alleyway. If it had really been Francesca standing there yesterday instead of you, Bianca, I guarantee that kiss never would've happened."

"How can you be so sure? You were obviously attracted to her enough to invite her to your hotel room."

"I won't deny she was the prettiest woman I'd seen in

Jackie Stephens

a long while. But attraction to her beauty is where it ended. And believe me, I was confused and angry with myself for wanting to kiss you when I thought you were Francesca. But I did it because my attraction toward *you* kept going beyond your pretty face. I may have thought you were Francesca, but I *knew* you weren't the same woman I'd spent two days with in Somerville. And I knew you weren't the same woman I'd kissed before, either. I just couldn't figure out why I liked you so much better— until I found out I'd never met you before now." He frowned inwardly, wondering why he'd been so damned open with that latter thought. He hadn't meant to tell her he liked her. But was glad he had when she smiled at him so soft and pretty and tucked her head down to hide the blush filling her cheeks. The shy stare she gave him through her long dark lashes melted his heart.

Bianca swallowed, trying to catch her breath, searching for her voice, both stolen in the wake of his endearing explanation and the desire burning in his blue eyes. "I like you, too, Kane," she whispered.

"I'm glad." His smile threatened to steal her breath again. "I thought you might not feel too kindly toward me after making you ride that mare. But I have to say, you did real well for not knowing what you were doing."

Bianca chuckled, rubbing her right hand against the back of her hip. "If it is supposed to hurt bad enough to make you wonder if death would be easier, then I did *very* well."

Kane furrowed his brow. "Your backside still hurting bad?"

"It is getting better." She stretched her legs out on the bedroll and leaned back against the saddle, patting the leather with one hand. "But that does not mean I am eager to get back on this thing in the morning."

"I'll try to keep it to an easier pace tomorrow. Or you can always just ride with me," he quipped. Hell, he'd welcome the chance to have her in his lap again.

She lifted one eyebrow in surprise, but there was a

light in her amber eyes that suggested she was giving it some thought. "As tempting as that offer is, now that I have come this far, I think I will try to conquer this torture chair just a bit more."

And I need to get a better grip on myself, and stop flirting with her. He needed to stop thinking about wanting to kiss her, too. She might like him, but he'd felt a definite "stay away" in that hard slap she had handed him, and he intended to honor it . . . until she said otherwise. Which he strongly hoped she would.

"I want to say again how sorry I am for the way I've yelled at you, and for being so rough with you at times."

She waved one hand dismissively. "There is no need. You had your reasons, and I understand your anger with Francesca. Especially for what she did to your papa." And if anyone was to blame for the aggravation they had been through, it was her sister. *For not telling me the truth.* "I am very happy that he is going to be all right."

Kane nodded, not doubting her sincerity at all. "Thanks." He shifted up onto his knees and reached for a narrow stick to stir the dying embers back to life. "I hope you understand, though, that I still intend to see Francesca answer for her crimes."

Bianca nodded, sighing as she stared into the tiny flames that sparked against the wood and slowly climbed higher. She understood that Kane was doing his job, and though he hadn't voiced it, she understood that he wanted justice for his papa. "Are you going to arrest me for switching places with my sister?"

He didn't answer but instead slowly reached for a log from the stacked pile and set it on the coals. Then another. And another.

Bianca's pulse slowed with dread, certain he was trying to find a way to tell her that he *was* going to do just that.

He slowly brushed the wood chips from his hands into the fire and finally looked up at her. "No, I'm not."

She released a heavy sigh. *"Grazie."*

Kane thought about telling her not to thank him, because he'd sat there pondering whether he could work this to his advantage somehow and claim another kiss from her for her freedom. And he had to talk himself out of following through on that stupid idea before answering.

He was *really* glad she wasn't Francesca. But one thing sure hadn't changed tonight: she was still driving him crazy.

TWELVE

Hailey leaned expectantly into Francesca's every word. Hope lit up her face as she listened from across the cabin's kitchen table. "Then Bianca is really safe?"

"Of course," Francesca assured her, tossing her pointed nose in the air, whipping her braid around until it rested on her shoulder. "I simply sent her on a pleasant vacation. She was in dire need of one."

Raimondo's pulse burned him because he did not believe a word of it. Francesca had always been a liar—a nice one at times, but still a liar. And this didn't make any sense. "Why did she tell no one?"

"I don't know," shrugged Francesca, haughtily straightening her posture, "Maybe she didn't think it was anyone's concern except mine." Her amber eyes, rimmed with chocolate challenged his right to question her.

Raimondo didn't like this one bit. He wondered what mischief the restless Francesca was up to this time, and whether Bianca was truly safe. But he didn't want to scare Hailey. He could see that Hailey believed because she wanted to believe. And he didn't see what good it would do to announce his suspicion that Bianca was not at all on a frivolous vacation but the victim of one of her sister's dangerous schemes. Just seeing the hope in Hailey's light-blue eyes warmed his heart. He did not want to snuff out that light of relief he saw there. And furthermore, he had no way to prove Francesca was lying. "Then what are *you* doing home?" he asked, by way of changing the subject. "You should be on the stage somewhere, no?"

"I am here to pack," she announced brightly, causing startled creases in her audience's foreheads. "It is time to broaden my career, signor Casale, thank you so much for asking. I happen to be on my way to Europe!"

"Europe?" they asked simultaneously.

"Yes," she said proudly, with an actress's flair. "So you see, there is no need to worry about us. Bianca is just fine, having the vacation of her dreams, and I will be leaving the country in a matter of days. It is a shame, though, that I won't be able to bid her *ciao*."

Dawn's golden warmth slowly chased the morning chill away. Bianca sat on a log near the river's edge where the falls rushed by, and listened to the birds loudly chirp their songs of greeting to the new day as she finished braiding the remaining ends of her hair, then coiled the rope at her nape. Holding it in place with one hand, she reached down with the other and plucked a hairpin from the small stack she'd piled in her lap atop Kane's folded blue shirt. One by one, she shoved the pins into her hair, anchoring the knot in place.

Then she reached for the other item she had pulled from her skirt pocket along with the pins. She leaned forward, bracing her elbows on her knees, and stared at the photograph Kane had returned to her last night. She was glad to have the cherished picture back, but it had also only added to the myriad restless thoughts about Francesca's unexplainable behavior of late, which had plagued her sleep throughout the night—thoughts that plagued her still.

Bianca knit her brow, wondering where her sister had gone, wondering if any proof really existed for Francesca to seek out.

Or was Kane right, and she had lied about that, too?

A sharp jab of uncertainty wedged its way into Bianca's heart, wanting to crowd out her last slice of hope that Francesca hadn't lied about everything. But Bianca wouldn't let uncertainty win. She couldn't. Deep in her soul, she still believed that Francesca would not break the bonds of blood. Her twin *would* be in Somerville as she promised. With proof.

Or a darn good explanation for all this, anyway!

Bianca sighed, knowing she'd spent enough time lost in her thoughts while she'd washed and gotten dressed, and that Kane was most likely finished saddling the horses by now and ready to leave. She stood clutching his shirt in one arm and slid the photograph back into her skirt pocket as she headed downstream along the grassy bank, thoughts of her sister fading and her mind filling with the other source that had occupied her mind way too much of late: Kane.

They had stayed up talking long into the night. He'd wanted to know if the things she had told him about living in Sicily and sailing to America were true, and she'd been glad to be able to tell him yes, that she'd only left out mentioning Francesca. He had also wanted to know how much truth about herself she'd had to stretch to keep him thinking she was Francesca. Bianca had been more than willing to clear up the misrepresentations, and to answer his other interests about her life in Galveston, her friends, her future plans. She had inquired into his life, as well, discovering he had a sharp mind and strong views about politics—and seeing more of his kind, caring heart whenever he'd talked about his family. But there was also a sadness she'd seen deep in his gaze that had left her wondering again about the person he'd lost to that bank robber's bullet, and why Kane didn't talk about him . . . or her.

The trees thinned as she neared their camp, and she spotted Kane standing beside the dying fire. His back faced her, but she could see the coffeepot in his hand and watched him tip it over and pour water onto the low-burning embers. The coals popped and hissed, and white smoke rose as the liquid slowly turned the red heat to gray ashes.

Bianca took the opportunity of his distraction to freely sweep an appreciative gaze up from the heels of his boots, along the worn denims hugging his sinewy legs, to the single leather holster strapped around his lean hips. The pearl handle of his Colt gleamed against the bottom edge of the black leather vest covering his back and broad shoulders. He'd rolled his white shirt sleeves back on his tanned forearms, and the black Stetson graced his head.

Her mouth went dry. He was such a handsome man. And she'd had to force herself not to secretly intrude earlier and sneak a glimpse of his tall, muscular body when he'd gone upstream to bathe while she made coffee and bread for their breakfast. She smiled. Bread that had turned out perfectly golden this time, and that he'd warmly complimented her on as he devoured more than half, along with the blackberry jam.

There wasn't a thing she didn't find appealing about this lawman—except perhaps his strong dislike for her sister. But Bianca could understand his reasons for feeling that way. Francesca had a great deal to answer for. And she knew Kane was a man driven by a deep sense of justice to make sure that her sister *did* answer for everything.

Bianca swallowed the apprehension that suddenly rose at the thought of her sister going to prison, and prayed with all her heart that this proof Francesca had mentioned truly did exist.

She started up the bank toward Kane, only then noticing the tense set of his shoulders and seeing the lines of aggravation marring his forehead when he spun around. "You were sure gone a long time."

She arched her eyebrows at his brusque tone and glanced beyond him to the saddled horses, both lazily chomping at the grass. She stopped, looking up into Kane's hard stare, wondering at his reaction. "I am sorry. I did not know you were in such a hurry."

He sighed and shook his head, his shoulders relaxing, his brow smoothing . . . his blue eyes softening. "I'm sorry I snapped at you. I was just starting to get worried that something might have happened."

The concern in his voice settled over her heart like a warm blanket. "Did you think I had run off?" She couldn't resist teasing.

"No." The somberness in his expression quickly dashed her humor. "Concerned about Bartlett being on the loose. And the fact that he could just as easily mistake you for Francesca as I did. Not to mention Devon Carson. Do you have any idea if he might know Francesca, or what he wants?"

Bianca shook her head. She'd been wondering that herself ever since the cowboy had approached her in Houston. Wondering if her first instinct had been correct and he did know something that might help clear Francesca of some of the charges. She frowned, also wondering how many more unanswerable questions were going to pop up before she had the chance to see Francesca again. None, she prayed. She had far more than she wanted already.

"Well, let's hope those hands from the ranch chased him off our trail for good."

"Maybe he knows something about where the gold is hidden."

Kane nodded. "That's certainly crossed my mind. But if he does know where it's hidden, then why follow us? Why not ride ahead and beat us to it?" He raised one hand and rubbed his chin. "Of course, it could be that he's in cahoots with Bartlett and is only supposed to make sure we don't get to it first. Or else he just somehow knows about Francesca and the gold, and he thinks you're her, so he's following us hoping to find it." He lowered his hand and shook his head in frustration. "But he's sure being mighty cocky showing his face so often if he's up to any of that. So it could be he's doing nothing more than looking for work, like he says—and just found you too pretty to pass up." He smiled. "Which is understand-able."

The smoldering flame in his blue gaze spread a warm glow through her body. "That is kind of you to say, but I do not think he would have offered to set me free if I were a stranger to him. It is more likely that he *does* know my sister. And perhaps we should try to find him and talk to him."

He shrugged. "We could. But something tells me he's going to show up again. Especially if he *is* looking for the gold. So we'll just wait until he does, then confront him."

Bianca released a heavy sigh, frowning. "Are you certain my sister is the one who took that gold, Kane?"

His expression softened with sympathy. "I'm certain she had it when she left that hideout. And I'm positive she knows where it's at now. It's only the in-between part that I'm having trouble figuring out for sure."

Sadness rose into her throat, and the hollow feel of betrayal swept across her chest. "I intend to find out why she has done these things."

"And you certainly have a right to know, too."

He lifted his hand, Bianca thought—hoped—to touch her face, to pull her close and kiss her again. Then she chided herself for the disappointment that settled hard when he only reached for the shirt she held.

"Let me stow that and this coffeepot away, and we'll head on out."

Bianca nodded, handing him the shirt, then walked beside him as they made their way over to the horses.

He raised one leather flap on the saddlebags draped over his buckskin and shoved the items inside.

Bianca walked on to where the mare stood a few feet behind Kane's horse, and stared at the saddle, feeling a twinge of hesitancy to sit on the hard leather again.

"Give me a second, and I'll give you a hand up." Kane finished strapping the flap closed on the pouch and walked over.

Bianca turned to face the mare and reached up for the saddle horn, swallowing at the warmth of Kane's strong hands circling her waist.

"We're leaving just in time. I've got a surprise for you this afternoon."

She froze, her heart thumping with delight. She glanced over her shoulder at him, his wide smile making her pulse race with more than just curiosity. "What is it?"

He reached up one hand and lightly tapped his finger against the tip of her nose. "It's called a surprise, darling, because you're not supposed to know what it is before-hand."

Excitement at his softly drawled endearment darted through her with enough intensity to make her knees quiver. And it thrilled her even more because it had sounded nothing like the "sweetheart" he'd always snidely called her when he'd thought she was Francesca.

Kane hadn't really meant that endearment to slip out, but he definitely liked the ardent gleam it brought rising in her amber gaze. He liked the flush that filled her cheeks. The smile that parted her lips was an invitation that sent his desire churning. He tightened the hold he still had on her waist, and with his other hand cupped her slender jaw, lifting her face as he leaned down and gently pressed his mouth to hers, reveling in her delicious softness, in her surprising hungry response that had him craving more.

He pulled her closer, encouraged when she turned into his embrace and circled her hands around his neck. He wrapped his arms around her and held her tight, the feel of her soft, full breasts pressing against his chest creating hot needles of ecstasy spiraling low in his groin. He devoured every luscious curve of her mouth, then traced his tongue along her lips and slipped inside at her opening welcome, exploring the recesses of her warm mouth, her sweetness as intoxicating as the faint taste of blackberries. The velvety stroke of her tongue sparring with

his in wild abandon melted his senses useless, save for
the passion swirling like a prairie fire through him.

A passion he still knew he shouldn't let rule him; a
passion he knew he had best rein in really quickly before
he lost all control.

Kane reluctantly ended their kiss and gazed down at
her. "Before I let you go, are you going to slap me again
for what just happened?"

Her thin eyebrows darted up. "Was it *me* you were
kissing?"

His heart thudded against his ribs. Oh, it had been
Bianca, all right. He'd never wanted to kiss Francesca this
bad. Never enjoyed her kisses as much as what he'd just
experienced . . . and wanted very badly to do again.
"Definitely you, Bianca," he whispered.

"Then you are safe." She smiled, lifting up and pressing her mouth to his, searing him with her sweet kiss—
and leaving no doubt in his mind, or his hardening body,
that he was far from safe with her.

He had to force himself to tear his mouth from hers,
to pull his arms away and step back. He swallowed at the
desire shimmering in her amber gaze, drawing him to
want to return to what they'd been doing. "We'd best get
going. We've got a lot miles to cover to reach that surprise."

And if they didn't leave now, they wouldn't be going
anywhere today, except down on the grass, where he
could strip her clothes off and make love to her beneath
the blue sky.

Devon shoved his hat brim down against the midmorning glare, then yanked his saddle up off the ground and
tossed it on top of the blanket spread across the bay's
back. He grumbled a string of curses as he hurriedly
tightened the cinch, not sure whether to be aggravated at
Francesca for roping him into this plan, or just with himself for oversleeping.

He knew one thing for damned sure. He was definitely more suited to being a gambler than a watch guard over some gal. He was also more used to riding in the opposite direction of any lawman, not chasing after one.

He slung his saddlebags over the bay's hindquarters, then heaved the bedroll on top and tied it down.

He was more used to staying up late and sleeping until noon in some hotel bed; and between the interference with his rest he was getting from the hard ground, and the sleepless night he'd lost after dodging those cowboys from the Circle F, the tiredness had finally caught up with him and he'd fallen dead to the world in the early hours before dawn.

Devon shook his head as he climbed into the saddle. And now the Ranger and Bianca had at least a good two-hour lead on him—maybe even three if they'd left at first light.

And to Devon's annoyance, that lead time increased when he reached the banks of the Brazos River fifteen minutes later and didn't take the time to ride all the way into their cold camp, just assuming they had headed out north toward Somerville in the same direction they'd been traveling. He realized his mistake forty-five minutes later when he still hadn't found their trail and had had to back-track to the camp, where he discovered they'd headed southeast instead.

An hour later, as he rode out from the stand of trees, he was on his fourth cheroot and still frowning his con-fusion over what had made them change direction. Devon smiled at the sight of the flat field of grass that stretched ahead for miles. He took a final draw on the cheroot, then stabbed the butt out against his chaps, and tossed it to the ground. He gathered the reins a little tighter in his hand and kicked the bay to trot, then to a flat-out run, welcoming the wind against his heated face, and the op-portunity to make up some lost time.

He'd traveled about a mile when the bay suddenly stumbled forward, throwing him out of the saddle as the animal fell to its knees. Devon flew over the horse's head, catching a brief glimpse of the prairie dog hole, and at the same time hearing the bone in the bay's leg snap. Then Devon hit the ground flat on his back, hard enough to send the air whooshing from his lungs. White stars swam in front of his eyes and blotted out the sky above. Neighing cries of horrific pain rent the air.

Devon closed his eyes, groaning.

Aw, shit! I just bought that horse. Now I'm gonna have to shoot the poor animal.

And then he was going to be stuck on foot.

Damn you, Francesca, why did you save my life? His debt was the only thing holding him to this scheme now. After seeing how quick Fairchild was to come to Bianca's defense from that coyote, Devon wasn't worried about anything happening to her. And fifteen hundred dollars sure wasn't worth all this trouble he'd had so far.

He should have demanded double that amount.

The noon sun hung high in the clear sky, but only a few thin shafts of pale light filtered through the pines and dappled the narrow trail that grew steeper as they neared the top of the thickly wooded hill. Kane glanced behind to see how Bianca was holding up on the mare, hoping she'd been more comfortable this morning sitting on the blanket he had folded over the saddle for extra padding. He'd been impressed with her quick grasp of his instructions earlier on how to handle the reins and smooth out her rhythm in the saddle, but he could tell by the way she was biting at her lower lip right now, and the way she held the leather straps in a white-knuckled grip around the saddle horn, that she was still nervous— especially riding up a steep incline for the first time. Kane smiled inwardly. But she was definitely doing a far cry better riding that mare than she had the first night he'd put her up there and headed out of Galveston.

He thought about all the times he'd ordered her to

climb into that saddle, and admired her courage for doing
it, and for enduring the pain to her backside. It still surprised him that she'd been able to stay silent about not
knowing how to ride before last night—especially when
he'd accused her so often of just pretending. He had to
give her credit for her stamina, and her determination to
stand by her twin. Even though it was misplaced.

Kane frowned. Francesca didn't deserve that kind of
loyalty. Not after the way she'd lied to Bianca about everything.

"You all right?"

She looked up and nodded, her lips parting in a small
smile that slightly creased her dimples and set his blood
aflame. Every time he gazed into her pretty face, joy sang
through him that she wasn't her sister. She looked like
Francesca, and she had the same courageous spirit as her
twin, but he was fast learning that Bianca was oh, so
much sweeter, so much more honest. So much more desirable. His body ached to feel her close to him again.
He faced forward, telling himself to rein in his lust. But
his mind refused to listen to the order as her pretty image
came swimming in.

A few minutes later the buckskin topped the hill. Kane
rode on a few yards farther, then drew the mount to a
stop along the narrow ridge and twisted around in his
saddle, waiting for Bianca to ride the mare up alongside.
"Now, just pull back on the reins, and bring her to a
stop."

She released the saddle horn and jerked too hard on
the reins. The sorrel stopped abruptly and tossed its head
back. Bianca gasped her fright, released the reins, and
reached for the horn again. Kane quickly leaned over and
grabbed the mare's bridle before the horse could rear up.

"That was a little too hard, but you'll do better next
time." He smiled.

She rolled her eyes, sighing heavily. "I do not think I
will ever be comfortable with this beast. Or that there
will be a next time."

Kane swallowed, biting back the urge to offer again the use of his lap, fighting back as well several wanton images of her in his arms. He released the mare's bridle and pointed toward the valley below. "Think you can handle it long enough to ride down there? Then we'll take a break for a while."

Golden delight flashed in her eyes, sending excitement dancing through Kane's blood. "Is that my surprise? You have brought me to a town."

"Part of the surprise, anyway."

"Is that Somerville?"

"No." Kane stared down at the couple of dozen houses and businesses that sat scattered along the stretch of road running through the middle of the small town. "That's Cushman. They've got a fairly good-size mercantile where we can stock up on some decent supplies for the rest of our trip. And there's a restaurant that serves up some mighty fine steak. I thought we'd have lunch there. That's the rest of the surprise."

She blinked, her smiled widening. "And it is a wonderful surprise, too. *Grazie,* Kane."

God, how he liked her accent. How he liked *her*. He saw her frown down at her skirt and brush at the dust that clung to the black serge. "You look fine, Bianca."

She peeked up at him through her thick lashes, making his heart pound faster. "You are sure?"

"Positive, darling," he whispered, his heart turning over at the blush that crept into her ivory cheeks. It didn't matter to him that her dress was drab and a little dirty, or that several shorter strands of hair had come loose and softly framed her face. She was the prettiest thing he'd ever seen. But he knew words weren't always enough for a woman, and he wanted her to be comfortable. "But I know the mercantile carries ready-made dresses. We can get you something new to wear before we go to lunch, if you'd like."

Bianca's face lit up with excitement. She glanced down, fingering the folds of her dusty skirt. "That would be nice." She looked up at him, the light in her eyes dimming. "But I do not have any money except for that hundred dollars Francesca gave me, and I would not feel right spending money that could be stolen."

Kane still had the money, not having returned it with the photograph because he felt certain that, considering she'd gotten it from Francesca, it more than likely was part of the stolen loot. "I'll pay for it; don't worry."

He could see her hesitation to accept his charity flashing in her eyes, then heard it in her voice, "I could not let you do that."

"I don't mind, Bianca. I'd like to do this for you."

She nodded. "I will pay you back when we reach Galveston."

Her smile was payment enough, as far as Kane was concerned. "Forget that. Just consider it another part of your surprise."

"Grazie."

He released the mare's bridle and leaned over to gather up the reins Bianca had dropped, wishing instead that he was leaning over to pull her from the saddle and into his arms. He handed the leather straps to her. "You ready?"

She nodded. "Now, all I have to do is kick my heels into her sides and she will go, is that right?"

"That's right. But don't kick her too hard or she'll think you want to run down this hill."

Fear widened her eyes *"Dio,* that is the last thing I want." She frowned down at the mare and leaned forward slightly. "Do you hear, *cavallo?* No running."

The sorrel pointed its ears back.

Kane suppressed his chuckle and didn't bother to tell her the mare was only trained to understand physical commands, not verbal ones.

"Now that you two have that worked out, I guess we can leave." He nudged his buckskin forward, keeping Bianca in sight out of the corner of his eye and smiling when she got the mare moving at a slow walk.

The trees thinned out along the gradual downward

slope, and the road widened. Kane slowed his mount, letting Bianca catch up, then nudged his horse into step alongside.

"How far is it to Somerville from here?"

Kane sighed. He'd been wondering all morning when she was going to bring up Somerville again, and was surprised she hadn't already questioned why they'd turned around and were heading southeast all of a sudden. "About sixty miles north."

"And how much longer will it take us to get there?"

Kane knew she really believed Francesca would show up there on June first, but he was still just as confident that she-devil sister of hers had other plans. "We're not going to Somerville."

She cocked her head in surprise. "Why?"

"We're going back to Houston. But I'm taking a different route. It's going to be faster to get there on horseback from here than to waste another two days riding to the closest town where the train runs. Once we get to Houston, we'll head back to Galveston."

She drew her eyebrows together. "If you are making this trip to take me home, you are wasting your time. I would rather go with you to look for my sister, or wait for her in Somerville."

Kane was surprised that taking her home had never crossed his mind. Surprised to realize he wasn't the least bit anxious to part company with Bianca. But no matter how much he liked her and enjoyed being with her, he was still a Texas Ranger with a job to do, and he couldn't take her along when he left the island this time—with or without Francesca. But Kane had a strong suspicion that he *would* find Francesca there. What better place was there for her to hide? And what better cover than to switch places with a twin Kane hadn't known about, so she could freely move forward with her plans of escape? Kane was just as certain that Bianca wasn't going to be the least bit happy with him when he *did* find Francesca and carted her off to jail to await trial—and a sentencing that could separate the sisters for a good long time.

"Well, it so happens we're heading back because I am looking for Francesca. I've got a strong hunch she's in Galveston, and I'm going to try to catch her before she hightails it out of the country."

Bianca gaped at him with appalled shock; then her amber eyes slowly narrowed as angry flames rose in them. "Francesca is not going to leave the country," she hotly protested. "And she is not in Galveston. I saw her leave on the train that same night you showed up behind the Tremont Restaurant."

"She could have gone back. Or she could be in Houston. I plan to search there, too. Whichever port, I've got to try to stop her from leaving the country with the gold—if she hasn't already."

"I do not know where she is, but I know Francesca has not left the country. She would not break her promise to me. She *will* meet me in Somerville on June first."

"Bianca." Kane shook his head, sighing. "I know you want to believe that, but I'm sorry, she's not going to be there. She's in serious trouble, and I don't think she intends to turn herself in, or give up the gold. She's not out looking for any proof. My guess is that she needed to buy time for a couple of weeks. Long enough to get the gold transported to a port, and it and herself on a ship sailing for God knows where. And she used you as a decoy to help buy that time."

Bianca bit at her lower lip, hating that what Kane said sounded more feasible than she wanted to admit. But until she talked with her sister again, Bianca refused to lose all faith that Francesca could explain her actions, or that she had a good reason for breaking the bonds of devotion they had shared all their lives.

"I know my sister, and you will see that I am right. We will not find her in Galveston." But at least while they were there, Bianca could let her godparents and her friends know that she was safe. And there would still be plenty of time for her to travel to Somerville and meet Francesca on the appointed day. A tightening in her gut warned that Kane might be right about Francesca's being in Galveston. Bianca frowned inwardly. *And if she is, then I will find out that much sooner why Francesca went to these lengths of deception.* Bianca swallowed. Lengths deep enough to break her heart.

"Well, for right now, what do you say we call a truce on your sister's whereabouts and just enjoy a nice couple of hours being out of these saddles?"

His smile was like a ray of sunshine warming Bianca's soul, making her want to forget everything but being with him. "I would like that."

As they reached the bottom of the grassy knoll and rode into town, Bianca saw several people milling about on the sidewalks that fronted the various buildings, and she felt a sense of relief that this time she didn't have to worry about hiding any handcuffs, or suffer gawking stares.

She lightly touched the rein to the mare's neck, not sure whether the animal turned toward the mercantile because of her gesture or because it was just following Kane's horse. But the triumph was solely hers as she gently drew back on the reins and the mare came to a smooth stop in front of the hitching post.

"Nice job."

The admiration dominating Kane's low voice, and reflecting in his blue gaze, sent her pulse skittering. *"Grazie."*

He dismounted, wrapped the reins around the post, then came and took the reins she handed him and did the same. Bianca stood up slightly and swung her leg over the mare's hindquarters, surprised how much easier she was finding it to climb in and out of this saddle. Her blood tingled when she felt Kane's strong hands grasp her waist as he helped her down. Her heart pounded against her ribs as he slowly moved his hands away, his fingers lingering to the last touch and driving her mad

with the desire to turn in his arms and melt against him
as she had that morning.

And she would have, she realized, if there weren't a
handful of folks standing out in front of the store and
watching them with curiosity, and if Kane hadn't backed
away from her at that moment. She walked beside him
up the steps, smiling at the folks that politely greeted
them, then followed Kane through the door into the
murky shadows that filled the large store.

"Howdy," the thin, dark-haired man called out from
where he stood behind the long glass counter.

"Afternoon," Kane replied.

"What can we help you folks with today?" the shop
owner inquired.

"Need to pick up a few supplies." Kane glanced over
toward Bianca, smiling. "And a new dress for the lady."

The shop owner nodded, then glanced over his shoulder and called out, "Martha, come on out here."

The brown calico curtain covering the doorway to the
back was shoved aside, and a young girl Kane guessed
to be about sixteen, her long black hair tied back with a
silk ribbon, emerged. "What is it, Pa?"

"The lady's looking to purchase a dress. You show her
what we have."

The girl nodded and came out from behind the counter,
smiling as she walked up, then led Bianca toward the
back of the store.

Kane allowed himself to drink in the sight of Bianca's
swaying hips as she walked away, but reminded himself
once again that he needed to keep a tight rein on his
attraction. He was surprised that it was becoming an issue
he was having such trouble dealing with. No woman since
his wife had ever captured his attention with such intensity. But given her obvious devotion to her sister, he
couldn't let himself forget the deception Bianca had
agreed to play, and he wondered again just how far she
might go to help Francesca get out of this mess. He
looked away, shoving that concern aside for the moment.

Right now all he wanted to do was look forward to the next couple of hours.

Thirty minutes later, Kane had purchased the supplies he needed, stowed them in his saddlebags, and stood leaning with one elbow against the counter, half listening to the shop owner converse with a couple of farmers who'd come in, and keeping his gaze on the curtains Bianca had slipped behind to change.

His heart was pounding with anticipation at seeing her in something besides the black uniform. But the vision that walked out seconds later was even more than he imagined. Kane straightened, swallowing as he unabashedly raked his gaze over the deep-mahogany-colored skirt clasped around her narrow waist. The gold-and-cinnamon striped percale shirtwaist had a tailored collar and leg-of-mutton sleeves that tapered at her narrow wrists and fit her like a glove, outlining her full breasts and bringing out the shine in her amber eyes.

"You look beautiful."

"Grazie, Mr. Fairchild." She smiled wide, stealing his breath. "Are you ready for lunch?"

His body was craving nourishment, all right, but what he wanted had nothing to do with food. He swallowed, reining in his raging lust. "Most definitely, Miss Rossetti."

THIRTEEN

It was the juiciest, thickest steak Bianca had ever sunk her teeth into. If it wasn't, at least it seemed so after days of living on a traveler's rations. The succulent meat made her mouth water, danced sweetly upon her taste buds, and filled her stomach comfortingly. The only thing that could make it any better was a glass of Chianti, which she ordered in haste.

With longing, Kane watched her lick her juicy lips. He nearly forgot about his own steak, he was so drawn to the sight of her delicate jaw rotating sensually with every chew.

She caught him staring and blushed.

He hadn't meant to make her lower her face. He hadn't meant to embarrass her. He only wanted to admire the beauty she was too modest to see in herself. He refused to release her from his probing blue stare. Damn it, he could look if he wanted. She'd done enough wrong to owe him that.

"Is there something on my face again?" she inquired, recalling the embarrassing streak of flour the night before and hoping she hadn't repeated the foible by splattering herself with steak.

"There's nothing there," he said, a smile creeping across his mouth as she brushed her cheeks just to make sure.

"Then why," she asked, feeling shy before his mascu-

line stare, "are you looking at me that way, Mr. Fairchild?"

*Because you're the prettiest thing I've seen this side
of the Colorado.* It was what he wanted to say. It was the
truth. But her coyness made him kind and he said only,
"Call me Kane, for Pete's sake."

She decided she liked that very much. Color brushed
her dimples as a glass of red wine appeared before her
plate. "Kane, then," she smiled, "Why don't you tell me
what you are thinking?"

"I'm thinking," he said, striking a match against the
edge of the rustic cedar table, "what's a pretty woman
like you doing with nobody better to cook for than a
lucky fella named D'Angelo?" They *had* said they were
going to have a friendly chat, hadn't they? Well, it was
time to start chatting. There were some things he wanted
to know about this gullible little lady who was running
away with his heart.

She swallowed as she watched him light his cheroot.
It suited his handsome face, dangling from the corner of
his mouth the way it did. She felt a fluttering in her nervous hands as she asked, "You mean, why aren't I . . ."

"That's right." He grinned at the hesitation in her de-
meanor that separated her so plainly from her shameless
sister. "I'd say I don't mean to pry, but I do. Can't say I
understand why there isn't some fella out there waiting
to paddle your backside for running off like this."

She stiffened defensively. "Well, there was someone."
She didn't want him to think there had never been. But
she was reluctant to speak of it.

"Go on," he said, tipping back his chair, "Tell me
about him. This is what you call a captive audience." He
winked kindly, pleased that it made her flush the way it
did. It was so easy to draw her feelings to the surface.
Her honesty, her complete ineptitude at hiding her
thoughts, made him wonder how pure and natural she
would be in his bed. If she couldn't hide behind her
clothes, if she couldn't be shy between closed thighs . . .

"His name was Antonio," she said, mercifully interrupting his frustrating thoughts. "We were engaged to be married, but it was Francesca he really loved. Not me."

"Then he was a damned fool."

Bianca looked up at him appreciatively. It wasn't so much that he'd said it, but that he'd meant it. She could tell. Did he really find her so appealing? The thought turned her insides to dough. "He'd known Francesca first," she confessed. Kane guessed she was using the biblical sense of *known,* seeing as there were a number of men no doubt who'd *known* Francesca in that way. "But she didn't stay with him, and I think he took me as a . . . a second choice." She bowed her head in shame. "When I learned of it, I broke the betrothal." She didn't wish to tell him the embarrassing detail of how she'd learned Antonio's affections for Francesca had never really died.

The hurt in her golden eyes made his gaze harden. How could anyone make Bianca feel so small? He wanted to clobber the bastard and he'd never even met him. What kind of a fool would want a trickster and a she-devil like Francesca when he could have something as soft and alluring as Bianca?

"It's your turn," she announced. "I told you something personal, and now you have to do it, as well."

He put out his cheroot on his boot heel, intentionally averting his eyes while asking, "What do you want to know?"

"Who died that day?"

Every muscle in Kane's body tensed as he slowly dropped his boot back onto the splintered floor. Of all things, she had to ask him . . .

"Tell me," she urged. "I know you don't want to, but tell me anyhow. Tell me who those bank robbers shot. I want to know." Why she needed to know, she wasn't certain. But she was craving a better glimpse at this handsome Ranger who could well be the pivot point in the lives of both her and her sister. She wanted to understand him.

He didn't know why he did it. Maybe it was her honest gaze, the way she looked at him as though she really cared. Maybe it was the affection that was growing so strong in his gut that made him want to do what she asked, to answer her question just to make her happy. Or maybe he suddenly realized that he wanted to talk about it. With someone. With her. But for whatever reason, he found himself leaning into the table and telling her plainly, "It was my wife."

"Dio! Your *what?*"

"My wife," he repeated, amused to see her surprise.

Bianca couldn't believe it. He'd had a wife? And she was killed? How awful! "I'm so sorry."

He nodded, no longer doubting her anytime she said that. He knew she had a heart of sympathy. Unlike her sister. "Natalie was the light in my life," he explained without shame or regret. "I reckon she had the blondest curls I ever saw. And the prettiest smile, too." *Next to yours,* he added silently.

Bianca could feel the pain that peeked through his blue eyes. She hung on his every word.

"She was just riding into town that day," he went on in a low voice, rather resigned. "My ma was with her, and a couple of ranch hands. And that's when the outlaws came by, shooting every which way, trying to escape the robbery. They didn't mean to kill her, but that's what they did. They killed her, and they kinda' killed me, too, if you think about it." He stabbed at what was left of his steak as if it were the head of one of those robbers. Bianca could only guess what he would do if he saw one of them now. She knew it wouldn't be pretty. And she didn't know the half of it.

There was one part Kane didn't plan to tell her—not today, not any day. It wasn't just Natalie they had killed, but their baby as well. He knew about it, all right. Natalie didn't know he knew, but he did. That was why he'd been carving that rattle. She'd planned to surprise him that

night by blurting out the news. Well, he planned to surprise her right back by shaking that rattle and telling her
he knew. That was why he had to get the rattle done fast;
that was why he didn't go with her to town. And it was
why he wasn't there to protect her. It killed him. It killed
him even worse when his ma told him the big fancy way
Natalie planned to tell him about the baby, whisking him
off to a hotel for the night. What a night it would have
been! If only they hadn't fought about his staying behind
before she left. If only they'd parted on good terms that
day. If only they'd known it would be their last chance
to say good-bye.

Bianca watched his face darken with every thought
and mourned for him. She could only imagine the pain.
She had never had such a longing to comfort anyone in
all her life. And yet, there was another feeling there too.
Dannare! How could she be so selfish? Did she really
feel jealous? Of the way he spoke of his wife, the way
he reflected upon her beauty and goodness? A terrible
piece of her wished he were speaking of her that way.
Oh, no. She was losing her senses. How could she be so
selfish? And so crazy? She pushed such wretchedness
aside and gazed into his sorrowful eyes, trying to comfort
him. Because he was a nice man, she told herself. Because he didn't deserve this, to be a widower and so
young. It was right that she should wish to console him.
He replied to her sympathetic gaze by tenderly squeezing
her hand. What a strong hand he had! She felt that he
could crush her between his fingers if he wished it. But
she trusted that he never would. He knew how to be kind.
He *was* kind. And she wished there were some way she
could take away his pain. For just one moment, she
thought she just might do anything to put a smile back
on his face. Anything.

Bianca sipped the last of the Chianti from the tin cup,
enjoying the warmth that lazily swam through her blood

and loosened her limbs, smiling at the memory of Kane surprising her with the bottle of wine that night. Pleasure swirled in the pit of her stomach as she recalled his saying that he'd bought it because he had seen how much she enjoyed the glass she'd had with lunch today. She took a deep breath, wondering what else he had noticed about her during lunch, remembering how the conversation had lightened after the tension of their confessions had pleasantly eased. She remembered how much he'd charmed her with his wit and attentiveness, remembered the admiring stares he'd garnered from the waitresses and several other female patrons but hadn't acknowledged even noticing. She remembered again the desire in his eyes when she'd walked out from the back of the mercantile, and that she had heard in his voice when he told her she was beautiful.

Bianca sighed, chiding herself again for being unable to get him out of her thoughts for longer than a few seconds all day. Especially now that she understood what drove him: his secret pain and his steadfast heart. She felt closer to him than ever. She set the cup down and leaned back against the saddle, staring up at the stars that littered the velvet sky.

"Would you like some more wine?"

She smiled, loving the way Kane's deep voice made her tingle, made her heart pound loud enough in her ears to drown out the crickets' songs that filled the night. She looked over to where he sat stretched out on a blanket across the fire, the low flames reflecting on his tanned face. *Dio, I wish he would kiss me again.*

She shook her head in answer to his inquiry, the languid flow in her veins—and her thoughts—telling her that the two cups she'd had tonight was plenty.

Kane's pulse raced at the flush that filled her pretty cheeks. He lifted the pocketknife he'd been carving with and pointed toward the leather pouches at the edge of the blanket. "You hungry for anything?" She'd refused his offer to fix supper when they had stopped and set up camp a few hours ago. Kane hadn't been all that hungry, either, and had contented himself with a few cakes of hardtack and some coffee.

"No, I am still full from lunch. That steak was delicious. So was the rest of the food."

Kane nodded, but he didn't remember the taste of the food nearly as much as he did his enjoyment at just sitting across the table and staring at her pretty face, loving how she listened and how she spoke from her heart. And later, in watching her absorb every detail of the restaurant. Hearing the excitement in her voice as she talked about the establishment she intended to open soon, and listening to her say the Italian names of the dishes she planned to serve.

She sat up, wrapping her arms around her knees. "I want to thank you again for lunch, and for the wine." Her smile started slow and spread wide, making his heart gallop. She ran one hand along the mahogany skirt. "And for my new dress. I really like it."

Kane swallowed. "I like it, too." He'd like to see her stepping out of it, too, but he reined those words back before they had a chance to jump out and give her a reason to send that cup sailing toward his head. "And you don't have to keep thanking me, darling, just consider it some of that penance you wanted me to do when I didn't believe you at first about hurting your ankle."

He frowned at the sadness that suddenly clouded her amber gaze and robbed her smile. "Did I say something wrong?"

"I was angry when I said that. I did not mean for you to take it to heart. You do not owe me anything."

"And I didn't buy you anything today because I thought I did. I was just teasing when I said that." He sat up straighter. "Truth is, Bianca, I wanted to take you to lunch because I thought you'd enjoy something besides trail grub. And I suggested the dress because I wanted you to be comfortable and not worried about how dusty your skirt happened to be." And because he liked her far more than he wanted to admit, and because seeing her happy brought him a joy he hadn't felt in a long, long time.

Her golden eyes burned bright with pleasure. "You are a kind man, Kane."

"We both know that can be put up for debate on occasion." He chuckled low. "But I'm real glad you think so." *Damn glad.* He leaned back and picked up the piece of wood, needing to get his mind on something else besides her. "Are you sure you don't want anything?"

Kane had to take a deep breath to keep himself from getting up and walking over there, and kissing her soft, full mouth, which he'd been wanting to do all day.

"I think I *will* have some coffee." She waved her hand as Kane made to rise. "I will get it. You keep on with your carving." She reached for her cup, then stood and stepped over to the fire. She leaned down, grabbing the bandanna and wrapping it around the coffeepot handle.

Kane turned his attention away from the nice curve of her backside and set his knife to the wood. He trimmed off another small shaving along one corner of the two-inch block of pine. From the corner of his eye he saw her straighten and, to his surprise, walk around the fire toward him.

"Why is it that you are not trimming that stick into a point, as you have done with all the others I have seen you carve on?"

"The other times I've just been whittling to pass the time." He shrugged, looking up as she stopped at the edge of his blanket near his feet. "It's a habit I picked up from my father. For as long as I can remember, I've never known him not to have a knife in his pocket. And any time he was outside and idle he was looking for a stick to whittle on." Kane smiled at the memories. He'd spent a good number of hours over the years sitting down at the barn or on the front porch with his dad, listening to his stories, talking about ranching and politics and life, and whittling a tidy pile of wood shavings between them every time. "But tonight I decided to make something."

"What is it?"

He tilted his head in a nod. "Come over here and I'll show you."

She took a sip of the coffee, then walked over and knelt down beside him, setting the cup off to the side.

Kane folded the knife closed and stuck it in his shirt pocket, then sat up away from his saddle and leaned close, intoxicated by Bianca's nearness, by the sweet scent of her sun-kissed skin. He held the wood in his palm.

She ran one slender finger along the carved corner. "It looks like a hoof."

Kane nodded, smiling. "It is. I'm carving a horse. For you."

Her chest rose and fell with her quickened breaths. "For me? Why?"

He gazed into her amber eyes, loving the delight that shimmered in her depths, wanting more than anything to lean across the mere inches separating them and kiss her. "I thought you might like a little something to remind you of the time you first learned to ride."

She nodded, running her finger along the wood again, then slowly across his palm as she pulled her hand back. Kane swallowed, feeling his dam of restraint cracking. "I will cherish it." Her smile stole his breath as much as her words, as much as her touch when she leaned over and pressed her lips to his cheek in a brief kiss.

He folded like a house of cards, dropping the wood and reaching up to cup her face with both hands, his need too strong to deny any longer. He claimed her mouth in a hungry kiss, and she responded eagerly, parting her lips to welcome him in, her soft, sweet taste sending joy singing through his veins and igniting full force the fire in him. Kane stroked one thumb across her smooth cheek, then ran his hands along her shoulders.

The feel of his warm mouth and the caressing stroke

of his tongue were as drugging as the wine she'd drunk, and oh, so much sweeter. The gentle touch of his hands roaming over her shoulders, then down along the sides of her breasts seared a path of delicious sensations swirling in the pit of her stomach.

Kane explored the lines of her slender waist, then circled his arms around her, reveling in the feel of her hands trailing a heated path around his neck, her soft breasts pressing against his chest as he pulled her to him. He delved deeper into the warm recesses of her mouth, his heart pounding with the force of a steam engine at full speed. He slowly slid one hand along her spine, then cupped her head, taking her with him as he leaned back against the saddle.

Dio, how she wanted this man, wanted him with a need that she didn't fully understand and didn't have the will or the strength to question as his hands roamed over her back, her hips, and created a searing path of liquid fire raging through her body. Passion rose up to claim her heart and scorched her with a need unlike anything she'd ever known. She ran her hands through his hair, then along the corded lines of his broad shoulders, reveling in his warm strength, in the feel of her hardened nipples against the muscled wall of his chest. He ended their kiss and pressed his lips along her neck, scorching her blood with growing desire. He retraced his path back up, then along her jaw, and claimed her mouth again, kissing her tenderly, rolling her gently onto her back. He half covered her body with his, cupping her head in one hand and slowly running the other along her waist. She could feel his manhood pressing against her hip, could feel the heat of his desire burning through their clothes and fueling her own surprising need for this man. She explored the lines of his back through his shirt, longing to feel his skin beneath her fingers.

Kane couldn't get enough of this sweet woman. He had to have more. He slowly slid his hand across her stomach, then up along her shirtwaist, letting his fingers brush the underside of one breast. He ran one finger along the valley between her breasts, then across one mound, circling the hardened nipple. Bianca's moans of ecstasy gently vibrated against his mouth. He filled his hand with the soft globe, his blood pounding in his ears as she arched into his touch and tightened her arms around him. Kane kneaded her, growing bolder and more urgent with the caresses he raked over her body. She stroked him with the same urgent exploration, her hands roving over his chest, his shoulders, his arms, searing his flesh with her tender touch. It crossed Kane's mind that this little temptress wasn't quite as shy as he'd first thought her to be, and he was surprised at the curiosity and jealousy that reared up at the man who'd taught her how to use her hands with such scorching boldness. He was surprised at the primal instinct that had him wanting to be the only one to teach her, the only one to have tasted her sweetness.

Then all thought fled from his mind, save his burning need to savor that she was in *his* arms now. He outlined the circle of her breast, brushed his thumb across her nipple, feeling it pebble even more at his touch. He moved his lips away from hers and trailed kisses along her jaw, at the tip of her small earlobe, then suddenly felt her freeze beneath him.

"Kane," she whispered.

He stilled at the fear in her voice, frowning as he lifted up slightly and saw her staring wide-eyed past his shoulder.

"Why don't you get your hands off my woman, Ranger?"

Bartlett's command set the hair rising on the back of Kane's neck, and shock instantly cooled the ardor from his veins. The sound of two gun hammers cocking reverberated in the strained silence and let Kane know the odds against him had just doubled. He met Bianca's gaze, saw the confusion swimming with the fear in those amber depths, and knew she had no idea who was standing behind them. Kane mouthed the words, "Stay quiet, and don't move"; then he slowly eased away from her, pushing up to his knees.

He started to rise.

"Stay where you're at, Ranger," Bartlett ordered. "And get your hands up where I can see them."

Kane lifted his hands into the air, cursing himself for getting so wrapped up in Bianca and letting his guard down.

"Guthrie, get Fairchild's gun."

Kane frowned, surprise swirling harder through his gut. He turned his head slowly and glanced over his right shoulder, recognizing the stout, leathery-faced cowboy walking up behind him. "What are you doing here, Guthrie?"

"Looking for that bitch." He waved his gun toward Bianca.

Kane hated the fear he saw in her eyes and wished he could take her into his arms and tell her that everything was going to be all right. But he didn't dare move as Guthrie pressed the barrel against his head and reached down to grab Kane's gun from his holster.

"And for my portion of the gold," Guthrie added as he took a step back.

His portion? Kane arched one eyebrow in dawning realization of how Bartlett had known about that rancher's gold being in the Somerville bank. The information had obviously come from a new partner, Guthrie—the rancher's foreman—and Kane figured he was the unknown accomplice who had helped Bartlett escape from jail, too.

"She can't lead you to any gold," Kane stated. "That's not Francesca."

"Of course that's Francesca," Bartlett snapped. "Don't you think I know my own fiancée?"

"Guthrie, bring her over here," Bartlett ordered.

"It's not her, Bartlett. That's her sister."

"Shut up, Ranger."

The cowboy walked over. Bianca sat up and scooted

back away from his approach. "Leave me alone. I am not Francesca."

Kane started to rise to her defense.

"You move another muscle and you're a dead man, Fairchild," Bartlett warned.

Kane sank back to his knees.

Bianca tried to twist herself free of the man's grasp. "Let go of me, you brute."

Kane tried to rise once more, and it cost him a knock on the head with the handle of a Colt. That was the last thing he knew.

FOURTEEN

The chill had seeped deep into Bianca's bones and only added to the ache in her body from riding all night. Dawn's light was just starting to crest before Bartlett brought the horses to a stop. Bianca's body ached from the nightlong ride; she wasn't sure she could even get out of this saddle. She was tired, too, and scared as Bartlett dismounted and came over to stand beside the mare.

"We'll rest for a couple of hours. And then you're going to take me to the gold; you got that, Francesca?"

"How many times do I have to tell you that I am not Francesca? And I do not know anything about the gold."

"Knock it off, Francesca. It was a good scheme to use with the Ranger, but I'm not that stupid. I know you better. And I remember you telling me how much you loved your sister, and you never wanted her to know how you never really made it as an actress. And I know you wouldn't want her to know about your trouble with the law. Or with me."

Something lurched in Bianca's heart. Francesca had never really made it as an actress? But her letters . . . She made it sound as though everything were going so well. Why hadn't she told Bianca the truth? More lies— only this one was a sad one. Francesca must not have wanted to disappoint her. *Oh, Francesca, how could you think I would look down on you? Aren't the bonds of blood any stronger than that?* She was beginning to wonder. And the wondering hurt.

Still, Bartlett had said "how much you loved your sister." So at least that much was still true. And that was enough for Bianca. For love alone, she would go on. There was still time for Francesca to explain everything. There was still hope. The important thing was, she mustn't let Bartlett know that he'd caught the wrong woman. She must fulfill her promise and give Francesca more time. "Very well, I will play no more games," she announced. "The treasure is hidden that way." She pointed toward Somerville.

Bartlett tipped back his black hat to get a better look at the worn trail ahead. Devilish blue eyes sparkled meanly from within a lean, handsome face. Bianca could see why Francesca had been drawn to this midnight-haired cowboy. In his black hair and suit, he looked like a demon in the most appealing sense of that word. "You better not be leading me on a fool's errand, Francesca. It'll be the last thing you ever do."

"I told you where the treasure is," she said bravely, "Now, do you want to quarrel or do you want to head on, *signor?*"

A firm nod was his reply. "All right, we'll head out after we give these horses a rest. But I'm warning you, Francesca . . ."

"You already did." She thrust her chin into the air and dared him to outstare her. He was surprised that he could not, and wound up dropping his chin before tying his mare's reins to the nearest tree. The leathery-faced Guthrie followed his example. So it was settled: they would head toward Somerville.

But for the first time since the start of this wretched journey, Somerville was not really where Bianca wanted to go. It was better than heading any other direction, but she would not be able to ride in earnest, not even be able to anticipate meeting her sister, unless she found a way to escape for a spell and search for Kane. All she saw before she'd been whisked away was Kane trying to come to her defense . . . so gallant. And then being knocked unconscious. If only she could have lied and told them the treasure was behind them, back at the camp, back where Kane might still have been unconscious . . . or worse. But she knew that was useless. They would never believe her, never turn around. And besides, she needed to be alone when she ran off to find him. Otherwise, they'd only kill him if he wasn't already dead. No, Somerville was the best place to head . . . unless she got a chance to flee. But what had happened to Kane after Bartlett knocked him unconscious? Guthrie had not let her turn around to see.

"What ever happened to that Ranger?" she asked as nonchalantly as she could. After all, Francesca would not have been so concerned about a man she'd only kissed— especially if she'd done so just to persuade him not to arrest her, which was undoubtedly what they thought.

Bartlett chuckled callously. "I reckon that depends. How well does he get along with a horse?" He and Guthrie shared laughter that made Bianca uneasy. She didn't understand what he'd meant by that, but she certainly didn't like the sound of it.

She had to find a way to escape. Somehow, she had to get back and save Kane . . . before it was too late.

Kane swallowed, his Adam's apple grating across the rope around his neck. He glanced up at the thick branch the end of the noose was looped over, and tugged at the handcuffs that bound his wrists behind his back, his curses muffled by the bandanna Bartlett had shoved in his mouth. And just to taunt him more, the outlaw had left his gun lying on the ground just a few feet away.

The buckskin shifted beneath him. Kane tightened his knees against the saddleless mount's sides. He'd managed to keep the horse still beneath the oak tree throughout the long, sleepless night, but as dawn crept over the horizon, he wasn't sure how much longer the horse would stand on this patch of dirt when a bed of grass and a flowing creek were less than thirty feet away.

Damn, he was in some trouble, and he wasn't having much luck figuring a way out of it, either. And he was worried sick about Bianca.

What has he done to her?

Bartlett was already a dead man just for kidnapping her. Kane didn't want to think about what else Bianca might be forced to endure, but he was unable not to, and it only made him that much madder that he couldn't get the hell loose from here to go after them.

He spied a rider in the distance. Could he be so lucky? Or was it luck at all? It might be Bartlett's accomplice coming around to finish him off. That wouldn't be so bad, he figured. Better than the torture of trying to keep the horse still. Except for one thing: he had to save Bianca. He had to live so he could get her out of Bartlett's coldhearted grasp. The rider grew nearer—so near, Kane could tell he was heading for him on purpose. This was no coincidence. That rider knew just what he was looking for and where to find it. It had to be someone coming to finish him off. None of his ranch hands would know to come looking for him, and they wouldn't be riding so hard as though there were some kind of fire. At last, it was the long black hair flapping around the rider's shoulders that gave him away. Devon Carson. What the hell was he up to now? And why was he now mounted on a snow-white steed?

Devon reined the mount to a halt. "Looks like you've got yourself in a little trouble there, Ranger." He grinned.

Kane furrowed his eyebrows at the amusement ringing in Carson's voice. His muffled words of aggravation only made the cowboy grin wider and deepen Kane's mounting anger.

Devon cocked his head and raised one hand up to cup his ear. "What's that you're saying, Ranger?"

Kane narrowed his stare. *Damn it, I can't wait to get my hand on that Colt.*

Devon looked around, his humor fading. He rode alongside the Ranger and ripped the gag from his mouth.

"You son of a bitch," Kane spat, "you're going to pay for that little bit of fun you had."

"Shut up. Where's Francesca?"

"If I knew that, she'd be swinging by her pretty little neck right now."

"But you had her just yesterday," said Devon, "Don't you know what happened to her?"

"I never had her," growled Kane, "I had Bianca."

Devon's green eyes smiled. "So you know about that, do ya?"

Kane's unshaven face grew murderous. "You mean *you* knew about it? You knew about it and weren't going to tell me? Who the hell are you, cowboy?"

Devon crossed his lean arms with cockiness. "Now, Ranger, is that any way to talk to the man who just saved you?"

"Hand me that Colt and I'll show you how I talk to lying, cocky-eyed cowboys who help out the likes of Francesca Rossetti."

"Quite a temper you got there. I'll tell you what. You talk a little nicer to me and I'll let you down out of that noose."

Kane tugged at his handcuffs. If only he could get them off without that lying cowboy's help. But he couldn't. "I'll tell you what," he said, "throw in telling me all you know about Francesca Rossetti and I'll agree not to arrest you as a goddamn accomplice."

Devon's smile was cocky. "You know, that's really not my idea of talking nicer."

"What do you *want?*" Kane snapped.

"You gotta promise me three things. One," he said holding up a finger, "that when I let you down from there you won't turn around and arrest me."

Kane looked up at the threatening noose and then down at his trembling thighs, which he'd been trying to hold steady for so many long hours. He nodded his acquiescence.

"Two," said Devon, holding up a second finger, "you gotta promise that when you get hold of that gun there you won't use it to give me a new orifice right through the center of my skull."

Again Kane grumbled and nodded.

"And three, you gotta promise you ain't gonna beat me to death."

"That's asking too much," he grumbled, but Devon could tell he didn't mean it. So he went to work letting him down. After all, he had an emergency on his hands. He'd been hired to take care of Bianca, and apparently, he'd blown it. He was going to need Kane's help.

Kane nearly fell from the horse the instant he was released from the noose. Devon had to steady the horse so it didn't run off ahead of him. Kane landed hard on the dusty earth, his knees buckling under, both feet asleep and filled with sand. He took off his boots and rubbed them, sighing heavily at his freedom and the pain that came with it. But he knew he couldn't waste too much time with his own suffering. Devon reminded him of that when he asked, "So what *did* happen to Bianca?"

"Bartlett took her. Bartlett and that spineless partner of his."

"Then we have to go after her," said Devon. "Do you think you can ride?"

"Oh, I can ride," Kane assured him with a hard squint in his eye, "but I'm not trusting you to go with me until you tell me what the hell you're doing and who you really are."

Devon figured he'd better tell him something or he might never get him up off that ground and after Bianca. And if anything happened to her . . . he could kiss his money and the value of his word good-bye. "Here," he said, thrusting a letter at the Ranger, "Does this explain it?"

With muscles that still trembled all the way to his pulsing fingers, Kane opened Francesca's message and read it with knitted brows.

To the most handsome Ranger in Texas,

By the time you read this, it will be June first, and I will have left Galveston and will be well on my way to foreign shores. I hereby inform you that the woman you have mistakenly taken into your custody is not myself, Francesca Rossetti, but my dearest twin sister, Bianca, whom I love beyond all words. Bianca has absolutely no knowledge about the crimes of which I am accused. She is as innocent as a dove, and in the name of justice, you must release her. I am the one you seek. Best of luck to you in finding me.

Love and fondest memories,
Francesca Rossetti

"No mention of the gold," Kane grumbled, wishing to strangle her for the *fondest memories* remark, but forcing himself to focus on the task ahead.

" 'Fraid I don't know about the gold either," said Devon. "I was just hired to make sure Bianca made it safe, and to make sure you got that letter after Francesca had enough time to get away."

"There's no time to waste," said Kane firmly, his eyes glittering with determination. "We've got to get Bianca before Bartlett . . ." He couldn't even think it. If that bastard had touched her, if he'd hurt her . . . "before Bartlett takes her too far away."

Devon nodded his understanding. He could see Kane was worried about more than just that. In fact, if he didn't know better, he'd think that shy little filly had gotten a hold of the Ranger's heart. Now, wouldn't that be something!

Kane remounted with a strength and determination difficult for someone in his condition. He nodded at Devon to hurry up and growled, "Let's go, you fool."

It wasn't until hours of riding in darkness that they finally slowed their pace enough to have another chat. It was Kane who broke the silence by asking, "What happened to that bay you were riding?"

Devon shook his head. "Broke its leg in a prairie dog hole. Had to shoot it."

"Where'd you'd get this whitie you're sitting on?"

"Bought her from a pretty little widow woman who owns a small farm about twenty miles east of here. That's after I carried my saddle and gear ten miles before I found her place."

Kane frowned. "Petite gal, with red hair and green eyes? Last name Sampson?"

Devon nodded. "You know her?"

"No. Stopped by her place a couple of days ago and bought a few supplies from her."

"Hard to forget a pretty girl like that."

Kane shrugged. "She was fair."

Devon arched his brow. "Are you half dead, Ranger? She was better than fair. Or is it that you've got your eye turned on someone else?"

Pain gripped him. He had his eye turned on Bianca, all right. But he'd let one woman down, years ago, and now he'd let Bianca down, too. He had to find her before Bartlett did anything to her. Kane prayed he wasn't too late.

"Sounds to me like you've got your eye on that widow."

Devon shook his head. "Naw. She had three young'uns hangin' on her skirt. And I'm not much for being around kids, or settling down. In my line of work, you spend a lot of time moving around."

"And just what line of work are you in, Carson?"

"Gambling."

"So, you're not a wrangler?"

Devon shook his head.

"Then why the cowboy garb?"

Devon grinned. "Didn't want to get any of my good suits soiled."

"Didn't want me recognizing you from any poster, either? Or finding out you're in cahoots with Bartlett?"

"Hate to disappoint you, Ranger, but I'm currently not wanted for anything. And I'm aiming to keep it that way. I've seen enough time behind bars to know I'm not in any rush to go back. I cut a deal with Francesca, yes. But I had no part in the robbery she helped commit, or in hiding any gold. But I did know she was being mighty secretive about something when she asked me to help her out."

"Why did you help her out?"

"Owed her a favor," he shrugged, "She kept me from getting a new hole in my head, compliments of a certain lady's husband, if you know what I mean."

Kane smiled and shook his head. It figured. Still, no man deserved to be indebted to the likes of Francesca. Not even a man who frolicked with other men's wives. Not even Devon Carson.

"And the money didn't hurt, neither," Devon was quick to add.

"But why did you come to the ranch if you were trying to follow us quietly?"

"Seemed like you were late heading out. Wanted to see if you were still there or if I'd missed you somehow. Thought asking for a job would give me an excuse to check on ya."

Kane nodded his understanding. He couldn't say he was too impressed with the cowboy's reasoning. But who was he to talk? If Devon had failed to protect her, well, he'd done twice as badly. He'd had his damned arms around her and couldn't keep her safe. He couldn't prevent his mind from drifting and his hands from coiling into fists around the reins. He would die if anything happened to her. Where the hell were they? What the hell was Bartlett doing to his girl?

* * *

"You're taking me on a damned fool's errand!" growled Bartlett, grabbing Bianca by the collar. "We should have been there by now. We should've been *somewhere*. What the hell are you trying to pull?"

"I'm not pulling anything," she begged him to believe. "I just can't find it. But I'm sure it's up ahead somewhere.

"How gullible do you think I am? You think I'm gonna take mercy on you 'cause of that pretty face of yours or that cute little fanny? Well, think again, darlin'."

"Jeremy, please." She hoped that by calling him Jeremy, he would remember the affection he once felt for her sister, and maybe let go of her collar. But it didn't work.

"You listen to me," he growled, "If we don't reach that gold in one more day, I will beat you. Do you understand me?"

Her wide eyes fell upon the muscles that bulged through his black shirt.

"Do you understand me?" he repeated.

Bianca had never felt so helpless in all her life. All she could do was hold her breath and whisper, "I understand."

He let her go, spinning on his boot heel, shoving a cheroot between his lips. "Let's head out!" he called to Guthrie.

Bianca was still recovering from the fright. What could she do? She didn't know where that gold was. If she'd known, she would have taken him there in the blink of an eye. It made no difference to her. But she didn't know, and she didn't know what to do about it. All she could think was to keep heading for Somerville and hope that by some miracle she'd gain some opportunity to escape and go find Kane.

She shuddered as Bartlett lifted her onto his lap and his faithful steed lurched forward. She couldn't bear to be so close to him, to have his arms wrapped around her after what he'd just threatened. But as the hours wore on, she forgot some of her immediate fear and turned her thoughts to larger problems. "Jeremy? Was I very helpful in the bank robbery?"

Bartlett snorted. "Yeah, darling, you were a real gem. Until you double-crossed me and ran off with the whole damn loot."

Why would he say that to Francesca if it weren't true? "Then the part I played . . . it helped you?"

"Of course it did. You stuck to the plan, didn't you? Couldn't've done it without all your scheming. Of course, the last part of your scheme didn't help me much. You know, the part where you ran off with my share. We hadn't really discussed that part." He laughed darkly, crushing her ribs as the gap between his arms narrowed.

Bianca was so confused, she didn't know what to say or do. Francesca had truly helped him plan. It had to be so. She could see no way for Bartlett to be lying, not when he thought he was speaking to Francesca herself. *Oh, Francesca. Is my love misplaced? What can you say when I see you again? What could possibly explain all of this? And Dio, where are you?"*

Francesca really was a beauty, thought Raimondo, cocking his head as he studied her face. He liked her sister better, but there was a real spark in Francesca's feisty eyes, and a seductiveness in the way she pouted her lips. He could see why a lot of young men had fallen for this one, though to him, there was only Hailey. . . .

"How did we get so old?" laughed Francesca, touching a cup of lemony water to her lips, "When did you become a man and when did I become a full-fledged woman?"

Raimondo loved her when she was this way—playful like when they were children and her schemes never caused quite so much harm. Only fun. "I don't know," he said, tilting back one of the chairs she'd set up on her shrimp boat's deck, closing his eyes against the late afternoon sun, trying to throw his voice over the waves. "But I remember when you and Bianca were so skinny, I thought it was because you are twins. I thought you were each as wide as half a person."

They chuckled as she thrust her breasts in the air. "I like to think that's changed."

Raimondo only shook his head. He'd never cared for her boldness. He liked shier, softer women like Hailey. But he was used to Francesca's ways and never faulted her for them. They suited her. She could never be anyone else but herself.

"One thing hasn't changed, though," she mused, her eyes growing cloudy in thought. "Even back then, I wanted to be an actress. When I was nine years old I saw Sarah Bernhardt in *Camille,* and I thought, 'I can do that. I can do it, too. I was made to do it.' "

Raimondo said nothing. He couldn't deny she was born to be an actress. He couldn't picture her doing anything else.

"That's why I'm so excited about Europe," she went on carelessly. "Things will be different there. I just know it. I know I'll be a *prima donna.* Just as soon as I get there."

Speaking of Europe reminded Raimondo of his uneasiness. "Francesca," he asked, "Bianca is really all right, no?"

"Of course," she said, stiffening. "I told you so, didn't I?"

Yes, but you are an actress. "Can you promise me?" he said. "Can you promise me that she will return? That all you say is true?"

He noticed something rise and fall in her throat, and the long silence that ensued. "Raimondo," she said at last, choosing her words very carefully, "I promise that I know exactly where Bianca is, and that she will return home safely."

Raimondo could think of no more to say. He had to grant her a nod.

"Then what about *your* future?" she asked, "What do you plan to do while I am in Europe?"

Raimondo coughed into his fist, then pulled off his cap, rubbed a hand through his black curls, and put it back on. The nervous fidgeting did not go unnoticed. "I plan to marry," he said.

"Oh?" Francesca raised an attentive brow.

"Yes," he replied without eye contact, "a bride is on her way to me now. Someone I haven't met, you understand."

Francesca leaned back in her chair. She knew all about arranged marriages. Many of her childhood friends had fallen prey to them. But she and Bianca were lucky. Her parents, though traditional, had never taken tradition that far. "I see," she said deeply. "I must say, I'm a little surprised signor Casale."

"Why is that?" He scratched nervously at his wrist.

"Because I thought your heart belonged to another."

He was surprised to look up and see her strong, insightful gaze. He blinked under the moon of her compassion.

"I saw the way you looked at signorina Tillman, Raimondo. I saw your heart catch in your throat, no?"

He couldn't deny it. In fact, he couldn't speak.

"And I saw the way she looked at you, too." Francesca leaned into the table, begging him to meet her eyes.

When he did so, he blurted it out. "I love her, it's true. But you don't understand . . ."

"Yes, I do." Her nod was comforting and rhythmic. "I understand. I'm Italian, too."

"But . . ."

"I know. It's your duty to your family. I know, Raimondo."

"So you see, I have to—"

"I do see," she interrupted, taking him chastely by the hand. "I see perfectly. I understand."

"I just can't . . ."

She shooshed him like a mother and squeezed his hand like a friend. "You don't have to say another word, Raimondo. I know all about it. I just want to leave you with one thought. As someone who loves you, as someone who was once your childhood friend."

He raised a curious brow.

"Pride is a lonely partner, Raimondo, especially if your bed is being warmed by someone you don't love."

With a kiss on her hand, he thanked her for the words, only gradually realizing how badly he had needed to hear them.

FIFTEEN

The midmorning sun poured across the glassy sky, promising an afternoon thick with sweltering heat. Kane already felt sticky under his black vest, and it wasn't yet noon. Even the occasional breeze nurturing his lungs with the scent of distant bluebonnets did little to stop the sweating. He didn't look forward to the long, hot hours ahead. He and Devon had ridden through the night, their eyelids heavy from exhaustion. Even squinting at the brightness that crept up on the day took more energy than they could afford. The only thing that kept Devon moving—and he was the less sore of the two—was his honor, and the feeling that he could never look at his reflection again if Bianca should be killed after he personally had been sent out to keep it from happening. And the only thing that kept Kane from falling unconscious and sliding off his saddle was the thought of Bianca in Bartlett's angry clutches. Whatever pain he was in, it was nothing compared to what those bastards might be doing to her right now. Every time he thought of it, he speeded up.

"Have you any idea where this trail is leading us?" Devon called out once.

Kane eyed the tracks suspiciously. The fools had done nothing to hide their trail; they'd been that sure they'd taken care of the one man who might follow them. "Looks like we're heading to Somerville," he grumbled. *That's a dangerous game, Bianca. Did you tell those outlaws the gold was hidden there? Darlin', they're gonna kill you when they find out you lied. Don't do this. Your sister ain't worth it.* It made him fume to recall the letter and to know that Francesca was not going to meet Bianca. That damned woman didn't deserve a sister like Bianca. Bianca should have kissed her sister good-bye long ago. If only he could have talked some sense into her while he still had the chance.

"You know, you look as pretty as the day I met you," said Bartlett, trapping Bianca by a live oak, a hand on either side of her face, caging her into his liquid blue stare.

Bianca had not thought of this. He'd been so determined to make haste when he'd snatched her away from Kane, then so angry about the gold, he had failed to remind her; and she had nearly forgotten: she was supposed to be his fiancée. It was only after another hard day of riding and finally making camp once more that he seemed to have the energy and the mind to bring it up. Oh, how she wished he hadn't! "You keep your hands off me," she warned, trying to duck under his arms, "I'm not your fiancée anymore, not after how you betrayed me."

"I betrayed you?" he asked, preventing her escape. "That's real funny, darlin', 'cause that's not how I remember it."

Bianca kept forgetting which was Francesca's true story. *Oh, Francesca, what is going on? If only you had told me more, I could have been of more help!*

"Seems to me you owe me an apology, little lady." His smile was so fierce, the shadow over his lip only adding to his threatening expression, that she wondered how she could ever have thought him handsome.

"I owe you nothing," she snapped, frantically casting about for a way to get out of this. Guthrie was no help. He was smoking a cheroot by the fire, listening to the evening crickets and watching Bianca's plight with amusement. That *bastardo.* He planned to watch!

"Oh, I think you do owe me something," grinned Bartlett, grabbing her around the neck without squeezing, just to show her how his hand spanned the whole breadth, just to let her know he could kill her. "And I know just the way for you to start saying I'm sorry." His free hand inched up the hem of her skirt, making her shake, making her grab at his choking arm, trying to push it away to no avail.

She remembered the way they'd bounced around in the saddle all day, how she'd felt his manhood pressing against his denims, rubbing against her bottom once or twice. How it had frightened her. And yet, she'd been so certain that all he wanted was the gold, and she'd been so worried about Kane, that she hadn't let herself believe this would happen. And now, here she was. "No." It was all she could think to say. *"Per favore,* no!" But his hand was rising with her skirt, and in a moment she knew he would be touching her somewhere so private, she couldn't bear to think. "No!"

"Shut up!" He dove in for an angry kiss, which she resisted with all her might. But he was stopped by the sound of a click.

"Hard of hearing?" asked Kane. "I think the lady said no."

Bianca's knees fairly melted in her relief. Bartlett's hands fell limp. It had taken a full night and day of riding hard, but with Bartlett riding at a slow, hunter's pace, it hadn't been tough to catch up to the campfire. Devon had his six-shooter on the red-faced Guthrie. And Kane was grinding his jaw just a few yards away, resisting the temptation just to pull that damn trigger for what Bartlett had nearly done to Bianca. *I'm a lawman,* he had to remind himself. *The bastard gets a trial.* But when he looked over at Bianca's tear-streaked face, it took every last ounce of willpower not to kill Jeremy Bartlett right there where he stood. "Get your hands in the air," he ordered. When Bartlett didn't comply, he stiffened. "I said get your—"

Bartlett grabbed his gun from the holster and spun around.

Bianca dropped to the ground, crawling away as she heard crackling all around like fireworks. She couldn't tell who was firing, who had fallen. It all just happened so fast. And all she could think was *getting away*. When the noise stopped and smoke wafted in the air, she found herself panting against a tree. She patted herself all over to see whether she'd been shot. She'd felt so many chills as she crawled, she didn't know whether they were from fear or from a bullet piercing her skin. But she was fine. All was still. And when she looked up, she noticed only one thing: Kane was still standing. "Kane!" She ran at him with her arms open wide. "You're alive! *Grazie!*"

He squeezed her so tight, she felt like a child in his powerful arms. He kissed her neck and rubbed circles into her back whispering, "Are you okay? Am I too late? What did he do to you?"

"I'm fine," she wept, more loudly in her relief. "I'm fine. You're alive. Oh, *la fortuna*. I was so scared for you."

"For me?" he growled, "Honey, you're the one who should have been scared. Do you know what they almost . . ." He couldn't finish. Of course she knew what they almost did. He didn't have to say it. The poor thing was scared enough as it was.

"How did you find us?" she sniffed. "I was trying to escape, trying to find a way to get back to you and help."

"Well, thank god you didn't pull anything foolish," he scolded her. "You just let me do the rescuing, you hear?"

"But how did you—"

" 'Fraid we don't have time to explain." He looked over her shoulder at the three reclining bodies. Bartlett's and Guthrie's chests were no longer heaving, but Devon's still was. "Jesus," he said, "we've got to get him to a doctor." He let go of Bianca and jogged to his partner's side. "You all right, cowboy?" He lifted his shaking hand.

"What is he doing here?" asked Bianca, cocking her head at the familiar face that had followed them all the way from Houston.

"For now," sighed Kane, "let's just say he's a friend. Come on. We've got to get him to a doc."

"What about the others?" she asked, squinting at the still bodies of her assailants.

Kane suspected she'd never seen a man shot before. He took off his hat to tell her. "Honey, they ain't going nowhere." He took her frightened hand and squeezed it, gazing at her sympathetically.

"Are you sure?" she asked with a flutter in her voice, "Shouldn't we . . . check to see whether it's not too late?" Her knees were shaking so at the sight of two men brutally shot to death that she couldn't find the courage to approach them herself and look closer.

"I'm sorry, darlin'." *Sorry only because she had to see it. Not sorry I shot 'em.* "They're gone. I know a dead man when I see one, honey. Now come on, we've got to get Devon here to the doc."

"But where?" she asked as he yanked her by the hand.

"Looks like you're finally going to get your wish to go to Somerville, darling."

The bath water melted away the dirt, the grime, the dust, and maybe even some of the memories. Bianca squeezed a cloth, letting the warm, soft droplets smooth away her cares. She let them drip from her slender legs, her small, weary feet, and even the ends of her dark-brown hair. As her muscles warmed and her pulse slowed, she felt the memory of Bartlett's cruel hold on her float away like the burrs in her hair. She let go of the image of his fierce eyes, his frightening hands, and the seething, cruel intent. She let go of the fear she'd held for so many long hours that Kane had come to even worse harm than she. And she let go of the memory of those motionless bodies, stilled by gunfire in the darkness. It wasn't that she blamed Kane for doing it. She knew he'd had no choice. But to see them lying there, dead like her mother from fever so long ago, pained her nonetheless.

She was grateful that Kane had covered their bodies and taken them himself to the undertaker, leaving her in peace to take a bath in the quiet, rickety Somerville hotel room. As a hot late-afternoon breeze brushed a torn white curtain and rattled the square window panes within their splintered wood, she said a silent prayer for Devon, who was with the doc in town. He hadn't looked good when they left him. He was shaking and sweating and wouldn't open his eyes. The doc said there was nothing they could do but leave him and check back later. So that's what they did. Only Kane had run off to have some kind of chat with his friend and partner, Caleb Wilson. About what, Bianca didn't know. All she knew was, it gave her some time to enjoy this delicious bath.

There was a knock at the door. "Oh, *Grazie, signorina!*" More rinse water! It was the fastest maid service she'd ever known. *"Buongiorno. Enter."* This bath was just going to get better and better. She closed her eyes and sank deeper into it as the door creaked open. "Right over here!" she called, sighing until she'd fallen chin-deep.

She heard footsteps and felt the maid standing over her, but didn't yet hear a reply. Gently she opened her eyes. *"Dannare!"*

Kane threw up his hands. "I'm sorry," he said, turning his back more slowly than he knew he should. "I'm sorry, darlin'. You said to come in." *And I couldn't look away.* Glory, what he'd seen was enough to drive any man over the edge. He'd seen her pert little breasts peeking up from that water, their tips hardening in the air.

"I thought you were the maid!" she cried. "I asked her to get more rinse water, and oh—" She was mortified as she crossed her arms over her breasts and sank deeper

into the tub. But she couldn't help feeling just a little
excited, too. She wondered how much he had seen. How
much she *wanted* him to see.

"I just came by to bring you something," he said, tossing a package on the four-poster bed, by far the fanciest
thing in the simple room. "Again, I'm real sorry. I didn't
mean to, uh . . ." He swallowed hard. He wanted to reach
in that tub and grab her. Put her over his shoulder, carry
her to the bed. He steadied his breathing and his manhood
both. "I uh . . . just put that there dress on and, uh . . .
meet me downstairs when you're . . ." He rolled his hand.
". . . dressed." Damn, he hoped she liked the dress. "I'll,
uh—I'll just get out of your way now." *Before I do something to make you sorry I didn't. Steady, steady.* "I'll be
waiting downstairs."

His anxious exit left Bianca with a wide grin. Why,
she had made him nervous! *Dio,* he was handsome when
he was aroused. She wondered what he'd wanted to do
to her. And whether she would have liked it. Her eyes
fell on the package. A new dress? She leaped from the
bath tub, barely feeling the chill as she carefully opened
the ribbon and the box. She hated for him to spend money
on her this way, but the thought of wearing something
new now that she was all fresh and clean felt so wonderful
that she knew she wouldn't refuse. And then she saw
it. . . .

If it wasn't the color of a perfect sapphire, she didn't
know what was. The sleeves were puffed generously
enough for a queen, and even the little buttons at the
wrist were of carefully carved wood. The skirt was so
full, with so many layers, it would rustle louder than her
petticoats. And the top would cling tightly to her bosom.
So tightly that she would have been ashamed to wear it
if Kane weren't going to be right there, protecting her.
She knew he'd never let anything happen to her. She
hugged the dress to her breast and closed her eyes. She
was touched. The dress was beautiful, and so was his dear
heart. If only they had met at another time, in another

place. If only they could run away and forget all that had been and was to come. If only . . .

Kane's breath caught in his throat the minute he caught sight of her, descending the rustic stairs in the dress he never dreamed could be so beautiful. Her brown hair looked so soft as it whispered against her ear, a few strands left waving and loose from the coiled braid atop her head. Her thin eyebrows gave a lift of character to her liquid-gold eyes laced in brown. Her skin, from her face to her collar bone, was like ivory kissed by the sun, completely unmarred, unblemished, and shining with golden perfection. Her nose was straight and narrow, her lips soft and shy. And that dress! It hadn't looked that way in the store; that was for sure. Her waist looked so tiny, all cinched up, and by contrast her breasts were pushed together and spilling forth, the dress allowing just a peek at their ripened tops. He glanced over each shoulder to make sure no man was staring, ready to offer him a fist if he was.

"I'm speechless," he said, tipping his hat.

Bianca flushed, her cheekbones rising high and her dimples enticing him. "So am I." She touched her skirts affectionately. "It's beautiful. *Grazie.*"

He was too moved to say, "You're welcome." He couldn't even remember the term. All he could manage to get out was, "There's an empty table if you'll join me." He nodded at a quiet one by the window and a fluttering old curtain. It was as quaint and bucolic as the floor, all splintered and wobbling for one leg's being too short. But the other diners had friendly smiles, and the breeze was soothing. From the window, they'd have a perfect view of the sun going down like an orange ball of fire. It was as homey a little restaurant as Bianca could have asked for. The kind she hoped to have some day.

He held out her rickety chair and saw to it she got settled in. She was smiling. Happiness made her so pretty.

Much prettier than when she was scared or suffering on that damn horse he'd made her ride. He chuckled softly to himself. It was just a little funny in retrospect. "Oh, Kane," she said, peeking behind the dusty old curtain so she could see the glorious flatlands in the distance, blessed by the hot breeze and the setting sun, "This feels like the most luxurious night of my life."

He bowed his eyes guiltily. He had something he knew he should tell her. But he just couldn't do it. He just didn't want her to stop smiling.

"Is everything all right?" she asked, squeezing together her thin, elegant brows.

"Yes," he said, forcing a pleasant expression. "Yes, everything's just . . . just fine, darlin'." How could he tell her about the letter? How could he tell her that Francesca would never arrive in Somerville, would never explain her actions, and had left Bianca on her own with nothing but a petty letter? There was a time he'd have done anything to have proof like that, to be able to show her beyond any doubt how wrong she was to trust in her conniving sister. But tonight he just couldn't break her heart. He'd tell her in the morning. Or the afternoon. Later. Just later. "Everything's fine."

Bianca smiled softly at his warm face, so handsome and tender in the dimming sunlight. And still so rugged. "I pray that Mr. Carson will be all right," she said in earnest, hiding the depths of her concern behind black lashes.

"I think we got him to the doc in time," he said soothingly, taking her delicate hand in his strong fingers. "We'll check on him in the morning."

Bianca nodded, basking in the feel of her small hand wrapped in his sturdy, protective fingers. "Won't you tell me now why Mr. Carson was following us?" she asked, "now that we have a quiet moment?"

It pained him, but he shook his head. "Not now, darlin'. I'll tell you soon, I promise."

She was about to argue, but the waitress arrived with

a bottle of wine. "This what you asked for?" she questioned Kane.

Kane turned to Bianca. "I ordered white. Hope it's all right. I know you like Chianti, but—"

"Do you have chicken?" she interrupted to ask.

The waitress nodded with pride. "Only the best this side of the Appalachians. Baked or fried."

"Then white wine will be just fine," she beamed. As the waitress poured, she hastily explained to Kane, "The wine draws out the flavor in the food, you see. A clashing bouquet or the wrong level of tannin, and the food will be ruined. But a crisp white with a tender piece of chicken. *Buono!* Perfect."

Kane chuckled softly. "Is that the future restaurant owner talking?"

"The *hopeful* future restaurant owner."

Kane lifted his tin mug, freshly filled to the brim. "Then let's toast."

"To my restaurant?" she asked. "It doesn't even exist yet."

"Then you choose the toast, darling," he drawled with a twinkle in his deep blue eyes.

With a gentle grasp, she lifted her cup to his. "To friendship," she suggested.

Their mugs hung together in midair, hesitant to part ways. Her soft amber eyes melted into the sharpness of his blue. "To friendship," he agreed with a lump in his throat. But when, a moment later, she licked a drop of wine from her succulent lips, he knew he could never ever settle for friendship. Not with her. Not ever.

"Is this where we part?" Bianca had never had such an evening. All night, the conversation had been light and breezy, their glances across the table flirtatious and exciting. The food was juicy and scrumptious, the wine tart and cool. When the night had painted the windows black, she'd begun to dread this moment: when he would walk her to her room, when the night would be over and they would have to part ways and, in the morning, get back to the business of real life.

"I reckon so." He was no happier than she was. Their banter had been so easy, her pretty face so gentle on his eyes, so hard on his heart. All night, he hadn't once thought about Natalie. And that had to be a first. He didn't want to go, but he figured he'd better. The way her breasts were stuffed into that dress, as though they wanted to be let out, he figured he'd better go fast before he obliged. He'd just give her one little kiss good night. No harm in that, he told himself.

He was wrong. The moment he bent down to kiss her, as soon as their lips touched, an urge spread across his loins that he could barely control. He wanted to tear that dress right off of her. He wanted to join bodies instead of mouths. He wanted to pick her up and toss her on that bed, to show her the ferocity of his yearning. Bianca responded to his rising desire with daring fervor. She melted under his touch, at the feel of his breath upon her quivering lips. Her tongue moved across his hot lips, tasting the faint sweetness of tobacco, the masculine burn of whiskey. For a moment, neither of them thought. There was no past, no future, no Francesca, no Bartlett. There was only their lips joined in an embrace and Kane's hands clasping fiercely at her backside.

"May I come in?" he asked, stopping the kiss by lifting her narrow chin.

She met his fierce eyes dazedly and whispered, *"Per favore,* come inside."

Her appealing accent melted what was left of his gallantry. "If I come in, I'm going to toss you on that bed," he warned, "and there's nothing on this earth that will stop me."

She swallowed as she nodded breathlessly. "In that case, I definitely want you to come in. All the way in."

He reached down and lifted her off her feet, turning sideways to cross the threshold. She couldn't believe how easily he lifted her, as though she weighed nothing at all. He kicked the door shut behind them and tossed her on the bed as promised. She fell in an alluring pose, long waves of shining hair tumbling about her shoulders in the commotion, one knee lifted, inviting him to contemplate what lay in the gap thus created. He fell on her even before he'd finished unbuttoning his vest. He couldn't resist. She was beautiful. He wrapped her in the strength of one arm while the other explored her body. Bianca sighed under his exploring fingers, yearning for them to travel farther, moaning when they cupped her breast, kissing him when they tore at her gown, nuzzling him when they squeezed her tiny waist and trickled over a round hip. At last, she thrust out her hips when the fingers threatened to open her legs.

"I don't wanna scare you, darling. After what you been through." His hand stopped abruptly.

But Bianca couldn't stop the yearning that was consuming her, or the love that was welling in her heart. She couldn't even remember Bartlett and his ugliness. She couldn't remember anything. All she knew was what she craved, and it was staring right at her. She ran a hand through his dark, sandy hair. "Do I look scared to you?"

He smiled. No, she sure didn't. She sure didn't. So he followed the urging of his loins and rolled on top of her, tearing down her stockings, squeezing her slender thighs. "I've wanted to do this for so long," he said, nuzzling her neck, giving her chills at the feel of his stubble against her delicate skin.

"And I've wanted you to." She opened her legs wide under the beckoning of his manhood. He lifted them around his waist, pulsing with need, struggling to free himself from his denims without missing a chance to fondle the sweet-smelling tresses under his rugged palm.

She ached from the wanting, burrowing her fingers in his thick hair, longing to pulse all around him, to learn his body's movements between her parted legs. At last he entered, filling her, sending sparks to her womb that drove her to the brink of madness. He stopped short when he felt her tense. It was the pain. The pain of maidenhood lost. Gently, he brushed her cheek with a callused hand that made her flutter all around his piercing manhood. The last thing he'd wanted to do was hurt her. But it was a pain she didn't mind bearing, not in his arms. And within moments, she was smiling again, urging him to thrust, digging her hungry fingers into his buttocks. He rode her with his hips and loved her with his lips, planting gentle kisses along her neck that caused a burning warmth to shoot down her spine. It started to look as if her moist lips might just part in ecstasy.

"That's it, sweetheart, come fly with me," he whispered, his heart thudding hard against his chest as he watched the moonlight's reflection dance with the ecstasy building in her golden eyes.

Under the command of his thrusts, she found her fulfillment. She cried out through the night, trembling all around him. The sight and sound of it was enough to make him find release as well.

"God, you're beautiful," he whispered huskily as their bodies melted in collapse. She clung to his shoulders, stroking the muscles that would protect her through the night. Lying on top of her, snaking his arms behind her for an embrace, he believed for a moment that he would never let her go. And she wished she could believe that, too. She snuggled into his hot, masculine-scented skin, more exhausted than she'd ever been before. She didn't think about what they'd done, or what they were going to do. She just thanked the heavens that, for one night, she had been to paradise.

SIXTEEN

An evanescent fog wafted just beyond their window, the flimsy old curtain dancing in a cool morning breeze, surely the last cool breeze of the day. Bianca stirred in his arms, finding a home in the nook of his shoulder. He kissed her sweet hair good morning. *Damn, she was beautiful.* Her hair tumbled across the pillows wildly; her shining, sleepy face was as fresh as the dim morning light. He took her oval face in his hand. "No regrets, darlin'?"

Bianca sighed placidly. "Mmmm." She snuggled deeper into the soft blankets and her warm cowboy. "No regrets, signor."

For that answer, he kissed her. It was a gentle brush of his lips, but she could feel the roughness of stubble. She felt deliciously humbled by the size of him, his arm muscles encasing her where she lay. "Thank you for last night," he said, brushing the hair from her forehead, penetrating her with his bright blue eyes, "And not just the end of it; I mean all of it. Dinner, talking, everything." She'd never know how much it meant to him, being able to get away from it all like that. Just spending a normal night with a beautiful lady in a rustic hotel. He couldn't remember the last time he'd been so at ease, so happy.

"I enjoyed it," she said with a sleepy smile. It had been a long time since she had a man's attention, that kind of intense attention that seemed to hang on her every word and cherish every flutter of her lashes. He'd made her

feel special. The way Antonio had . . . before she'd found
out she wasn't special to him at all but only a second-rate
substitute for her sister.

Their eyes locked, sharing a moment of love and ado-
ration. But when another cool breeze sent a chill through
their bones, they found themselves sharing a hopeless
smile. There was definitely a problem here. Last night,
they'd pretended it was all roses and kisses. But the truth
was, Kane was on his way to arrest her beloved sister.
He didn't know how yet, but he was going to do it, no
matter what it took. It was the kind of man he was. He
couldn't forget he had a job to do, couldn't forget how
he owed it to his father—not just because he had happened to fall in love. And here he was. He hadn't even
told her about the letter yet, hadn't even told her what
her sister had done to her. He just couldn't bring himself
to, and he knew that when she found it, it would destroy
her world, her faith in her sister, her trusting heart. Oh,
damn it. This beautiful night between them was about to
fall apart, and she didn't even know it.

But she knew more than he thought. She might not
have known about the letter, but she knew that Kane was
still going to arrest Francesca the first chance he got. She
wouldn't have doubted it for a moment. She knew what
a determined man he was. And when it didn't involve her
or her sister, she loved him for it. But she was just as
stubborn as he. She would hold her sister innocent, however impossible it seemed, until Francesca looked her
right in the eye and said she was guilty. She knew that
Francesca had lied, that she was more involved than she'd
let on, but until she got the chance to hear everything
from Francesca herself, she would not condemn her. And
she would not help Kane do so. Not until she'd heard her
sister's side of the story. If he arrested her before that, it
would be against Bianca's will and, if necessary, over her
dead body.

"We have a problem, don't we?" he muttered, knowing
her thoughts were heading the same direction as his.

Bianca reached up and touched his handsome face. "Don't talk about that," she said. "The morning is still young. We still have right now."

"I reckon we do," he said, squeezing a rough hand between her tender thighs. "Are you ready to steal another moment?"

"Oh, yes," she said, wrapping her arms around his rugged neck, "let's not let the morning get away."

The moment he bent down for a kiss, a fire spread through his loins that was uncontrollable, all-consuming, and made him forget once more what awaited them in the cruel world beyond their bucolic little sanctuary. She opened her legs and welcomed the joining, forgetting all the heartbreak and sorrow of days gone by. As he rode her gently and lovingly, she sank deeper and deeper into the madness of her hope and her love of this handsome Ranger whose love prodded wishes she dared not entertain. She knew, even as she opened her mouth wide in her ecstasy, that this stolen magic could never last.

"I pray Mr. Carson will be all right."

Kane worked out his frustration with an anxious pace. He didn't like being kept waiting in the doc's office, and grumbled to himself that he'd better have good reason. But when he looked up at Bianca, he couldn't help smiling at the way she closed her eyes in prayer. He didn't know how he could ever have thought she was her sister. Couldn't believe he'd ever mistaken her warm sentiments toward his father, his sister, and now Devon for her sister's chicanery. Her heart was so honest. "I hope so, too," he said, wrapping his arm about her waist.

"Where will we go once we're sure he'll recover?" she asked, tender curiosity showing in her wide amber gaze.

"Back to Galveston."

"But I told you," she said, "My sister will not be in Galveston. She'll be right here in Somerville exactly on June first."

Kane winced. All right, there was no more putting this off. "Bianca," he said, taking her feminine hand, "I have something to tell you."

He found a rickety old chair by a window and urged her to use it. "Come here, honey; sit down."

Bianca was wary of the urgent expression in his penetrating eyes and found herself taking her seat with caution. "What is it, Kane?"

There was nothing to do but draw the letter from his shirt pocket and unfold it before her eyes. "I think you'd better read this, sweetheart."

She took it with an unsteady hand, keeping her eyes fixed on his until the last moment. Then she bowed her chin and read. Kane swallowed a lump in his throat as he watched her eyes skim the page. He wished he'd never had to tell her. "No," she breathed, clasping her throat. "No, Francesca would never do this to me. Where did you get this?"

He nodded at the doc's back room, sealed by an old wooden door. "Devon Carson brought it. That's why he was following us, Bianca. Francesca hired him to see you safely to Somerville, and then to give me this letter."

She was shaking her head slowly and in steady rhythm. "I don't believe it. She wouldn't abandon me. She promised she would meet me here! Maybe Mr. Carson wrote the letter."

He wished it were possible, but he tipped his hat in apology. "Look at the cursive, darlin'. Whose writing is that?"

It was Francesca's, all right. She scanned it closely, searching for any sign of error, any indication that someone else was trying to copy her penmanship. But it was perfect—exactly Francesca's tall, thin lettering. And for the first time, Bianca admitted the truth. There could be no justifying her sister. "I'm going to kill her," she whispered. But she didn't mean it literally. Kane knew she didn't. She was just so hurt.

"I imagine she thought that the letter would make up

for it," he said, trying to assuage her pain. "She probably figured you wouldn't mind so long as you were set free."

"She figured wrong." Bianca's eyes were blank in her fury. One little letter of exoneration did not make up for all the danger her sister had put her in, did not make up for the lies. So many things could have gone wrong. What if the letter had never arrived? What if something had happened to Devon Carson a little sooner and he hadn't made it. Would she have let Bianca hang for her crimes? And what if Kane and Devon hadn't saved her from Bartlett? And most important, did she intend never to explain the lies? Obviously, that was exactly what she had intended. Bianca felt betrayed beyond reason.

"You understand I'll have to go after her," he explained gently. "Since that letter got to me before June first, I've still got time to stop her from leaving Galveston. You understand that's just what I'll have to do."

"I'll go with you," she replied stoically. "I'll go with you when you arrest her. I must ask her why. I must hear it from her lips."

Kane's nod was slow and understanding. He wished he could erase the hurt.

The doc interrupted his thoughts by bursting in. "You can see him now," he announced.

Kane grumbled about the wait but then turned on his boot heel to help Bianca up from the chair and plant her hand in the crook of his arm. "Come on, honey. Let's go see that good-for-nothing cowboy." He winked.

Bianca followed dazedly behind him to a hard cot in the back room. These were not the most luxurious accommodations she'd ever seen in a doctor's office. The shelves were cluttered with bottles and jars, some of them labeled, others not, all of them threatening to topple over with the *thunk* of Kane's boots. The cot seemed to be an afterthought in the cluttered room. But Devon didn't seem to mind it. In fact, he looked pretty happy just to be alive as he smiled up at them. There was weakness in his limbs, but strong life in his green eyes. "Well, look what the cat dragged in," he grinned cockily. "Ohh, I didn't see you, Bianca. No offense, but you're looking mighty lovely. I was talking about the ugly Ranger there." He winked playfully.

Kane frowned. "Well, looks like this'll be a short visit."

Devon chuckled as Kane pulled up a chair. "By the way Ranger, did I thank you yet for saving my life?"

"I don't remember."

"Well, consider yourself thanked. I owe you one."

Kane's nod was slow and steady. "I think you already paid that debt." His thighs trembled as he remembered being on that horse with a noose around his neck.

Devon nodded a truce.

"I'm afraid I'm the one indebted to you both," said Bianca meekly, "Mr. Carson, you never would have taken that bullet if it hadn't been for me. I don't know how to thank you both for saving me."

Kane already felt pretty well thanked. He recalled her sensuous body moving under his in the moonlight. *Devon sure as hell better not be thinking he should get thanks like that.*

"I was just doing my job," said Devon cautiously, giving her an unusually serious nod.

Bianca bowed her head. She didn't want to be reminded of his job, of Francesca and her deceit. "Well, I'm glad to see you're doing well, *signor.*"

He rubbed the stitches in his side. "I think I'm gonna be all right. If that Guthrie was aiming for the heart, someone should've told him I don't have one." He chuckled boyishly. "You got a cheroot I can puff on, Ranger?"

Kane patted his empty shirt pocket. " 'Fraid not."

"Ah, can't wait to get out of this doc's office, then. This is no kind of a life." Devon leaned back and closed his eyes, maybe dreaming about getting out and chasing some pretty women, or maybe just too exhausted to keep talking.

Kane took Bianca's hand. "We should leave him to rest," he whispered, "It looks like he'll be just fine."

Bianca said a silent prayer of thanks, then swallowed.

"Come, we've got to get a move on. Train to Houston leaves this afternoon, and I think we'd better be on it." He looked at her tenderly and with warning. " 'Fraid we've got some ugly business in Galveston, honey."

Strand Street was buzzing by late afternoon. The mule-drawn trolley was forced to linger at every stop as the crowds fanned themselves, waiting patiently to board or disembark. The elevated walkways were packed with shoppers undeterred by the brutal sun beating down on their hats. There was a ceaseless jingling of bells as merchant shops were patronized and abandoned over and over by tourists and customers eager to sniff a new scent of perfume or rest for a long, hot meal. It was to Hailey's great surprise that through one of those doors came none other than Francesca Rossetti, a new bottle of perfume in hand. "Hailey!" she cried, grinning broadly. "What are you doing here?"

"What am *I* doing here?" Hailey glanced enviously at Francesca's new perfume. "What are *you* doing here?"

"Oh, nothing." She shrugged brightly. "Just a little shopping."

Judging by the bulging ribboned packages tucked under her arms, Hailey would say she'd done a *lot* of shopping. "I see."

"Well, I'm so glad I ran into you, Hailey. You're just the person I wanted to see. Do you have time for an early supper?"

"Uhhh . . ." *Time? Yes. Money? No.* "I'm afraid the business district is a bit pricey for me, Francesca."

"Never mind that! It's my treat. Come!"

Before Hailey knew what had happened, she was being led by the arm to Ritter's, a fine restaurant indeed. And truth be told, she wasn't fighting much. Secretly, there was nothing she wanted more than to try their tenderloin of trout, though she hated for someone else to pay. "Francesca, are you sure that you . . ."

"Yes, yes, I need to talk to you. And besides"—she tossed her chin, and would have tossed her hair as well if it hadn't been coiled so neatly at the base of her long neck—"actresses don't have to worry about money, you know. We get plenty."

Hailey lowered her pale-blue eyes. Being an actress certainly did sound glamorous, at least by all Francesca's accounts. She wished she were as lively and daring as Francesca. She wished she wanted to be an actress. But she knew she would never be anything but simple and ordinary Hailey. Oh, well, it couldn't be helped. "What did you want to talk to me about?" she asked, settling into her seat, glancing out the window, which overlooked the fancy tourists and passersby, delighting in the aromas which rose so temptingly from the kitchen.

Francesca tried to look casual, though a warm smile curved her red lips. "Raimondo, actually."

"Raimondo?" Hailey sat up erect, excited even to hear his name. She'd been thinking about him every day and every night. Especially at night. Especially when she lay in her bed—alone—and imagined his handsome dimples. "What about him?"

"Tenderloin of trout for two," Francesca told the waitress. "It's the best thing they serve," she explained to Hailey. "Trust me."

Hailey already knew that. She might not have had the money to eat in a place as fine as this, but she knew all about it. She spent more time than she should studying and coming to know the lives of those more fortunate than she. Especially when cleaning at the hotel. She was always hearing the gossip of the rich and overly pampered. She'd heard Ritter's tenderloin of trout mentioned many times in passing. But she never thought she'd be eating it herself!

"I was thinking," said Francesca, tapping her chin with

long, dainty fingers, "that Raimondo really shouldn't marry someone he doesn't know at all. What do you think?"

Hailey felt a knot form in her tearful chest. It was a moment before she swallowed and replied, "I think he must follow his own path. I can't choose for him."

A warm light softened Francesca's worldly gaze. "Are you so willing to let him go?"

Hailey was startled by the comforting texture of her voice, by the unusual sincerity in her eyes. In fact, Francesca's caring rendered her momentarily speechless.

"I saw the way he looks at you, Hailey. And you at him."

Hailey flushed in embarrassment. "I know," she replied when she was able to look up from her lap, "I know he cares for me. And I . . . feel the same way." That was an understatement. But she couldn't tell Francesca the truth. Couldn't explain the long nights of loneliness, of lying in her bed, imagining their wedding day, and other outrageous fantasies. "But if I push him, he will resent me. Don't you see that? Even if I could convince him, and who's to say I can? Even if I convinced him, he would never forgive me for it. He would always resent the woman who urged him to betray his loyalty, to alienate his family, to lose the respect of some friends. Marriage is hard, hard work, Francesca. There will be difficult times ahead; there always will be. And in those times, you need a marriage built on firm ground. Not a marriage where one person pushed the other to betray himself."

Francesca's smile was rich; her sparkling eyes were savvy. "You speak very well, signorina Tillman."

Hailey bowed her head.

"So why don't you use some of that nice talking to go talk some sense into Raimondo?" She winked kindly before taking a sip of water, "You've almost persuaded me to let the subject drop. And if you can do that, I promise, you can convince anyone of anything." They shared a genuine smile. "Go talk to him, Hailey. Tell him how you feel. Don't let him slip away."

She fidgeted with her napkin. "I can't."

But Francesca startled her by taking her hand and looking deeply into her vulnerable eyes. "You must," she said, giving her a firm squeeze. "You must."

"But his family . . ."

"It's your only chance, Hailey. Once he marries, it's all over. This is your only chance. Take your chance. Take it."

Hailey felt empowered by Francesca's determination. "Do you really think?"

Her strong nod, eyes closed, was her adamant reply.

Hailey felt a flutter of excitement, a sense of encouragement and hope. "I'll think about it," was all she could promise. "I'll give it some thought."

Francesca's heart was warmed. For now, that was all she could ask.

They missed the train to Galveston. Kane kicked a bench on the Houston platform. But he'd hoped that train might take them to Houston a little faster so they could make the switch. It was too late now. Another wouldn't leave till morning. And he couldn't ask Bianca to ride with him through the night on horseback. It would be too hard on her. She just wasn't a good enough rider yet. "Well," he said, tipping his hat politely, "Might as well make the best of it. I figure we can at least find a good hotel for the night. Should be plenty here in Houston."

Bianca could see his frustration at losing so much time. He was such a determined man, so fixed on his job. She wouldn't let him lose even a minute on account of her. Just because she wasn't a good rider didn't mean she couldn't be a determined one. "I say we ride."

Her graceful smile sparked a light in his heart. He sure wished he could take her up on her kindness; he really wanted to hurry. But he couldn't put her backside through another hard ride, and without any sleep, to boot. "No, honey," he said, resting a strong hand on her narrow shoulder, giving it a tender squeeze. "We might as well just rest. I don't want to push you so hard."

"You didn't," she grinned. "I'm pushing myself. Come on, Ranger. I said ride."

His grin was so broad it made his eyes sparkle. "You're really something, Miss Rossetti."

"Well, now, I didn't say we shouldn't stop at all," she teased him, trying to flirt. She wasn't much of a flirt, though, he noticed with delight, because the harder she tried, the redder she blushed. "I still think we should stop. Once we get out in the grasses. Once we're under the stars."

He took her meaning, that was for sure. The mischievous spark in her eye was a little uncertain, a little shy. But his own strong eyes gazed down at her and twinkled blue, and a steady nod came over him. "You sure you want to be tempting a rugged old Ranger like that?"

She looked up boldly and draped her warm arms about his neck. "You're the one who tempts *me,* Ranger. I'm the one you should worry about."

With a humorous spark in his eye, he bent down for a kiss, consuming her sweet lips, parting them with his fervent tongue. And when his hands slipped over her round little bottom and he felt the passion the gesture stirred in her ardent mouth, he knew there was going to be quite a fire under the Houston stars tonight.

SEVENTEEN

"I really did enjoy our meal. Thank you, Francesca."

"You're quite welcome. I'm glad we had this chance to get to know each other."

Francesca took Hailey about the waist and rested her head on her warm shoulder as they walked along the sidewalk. "You're a special person, Hailey. I can see why Raimondo is crazy about you and why Bianca counts you among her friends."

Hailey didn't feel special. In fact, she felt guilty over how much she had enjoyed the meal. She hated for Francesca to spend her money on something so frivolous as fine food, especially for her sake. But she had to admit, she'd never tasted food so delightful on the taste buds. Even the coffee was the smokiest and best she'd ever had. The company had been truly enjoyable as well. It was a shame Francesca was going to be running off again so soon. She would have liked to get to know her even better. She had sensed they both felt that way as they'd lingered over coffee and dessert long enough to make the waitresses grow impatient.

The streetlights on Strand Street were glowing brightly, competing with the rising moon. It was a crisp evening mellowed by a warm breeze. The women hated to part company, but it was time to go. They stepped just beyond the streetlights, where their evening plans took them on different paths. But before they could finish their hug, a shadow spread over them both.

Hailey screamed.

But her voice was silenced by a stifling hand, smooshing her nose and lips shut. Wide-eyed, she found that she could barely breathe! But she could see. She could see that someone had a knife to Francesca's throat. And even in the dark, she began to recognize the outlines of his beady eyes and the ring of brown hair like a curtain around his balding head. It was Avis Murdock!

"You've caused me a lot of trouble, Bianca Rossetti." He was pressing the knife so firmly into Francesca's throat that it made a deep dent, though there was not yet a drop of blood. "And I'm not talking about that stew you dumped in my lap."

Hailey tried to free her lips, tried to cry out, "That's not Bianca!" But she couldn't make even a sound. She thought she might suffocate.

Francesca's eyes were bitter and hard. She was so calm, it put Hailey in awe. Her hand was gradually lifting up the hem of her skirt, as though there were something hidden in her stocking. *Francesca,* thought Hailey, *why don't you tell them you're not Bianca? Why don't you save yourself?* But Francesca was no coward. "Were you afraid to face two women alone?" she asked coldly, "Did you have to bring one of your thugs?" She sneered at the man who grasped Hailey.

"I've had about enough of your smart tongue and of *you,*" he growled. "If one more Casale brother waltzes into my office on your beck and call, I'm gonna slit this pretty little throat of yours. And you!" he growled at Hailey, who recoiled into her own assailant, trying to escape the boom of his voice and the threat of his stare. "Don't think I don't know what you told those boys." She shook her head wildly from side to side, unable to speak but doing everything she could to communicate. "Yeah, I know you opened your fat mouth," he snarled. "I seen you with them; I know what you probably told them." She kept trying to protest, but it was hard when she was turning purple from lack of breath. "Yeah," he smiled wickedly at her fright. "I think it's 'bout time you and I had another talk, huh? Would you like that? I bet you would." Frantically she struggled with all her might, tearing herself left and right to be free from her assailant's clutches, but nothing worked.

Until Francesca shoved Murdock and sent him stumbling with his own knife. As he tumbled backward, she drew her derringer and grinned. "I think you're the one who needs a talking to," she drawled, a determined light in her golden eyes. He looked up pitifully. She looked as if she knew how to use that thing. *Damn it.*

But his partner let go of Hailey and leaped at Francesca, wrestling the weapon from her hand. Murdock scrambled to his feet.

Both women were carried kicking and struggling into a darkened alley.

Raimondo paced back and forth along the dock before the Rossettis' shrimp boat. *Dio,* where are you, Francesca? He needed to talk to her, needed more advice. He needed to hear from the one person he knew would give him exactly the advice he craved. To go ahead and follow his heart. Yes, that's what he wanted. Not an honest opinion, just the *right* opinion. He wanted a push; he wanted a shove. He wanted to be told once more that if he confronted his papa and said he would absolutely not marry this stranger, that he had already met another, he wasn't really a traitor and a bad son. Well, since Francesca wasn't home, perhaps he should visit Hailey. No, that would only lead to trouble. He'd just wind up putting his arms around her, holding her close, telling her sweet words from his heart. Kissing her. He could still remember their kiss. How he wanted to do that again and again and again. No, he'd better not go to her house. He had already led her on badly enough as it was. *Dannare, Francesca. Where are you?*

Footsteps raced at him, but they were too light and

rapid to be Francesca's. Raimondo held his cap down against the wind and peered into the distance. He was surprised to see a little boy. And not just any little boy. It was the one who'd stolen from the candy store. "Stefano?"

Stefano stopped before him and clutched his knees, panting out every breath. "I . . . are you . . . are you the one who's friends with that girl?"

Raimondo needed a little more information than that. "Which girl?"

"You're the one from the candy store, aren't you? The one with that nice lady?" He panted and puffed and spat on the ground.

"I didn't know you knew about that," said Raimondo. "Did the shopkeeper tell you?"

He gasped through his nods. "Yes, sir. I know what you did. Thank you, but . . ." He was very moist in the face. Raimondo could see he'd been running a long time.

"What is it?"

"Your friend," he panted. "I didn't know what to do. She was back in town." He jerked a thumb behind him. "Some men grabbed her and I think they were hurting her. I didn't want to go to the police. But I saw you here."

Raimondo stiffened. "Grabbed her? *Dannare!* What are you saying?"

"I don't know," he said. "I didn't understand it. She was with a friend. A thin lady with a pretty face. And two men grabbed them. One of them was bald, I think."

Murdock. That *bastardo.* "Come on!" cried Raimondo angrily. "Take me to them!"

His fists were already clenched for a fight before they'd even jogged from the docks. Raimondo wanted to run all the way to the business district, but Stefano's legs were too short, so he had to slow down. Terrifying images danced in Raimondo's darkening mind. What was Murdock doing to Hailey? He could only imagine her fear, the way she must be shaking, her muffled cries for help. He would kill that Murdock! He'd pound his skull into the bricks. How dare he touch her! How dare he lay one filthy hand on her pretty face! "Are we almost there?" he asked impatiently of the boy, who struggled valiantly to keep up.

"Just around this way," he panted. "I'm going as fast as I can."

"I know."

They walked another block under the taunting orange glow of lamps beckoning their way. But they still weren't near, and Raimondo was surprised to hear Stefano's little voice. "Can I ask you something, signore?"

"It's not a good time, Stefano. We have to save my friend."

"I know," he said, "but it's just one little thing." His dark eyes looked up at Raimondo imploringly.

"What is it?"

"Why have you been asking about me?"

Raimondo nearly stopped in his tracks. "You know about that, too?" he asked. This little boy was quite the sleuth.

"Yes, I know about that. I heard you were asking about my papa, my name, my life. How come?"

Raimondo really liked this little kid. He was direct. He said exactly what he thought and asked exactly what he wanted to know. Natural qualities for a street urchin, he supposed. "I asked about you," he said with a comical tilt to his head, "because I was trying to impress a girl."

Stefano laughed delightedly at their shared secret. "Ohhh. That makes sense." His grin was more like a wink. He felt as though he and Raimondo had just had a real talk, man to man.

Raimondo grinned and privately added, *A girl who's a good judge of character. What a spunky little boy he is. No wonder Hailey liked him right away. She's smart.*

"Over there!" cried Stefano, worry furrowing his small brow, "I saw them take the ladies in there."

Raimondo backed himself against the building, shoving a fist in his palm. He motioned for the boy to be quiet as he took a quick peek around the corner. He saw nothing. He shrugged in confusion at the boy.

"The alley wraps around," said Stefano. "Maybe they turned the corner at the end to get farther from the street. I'll go check if you want."

What a brave kid! But Raimondo couldn't send him off alone to face danger. "Stay with me," he said, squeezing both his shoulders, "We'll both go look."

Silently, they crept into the alley, tensing when they heard muffled talking somewhere in the distance. Raimondo kept a tight hold on Stefano, prepared to grab him if there was any sign of trouble. But they reached the crook in the alley's L without any trouble. Again Raimondo flattened himself against the wall; again he motioned for Stefano to stay quiet; and again he took a peek.

Murdock was holding Francesca, clutching her around the waist and squeezing her cheeks together brutally, forcing her lips to purse. But the younger man, his accomplice, was having to chase Hailey around the dead end. She had broken free of his grasp and was waving a pipe at him, threatening to use it if he came any closer. Raimondo flung himself back against the wall before he could be seen. He sighed heavily. "All right, Stefano. Do you know what we have to do?"

The boy nodded. "Create a distraction, right?"

"Right."

"I'll go find something to light on fire."

"No, wait, wait." He stopped Stefano by the tail of his shirt. "There's no time for that."

Hailey's voice cried out through the alley. "You let her go! You hear me? I'll use this! I will!"

Raimondo peered around the corner and saw that Hailey was swinging a pipe around, fending both men back out of range. But Murdock had his knife to Francesca's throat, and looked fully prepared to use it if Hailey came any closer. His companion's hands were tossed helplessly in the air as he visibly schemed for a way to surprise Hailey and take that pipe.

"Okay," said Raimondo, "I need you to . . ."

Stefano broke into a smile and then gave a high-pitched scream, so piercing that even Raimondo wanted to cover his ears. And what vocal cords! It seemed there was no limit to his breath.

"That'll do it," Raimondo shrugged.

He raced into the alleyway, where Murdock's companion was covering his ears, scrunching his face in pain. Murdock looked as though he wanted to do the same, but couldn't because of the knife he had to hold to Francesca's throat. But he was squinting off in the distance, trying to see what the noise was, and that was just enough distraction to make him loosen his grip ever so slightly. When Raimondo leaped on his back, choking him with both arms, he dropped the knife. Hailey swung out and knocked down the companion. Francesca stumbled to the ground, scrounging for any kind of weapon. But she didn't need one. Raimondo let go of Murdock's neck, turned him around, and punched him square in the jaw. "Don't you touch my woman!" he spat, giving him a good kick in the ribs. Murdock looked unconscious, but Raimondo gave him one last kick to be sure. Hailey couldn't believe she'd truly rendered the other thug unconscious. She covered her mouth in shame, shock, and maybe just a little pride.

Raimondo looked up through the moisture beading on his black curls. "Hailey!" He ran at her and swept her up in his arms. "Hailey, are you all right? Did he . . . What did that *bastardo* do to you? Are you—"

"I'm fine." She was nearly weeping, though, she was so relieved to see him. "Oh, *thank you,* Raimondo. Thank you. How did you know we were here?"

As soon as he could bear to put her down, he nodded over to Stefano. "The kid told me," he said.

Hailey squatted down, placing both hands on her knees. "It's nice to finally meet you. It looks like I owe you a favor."

The boy shrugged. "No, I didn't have anything better to do tonight."

She grinned brightly at Raimondo, who said, "He's a great kid, eh?" He scruffed up the boy's black hair. "I have a feeling we're all going to be good friends."

Francesca cleared her throat. "Does anybody remember that I'm here?"

Raimondo laughed good-heartedly and helped her to her feet. "You all right?" he asked in all earnest.

"Yes," she said hotly. "How humiliating!" She tried to neaten up her hair but could tell it was no use. She was furious with herself for having been disarmed, for having lost the fight and having to be rescued. It was not exactly her style. "Who were those men, anyhow?"

"It's too long a story," said Hailey, dropping her head onto Raimondo's chest. He comforted her, stroked her back, and kissed her hair. She knew it was his way of telling her it was all right. In his slender, muscular arms, she felt so safe and protected. She wished she could stay there forever.

"Well, whoever he is," declared Francesca, spitting on the unconscious body, "he's lucky he didn't try any of that with my sister or I would have killed him tonight. I promise you." Nobody doubted that one bit. They could see the ferocity in Francesca's determined glare.

"Come on," said Raimondo, "I don't think Avis Murdock will be bothering anybody for a very long time. Come on, now. Let's get you ladies home." He led Hailey through the dark alley to the safer, busier street. He kept her in his arm so she would know she was safe. And after they'd walked a few blocks, he whispered, "Hailey."

She sniffed. "Yes?"

"Hailey, that's the last straw. I'm talking to my papa."

"What?" She drew away from his warmth just long enough to look him in the eye. "What are you saying?"

He forced her head back onto his shoulder, pressing it there and holding it secure. Then he kissed it. "I love you," he whispered. "I know now that I can't ever see you hurt. That means I have to keep an eye on you. And that means"—he took her hand to his lips—"I need to marry you."

"Oh, Raimondo!"

But before she could go on, Francesca interrupted. She had not been listening to them and turned around to ask sharply, "Will you all come to my boat for drinks? I think we could all use one." There were nods all around, so she spun back around to lead the group.

As soon as it was private again, Hailey whispered, "But what about your family?"

Raimondo squeezed her waist. "I choose you." He kissed her hair. "I choose you."

Hailey imagined she should be happy about that. And in a certain way, she was. But in another way . . . she couldn't help wondering. Was she going to be the cause of an unbridgeable rift between him and his family? Would he hate her someday for this? She took his strong hand and squeezed, wishing that this were really the happiest night of her life, just as she'd imagined for so long that it would be.

Francesca danced gaily about her cabin all morning, imagining herself onstage in some exotic European city. She hadn't decided which one. Prancing about in the dim, foggy light, she imagined herself playing one leading lady and then another, and then one entirely of her own invention. *"Grazie, grazie,"* she said, bowing to her pretend audience. Then she danced up the stairs, a plate of hot food in hand, deciding to take her breakfast on the deck. It was foggy and cool up there, though Francesca barely noticed it. She was lost in her daydreams, consumed by the excitement of her voyage to come and of the hope that her dream of being a star was finally going to come to pass. Not falsely, like the embellished, embarrassing words written in her letters home. But truly. People would see her and say, "That's Francesca Rossetti! The brightest star this side of the Atlantic!" She'd been hoping for this all her life, sure somehow that it would come to pass. It was just taking a little longer than she'd expected. She was still delighting in the applause drumming so welcomingly in her mind when she spun around for one final bow, and . . .

"Bianca!"

Bianca did not look like an appreciative audience. Francesca was startled by the dark fury reflected in the face so similar to her own. Bianca's hands were on her hips, her hair blowing naturally in the morning breeze, falling free from its bun as if she'd been on horseback all night. Her eyes were quietly murderous. "You must be surprised to see me."

Francesca feigned a grin. "Yes!" *Dio, this was going to be awkward.*

"How could you do it?" her sister cried out. "How could you trick me? How could you tell me you were innocent, that Bartlett had deceived you, when you were his accomplice all along?"

"Wait, Bianca. Wait." Francesca threw up her hands as a barrier between herself and her sister's fury. "Please listen to me. What I told you is true. Some of it, that is."

"Which part?!" she cried. "I have searched and suffered and all I've found are lies! *Your* lies!"

"No. You don't understand. Please sit down."

"Sit down? I cannot sit! I'm furious! You lied to me, Francesca!"

"No, no, Bianca." Her voice came out on a ragged breath. It hurt to see her sister's hate run so deep. She had never intended . . . "Bianca, what I said is true about Bartlett. Yes, I helped him plan the bank robbery. And I seduced the Ranger for him. But that's because he threatened to kill me if I did not. Bianca, you must believe me. I was in love with Bartlett. I didn't know anything about bank robberies until after we were engaged and he asked me to help. I told him no. You must believe me, I told him no. I told him I would go to *la polizia!* But he took me by the throat and said he would kill me if I did. And so I helped him. I helped him plan, and I helped him execute. But I was furious! I couldn't let him win. I couldn't let him treat me this way! So I played a joke on him. I took the gold for myself and ran away with it." A proud smile crossed her cherry red lips. "I would have liked to see the look on his face when he found out."

"It is wrong to steal!"

"But I didn't steal it, Bianca. I only hid it. I swear to you, I have not used that money. The hundred dollars I gave you was honest money. I've been spending what I saved, and what I got . . ." She grumbled the last of it. ". . . selling the Ranger's rifle." She coughed into her fist. "I got a good price."

"I cannot believe you, Francesca! You were going to use that gold to get to Europe! Yes, I know all about Europe and the letter."

"No, Bianca. No, I was going to give the Ranger a map to the gold. Honestly! I have not touched it. I only took it to play a joke on Bartlett, which he deserved! As soon as I was gone, I was going to send Fairchild a map so he could return that gold to its rightful owner. Really, Bianca! I swear it."

Bianca's gaze lost some of its wild fury, but it cooled only to a somber glare. "You still shot Kane's father."

Francesca lowered her eyes in shame. "Bianca, he had cornered me. I was scared. Do you know what the Ranger would have done if he'd caught me?" Her eyes were imploring. "Do you know what they would have done? Bianca, they would have killed me. I was scared. I never meant to pull that trigger." She crossed herself to the Father, Son, and Holy Spirit. "Please forgive me."

She looked up with sincerity. "Do you know if he lived?"

Bianca bowed her head in thanks. "Yes," she whispered over the sound of the waves. "I believe he will be all right."

"Thank God."

"But you will not be!" cried Bianca. "After all you have done, after all the lies! How could you?! How could you lie to me? How could you put me in such danger?"

"Should I have told you I shot an innocent man?" Her thin brows shot up in alarm. "Bianca, you were my only hope! You would not have helped me; I would have hanged. And . . . you would not have loved me anymore." Her eyes drooped miserably.

"Oh, Francesca." Bianca crossed her arms against the wind and paced. "Do you think my love is so weak? Are the bonds of blood nothing to you?"

"They are everything to me, Bianca! But I didn't want you to hate me. And I didn't think you would come to any harm."

"You didn't think! That's right, Francesca. You didn't think at all. I could have been killed! You know, your wild schemes were very cute when we were children, but it's not so cute anymore. I don't think you're clever, and I don't think you're amusing. The fix you got me in was dangerous!"

"I'm sorry."

"I don't know whether you're truly sorry now or not, Francesca. But you will be. You'll be sorry the moment I turn around and leave, because I have brought the Ranger with me. He let me come first so I could hear your story. Yes, he trusted me because he's a good man. But now I'll go tell him I've found you, and for once you'll have to face the consequences of your own actions!"

"Bianca, no!" Francesca saw her whole life's plans

collapse in the drop of a noose. *"Per favore!* I know you're angry with me. You have every right. But do you wish to see me dead? Do you truly wish to hand me over like a common criminal? Your own sister? When you *know* it was Bartlett who got me into this fix!"

Bianca closed her eyes against her sister's desperate pleas and her own torn heart.

"Bianca, they will kill me. They will *kill* me."

Bianca knew this might be true. She'd heard Kane say it himself. Her own sister. Furious as she was, could she turn her own sister over to be hanged? "Francesca," she said softly, "You have really hurt me."

"I know," she said. "I was careless; I was thoughtless, but—but Bianca, I was desperate."

Bianca sighed heavily. She knew she couldn't do it. Her sister had lied, been reckless, taken an outrageous gamble with Bianca's own safety, and even been cornered into shooting a man. She wanted to see her punished. And she was so hurt that she'd not been trusted with the truth from the beginning. But to turn her over to the hangman? To watch her own sister, no matter how thoughtless, swinging from the gallows? Because she herself had turned her in? She couldn't.

"All I ask," said Francesca, "is that you give me this one chance to escape. I'll hurry. I'll go right now. Just tell one little lie for me. Just tell the Ranger that I'm on my way to turn myself in; keep him occupied, and wait for my ship to sail. I should be gone by tomorrow morning. That's all. Please, Bianca, don't turn me over to be killed."

Bianca bit her lip, trying to drown out the raging voices in her head by drawing a little pain. "What about the gold?" she asked. "You said it would be returned to its rightful owner.

"I'll tell you where it is. You and the Ranger can go get it. Just please, stall him while I escape."

Bianca bent her head in anguish. When she lifted her chin, her eyes, though sorrowful, were perfectly determined, and her voice as sturdy as the old boat on which they'd been raised. She said, "Go, Francesca. I will not let you hang."

EIGHTEEN

"How'd it go, darlin'?" Kane's voice was as tender as the hand on Bianca's cheek.

"Fine, thank you." Her face was bowed in the breeze. Kane just figured it was painful to see for herself what a liar and she-devil her sister was.

"Why don't you just stay here while I go do what needs to be done?" He patted her shoulder affectionately. "There's no need for you to watch this."

"Wait!"

He stopped in mid-saunter.

"Uhhh . . . she agreed to turn herself in."

Kane touched the brim of his hat. "Well, that's nice. It'll make things a little easier, I reckon."

"Tomorrow morning," she said.

"What?" His scowl was impatient.

"Please, Kane." She thought she might make herself sick as she went on, eyes averted, rambling out her horrible lie. "I promised her we'd give her time to say goodbye. To all our friends, to the island, to everything she's ever known. I promised, Kane. Just one night."

He looked down at her frantic little hands clasping and unclasping in her anxiety, at her trembling, pretty pale lips. "I can't take her word for anything, darlin'. You know that. I let her have a few more hours, next thing I know she'll be hightailing it off this island."

"Then take *my* word for it," she implored. "I swear to you. She won't leave." That hurt. Saying it, knowing how she was deceiving him, someone she had come to love. It hurt.

"Darlin', I'd be a fool." *Damn, if there's any woman who could make me turn a fool, it'd be you, though.* "What-all did she say to you?"

"That she's sorry she shot your father, that she panicked."

His eyes darkened furiously.

"And that she never intended to use the money. She was only getting back at Bartlett because he made her help with the robbery. He threatened to kill her if she didn't."

He cocked his head in lieu of a nod. "I can believe that, I s'pose. Sounds like something Bartlett'd do. But that doesn't change what she did to my father. And besides, her word ain't exactly proof."

"But . . ."

"Never mind," he said, taking her around the shoulders in a firm embrace. He wanted to comfort her. He knew how hard this all was on her. "No need to figure it all out now. Maybe Bartlett made her; maybe he didn't. If you want, I'll try to believe he did. But I've still gotta put her under arrest."

"But please, Kane! Please just wait! I promised her I'd let her have one last night."

"Darlin', you shouldn't promise things you can't control."

"Please!"

One more "please" and he thought he might just melt. Was that all he had to do to make her feel better about this whole thing? Just give in to this one request? It seemed like a small price to pay if it meant she might forgive him for what he had to do. If it meant they might still have a chance to get past all this ugliness and stay together in the end. His heart pounded with a new hope. "All right, darlin'. I'll give her one night. For *you.* Don't you forget this." He kissed her tenderly on the crown of her head.

266 *Jackie Stephens*

"Oh, *grazie!*" she cried. "Thank you, thank you! How can I ever thank you enough?!"

He wrapped a lazy arm around her shoulder. "How 'bout showing me around this island?"

"Of course!"

"They've got some pretty beaches here. Wanna find us a nice hotel? I want one looking out over the ocean. We can take dinner in our room," he added with a quick, enticing squeeze to her backside.

Bianca's heart fluttered, and then it fell. *Oh, lord, am I doing the right thing?* It just didn't feel right. It felt terrible. "Yes," she said, "I'll find us a nice room to rent." And why not? It would probably be their very last night together. Her very last chance to know love. In the morning, they would be enemies. Another love lost—and once again, because of her sister.

There was only one way to do it, and that was directly. No pacing before the dock, rehearsing his lines, no settling in for a lazy conversation and working his way to the point. He had to be bold. He had to walk right into his parents' cabin and announce, "I am not marrying Adrianna!"

His papa faltered with his cigar. His *mamma*'s plump face went pallid, her loaf of fresh bread threatening to tumble from its pan under her trembling fingers. Neither of them spoke.

"I know this is a shock," he explained more humbly, "but I am a man, and I have made a decision. My heart belongs to Hailey Tillman and no other. I must marry her, Papa."

His parents exchanged looks, and for one moment, Raimondo thought they were calmly considering his declaration. But *la fortuna* was not shining so brightly upon him. Within a minute, his father leaped to his feet and shouted, "You will do no such thing!"

Raimondo thrust his square chin up into the air. "It is

my decision, Papa. I am sorry to disobey you, but I am not sorry to take Hailey Tillman as my bride. I—"

"You are not my son!" he cried, his face heating from red to purple and back again. "Would you shame me? Would you have Adrianna arrive on these shores only to be sent back to her family in dishonor?"

Raimondo offered a slight bow of his head. "I am sorry for Adrianna," he admitted, "but I would be more sorry for her if she were to marry a man who loves another. It would not be fair to her."

"Ah!" shrieked Rosa, "now, he is considerate! Now, he says he is not doing this for himself. Talk some sense into him, Vito." She shook her head furiously.

"It is a boy's duty to marry the one his papa chooses!" he cried.

"I am sorry. I cannot."

"Then expect no wedding gift from me!"

Raimondo's determined face fell just a little.

"That's right!" cried his papa, "If you marry this woman, I will not give you your own vessel as I did your brothers. You will have no way to support her. You will be an islander with no boat! No home! No wage!"

His mother nodded her approval. "It's what you deserve!" she averred.

Raimondo's heart lurched. He had not thought of this. All of his life, he had assumed, as he was taught to do, that when he became a man and had a bride of his own, he would also having a shrimping boat. It was tradition. He would do the same for his sons someday, and they for theirs. How could he marry Hailey without one? Well, he'd just have to manage. He didn't know how. But he would not back down. "Then I will starve," he said calmly, "but at least I will not have betrayed my heart." He spun around and left them, their mouths gaping wide.

Hailey was waiting for him outside, biting her nails to the quick. "How did they take it?" she cried, running at him with open arms.

"I would say, mmmm, not too well." He welcomed her hug and returned it with a tender kiss.

"Oh, no!" She pulled away and cupped both her cheeks. "Does this mean we can't . . ."

"Nothing could mean that," he assured her, gazing into her sweet eyes with determination. "I will marry you no matter what they say."

"Oh, Raimondo!" She was touched. It was the answer to all of her most impossible dreams, ever since the day she'd first met him. And yet . . . "Can you really be happy, Raimondo, knowing that they are so angry?" She didn't want to discourage him, didn't want to lose him, but it scared her. She just couldn't bear to be the cause of his misery.

"They will come around," he said, though he wasn't at all as sure as his casual posture and lazy nod let on. "I'm sure once they recover from the shock, everything will be fine. Except . . ."

"Except what?"

"Well, it looks like I won't have a shrimping vessel."

"Oh." Hailey lowered her face, worried.

The moment he saw her concern, the impulse to tell her he'd take care of her somehow overwhelmed him. He was a man. He must not let her worry. "I'll ask the bank for a loan," he told her. "Then I can buy my own boat. Please, Hailey, don't worry. I'll take care of you. I promise."

She wasn't at all sure the bank would give him what he asked. But if a boat was the only thing keeping them apart, she thought she should reassure him. "Raimondo?"

"Yes?" He brushed her cheek with a friendly knuckle, loving the feel of her ivory skin.

"I've had nothing all my life," she said soothingly, "You don't need to worry for me. I don't care how we make a living. We'll survive. I don't need much. I know that together we'll survive."

He took her in his arms and squeezed mightily. How

could he have found a better woman than that? He was more sure than ever: he'd made the right choice. "I love you, Hailey."

"I love you too, Raimondo," she nearly wept into his shirt. But behind her elation there was still deep sorrow. Just as she had feared, she had come between Raimondo and his family. She had cost him his *mamma* and papa. How could she live with that?

"You sure picked a pretty hotel." Kane's heavy boots were a little out of place on the beach, but it was midnight and nobody seemed to care.

"You bought us a wonderful meal," said Bianca, "I enjoyed it."

The stars were like rips in the sky's primordial black cloth, peeks into the bright heavens above. The water lapped at the sand, blessing them with a warm, salty breeze and a rhythmic sound to steady their heartbeats. In the clear, black night, they felt like the only two people on earth. But they weren't. The beach was strangely crowded, thought Kane, especially at the midnight hour. "Doesn't anyone ever sleep 'round here?" he asked cheerfully.

Bianca blushed, but he couldn't tell in the darkness. "There is a reason for the crowd," she confessed.

She said it as though she was concealing some mischief, but he couldn't think of what it might be. "What's the reason?"

"Look carefully," she giggled.

He looked around him at the menfolk and the womenfolk strolling, laughing, sometimes running in the waves under the stars. Everything looked pretty normal except for the hour. Except . . . "For Pete's sake!" He put a hand at Bianca's temple, yearning to protect her from the view. "Some of these menfolk ain't wearing a thing!"

Bianca giggled brightly, assuring him there was no

need to protect her from the sight of them. "It's nothing I haven't seen before," she smiled. "Nude bathing is popular on the island. People did it so often, the city finally put a restriction on it. Only between the evening hours of ten and two. That's why everyone comes out here at midnight."

Kane peered at her suspiciously. "And did you? Did you ever . . ." He swallowed hard. The thought of other men having a look at her bare flesh—it was enough to make him take a swing at every man on the island.

"No," she replied in earnest. "No, I never have."

A smile crept across Kane's hard face. A delicious idea was dawning. "Then let's say we make it a first."

Bianca gasped. "You mean you want me to . . ."

"Not here," he said firmly. "Not where these other fellas can see you. Let's head on down the beach." He fondled a wisp of her satiny hair. "Let's do it, just the two of us."

Bianca liked that idea very much. She nodded rather than spoke. She wanted to hide the sinful thrill he would surely hear in her voice. She nearly swooned as he took her tiny hand and led her down the sand.

Their walk was silent save for the crash of the waves and the laughter of couples, young and old, splashing all around them. But they did not speak to each other until they were far from the crowds, far from the noise, and sure that they had found a private haven. "Should we undress here?" she asked, peering over each shoulder to make certain they were alone.

"I don't know about the 'we' part," he teased, "but I'd sure like to see you wiggle out of those clothes and into that water."

"You first!" she laughed brightly, tugging at his vest. "I will not undress alone!"

His laughter set off a spark in his eye. "I s'pose that's fair. Now, come here." He motioned with a twitch of his finger, and she obeyed.

His kiss touched her lips with a voracious need that

had been growing since the first mention of nude bathing. Since the image of her breasts, naked before his eyes and dripping with salt water in the moonlight, had first shot into his mind like a bullet. He took her mouth with ferocity, trusting that he could be virile with her, that she would not be afraid. His hands fumbled uncontrollably with her buttons, and to both his surprise and delight, her hands seemed equally busy. She was tearing at his vest, then his shirt, trying to bare him to the starlight. He helped her, tugging down his own shirt as they kissed, revealing a mountain range of muscle that heightened her hunger and made her work more frantically to relieve herself of the bindings of her own gown.

When they were both bare to their lovers' gaze, he lifted her in his strong arms and carried her toward the water, the waves lapping at his feet and then his ankles. Bianca allowed herself to be draped like a doll in his clutches, her arm flying out to the side, skimming the water's surface until gently he put her down on her feet. She felt the tips of her breasts harden in the cool water. So did he. For soon, they were pressed against his beating heart, where they tickled the hair of his chest and rubbed themselves to ecstasy against his muscles. Bianca dipped her head under the waves, then rose, her long hair straight and dripping with clear water. It was a sight more beautiful than he could bear. He pressed himself against her, letting her feel his manhood, seductively warning her of what he was going to do. She grasped his buttocks and said, "Yes."

So they swam a short way, clutching each other, letting the water cool their most private places. And then he took her by the hand and led her to the sand once more. He stopped her from instinctively grabbing her gown and held her captive in a kiss, forcing her arms to her sides. Bianca made herself fall backward, pulling his strong body down with her. His body glistened with droplets of water in the starlight. His sandy hair was made dark by wetness, his blue eyes sharp against the black night. She

272		*Jackie Stephens*

opened her bare legs to his magnificence, inviting him
to plunge into her. It was an offer he was all too ready
to take.

He pierced her womanhood, making her moan with
delight at having her emptiness filled. His hardness
stroked her from the inside, his hands pinched lightly at
her full breasts, still adorned with tiny droplets of water.
"How does it feel, darlin'?"

Her breath came out in gasps. "It feels like heaven."

He smiled because that was what it felt like to him,
too. He didn't think he could ever feel this way again,
not after losing Natalie as he had. But here she was, a
new woman, a new hope, and a brand-new feeling of
love. He burst open inside her, groaning out her name.

Bianca, she heard. And her grin was unmistakable. It
was her name. Not Francesca's. *She* was the one he loved.
She gave in to her own wild-eyed shudders, holding on
to his powerful shoulders to keep from flying away. She
was beautiful when she moaned. Kane watched her lips
part and listened to her feminine little cries and thought
he could die right then and there and be a happy man.

He rolled to her side and squeezed her. "I love you,
darlin'."

Bianca buried her face in his strong, hot chest. How
could she feel so wonderful and so awful all at once? "I
love you, too," she said, fighting to keep back a sob.

He lay there for a minute, basking in the aftermath and
peace of their love, squeezing his lady to his side, gazing
up at the stars whose beauty didn't equal that of her amber eyes. After a while, he said, "Well, I reckon we paid
for that hotel room. So should we go on and sleep there?"

Bianca nodded miserably.

He noticed her distress and said, "Don't worry, honey.
I know it's gonna be tough tomorrow. But like I said,
there's no reason for you to watch. I know you love your
sister. I know how you feel. So why don't you just stay
in our room tomorrow while I do what I have to do. It
would probably be better that way, honey."

But if there was one thing of which Bianca was very certain at that moment, there was *nothing* that was going to make what she said to Kane any better.

NINETEEN

When the fog blanketed Galveston the next morning, Kane woke up in his hotel room, very much alone. He rolled over, expecting to find Bianca within reach, planning to hold her close and give her a good-morning kiss. Planning to let her speak her anxieties, tell him how she felt, so he could hold her and kiss her and tell her he understood. But there was nothing. His searching arm fell upon an empty pillow. And his eyes gradually opened to the pale-blue light of morning. "Bianca?"

Nothing.

"Bianca? Are you bathing?" He got up, his heart pounding in his chest, and swung open the door to the adjoining room. There was an empty bathtub. "Bianca?" He gazed around and saw nothing. Not a dress, not a pair of stockings, nothing. Every trace of her was gone.

His fists trembled; his eyes narrowed to slits. He didn't want to believe it. "Bianca!!!" He didn't care whether the whole town heard him. He called her name out the window, where his voice dissipated in the ocean's loud waves. He called her name down the hallway, waking more than a few disgruntled hotel guests. She was gone. He raced down to the front desk, pulling on his shirt as he ran, his feet still bare, and demanded, "Where's the woman I checked in with? Have you seen her?"

"Yes, sir," said a spindly old man with a ridiculous long, horseshoe-shaped mustache, "She left hours ago."

Betrayal. It didn't take a damned genius to figure out

where she'd run off to. Or why she'd chosen this morning to do it. He wondered whether this had been her plan all along. To help Francesca get away, to seduce him so he'd trust her to give them the time they needed. *Like sister like sister.* Damn his foolishness! When had she first decided? He wondered. Was it after she talked to Francesca? Or was it when she had asked to see her sister alone in the first place? Or was it back in Somerville, when she'd said she would come along? Or was it a long time before that? It didn't matter. He'd been duped! He cursed himself for trusting another Rossetti woman. *By now, they're probably both hightailing it off this island.* How could he have thought Bianca was any different from her sister? *Because she is.* He had to remind himself. *She is different. I could see it; I could feel it.* But she wasn't different! She'd made a sorry fool of him! She'd looked in his eyes and asked him to trust her. To take her word! She'd sworn Francesca wouldn't run off. All lies. And their love . . . a lie, too.

He thought his heart might just break open and bleed on that hotel floor. But he didn't have time to let it. He had to go after those two gals. And damned if he wasn't going to strangle them both.

"I will miss you," Bianca wept into her sister's red dress. But her tears weren't just for Francesca. They were for Kane, too. Francesca would never know what this "little lie" had cost her.

"I will miss you, too," said Francesca. "We only have each other now."

Silently they both remembered their mamma's death, and their brother to that cursed fever. And now their papa. "We've been through so much together," Bianca whispered.

"We've always needed each other." Francesca rocked her sister back and forth in their embrace. It seemed no one would ever understand the ties that bound them. And they didn't need to. The only people who needed to understand were the twins themselves. They knew how much they meant to each other, different as they were.

"You'd better go," Bianca warned. "The ship is getting ready to sail."

Francesca sniffed back a tear and straightened up. "How do I look?"

Bianca shook her head expressively. "You're beautiful, Francesca. You've always been beautiful." *You don't need to seek the applause. You don't need to stand on a stage. You don't need everyone's approval. Can't you see you're good enough?* But she didn't say any of those things. Francesca had to find her own path. And if hers led to the roar of appreciative crowds, then so be it.

"I won't ever forget what you've done for me," Francesca promised her.

Bianca eased the tension with a chuckle. "Well, I should hope not!" But her face grew stern as she added, "You won't ever be coming back, will you?"

Francesca looked just a little scared for the first time. "No. I can't." She took one last glimpse at the shores of their girlhood. "This will all be a memory to me." She blinked back some tears as she gazed out across the waters, where the shrimp boats fought to stay upright. "If I come back, they'll have to arrest me. And you know I can't let that happen. Not with the punishment of death hanging over me."

Bianca nodded her understanding. "Then is this really good-bye forever?"

Francesca took both her hands and squeezed. "Goodbye forever, Bianca. My only family, my only love."

They squeezed each other with all their might, and might have lingered in their embrace forever if the crowds had not begun boarding. "Oh, you'd better go!" cried Bianca, "Hurry. You can't miss it."

Francesca seemed to agree. She gave her sister one last kiss, then looped her valise over her arm and walked proudly along the dock, her slender form growing smaller with every step. "Run, Francesca," Bianca whispered under her breath. "Run. Whatever happens . . . just run."

She sighed her enormous relief when the ship finally pulled away from the docks, sealed and protecting her sister, carrying her to safer shores. Francesca would be all right. Bianca had saved her life. It was over. The ship was moving. No one could stop it now. The relief was thrilling!

She was grabbed by the elbow. Instinctively she tried to jerk her arm away, but her assailant's grip was merciless. His fingers dug into her flesh, bruising her and making her gasp.

"What the hell do you think you're doing?"

"Kane! Please, my arm!" She tugged and tugged, but he wouldn't let go.

Then he let it go so quickly it sent her stumbling back. "You double-crossing, good-for-nothing she-devil. I oughtta whip you for what you've done."

"Kane, please! Listen to me."

"I'm done listening to your sister *and* you."

It pained her to hear him speak of them both in the same breath. But she had more urgent concerns. He looked as though he was going to thrash her. "Kane, she's my only family. She's all I have!"

"I'm all you have!" he growled. "That is, I'm all you *did* have. Now you got nothing."

"Kane!" she cried as he turned his back. "Please believe me! It's not that I don't feel bad about your papa!"

He whipped around and lifted his open hand. For just one second, she thought he was going to strike her. He thought so, too. But he saw the fear in her eyes and he just couldn't do it. He put his hand down. Instead, he spat. "Don't you talk about my pa. Never! You hear? You conniving harlot."

He didn't know how he'd wounded her. That was what she told herself. He just didn't know. He never would have called her such names if he'd known what it would do to her heart. But she understood. She deserved it. She couldn't blame him for his anger, so she tried harder to explain. "Wait, Kane! She told me where the gold is. You see?" She unfolded the carefully drawn map in her skirt pocket. "Look. It's the gold! Francesca wants it returned to its rightful owner. So you see? She's not so bad as you think. She—"

He yanked the map from her hand and kept on walking. Bianca was left weeping at his turned back. She loved him. *Dio,* how she loved him. Of course he was angry. But he would come to understand, wouldn't he? She watched him light a cheroot, as though he were going to blow her memory out with the smoke. Surely, he would calm down and they could talk. They could at least talk.

But it wasn't to be. When she tried to find him at his hotel that afternoon, she was informed that he had left. That he had said he would never be back to Galveston. Where did he go? The clerk didn't know. Had he left anything behind? Any message? No.

She gazed out the window at the sands where they had made love. It was over. Her heart pulsed with aching. She remembered him touching her hair, loving her. He was gone. Like the love in his heart. Gone like her sister. Bianca had no one left. It was over.

"Buongiorno! Hailey, it's so good to see you!" She had no idea how good. Just when Bianca had been hiding in her family's cabin, listening to the silence all around her in the dark, wondering how big a role silence would play in the rest of her life, she'd been interrupted by footsteps on deck and then Hailey's gentle calls. It was exactly what she needed right now! To be reminded she wasn't alone.

"Well, it's good to see you, too, Francesca." Hailey was taken aback by the enthusiasm of this welcome.

"I'm not Francesca."

"You're what?" She peered more closely, then slapped both hands over her mouth. "Bianca! Bianca, is it really you?!" She threw her arms around her old friend, squeezing and gasping, nearly bursting into tears. "How was your holiday? Was it as heavenly as Francesca said? I had no idea you were in such need of rest!"

Bianca squinted curiously over her friend's shoulder. "My holiday?"

"Yes! How was it?"

"Uhh . . . very relaxing."

"That's odd," said Hailey, rubbing her tense shoulders. "You don't seem very relaxed."

"Come," said Bianca, breaking into a warm smile, "we have a *lot* of catching up to do. *Per favore,* come downstairs."

Hailey was anxious to follow. She was so delighted to see her friend! And yet, she was surprised when she reached the bottom of the steps. "Where is Francesca? Isn't she here, too?"

"Gone to Europe," said Bianca, lifting up a pot of coffee. "Would you like some?"

"Thank you," she said, taking a seat at the kitchen table, "but I can't believe she left so soon, and without saying good-bye," she added as her tin cup was filled and the aroma rose to her nostrils.

"Well, she was . . . in a hurry. But she told me to say good-bye." It was a lie. But in Bianca's heart she knew that if Francesca had thought of it, she would have made that request. She just had a way of failing to think of things. In her heart, she had meant to say good-bye.

"Well—oh! How strong did you make this coffee?"

Bianca giggled and flushed. "I'm sorry!" she said, whisking away the cup, "Let me make another pot. I wasn't thinking—wasn't expecting guests. I'm afraid I've gotten accustomed to having it rather strong."

"On your holiday?"

"Uh . . . yes. On my holiday. Hailey, we really need to talk. About my holiday—"

"Wait! Before you go on, I must tell you something."

She looked so anxious, Bianca felt obliged to be interrupted. "Yes?"

"I'm getting married!"

"What?" Bianca plunked herself down in her seat. "To Raimondo! Tell me it's to Raimondo!"

"Yes!" cried Hailey in surprise. "How did you know?"

"Oh," said Bianca with a twinkle in her golden eye, "I just had a suspicion. Ever since you two first met. But Hailey, that is so exciting! I'm so happy for you both!"

"So am I!" she laughed. But after a moment of sharing a grin, her cheekbones fell just a bit, along with her chin.

Bianca peered cautiously. "What is the matter?"

"Well, it's just . . ." She couldn't bring herself to look up. "It's just that his parents . . . They wanted him to marry someone else. They—they won't speak to us."

"Oh." Bianca could remember well the stern brows and booming voice of her godfather anytime his temper was riled. She imagined there had been quite a scene when he was told. "Well, I'm sure they'll come around, Hailey. The Casales's tempers are fierce, but their tantrums don't last. One minute it seems the brothers are going to kill each other, and the next they're all friends again. It's just the way they are. I'm sure his parents will calm down, and when they do, everything will be back to normal."

"I hope you're right," said Hailey. *God, how she hoped.*

Bianca hoped, too. She was not nearly as sure of her words as she let on. In fact, though all she'd said was true about the Casale temper, it was also true that refusing to marry the woman of his parents' choice was by far the most serious breach of tradition any Casale man had dared. She wasn't at all sure that Hailey and her new love would find peace along their chosen road. But she prayed that they would.

Quietly Hailey wrung her hands in thought. She tried

to believe Bianca and said a silent prayer for Raimondo's sake that his parents really would change their minds someday. But then a thought occurred to her: she had interrupted Bianca. Bianca had tried to tell her about her holiday. How selfish! "Oh, I'm so sorry," she pleaded. "I got so caught up in my own problems, I nearly forgot. Please. Tell me all about your trip. Where did you go?"

Bianca considered lying. It would have been so much easier than telling the truth. But she just couldn't do it. Lies had caused nothing but havoc in her life thus far. Lies had cost her the man of her dreams. She was finished with lying. "I wasn't on holiday. I was under arrest."

"What?!"

Bianca spun forth her tale in all its gruesomeness and splendor. As the lanterns dimmed and the waves grew louder in the darkness beyond the cabin, she told her about Francesca and her true troubles. She told her about the switch, about the plan. And about Francesca's betrayal. A tear caught in each eye as she recounted her memories of the Ranger who had loved her and had seen her safely back to Galveston. She told Francesca's side of the story: how she'd helped her sister escape, and the price she'd paid for her love. Hailey was wide-eyed throughout most of the story. Her own troubles seemed a little petty all of a sudden. In fact, if the story had been spun by anyone but Bianca, she might have suspected a lie. It was just too dramatic! But Bianca was in earnest, she could see that. And her story was true.

"And now he hates me." Bianca wept into her skirt, soaking it on both sides. She let it all go: her love, her sorrow, her bitter decision. "The one man who ever loved me," she sobbed, "now hates me such as none ever has before."

"Bianca, no! No." Hailey rose from her seat and knelt

by her friend's kid boots. "If he really loves you, Bianca, he will forgive. He will come back."

"You don't know him," she sobbed. Hailey had never seen Bianca in such a state of suffering, and realized just how much she must truly love this man. "He will never come back," Bianca assured her. "If you knew him, you would understand. His heart is like a trapdoor. It's open or it's shut. But never in between. He's strong, and he feels betrayed. And he's right! I did betray him. He has every right to scorn me. Oh, Hailey, I just knew by the look in his eyes when he walked away. There was no more love there. To him, I had become just like Francesca. I was nobody to him now. I was just another liar." She leaned down and sobbed into Hailey's shoulder. "He'll never come back."

Footsteps sounded on the deck.

Bianca sat bolt upright, furiously fixing her hair. "I must look awful," she said, wiping off the tears, which had stopped flooding in her surprise.

Hailey patted her knee and said, "Don't worry. You look fine. You don't have to pretend everything is all right, you have reason to cry. I cry for you, too."

"Francesca? Are you here?"

Bianca smiled. "Raimondo? Is that you?" It had sounded like him.

"Yes, Francesca. May I come down?"

"You see?" asked Hailey, "It's only Raimondo. You don't have to hide your feelings."

"Oh, no, Hailey." She winked fondly. "I will not ruin our evening by sulking. Come down, Raimondo! *Per favore;* I'll cook some dinner! Can you stay for dinner?" she asked Hailey.

"Your cooking? How can I refuse!" She licked her lips in anticipation.

"Bianca? Is that you?" cried Raimondo, immediately recognizing her more slender face, not to mention the fact that she'd offered to cook. "How are you? Where have you been?"

Bianca and Hailey exchanged looks.

"It's a bit of a long story," said Hailey with a twinkle and a grin, "You'd better sit down, my love."

TWENTY

Two weeks had passed, and the pain had not subsided. Every night, Bianca slept with the little horse he'd carved for her, clutched in her palm. She wondered whether he now regretted the gift. It hurt to know that he probably did. That he probably winced every time he thought of it. Helping Francesca had felt so noble and so right at the time. Then why did she feel so worthless? Hailey and Raimondo were keeping her good company. Raimondo was staying in her shrimping boat, since he could no longer go home. He hadn't wanted to, but she made sure he didn't see it as charity. She made sure he knew how much she needed not to be alone at a time like this. And after hearing her tragic tale, he came to believe her. And he never let her spend any time feeling abandoned. He stayed up until she was tired. He rose before she did. He made sure she never sat in the dark, alone and frightened.

She spent her days wandering at first. She didn't have anywhere special to go, but she wanted to enjoy the sights and sounds of the island. She wanted to watch the children play and collect seashells because they were there. She collected them like memories, to keep her warm and sane in the cold, lonely life ahead. But one day, she remembered an old dream about a restaurant. It had been weeks since she'd thought about that. And as long as she was out wandering all day long, she imagined she could be on the hunt for a vacant building. Something small that she could afford. It would have to be very small, indeed. The first two days of searching turned up nothing. The business district seemed full. She'd only found one place for sale. It was a beautiful space with tall ceilings and plenty of windows, tucked inside a Victorian building between two banks. The moment she saw it, she imagined it buzzing with customers, and knew it was exactly the building of her dreams. A pricey dream, and one she wasn't sure she could afford.

"I know a way you can buy it," said Raimondo, sipping a hot cup of coffee in the dawn's early light.

Bianca was scurrying around the cabin, getting ready to head out for another day of searching for a less expensive place. "How is that?"

"You can let me buy your shrimp boat."

Bianca looked up at his tanned, youthful face, adorned with black curls falling over his brow.

He put down his coffee mug. "Let me buy it," he prodded. "I need a shrimp boat. You need money. With this sturdy vessel in mind, I know the bank will give me a loan. Why don't you let me buy it?"

Sell her home? Though selling the boat had been her plan all along, Bianca suddenly found herself hesitant to let go of everything she'd ever known. "But where will I live?"

"You're family, Bianca. You can live here with us. . . ."

"No! No, I will not be the spinster intruding on a happy married couple. I will not."

"Well, then, just until the restaurant pulls in enough money for you to buy something else. Until then, you stay with us."

He said it as though he were the one begging a favor, but Bianca knew better. He was trying to help her. He could have bought any shrimping vessel he wished. And the other ones did not come with an old maid on board. "I don't want you to sacrifice."

"Is having a friend nearby a sacrifice? No. It's what we both want. I discussed it with Hailey. And besides."

His wink held friendly mischief. "When you're rich from the restaurant, you'll be in our debt."

Bianca grinned brightly. "Oh, Raimondo! You are a true friend!" She wrapped him up in her arms and breathed out a sigh of relief, breathing it back in with a tingle of excitement. She was going to pursue her dream! "How can I ever thank you?"

He said she didn't have to, but she had a better idea. There was something she could do for him, or at least try. So she left him with the scrumptious hot breakfast he deserved and trotted off to the only people she knew who could put smiles on her best friends' faces: the Casales.

"Bianca!" Rosa's plump cheeks rose in adulation. "What brings you by this morning?"

"I just wanted to see my favorite godparents!" she beamed, struggling to breathe through Rosa's strong hug.

"And we are always glad to see you. You have not been around often enough since your return. And you still have said nothing about your holiday. Where did you go?"

"I'll tell you all about it another time," said Bianca, though she imagined she never would. "Where is Papa Casale?"

Rosa shot her a friendly look of faux frustration as she led them down the stairs. "Oh, he and the boys are out. I'm left here to do all the baking and cleaning as usual. Come down into the cabin; sit down; have something to eat."

"Oh, no, really I mustn't. I only wanted to chat."

Something sounded serious about the way she said that. Serious enough to cost Rosa her smile. "Well, have a seat, then. Have a seat." She offered the most comfortable chair she had. She wished she had even better for her goddaughter.

As soon as Rosa had plunked herself down with a cool cup of tea in hand, Bianca blurted out her mission. "Rosa, I wanted you to know that Raimondo is staying on my boat."

Rosa scowled at the mention of her son's name. She turned her cheek and pursed her lips with the stubbornness she was famous for. "Then I hope you will talk some sense into him, no?"

Bianca shook her head back and forth until Rosa spared a glance at her from the corner of her eye. "I think his decision is final, Rosa. I *know* his decision is final. There is nothing any of us can do."

She ground her teeth a bit before tossing up her hands melodramatically. "Well, then, he is not my son. That's all."

Bianca nearly chuckled but caught herself. There was absolutely no sincerity in Rosa's feisty proclamation. Her insight was only confirmed when Rosa clumsily added, "He is all right, though, no?"

"Yes," Bianca kindly assured her, "He is doing just fine."

Rosa tossed her head. "Well. That is good for him, I suppose. It doesn't concern me. As I say, he is no longer my son."

Bianca sighed warmly. She had always loved Rosa, the tight and proper way she tied her black hair in a bun, as though she didn't care how it looked, just so long as it was fit for work. She loved her ample figure and her round cheeks, evidence that she enjoyed her own cooking as much as the men of the house did. She loved that she was a short person who walked as though she were tall. And most of all, she loved the caring in her dark eyes, which she frequently hid so well behind a false air of traditional stubborn drama. "Rosa," she said, leaning forward in her seat, "I know you better than this. I have been your goddaughter for a long time. I know you love your boys."

"Two of them, yes. Just two."

Bianca laughed. "Oh, Rosa, there is no one else like you in this world. I adore you."

That sentiment was enough to put a smile in Rosa's black eyes. She loved Bianca, too. There was no secret in that. She had nothing against the sister. A little wild, that one. But she had her merits. Bianca had always been her favorite, though. Soft-eyed and sincere, Bianca also had a deep, inner strength. Not the brazen, hardheaded kind that her sister had. But the gentler strength of someone more rooted. Rosa admired that in a woman. She herself lived a life of solitude among men. She hadn't planned it that way. She'd always pictured a daughter. But God hadn't pictured it the same way, and somehow, she'd wound up in a house with a husband and three sons. She had learned how to stand up for herself. There was no other way when surrounded by men day in and day out. She'd had to learn how to make herself heard. So Bianca's deep strength resonated with her, and her love for the girl was well known. "I am furious with him," she spat. It was a gift, that moment of honesty, and Bianca knew it. It was the older woman's way of saying she was ready to talk.

"I know you are," said Bianca, "and I understand. But what good is it to punish him?"

"Bah! He deserves to be punished! My marriage was arranged, and my mother's, and her mother's. None of us complained. Well . . ." She tilted her head with a twinge of humility and humor. "Maybe we complained. But not out loud to our parents!"

Bianca joined her in a brief laugh. But then she reminded her, "I didn't ask whether Raimondo deserved to be punished. I asked what good it does." Rosa looked momentarily speechless.

But Bianca knew it wouldn't last, so she took advantage of her moment of silence and added, "Which would you rather? Know that you had soundly punished him, given him what he deserved, and never see him again? Or have your family together? Know that Raimondo is safe and sound, have him be a part of your life as you age?"

"What makes you think I am aging?" she asked curtly.

Bianca grinned. "All right, Rosa. You are quite right.

But then, in your eternal youth"—she winked—
"wouldn't you rather spend it with Raimondo in your
life?"

Again Rosa said nothing.

So Bianca went on. "You will like Hailey," she ven-
tured. Rosa flicked her wrist dismissively. "No, you
will!" Bianca promised. "She is gentle and kind and sincere. And I know that the only thing that could make her
happier than being Raimondo's wife is having the blessing of his mamma."

Rosa scowled at being patronized.

"It is true! You should see how she suffers, worried
that she has robbed Raimondo of his parents' love. It is
killing her."

Rosa peered suspiciously. "Is that the truth?"

"Yes, Rosa! If you knew her, you would know it is.
She cares about nothing but your son and his happiness.
She doesn't want him to lose you."

Rosa bowed her head. She was considering.

Bianca had one last sentiment to toss her before she
rose. "Rosa, I promise you that Raimondo is getting married to Hailey whether you like it or not. No amount of
punishment will change that. He is a determined man. I
think you know your son."

A tiny smile peeked out behind her sternness.

"That part, you cannot change," said Bianca, "but the
rest is up to you. Whether you shun him, whether you
lose him, whether he lives in poverty, that is up to you.
I ask that you consider whether it wouldn't be worthwhile
for his sake, for Hailey's sake, and for your whole family's sake that you forgive him and stop this pointless
punishment." She got up to leave, prepared to let Rosa
think about it without committing. But she was stopped
by the stubborn old woman's voice.

"Bianca."

Bianca turned around attentively.

She was surprised when Rosa offered her a determined
nod. And even more surprised at her firmly spoken

words. Rosa lifted up her proud, full chin and announced, "I will talk to Vito."

Their smiles joined across the room.

Three weeks, four days, six hours, and about twelve and a half minutes since Bianca's betrayal, Kane had nearly forgotten all about it. He never thought anymore about her ivory skin, touched by moonlight, dripping with sea water, and succumbing to his every touch. He never looked back on the way she'd looked that night in *his* dress of sapphire blue, laughing with her eyes, speaking warmly with words of compassion and good humor. He could barely remember her amber eyes, laced in chocolate brown, framed by sooty lashes, and the way they widened every time he kissed her. He couldn't recall her sultry voice or that adorable accent that lent character to every word she spoke. No, he was good and over that lying she-devil. The name Bianca didn't even make him wince. It just made him squint his eyes in wonder. Who was that?

All right, maybe he was kidding himself. Maybe he thought of her sometimes. But he didn't like to. Her betrayal had been the last straw. He could never love a woman again the way he'd loved her. He could never again bring himself to care. Not after the way she'd betrayed him. And he'd trusted her—that was the worst part. He'd really thought she was special; he'd really believed her when she lied. He'd been blinded by love, and he knew it. Hell, Bianca wasn't even a good liar. Any fool could have told she was fibbing by the way she didn't meet his eyes. But not this fool. He'd been so blind, he believed he must be the biggest fool this side of the Colorado. And him being a Ranger, too! He should never have let down his guard. He should have been smarter. He'd been taken by a Rossetti woman—again.

That was it. No more women. Ever since he'd been home, he'd been steadily at work. He and Caleb wrapped up the investigation on the Somerville bank and cut their losses. Francesca's map had been true. It led Caleb to the gold, and he returned it to its rightful owner. Two suspects dead, two in jail, one gone forever. Four out of five—not bad. It was time to move on, time to put this nightmare behind him. And looking at that pretty new face scrunched up in the afternoon sunlight that streamed through the window into the room seemed like a darn good start.

"Charlotte, that's the prettiest little girl I ever saw."

The new mother was beaming with pride, her face pink and moist as her new baby girl's. "Thank you, Kane."

The baby had come earlier than expected, scaring the whole family into a frenzy. They had all feared the worst, another miscarriage. Charlotte was so fragile, so wounded by her earlier misfortunes, they feared that losing another baby would be the end of her. But she seemed to know that, too. And she'd held on. Early or not, she was going to give birth to that baby, and the baby was going to live. She had been determined. And nobody had doubted that it was because of her surprising burst of stubbornness that Rachel Mebane Caldwell was born, a healthy and happy infant. "I only wish I'd been here to see you through it," said Kane. He gazed fondly at his bedridden sister, still too weak to go about her daily chores. But she looked beautiful, her caramel hair tossed over one shoulder in a braid, her face glowing with motherly joy.

"Well, I wish you had been, too," she said, kissing her baby's forehead, and making her smile, "but Marcus was wonderful. And so were Ma and Pa."

Kane nodded in gratitude. He wasn't surprised Marcus had been supportive. He was a good husband, and Kane loved him for it. But knowing how worried he'd been, he was a little surprised the fella hadn't passed out on the floor the moment his wife went into early labor. "Well, I'm gonna be around a lot more," he promised. "A whole lot more."

His father's voice called out behind him. "I'm glad to hear that."

Kane spun around. "Well, hello there, Pa. I didn't hear you come in."

"Wouldn't miss another chance to see my granddaughter." He hobbled in, almost completely recovered, suffering now more from age than from Francesca's bullet. Beth Fairchild, wiping her floured hands on her apron, followed closely behind. She visited her new granddaughter no less than sixteen times a day, by Kane's reckoning.

"Oh, there she is!" she beamed, tossing her arms out to the sides. "My little girl and her little girl! Oh, let me see you both again!"

Kane thought this would be a good time to take his leave. With a bright smile and a tip of his hat, he announced, "I'm gonna go see if Marcus needs some help in the stable." *Someone has to work while everyone else is cooing over the baby.* But he was so happy for all of them, he didn't care how long this went on. It was so heartwarming to see them all so happy. And his own welcome home had been just as touching. He really did feel at peace now that the whole ordeal was over. No more chasing, no more fury. Just home on the ranch. Not a bad life for a man. If only he had someone to share it with.

His father caught him by the elbow on his way out the door. "Son . . ." He nodded in that way of his, that way that said if he were a man of more words, he'd go on forever. But as it was, all he said was, "I'm real glad you decided to stay."

Kane nodded in earnest. "So am I, Pa. So am I."

With that, he left them all to their cooing and headed on over to the stables. Marcus was always such a hard worker. If Kane had had a new little girl like that, it would have been months before he was pulling a regular day of chores again. He didn't know how Marcus could pull himself away. But he understood it. He wanted to make sure everything was taken care of; he wanted to make sure his wife and his new baby didn't have anything to worry about. It's the kind of man he was, and the reason Kane was so glad to have him for a brother-in-law. When he found him in his denims, bending over a horseshoe, and hammering away with his short black hair flopping with every swing, he couldn't help but smile. "Need some help?"

Marcus wiped the sweat from his forehead. "Wouldn't refuse it, that's for sure."

Kane looked around for a hammer. "I know I've said it before, but that sure is a pretty little girl you got."

"Thanks." Marcus beamed so proudly every time someone said that, it didn't look as if he could ever hear it often enough. "Hope you won't think it's just fatherly prejudice if I say she's the prettiest little girl in Texas."

Kane laughed loudly. "I wouldn't deny it. No, I wouldn't." Marcus eyed him closely as he settled himself onto a stool.

"You lookin' at something?"

"No," said Marcus, ready to get back to work. But something stopped him and made him change his mind. "Actually, yeah. You know, I keep thinking about that story you told at the table when you first came home. Is all that really true?"

Kane looked at him as though he'd gone mad. "You think I'd make that up?"

"Naw. Naw, of course not. It's just really somethin'. So that little girl who stayed out here . . . She never shot your Pa? She wasn't no bank robber or nothing?"

"That's right." He tried to look busy as he shuffled through a pile of unfinished horseshoes.

"Damn, if I'd known that, I wouldn't've been so unfriendly."

"Neither of us would. Pass me a swig of that water, would you?"

"I just don't understand," he said, handing over the canteen, "So that Francesca Rossetti—you never did catch up to her?"

"That's right." He tried to be very engaged in the swigging.

"She just sailed away before you could get to Galveston?"

Kane put down the canteen as if it pained him. "Something like that." He closed his eyes for a moment.

Marcus scratched at his square jaw. "What is it you left out? I know there's something."

He wouldn't have told anyone else. But Marcus . . . Marcus was the kind of man who made him want to spill everything. He was a man's man, a real cowboy. And he was just gentle enough to understand. "Bianca helped her sister get away." He said it to a bed of straw, not to Marcus.

To his surprise, Marcus only shrugged. "Well, I s'pose that makes sense. They're sisters, after all."

Kane narrowed his eyes, capturing his brother-in-law in a merciless gaze. "She tricked me to do it. I . . . I'd gotten soft for her."

"Well, yeah," he chuckled, "I kinda assumed so. She was a real nice-looking lady. I figured after you found out she wasn't Francesca, and the two of you were still on the trail, well . . . I didn't figure I even had to ask."

"Maybe you didn't hear the first part. I said she tricked me."

Marcus only shrugged. "I guess she had to if she was gonna help her sister."

"I trusted her!" Kane threw down his hammer and rose to his feet. His face had grown hot; his hands had closed into fists. "I trusted her, damn it! I . . . I loved her."

Marcus wasn't even slightly intimidated. He didn't get up from his stool and he didn't avert his eyes. He just said, "You trusted her to do what?"

"To—to—"

"To let her sister hang? That's a funny thing to trust someone about."

Kane sneered. "I mean that I trusted her to love me, like she said she did!"

"Oh." Marcus's gaze flitted about the barn. "So she stopped loving you?"

Kane bit back his reply. That wasn't what he'd meant. Not exactly.

"Oh, I see," said Marcus, "She didn't stop loving you. You just walked out on her because she wouldn't turn her sister over to you. I see. *You* stopped loving *her.*"

Kane didn't like the taunting in his tone. "What are you trying to say?" He never thought he'd sneer at his brother-in-law the way he had just then, but he couldn't help it. This was a very tender topic, and he didn't much appreciate being mocked.

Marcus answered sharply. "I'm saying she did exactly what you would've done. You telling me you'd have turned me over to the law? You telling me you'd let Charlotte go on trial for a bank robbery she got threatened into? Hell no. You'd fight like hell."

Kane couldn't believe it, but he actually cracked a smile.

"Yeah, you know it, Ranger," Marcus winked. "She didn't do anything you wouldn't have done. If you're mad, it's 'cause she's too much like your own damned self."

Kane sat down in the sweet-smelling hay, his arms propped up on his knees. "You know what? You're damned right."

"I know I am. And you know what else?"

"What?"

"Last time you were here, you said you would never come back to this ranch. You planned to spend the rest of your life running no place, leaving all your family behind. And now look at you. Ready to settle right in. I think something's changed in you."

Kane had never thought about it before, but Marcus was right. The old white clapboard house was no longer haunted by the ghost of Natalie. Its halls didn't echo with longing. The smell of pine wafting through his room every morning no longer made him want to cry, wishing she were there to smell it, too. Bianca had helped him move on. She'd made him believe that he had his whole life ahead of him still, and that there was still joy to be found. "What the hell am I doing here?" he asked Marcus. "I left Bianca at the docks!"

TWENTY-ONE

Devon Carson figured he'd upheld his end of the bargain. Not everything had gone the way it was planned, that was for sure. But he had delivered the letter, even if he'd done it a little early. And he had seen Bianca safely to Somerville, even if he had a little help from the Ranger, and even if she'd headed on out to Galveston the very next day. That was good enough, he figured, for a deal with the likes of Francesca Rossetti. He could sleep at night knowing he'd at least followed the letter of their agreement, if not the spirit. Especially since this little adventure had cost him a hit in the chest that still smarted.

He didn't have anywhere special to go, now that he'd been let out of the doc's care. In the old days, he would have gone out in search of some more trouble, first chance he got. But every time he thought about gambling again, he thought about the debts he owed, and the men who wanted to thrash him, and the jail cell he'd gotten to know just a little too well. It didn't sound like so much fun anymore. Maybe he was getting old. Maybe that last little job and the bullet he took had gotten him thinking. He really was going to die someday. Maybe running away from everybody and everything wasn't how he wanted to spend the days he still had left.

For some reason, his horse headed east, and while he tried to figure out where he was being taken, he saw the sun, round and small like a Brazilian orange, falling behind a little white farm house on a pretty little plot of flat acreage. It was pretty—really pretty. And so was the woman who lived there, if he remembered right. He knew he didn't want her; he knew he couldn't do anything to endanger the freedom that had brought him this much happiness so far. . . . Hmmm. But he just wanted to say hello. Since he was there anyway. Since his horse had made him come.

She skipped out of the front door, a delicate hand over her brow to block the sunlight. She had beautiful red hair tied in a short braid. It was orange like the setting sun, and it was that frizzy texture that women hated to have but Devon really preferred. Her eyes were green ovals, and she was speckled with pale freckles all the way to her eyelids. She was a petite little gal, the kind he could toss over his shoulder and never feel the weight. "Why, Mr. Carson!" She looked so happy to see him, he wasn't sure whether anyone had ever looked that pleased to see him in all his life. It felt kind of good.

"Howdy, ma'am." He tipped his hat and dismounted the horse she'd given him a while back. "Hope you don't mind; I came on back just to thank you again for this fine animal here. Served me well." He was glad he'd thought of that. Though where in his mind it had come from, he sure didn't know. The only thing he was aware of thinking was what a pretty gal she was, and how much he hoped she'd invite him inside.

"Well, I'm very glad to hear that," she called out. *And he looks mighty handsome riding it.* She couldn't help adding that to her thoughts. Ever since she'd first laid eyes on the handsome cowboy, with his deep-brown tan, that fit, lean body of his, and the black hair that fell to his shoulders, she'd hoped to see him again. There weren't a lot of handsome men who came riding out to see her, not knowing she had three young'uns hanging from her skirt. Sometimes she felt like a leper.

"Something sure smells good." He held his hat over his heart as though he were singing to her.

Mrs. Sampson grinned. "That's fried chicken. The

children and I are just about to have supper. Would you care to join us?"

Oh, that's right—young'uns. That was another reason he shouldn't have come by. Visiting a widow with three mouths to feed was just like asking to be roped into sticking around, helping out, settling down. No man in his right mind would come by and give her the chance to start hinting, pressuring, sobbing about her hard luck. But that chicken sure smelled good. "That's kind of you, Mrs. Sampson. Don't mind if I do." He wondered whether he ought to be calling her "Mrs.," her being a widow and all.

She answered that question by saying, "Call me Marion."

Marion. He could have guessed that was her name. He wasn't sure how, but somehow he already knew it. She just looked like a Marion.

It turned out she had two little girls and one little boy. The girls were the spitting image of their mother. Red-haired and freckled, they were about as pretty a pair as Devon had ever seen. Their dresses were just a little too big, so they kept tripping on their hems in a way he thought was kind of adorable. He didn't have to ask why their clothes didn't fit. He could see Marion didn't have much money, judging by the sparse furnishings and the way some of the kitchen walls were starting to rot and hadn't been replaced. The farm looked to be in pretty good shape. She must have been good at hiring hands and keeping an eye on them. But there was more that needed doing, and he reckoned there was a limit to how much she could do by herself, with three kids to tend on top of everything else. She probably made their clothes big so they'd wear them a long time before she had to buy more cloth.

"What's your name?" he heard himself ask. The kitchen was in bad shape, but it was friendly and full of light from the red Texas sunset, and supper smelled welcoming.

The little girl turned away, a finger stuffed in her mouth.

"Nichole's shy," her sister explained boldly. "She doesn't know how to talk to strangers."

He could see the other little girl didn't share her phobias. "Is that right? Well, then, what's your name?"

"Lindsay."

Lindsay was going to be a heartbreaker when she grew up; there was no doubt about that. Just as pretty as her ma, and as outgoing as a little actress; he couldn't help thinking it was a shame there wouldn't be a man around to chase off the boys who'd be coming around, up to no good. He wondered whether Nichole might not have been more sure of herself if she'd had a prettier dress to wear. He'd sure like to buy her one, he thought, patting his pocket. But he quickly shunned the thought. He couldn't spend his money on little kids who weren't even his own. His money was his. There were bottles of whiskey out there with his name on them.

For the first time, he noticed the little boy, standing in the corner, his arms crossed as though he was watching over the family. He couldn't have been older than ten, but Devon reckoned that was the same age he was when he'd started getting that look in his eye. The look that said, *Don't mess with me. I might look little, but I don't feel little.* "How about you? Who might you be?"

"None of your business," he answered. He was the only child who didn't look like his ma. Looking at him, Devon could make a pretty good guess as to what their pa had looked like. Straight chestnut hair and very pale skin. Judging from that hard look in his eye, Devon was pretty sure Marion would have her hands full some day. When that boy was old enough to ride and shoot, he didn't see how she'd be able to control him, all alone as she was. He found himself wishing there were somebody who could help. Not him, of course . . . but somebody.

Marion spread a cloth of piping-hot buttermilk biscuits before her guest and children. The steam warmed Devon's

face, and the sweet-and-sour scent made his mouth water.
"This looks mighty fine, ma'am." Juice was trickling between the wrinkles in the fried chicken's batter. He
couldn't remember the last time he'd had a meal this
good.

"Oh, I hope it came out all right. And I do apologize
for the commotion. Is your home as unruly as this one,
Mr. Carson?" Marion's gaze was both friendly and apolo-
getic as she finally got the children to settle down in their
seats and was able to take her own.

Devon glanced around at the children, who seemed
pretty well behaved to him. She must have had high stan-
dards to call them unruly. But that didn't surprise him,
he supposed. If she was planning to raise them to be as
mannerly and pleasant as she was, she'd have to be strict.
He liked that about her. "Don't reckon I have a home,"
he said in answer to her question.

"Oh, I see." She lowered her gaze to her fork, making
him wonder whether she took pity on him. "I'm sorry."

Something about that bothered him. He just couldn't
have her feeling sorry. He was a rambler, happy to be on
the trail. Was she trying to find some fault in that?
"That's the way I like it," he added. "I'm not a man who
could be saddled with a house and farm."

"I see," she said with a smile that put him at ease. He
could see she hadn't meant any harm. He'd overreacted.
*Those pretty eyes are enough to put any man a little on
edge.*

"I'm sorry, ma'am. I didn't mean to snap. It's been a
while since I've had real company like this. I guess my
manners are a little out of practice."

"Oh, no! You didn't say anything wrong. Please, I'm
very interested in your life. Why don't you tell me? What
is it about traveling that you enjoy so much? I've often
wondered what it would be like, to be so free."

Well, that was easy to explain. Being out on the trail
was everything a man could want out of life. Out there,
he had . . . well, he had . . . He tried to remember. There

were the fast women, of course. They were fun. Except
when they took him for his cash and moved on to the
next man as if he hadn't been anything more to them than
a yawn and a sigh. He gazed longingly at Marion's gentle
face and attentive smile. There were the nights on the
bedroll, shifting on rocks and waking up with a sore neck.
He thought about the warm bed upstairs, and the way
Marion must look with the morning sun shining in her
fiery hair. There was the trail food. . . . He took another
bite of juicy chicken, savoring its spicy crust. There was
getting jailed and shot, and—what in hell was he thinking? "There's nothing I like about it," he said. Marion
raised her eyebrows in surprise. Devon was so surprised
to hear it come out of his own mouth, he couldn't think
what to do except to keep on going. "I mean, I used to.
When I was a kid, all I wanted was to be free. But that's
the thing about it, Miss Marion. After a while, I don't
think I *was* free anymore. I don't know when it happened,
but somewhere along the line, it was like I became a slave
to the trail, to being on the run, to living in a way I wasn't
enjoying anymore, 'cause my pride wouldn't let me settle
down." It was the most honest thing he'd ever said in his
life. He didn't know where the words had come from,
but they just kept coming. "Do you know? I was as
trapped as all those married men I laughed at. I just didn't
know it."

Somehow, he expected Marion to scold him for his
confessions, but she didn't. Her adorable smile was understanding, and it made her pretty freckles crinkle up in
the dim light. She poured him a glass of sweet lemonade,
sparkling with the red sun that made its way through the
kitchen windows, and said, "I understand just what you
mean. I made the same mistake once. I ran away from
home when I was a girl."

"Really?" Devon tried to absorb that. Cute little
Marion? A runaway?

"Oh yes!" she laughed prettily. "Ran away with my
husband, just to escape my stern parents. Before I knew

it I had three babies, a farm to run, and no husband to help me. Some break for freedom, eh?" Her laughter was so welcoming, he couldn't help but join in.

Before he knew it, they were chatting gaily, sharing heartbreaking stories with a sense of humor, holding each other's eyes captive, and finding comfort in each other's memories. Devon helped put the children to bed, finding that the girls fit snugly in his arms, as though they belonged there. In the pitch black of night, when the crickets chirped through the windows and they were alone at last, Marion put a piece of steaming apple pie under his nose. "Darlin', you're gonna make me fat," he remarked cheerfully, but he didn't hesitate to taste it. It was tart, hot, and delicious.

"So tell me," she asked, thrusting a fist under her chin and leaning across the table with a gentle attentiveness he thought was so charming, "If you let yourself choose, if you let yourself be free, what would you do now? Where would you go?"

He stilled his fork and pondered. He knew the answer. At that moment, anyhow, he would choose that little redhead looking into his eyes as though he was somebody who mattered. He'd never felt so sure of anything before. But he wasn't ready to admit It. "I don't know, Marion. I don't quite know."

She took his hand under the cool moonlight that poured through the window and gave it a welcoming squeeze. "You know, it's never too late to be free."

His nod let her know he knew just what she meant. He returned her squeeze with his fingers' tender strokes and met her eyes frankly. She could tell he was ready to talk. He was ready to think about it. And soon, he might just be ready to settle down.

Bianca's shrimp boat was alive with festivity. "To the happy couple!" This had been shouted out so many times by friends, neighbors, and others who had stopped by for the party, whether or not they knew the honored guests, that Bianca didn't even lift her chin each time it was called anymore. She was too busy cooking. All of her guests would be potential customers once she purchased that lovely space in the business district, and she didn't want to take any chances. She wanted to make sure they remembered the food!

"To our hostess!" cried Raimondo, his arm snuggling Hailey to his side as it had done all night. "When Bianca Rossetti opens her restaurant, we will all be too spoiled to cook!"

Many toasted to that, for they had never had such excellent Italian fare. Bianca beamed with pride, then remembered the cannelloni, and raced down to the cabin to fetch it. Hailey smiled as she watched her friend rush away. She was already thinking like a businesswoman. This wasn't a party to her; it was a promotional opportunity. Hailey shared a laugh with her husband-to-be. As long as her lovely face was so near, he stole a kiss. They just couldn't stop looking into each other's eyes. They couldn't believe it was happening. They were really getting married come Sunday. They could kiss openly with everyone's blessings—even those of his parents. It was Hailey's dream come true. Since the first day she'd met him, she'd imagined herself gazing into his eyes, surrounded by friends, planning their wedding. But it was the first time any dream of hers had actually come true.

Stefano could say the same. After being alone on the streets, a nuisance to strangers and unwanted by his own grandfather, he had finally made a friend. Raimondo was just the sort of man he wanted to grow up to be. He was funny and smart and he spoke to him man to man, not as if he were some kind of little kid. Hailey was a nice lady, too. They'd told him moving in with them didn't have to mean they were his parents. Not if he didn't want them to be. But perhaps, they'd suggested, perhaps he might just live with them for a while and see what it was like. He liked that very much. Especially since it meant

he got to eat every day for a change. Raimondo said he
was a big help because he would help protect Hailey
whenever Raimondo wasn't around. He said he'd teach
him how to shrimp, and that one day, when he grew up,
he'd give him his own boat. Just like Raimondo's own
father had decided to pay for Bianca's. . . .

Rosa Casale kissed her husband on his well-fed cheek.
"Are you enjoying the party?" she asked as the two of
them gazed at their handsome son, so happy beside his
chosen bride.

"Yes, it's a fine party," he grumbled, "I just . . ."

"Now, now. Stop pouting. It doesn't do any good, you
know."

"I know," he sighed.

"And Hailey is a nice young lady. You said so yourself."

"Yes, but that was before she made my son become
disobedient."

"She didn't make him do anything, Vito. No one can
make your son do anything he doesn't want. Isn't that
the lesson you learned?" She kissed him again. "He's
just as stubborn as his papa."

Vito squeezed her to his side. "You're right, Rosa."

"I am always right. How long have we been married
and how often have I been right? One out of two? Two
out of three? No. Every time, that's how many. Every
time."

"Yes, Rosa," he beamed.

"At least they are happy," she said to the wind. A
breeze caught her raven hair, pulling a strand free from
her tight bun. "Besides, Vito, what kind of a bride was
that you chose?"

"I chose?" he asked indignantly, "What do you mean
I? We chose her together."

"I don't remember it that way, Vito. I think she was
all your idea. You were the one who . . ."

"Oh, never mind. Just promise me you won't ever tell
Raimondo what became of her."

"Oh." She crossed herself. "Never. I swear."

Adrianna had arrived at the docks a week ago. Mamma and Papa Casale had met her there, both of them wishing desperately they could be somewhere else. They didn't want to tell her that their son was a failure. They didn't want her parents to learn they'd lost control of him. It was shameful. It was the end of their reputation. But they could hardly leave the girl stranded, having journeyed all the way from Italy. It was hard to say whether they were more perturbed or relieved when she waltzed off the boat with a handsome stranger on her arm. "Are you signore and signora Casale?" she had asked.

"Why, yes. And this is . . . ?" They had both looked very warily at her handsome companion.

"This," she'd said, tossing her head, "is the man I intend to marry. You and my parents certainly have a lot of gumption thinking you can choose a husband for me. But I think you're all pathetic. My parents wouldn't let us marry, and that's why we've come all the way here. To get away from them, to inform you that you'll have to find your son another bride, and to build a life for ourselves—far away from you all! Come now, Guido. According to my schedule, the train to New York leaves not too far from here. Signore Casale, can you tell us which way to Houston?"

Rosa broke away from her thoughts. "I'm very sure, Vito. You're the one who picked her."

"Eh, it's too bad," he said, chewing his lip. "They would have been a nice couple, eh? Both of them too disobedient for anyone else."

Rosa pinched him for his joke. They laughed and hugged and watched their three boys with pride. "Vito?" she asked, gazing into the face that was as familiar as her own after all these years, "Do you ever regret that our parents had us marry?"

"Of course not," he said gruffly. "How can you ask such a thing? You are a good wife. You have given me three good sons. Well, two good sons. Two and a half."

She smiled. He caught her eye, and again they laughed. "We have the same sense of humor," she observed.

"Yes," he agreed, "I don't see how we could have survived all the years, all the struggles, without it."

"Our marriage is a strong one," she agreed, "but maybe we were lucky. Maybe our parents' way, *our* way was not the best." She gazed curiously at her son in all his delight and loving glory, his arm wrapped so proudly around his blue-eyed lady. "We were never so excited as that."

"We were too scared to be excited," he reminded her. "Especially you. A wedding night is always scary for a bride. More so when she's barely met the groom."

"But it's more than that," she said, resting her head on his shoulder. "Look at him. Look at her. There's something they want that we never even thought of wanting. Do you see it?"

"Yes, I see it," he grumbled.

"What is it? What is it that makes them do this? Abandon all of our old ways like this?"

"Ignorance," he said, "They are being foolish."

"Maybe. Maybe you are right, Vito."

"Many young people are doing this," he reminded her. "Forgetting they are Italian, leaving our heritage by the wayside. Just for a bit of fun that won't last. Marriages aren't held together by the magic of true love. They're held together by commitment, by holding values. These young people won't remember that. They marry for the wrong reasons. I worry for my son's future. And for the future of his sons."

"You could be wrong, Vito." She patted his ample belly. "You usually are, after all."

He chuckled gaily at the wife he'd come to love so well. Every year, she brought him new surprises and new joy. He prayed that Raimondo would find the same thing with his own chosen bride. *"Chi lascia la via vecchia per la nuova, sa quel che perde e non sa qual che trova,"*

*he said. Whoever forsakes the old way for the new knows
what he is losing, but not what he will find.*

Bianca found the quiet of the cabin below to be a little
more comforting than she'd expected. She had come
downstairs only to fetch dessert. But once she settled
down in her rustic kitchen chair, she found herself none
too eager to get up again. She needed to breathe. She
needed to be away from the crowd. She needed to take
a break from her duties as hostess and waitress. She
needed a strong cup of coffee, the kind she'd once enjoyed on the trail. She needed the darkness, the peace,
the gentle rocking under her feet. And as much as she
hated to admit it, she needed to get away from the celebration of lovers on their way to wed. It was breaking
her heart.

Oh, she was happy for Raimondo and Hailey. Of
course she was! How could she not be? They were her
dearest friends, and they were both such kind people.
They deserved this bliss, this time to celebrate their joining. Hailey had never had someone to take care of her
before, and Raimondo, she knew, would do a brilliant
job. In fact, Hailey had already quit her job as a maid at
the hotel. Raimondo had insisted on it. And now she was
back to what she truly enjoyed. Enjoying the waves, picking up seashells on the shore and painting them, selling
them with pride, and no longer because she so desperately
needed the funds. Hailey's life in her lover's arms was
brand new and wondrous. Even a little boy had been
saved in their joining. Of course Bianca was happy for
them.

She was only unhappy for herself. She missed Kane.
The little carved horse was always there to remind her,
of what she'd had, of what she'd lost, of what she'd chosen
to throw away. She could still remember his anger at the
docks. He hadn't looked like a lover scorned, but more
like a man with an enemy. Pure hate. That's all she'd seen

in his eyes. Maybe he just hadn't loved her as much as she'd thought. There had certainly been no traces of love in his cold blue eyes on that day. He had nearly struck her down. She'd sensed it. What kept him from it, what made him turn away, she didn't know. All she knew was that she would rather he hit her than turn around the way he had and leave her to this frightening solitude.

She missed him so badly, she bent her head, prepared to start weeping. She barely noticed the long shadow descending the stairs, then stretching across the brown wall. The outline of a Stetson spidered across the ceiling, but she didn't notice—not until she looked up with a sniff to see what had blocked out the light. He was standing in front of the lantern, the dim flame casting shadows on his stubbled jaw, his hat shadowing his stern eyes. She'd forgotten how tall he was. "Kane?"

He took a step forward. His black denims clung to his muscular thighs. His leather vest smelled like tobacco and gin. His spurs clanked as he approached. "What're you doing down here?" His voice was low and soft.

Bianca tried to straighten her posture. "Hoping you'd come?" It was the best answer she could think of. And the most accurate.

Kane stepped out of the lantern's path. She could see him more clearly now. She could see the anger drained from his handsome face. "Mind if I join you?"

"Of course not. Please sit down." It hadn't sunk in yet. She didn't believe he was standing there, and hadn't tried to comprehend why. All she knew was that she'd just drunk the last of the coffee and she'd better put some on. "Are you well?" she asked nervously, fumbling with her kettle. "Is your papa well? Charlotte?"

"They're all just fine," he told her, slouching down in a seat. He stretched his legs out in front of him and took off his hat. "Charlotte had a baby girl. Prettiest thing I ever saw. And my pa's walking around now."

"Oh, thank heaven!" She set the kettle to boil. "I'm so relieved, I can't tell you!"

"And you?" he asked softly. "You're all right?" *Don't tell me you've found another man. I wouldn't blame you, but that's the one thing I can't hear.*

"I'm fine! Yes, yes. I uh . . . I'm going to buy a restaurant."

He raised an interested eyebrow.

"Yes, I got the money by selling this boat. Raimondo's buying it, or, actually his papa now. I'll stay here with them while I save. Do you want anything to eat with this?"

She tried to put an empty coffee mug before him, but he stilled her hand. It gave her a thrilling shudder just to feel his fingertips wrapped around her wrist. And when she looked up, she found that the sincerity in his gaze, the intensity of his stare, gave her shivers. "Running out on you was the stupidest thing I ever did," he said in a husky voice.

Bianca dropped her eyes. "No. No, I understand. I betrayed you."

"I would've done the same thing," he said.

Bianca looked up in her disbelief.

"That's right." He smiled, lifting the corners of his dark, stubbled mouth. "I would've done the same damn thing."

Bianca threw herself into his arms. "Kane." He hugged her fiercely, but it wasn't enough. He had to stand up; he had to swing her around. He had to squeeze her till every inch of her body was warmed by every inch of his.

"I love you," he said. "I loved you from the first day I saw you. I loved you when I was dragging you 'round town in those damned handcuffs." She laughed into his shirt. "I loved the way you played that trick on me to save your sister. I loved everything about you, right from the start. And I still love you, Bianca."

"I love you, too," she whispered in his ear, heating it with her breath.

"Then come away with me," he said, putting her down,

letting her out of the hug so he could take her hand. "Open that restaurant in Flat Rock, Bianca. Be my wife."

She touched her flushing cheeks, and paused for just a moment. She was so overwhelmed. Leave everything behind? Raimondo? Hailey? Use the money to buy a restaurant in Flat Rock instead?

Worried about her hesitation, Kane got down on one knee. "I'm gonna tell you something," he said plainly, capturing her eyes to make sure he had her attention. "A long time ago, I was building something. Just for me and the missus. Natalie." Her nod was sympathetic. "It's just a little ranch, not far from my parents'. But I was building it for me and the woman I love. Well, I did love Natalie. There's no doubt." He bowed his head in reverence. "But now I know. My ability to love didn't die with her. I still have a heart. And it belongs to you now. Now, it's not finished yet, but I figure we can finish it together. It was made for me and the woman I love. And Bianca, that woman is you now." He kissed her hand and asked, "Say yes, honey. Say you'll be my wife."

"Yes!" The word sprang out before her, beckoning her to follow. "Of course!"

He got up on his feet and swung her around. She had never been so glad she was still alive. "Oh, Kane," she called carelessly, "that day on the dock, you were so angry."

"I know," he said between kisses to her ear, "I've got a bad temper. I know."

"I thought you were going to hit me. I really did."

"Hey, now," he said sternly, pulling her to arm's length, "My temper's not *that* bad. You hear me?" She was moved by the sincerity in his eyes. "I may've been angry. I may've *wanted* to. But I will never lift my hand against you in anger. You got that? I will never lay a hand on you."

She nodded her belief.

"Unless it's this kind," he added, giving her bottom a squeeze.

Bianca laughed as she pushed him away. He laughed, too, and she couldn't believe how handsome it made him. "Come," she said, grabbing his hand, "Let's go tell the others."

"Others? Who?"

"All those people upstairs! I have to introduce you to Hailey and to Raimondo. You will like them. Come!"

He chuckled as she tried to pull him up the stairs. "Wait there, darlin'. Hold on."

"What is it?"

He tugged her back into his arms and lifted an eyebrow. "I came all the way out here thinking about nothing else. And now here I am, alone with you in this cabin, and I haven't even got the chance yet."

"Chance to do what?"

"To kiss you." He bent his face over hers and leaned down. Bianca's lips parted in welcome, delighted by the faint taste of tobacco and the soft force of his demand. She was breathless by the time it was over, and could hardly think of anything to say.

"Come on," he said, turning her around in his warm arms, "Let's go meet some folks. And after we've cleaned up, why don't you go ahead and pack. Because you know what we've got to do."

"What's that?" she inquired, leaning back to look at him.

"It's time to finish our long journey home."

EPILOGUE

Eighteen months later

The winds kissed the meadow, carrying in the scent of sweet grass past the verandah edged in black iron, through the bedroom window that spanned the wall's height, and into the folds of the letter in Bianca's ivory hand. The letter crinkled in the breeze, but she fought to keep it open. A placid smile softened her face as a shimmer of sunshine wavered on her cheek. The room smelled of sawdust, but it was a smell she'd learned to love. The whole three-story clapboard house smelled that way, and she'd come to view it as the scent of her and Kane's efforts to build something solid and homey—together. She sighed at the four-poster bed draped in blue satin, the only piece of furniture that didn't comply with Kane's bucolic decorating sensibilities. He liked everything to be in the style of Texas, and Bianca agreed with his taste. But not when it came to the bed. Her bed she had wanted adorned in the style of luxury, a luxury she'd never had as a child. And Kane had agreed, especially on the satin, which felt slick and cool in the wee hours of their love-making.

"Are you finally taking a rest?" His voice startled her so thoroughly that she touched her swollen belly. "I'm sorry, darlin'. You okay?" His concern was extreme as he knelt beside her on the dusty floor speckled in dots of sunlight.

"I'm fine." She pecked him lovingly on the cheek. "And I plan to get back to work. The curtains on the second floor need to be hung, and I have some polish for that old bureau we found. The kitchen needs—"

"Whoa, slow down, there, darlin'. You shouldn't be working so hard in your condition."

There was a flutter in her womb as he gently stroked the baby within. Bianca could not get over it. She couldn't believe she was going to have her very own baby. Kane hadn't stopped grinning since he'd found out. "I'm not working too hard," she promised him. "I just want our home to be perfect."

"It is perfect," he said. "How could any home with you in it not be perfect?"

"More perfect then," she beamed.

He kissed her tender cheek. "Well, between all you've been doing 'round here and running that restaurant, I don't see how you get any sleep at night."

"But the restaurant is a huge success," she reminded him. "It's the most popular in all of Flat Rock. I've been getting customers from all over these parts. Soon I'll have to hire a second chef and teach him all my recipes. With the baby, I just won't have time to cook for the whole state! I'll still run the finances and supervise, though. *Dio,* that reminds me: I need to hire a new waitress. All the customers have been complaining about the one I have."

"Why's that?"

"I am not sure. Something about threatening to poison their food if they don't leave a generous enough tip."

"As the new sheriff of Flat Rock, I would have to object to that," he winked.

"Yes, that is my thinking as well."

Her smile set off a twinkle in his eye. "So what is it that's got my busy wife finally sitting down?"

"Oh." She held up the letter. "It's from Raimondo and Hailey. They say they are doing very well."

"What else?"

"They are expecting a baby, like we are. Their second, they call it, because they think of Stefano as their first."

He nodded.

"I think they still feel strangely about accepting my shrimp boat. But I explained to them that I didn't need the money, how you insisted on buying my restaurant for me. That it was your wedding gift to me. I know the Casales need their money, and Vito can use his for something else now, which will help them. I told them I don't need my old shrimp boat. But I think they still feel strangely about taking it." She sighed heavily. "Well, at least their family is together again. At least his parents have accepted it. Someday they'll come to understand that I really *wanted* them to have that shrimp boat."

"Well, they've been good friends to you," he said. "They deserve it."

"Do you know who else has been a good friend?"

"Who?"

"Charlotte. And your *mamma*. All of your family has been so welcoming. I think they've almost forgotten about when they first met me." She lifted her apron and blushed into it. "I'm so embarrassed every time I think of that."

Kane chuckled at the memory, which seemed of so long ago. "They all love you now, Bianca. They say so all the time. Especially my pa."

"I know." Her voice was soft as the flickering sun. "I love them, too. I look forward to our Sunday dinners together all week."

He noticed a trace of regret behind her joyful professions. "What's the matter, darlin'?" He smoothed a strand of dark hair from her temple. She didn't answer, but he had a good guess. "Is it Francesca?"

She bowed her head regretfully. "Every time I hear of the beautiful actress who has stolen the heart of Europe, I know that it's Francesca. I know she is only using a stage name. And I'm so happy for her! But sometimes, I wish . . ."

He lifted her chin. "You wish what?"

"I wish I could see her again some day. I wish she could visit. I just wish . . ."

"Well, maybe some day she can."

Bianca cocked her head suspiciously. "What do you mean by that? You know Francesca can't come back to Texas. She's being hunted; she's—"

"No, she's not."

"What?"

Kane coughed into his fist, averting his eyes. "All right, darling, I'm gonna tell you something, but it has to be our little secret. Only you, me, Caleb, and Marcus know. All right?"

"All right."

"Well . . . when I got back from Galveston that time, after our fight, I . . . didn't exactly tell the truth in my report."

"What?"

"I told Caleb," he added defensively. "Caleb's my partner. I told him, and I told Marcus. But the report I filed . . . well, it said Francesca got shot in the chase."

"Kane! Why?"

He ran a coarse thumb over her tender lip and gazed at her in earnest. "Because I didn't want to risk some bounty hunter getting some notion to cross the sea and kill her. Because I didn't want my girl to lose the only family she had."

Bianca's lashes fluttered. "But Kane, you were so angry with me then. You hated me."

"No," he chuckled, surprised that she could have thought such a thing, "I never hated you. I was angry, yes. But I never hated you. In my heart," he said, patting it firmly, "I didn't want you to lose her."

"Does that mean," she asked, overwhelmed by the revelation, "that you're no longer angry at Francesca?"

He didn't want to go that far. But what he *could* say was, "It means that my love for you is stronger than my anger for what she did."

Bianca put a trembling hand to her breast. "Kane, I love you. You'll never know how much."

"I do know," he said, wrapping her up in his arms, "because I love you just the same."

They embraced in a huddle on the dusty floor as the sun turned to an orange ball across the meadow and shone through the verandah upon their hands, folded together over Bianca's round belly, ripe with tomorrow's promises.

More By Best-selling Author
Fern Michaels

Romantic Suspense from

Lisa Jackson

Stella Cameron

"A premier author of romantic suspense."

__The Best Revenge
0-8217-5842-X $6.50US/$8.00CAN

__French Quarter
0-8217-6251-6 $6.99US/$8.50CAN

__Key West
0-8217-6595-7 $6.99US/$8.99CAN

__Pure Delights
0-8217-4798-3 $5.99US/$6.99CAN

__Sheer Pleasures
0-8217-5093-3 $5.99US/$6.99CAN

__True Bliss
0-8217-5369-X $5.99US/$6.99CAN